MW00355641

Alimony's Treasure

Michael W. Hinkle

Alimony's Treasure

Copyright © 2022 Michael W. Hinkle. All rights reserved. No part of this book may be reproduced or retransmitted in any form or by any means without the written permission of the publisher.

Published by Wheatmark®
2030 East Speedway Boulevard, Suite 106
Tucson, Arizona 85719 USA
www.wheatmark.com

ISBN: 978-1-62787-932-3 (paperback)
ISBN: 978-1-62787-933-0 (ebook)
LCCN: 2021923622

Bulk ordering discounts are available through Wheatmark, Inc. For more information, email orders@wheatmark.com or call 1-888-934-0888.

Prologue

In October 1896, outlaws overtook Sir Lawrence Alimony in Oklahoma's Indian Territory. He was twenty years old and barely fifty inches tall. If the army patrol from Ft. Reno had been closer when they heard shooting, they might have arrived in time to save Sir Lawrence and Pete McGuire, his friend, driver, and protector. Sadly, by the time the soldiers arrived, McGuire and Sir Alimony were dead. In the ensuing shootout between the robbers and troopers, all four outlaws perished. The absence of signs of physical injury to Alimony's tiny corpse—which the brigands stripped and left naked in the dust—suggests he died of a heart attack. No doubt the outlaws scoured Sir Alimony's body and possessions, seeking clues that would lead to the fabulous treasure he was known to have with him when he boarded the ship at Liverpool en route to California.

In the tragedy's aftermath, the troopers collected Sir Alimony's scattered possessions and put them into the remains of his steamer trunk. The tiny Englishman and his friend Pete received as respectful a burial as circumstances permitted. As the burial detail rode away from the scene of Alimony's last stand, they neglected to find the boots that the outlaws pulled from Alimony's feet and tossed carelessly into a nearby Chickasaw plum thicket.

As of January 1973, the location of Alimony's treasure remained a mystery.

One

When Dale Hopper climbed into the Rambler to start his first day on the job at the Oklahoma County Zoo, he had no intention of getting on permanent. The reason he and his pal Vernon Cord answered the ad was because this job was supposed to be a three-month gig. The timing was perfect. Short-term commitment with full-time wages would go a long way toward putting enough coins in their jeans to bankroll their trip to California when spring rolled around. Without this extra cash, their '59 Chevrolet school bus would never be road-ready. They couldn't head out to the West without a starter solenoid, some tires with a few miles of tread life, and a tape deck.

The trivial money they earned singing and playing the blues at the Blue Buzzard Saloon was enough to keep the rent paid, but that was about as far as they could stretch it. They planned to drive the bus to California, where, according to reliable gossip, throngs of limber ballerinas yearned for the coming of some long-haired, free-spirited, guitar-playing Oklahoma boys. Hopper figured he and Cord were just the fellas to make those ballerinas' dreams come true.

The cold north wind hit him in the face when he opened the Rambler's passenger door and stepped into the zoo's parking lot. Hopper zipped his faded fatigue jacket and pulled the collar over his ears.

Cord fumbled around in the backseat to retrieve their aluminum lunch bucket, which contained a couple of bologna sandwiches, some potato chips, and a pair of oranges. Hopper didn't wait. He trotted toward the shop, hoping to find it warm inside. He double-timed across the parking lot, uttering an incantation against the chill: "Lord, let there be ballerinas . . . let there be bouquets of beautiful, lustful ballerinas."

Cord sprinted to his side, cursing the goddam cold. Frosty vapors rose from his lips as he spoke. "I know this is supposed to be a temporary deal, Hopper, but it sure as hell feels like we're stumbling into a cage with a door locking behind us. I'm starting to get a bad feeling about this."

Hopper felt obliged to rotate Cord's thinking away from the blustery here and now and angle him toward the sunny soon to be. "Relax, buddy. Nobody can lock us in. Just remember the magic words: 'we quit.' Speak these words, my son, and, voilà, cage door opens, and out we fly. We can bust out anytime we want."

Lunch bucket under his arm, Cord pushed his hands deep into his pockets. "Well, cage or not, I'll be glad to get inside. Surely they got coffee in there. We need a thermos."

Hopper, halfway to the door, stopped in midstride, squinting at the northeast corner of the building. Cord paused, his hand on the doorknob. "Come on, Hopper. I'm not gonna stand here freezing until you're done sightseeing."

Hopper hesitated, shivered, and then caught up. "Did you see that?"

"See what?"

"I thought there was somebody lurking around that corner of the building, watching us."

"It was probably a security guard eyeballing us. It ain't every day a high-dollar Rambler comes rolling into their yard."

"I don't know, Cord. It looked like . . . Well, never mind. Let's get inside." Whatever Hopper thought he saw, he shrugged it off. After all, his imagination was legendary for its habit of putting flesh on bones that weren't there. Sometimes he had to muster his concentration to maintain a reliable line between internal creations and the real world where everybody else lived. His hippie friends made allowances for his spells and eccentricities. They accepted his mental peculiarities with a mixture of amusement and reverence that, in ancient times, would be reserved for the community soothsayer.

Hopper blinked as he stepped into the shop. Déjà vu. It was like walking into the barracks at Fort Polk for the first time. The flashback wasn't sparked by any physical similarity; it was a feeling, like stumbling into an orderly system with languages, symbols, and logics all its own; procedures and methods that wouldn't be visible or understandable to somebody on the outside looking in. He groaned. Worlds with routines and standard operating procedures always had a way of getting snagged on a fella's rough edges—and he had plenty of those.

Hard-edged, sharp-bladed tools lined the walls—shovels, axes, saws, loppers—implements that wouldn't work without muscle and sweat applied to the blunt end. Golf carts, pickups, mowers, and other machines were arranged on the concrete floor in workmanlike order. Overhead fluorescent lights made everything look cold and sterile. The air smelled like oil, rubber, cigarettes, chemicals, and a variety of thick odors Hopper found unfamiliar and disorienting.

The melancholy chorus of Ray Charles's "Here We Go Again" drifted from an old radio in the corner, where two men heave-ho'd large white and green plastic bags onto a pickup. Two other men bent over square-nosed spades, raking the edges with metal files. Everybody seemed to know what to do, and they were busy doing it.

The only one paying attention to the newcomers was a string bean leaning against a golf cart, toothpick wagging side to side in his mouth. He inspected them as someone might eyeball a couple of piglets at a prayer meeting. Since he was much older than the rest and stood idle while everyone else was buzzing, Hopper assumed he was a supervisor.

Hopper was about to approach the string bean when Cord nudged him. "There's the coffeepot. Let's get some." The idler's eyes followed them as they crossed the shop to the coffeepot, which shared a metal table with a box of sugar, powdered creamer, a box of dominoes, and an assortment of outdoor and automotive magazines.

Cord poured industrial black coffee into a white Styrofoam cup. Hopper did the same, adding clumped creamer. Putting the Styrofoam to his lips, Cord grimaced. "Yep. We should've brought a thermos. This stuff tastes like it was made out of old tires boiled in muddy water."

Hopper nodded. He tried to salvage the cup's contents by pouring in a load of sugar. Cord thumbed toward the men loading the fifty-pound bags onto the pickup.

"You reckon we oughta lend a hand?"

Hopper shook his head. "Let's not peg ourselves as heavy lifters. I figure we should stand still and let everybody get a look at us. With this long hair of ours, we're probably the only undomesticated animals on this crew."

The lanky man sucked in his stomach and strolled to the coffeepot. "You two are the new men, ain't ya?"

Hopper's first inclination was to compliment the guy on his keen powers of observation, but he opted to be polite. "I'm Dale Hopper, and this big fella is Vernon Cord."

The lanky man gave a knowing grin and pointed at them with his toothpick. "You two was hired to clear the west forty, right?"

Hopper's smile concealed his irritation at the guy's density and bad manners. "Sorry, fella, I didn't catch your name. Like I said, I'm Hopper, and this is Cord." He extended his hand.

The string bean returned the toothpick to his mouth, bit down, and spoke through his teeth. "My name's Podd." He shook Hopper's hand twice and reached over to Cord. "I'll probably be breaking you in . . . you know, getting you lined out on the ground-crew routine. I'm sort of the senior man around here."

"Well, to answer your question, Mr. Podd, we're hired on temporary. Not sure what the job is."

Podd's sly smile returned. He put a finger against his hawkish nose. "You'll be clearing the west forty. You probably don't have no idea what that means."

Hopper tossed his half-full coffee cup into a nearby trash can. "We're all ears, Podd. Suppose you tell us what it means."

Podd leaned against the shop's metal wall, his arms folded. As if preparing for a lecture, he cleared his throat. "They'll probably say you was hired to get ready for the big cat exhibit going in over there, and they can't spare none of us regulars right now. That ain't the real reason, though. They're putting you fellas over there because none of us wants any part of that ground."

Cord frowned at the shorter man. "Well, now, Mr. Senior Man around Here, if clearing the west 40's going to be our job like you say, suppose you start breaking us in by telling us why none of the regulars wants to work over there."

Podd, obviously on the lookout for eavesdroppers, tucked his toothpick behind his right ear, speaking in a subdued voice. "Years ago, the old-timers hauled carcasses of dead zoo animals over there to bury 'em; birds, snakes, apes, bears. But that ain't the reason we don't go over there. The real reason is—"

Before he could say more, the shop door banged open, and a short, animated man in overalls strode in. The temperature seemed to rise a few degrees as if he carried an outsized, overheated magneto in his pocket.

Podd produced a shop rag apparently from thin air and got busy cleaning the metal table around the coffeepot. The newcomer, moving like a motorized fire plug, stormed across the shop, slinging instructions as he might broadcast seed. He pulled off his faded blue watch cap, jamming it into the pocket of his well-worn work coat. A tumble of red hair spilled out. The whole place shifted into another gear. Podd might be the senior man, but this guy was clearly the top dog.

"Wes, you and Ed load number-three pickup with the tools these guys will need for a day bare rooting hackberries. Don't forget the water can."

Podd showered the short redhead with a lopsided grin. "Mornin', Les. I was just cleaning up a little bit and telling these guys—"

"Podd, I need you to clear the barberries out of the bed over by main concession. Mr. Neyland says we gotta replace those with cannas. Let's keep him happy and get them thorny barberry bastards out of there— today, Podd."

Podd's thin frame shifted into gear and started moving. He stopped after a couple of steps, a puzzled expression on his face. "Say, Les, didn't we just put in them barberries last year?"

"Yep. And we're liable to yank the cannas and plant barberries back next year if Mr. Neyland says so. Now let's move. We're burning daylight." Les stepped over to Hopper and Cord, extending a thick calloused hand. "Which one are you?"

Hopper marveled at the strength in the grip. "I'm Hopper."

"I'm Lester Buntz, grounds crew supervisor." He pumped Hopper's hand and turned to the other man.

"You're a big fella, ain't you, Cord?"

"I'm bigger when I'm warm."

Buntz gave a snort that served as his chuckle. "Well, since this job's temporary, you won't be here long enough to get too big for your britches. You guys know a hackberry when you see one?"

Cord looked at Hopper. "We know a hackberry when we see one?"

Hopper came right to the point. "Nope."

"That's okay. I'll show you in two seconds. First, I gotta take a leak. Podd, get these guys some gloves."

Podd hurried toward a metal cabinet as Buntz disappeared around a corner. The instant the boss was out of sight, Podd returned with two pairs of leather gloves: large for Hopper, extra large for Cord. Keeping his eyes on the corner, he spoke in a conspiratorial tone. "You guys be smart. Don't get separated over there."

Cord frowned. "What the hell are you talking about? What's so damn scary about working over there?"

Podd winked. "I'm just telling you. Even Buntz don't go by himself. Reason being 'cause it's haunted."

Hopper, stunned by this declaration, was about to call bullshit when Podd interrupted. "Shush, here comes Buntz."

The stocky redhead pulled on his watch cap as he strode past without slowing up. "Come on, boys; it's a workday." As he pushed open the shop door, he spoke over his shoulder. "Get after them barberries, Podd."

Hopper hesitated at the door and looked back. Podd mouthed an exaggerated "Be careful," drawing his thumb across his throat.

Two

The cold didn't seem to bother Buntz as he sped the golf cart west toward the zoo's front parking lot. It sure as hell bothered Hopper. He pulled his collar around his ears, glancing at Cord, who looked as bothered as he was. Buntz talked nonstop, loud enough to be heard over the wind.

"I don't have time to get you boys oriented today, so I'll just lay it out quick and dirty. First, a couple of smart guys that had their eye on the future might get on permanent if they did me a good job."

He waved his left arm at the zoo premises flashing by as they raced along the north access road. "This is all about to change. Talk around here is that the Kronesons made a killing in oil and gas over the last couple of years, something about OPEC and international whatnots. Anyway, they're about to pour tons of cash into this place. The big cat exhibit you guys are working on is the first step.

"For now, you two are listed on the payroll as Animal Tech One, which means you're the lowest form of animal life in the zoo. Even butterflies in the Patagonia exhibit outrank you guys on the food chain."

Hopper spoke through his collar. "Animal tech? They told us when we interviewed we wouldn't be working with animals. I agreed to take the job on condition I wouldn't be fooling with caged animals—especially snakes; snakes are a deal buster." At the mention of snakes, Buntz shot a glance Hopper's way. Hopper couldn't figure whether Buntz was surprised, amused, offended, or just curious.

"Don't worry about none of that. You're called animal tech because it's one of Mr. Neyland's new accounting deals. Everybody on the payroll is an animal tech something. But no matter how you're listed on the books, it ain't normal for anybody on the grounds crew to screw around with animals. We might have to go someplace and pick up a crate or drop one off, but you guys most likely won't be doing any of that. For now, all you have to do is concentrate on giving me a fair day's work. Do that, and I'll do what I can to make a permanent slot for you. Then, soon as I can, I'll bump you up to Animal Tech Two."

Cord muttered into his chest, "Gosh, Mr. Buntz, that would be great."

"Call me Buntz or Lester or Les—and you're welcome." Hopper and Cord exchanged a glance. "Next, don't pay no attention to Podd's bullshit." Without slowing the cart, he took his eyes off the access road and studied them. "You two ain't superstitious, are you?"

Cord mumbled, "I believe it's bad luck to run your ass off the road in a golf cart."

Hopper elbowed him in the ribs. "Don't mind him Mr. . . . Les. He'll cheer up once he gets limber and works up a sweat."

Buntz ignored the wisecrack. "There ain't nothing to any foolishness about the west forty being haunted. I'm going to spell out the facts. Then I don't want to hear no more about spooks. Get me? Talk like that don't do nothing but upset the ignorant and weak-minded. Podd can't keep his superstitious old trap shut. That's one reason he's been here fifteen years and he's still Animal Tech One, just like you guys. I'm gonna put your mind at ease. Then you just forget all that haunted forty nonsense."

He told them about two men traveling through Indian Territory in the 1800s. "They got cornered by a bunch of outlaws. Both travelers got killed in a shootout. Some historians claim it happened near here, maybe on the forty. Nobody ever found anything to prove it one way or the other. Then, about five years ago, me and Podd was digging up plum trees to plant in the prairie exhibit. We found a couple of fellas curled up and froze. Just some poor hobos that wandered off the highway looking for a place to keep warm."

Hopper felt a shudder course through him, which had nothing to do with the weather. He resisted the seed of suspicion that there might be something creepy about this place. Buried animal carcasses and frozen hobos didn't need to be perched in his imagination.

He strained to focus his thinking on warm days in California, when Buntz stopped on the west edge of the parking lot. As Hopper stepped off, Buntz gripped a handful of his coat sleeve. "I'm serious, boys. There's all kinds of varmints in there: feral cats, turkeys, coons, possums, coyotes—lots of critters that make noises that sound strange to folks who don't know what they're hearing. But everything living in there is harmless except ticks and hornets, and they mind their own business in the wintertime. So if you hear something, don't let your imagination run away with you. Be grownups. Do what you're paid for, and this'll be the best damn job you ever had. Trust me, this ain't the time for any of us to be drawing attention to what we do over here."

Hopper felt edgy about the whole deal. He pushed it to the back of his mind and joined Cord in assuring Buntz they had no fear of ghosts, evil spirits, or stuff like that. They promised to keep their mind on their work and do nothing to upset grounds crew morale. Buntz gave them a happy smile. "You fellas are gonna work out great. Now I'll show you how to bare-root a hackberry."

He strode to a thin tree on the edge of the parking lot and knelt, pointing to the gray warty bark. "This here's a hackberry." He ran his hand down the rough bark like he might stroke a beloved pet. "Hackberries is one of the best trees God ever put in the garden of Eden. Most people don't know it, but their little fruit is real tasty. You can eat them right off the tree in fall and early winter. You don't need to pamper this tree." He caressed the bumpy surface again, eyeing it lovingly.

"Treat it right, give it a fair chance, and it'll find water on its own. It'll do fine in any decent Oklahoma soil. In return for a little care, this tree'll give you shade, good fruit, and pleasure your eyes." He pointed to the soil under the leafless limbs. "Start out about three feet, dig down a foot or so. Get under the tree. Cut all the roots. Find the tap root. Cut that. She'll come right down. These are tough trees. If you don't waste time getting them back in the ground, they'll be fine even if there ain't no soil left on the roots."

He stepped close to Cord and looked intensely into his eyes. "If it'll add any enthusiasm to your work, you should know that whatever we can't get out of here by April is gonna get pushed over by dozers and burned." He arched his eyebrows as if they were sharing a secret that required no elaboration.

Buntz stood quietly, shifting his gaze into the west forty. Hopper hugged himself to stay warm while Buntz finished his meditation. Buntz shivered and studied the two men watching him, all three standing silent in the cold. Buntz coughed, an embarrassed expression on his face. He pulled a heavy wad of metal keys tethered to his belt on a thick ring. He inspected keys until he found what he wanted. He worked a key off the ring and flipped it to Hopper. "This is the key to the gate." He pointed to a dirt road leading off the northwest edge of the parking lot. "When you get in there, get me a dozen hackberries. That'll do for your first day. Now let's get back to the shop. Your truck ought to be ready."

In the parking lot, a faded green '62 Ford F-100 standard-bed pickup stood idling. Buntz pointed. "That's yours." Cord slid under the wheel as Hopper got in on the other side. Cord shifted the manual transmission into reverse. Buntz tapped on his window. He was talking before Cord got it rolled down. "Just one more thing. You two stay together while you're in there. I . . . uhhh . . . I don't want nobody wandering off and getting lost."

Alarm bells went off in Hopper's head, but before he could ask how the hell a fella could get lost in broad daylight on a forty-acre piece of ground bounded on the east by an asphalt road, Buntz was already switching on his golf cart. "I'll be checking on you," he yelled, driving south toward the zoo premises, his left leg dangling off the machine.

The full weight of the situation pressed on Hopper once they parked on the forty and Cord killed the engine. Hopper knew from experience that occupational vertigo was common but temporary. It passed once he figured out the job's mechanisms, shortcuts, and pitfalls. As for the cold, with enough warm gear, infusions of hot coffee, and occasional timeouts in a warm pickup, he could adapt. He put zero stock in Podd's nonsense about the forty being haunted. Still, Buntz's insistence that they stay together caused his anxiety level to go up a tic. He wasn't buying this "I'm afraid somebody will get lost" bullshit. But, like Buntz said, everybody was a grownup. If Cord could work in an animal graveyard that might be haunted by a bunch of dead hobos, so could he.

They sat quiet in the pickup, knowing cold labors waited. The warmth began to melt. Decision time. Cord took a deep breath. "Know what we ought to do? We ought to drive right back to the shop and quit. I didn't sign on to watch over my shoulder for spooks while freezing my butt off digging up trees."

Hopper was relieved for the excuse to laugh. "You heard Buntz. Keep your eye on the future, and you'll be Animal Tech Two with an office and a secretary before you know it."

"Screw that." Cord snorted. "On April twenty-third, if I don't get fired or demon possessed, my three-month sentence doing hard labor in this place expires, and I'm headed for California."

"Whatever you say, amigo. In the meantime, let's earn our pay." Hopper pushed open the creaky door, shuddering as the wind stung tears from his eyes.

They had no problem locating their first hackberry, a sturdy tree about nine inches in diameter. The earth around the roots was soft and moist. As they dug deeper, the ground became hard-packed clay. The roots grew thicker as they penetrated deeper into the soil. Hopper was happy to be absorbed in the work. He was also pleased to discover that as he concentrated on the job, the cold didn't matter so much.

Each time their spades exposed another root, they used loppers to cut it back near the trunk, allowing access to the roots disappearing into the soil under the tree. In a surprisingly short time, their efforts exposed the taproot. Cord got out of the hole they'd dug around the tree and pulled against the trunk, giving Hopper an angle on that last root anchoring the hackberry to the earth. With well-aimed ax strokes, Hopper severed the taproot. The hackberry groaned and came to rest at their feet.

Gnarly roots and leafless branches clawed upward as if tearing, motionless, at the sky. Hopper shook his head. "A couple minutes ago, this looked like a tree. Now it looks like trash."

Cord nodded. "Yep, but if Buntz is right, this little fella will be real happy once we get it planted someplace else. And I guess it's better to get uprooted and transplanted than bulldozed and burned."

Hopper appreciated Cord's happy-ending view. "Let's get this loaded and go find another."

They had four trees down and loaded in three hours. As the sun got higher and they warmed to the work, they shed their coats, tossing them in the truck bed. Hopper drew a cup of water and handed it to Cord and then drew one for himself. "What do you think, Cord? Not so bad after all, eh?"

Cord took a long drink and tossed the remaining water onto the brown prairie grass. "If we can do this every day for three months and it keeps from raining or snowing on us, I believe I can handle it."

By unspoken agreement, they ended the recess. Back to work, they fell into an easy rhythm. Hopper enjoyed the varied bird songs drifting from the surrounding trees. He was amazed at the multitude of feathered residents who stayed put in their Oklahoma home, even in the dead of winter. He found himself appreciating these nondescript little songsters who fought it out through the cold months while their flashier cousins took their bright feathers and headed South. *You all can stay if you want,* he thought, *but as soon as my wings get feathered, I'm flying out of here.*

All thoughts of haunted acreage evaporated in the unexpected pleasures of the simple outdoor work—until Cord jerked upright, frowning. "What's that?"

At first, Hopper thought Cord was making a lame attempt at haunted forty humor. But Cord wasn't a good enough actor to fake his alarmed expression. Hopper strained to hear. Nothing. In an unsettling coincidence, the wind noise died off, and the birds stopped singing. "What was it, Cord?"

Cord shook his head. "I don't know. Sounded like something big coming from over in that brush." He nodded to the west. Hopper squinted, listening. Still nothing.

"Cord, you fraidy cat, there ain't anything out there except a rabbit or something. Don't be so damn skittish. I won't let anything hurt you."

Cord blushed, gave a short nervous laugh, and started back to work. But the next instant, he was standing tense and alert, again clutching his shovel. "There's something out there."

Hopper's urge to laugh stopped in his throat. There was something, and it was no damn rabbit. He could hear it coming. With a firm grip on his shovel, he strained to isolate the sound's location. Cracking, moaning noises rose from the brush as the thing—whatever it was—drew closer. Hopper's imagination conjured images; ghostly remains of frozen hobos mounted on skeletal camels rushed out of the trees, hungry to feast on the flesh of a pair of green Animal Techs One.

"What do you reckon we ought to do?" Cord spoke through clenched teeth. The cracking and groaning grew louder as the *something* approached, picking up speed.

"I think we ought to stroll over to the pickup for a drink of water. I'm sure thirsty; how about you?"

"Yeah. I'm dry as a bone."

"Bring your shovel."

"Don't worry. I ain't going no place empty-handed." Hopper whistled casually, glancing over his shoulder, as they sauntered toward the truck. Whatever was coming got noisier and sounded bigger with every step. They were halfway to the pickup when a man-like apparition stepped from the underbrush, staring at them with menacing intensity. Hopper and Cord stood rooted, gripping their shovels as the apparition lurched toward them, bony hands outstretched. The tangle of dry twigs and dead leaves littering his disheveled hair gave him the appearance of someone who'd been lying under bare winter trees for ages. His long gray/black beard, wind-whipped and seeming to pull him forward, had acorns and small pinecones woven into it.

Cord whispered, "Jesus, Hopper, you reckon it's the ghost of one of them hobos that froze in here?"

Hopper tightened his grip on the shovel and tried to devise an explanation more benign than ghosts. He couldn't find one.

As the apparition drew closer, Hopper saw, beneath the tangle of wild hair and bizarre beard, the wrinkled face of an old man, smiling. Clutching something in his gnarly outstretched hands, the apparition stopped about twenty feet from them, speaking in a surprising loud, clear, reassuringly human voice. "For you."

When they didn't react, the old man made an offering gesture, saying again, "For you."

Hopper studied as much of the wrinkled face as he could see beneath the tangled beard. This was no spook. This was a wind-blown old guy wanting to give them something. The outstretched hands appeared to hold nothing but forest rubbish. Hopper sensed the old man was pleading for something. The weirdness level remained elevated, but Hopper felt the menace index dropping.

He decided he could go a long way toward normalizing the situation by opening a dialogue. "Hey old-timer, we got water in the truck. You thirsty?"

The disheveled wood spirit nodded, lurching forward, hands still outstretched. Cord mumbled, "He ain't drinking out of my cup."

They kept a wary eye on the old man stumbling behind them to the rear of the pickup. Hopper could see that what he took to be rubbish cupped in the thin, knobby hands was really a collection of soil-covered root bits. With an unsteady gait, their wild-looking visitor stepped closer, bringing his hands nearer to Hopper's face.

Hopper edged back. "Thanks, fella, but you probably ought to hold on to those."

"I have plenty. You need this . . . for tea. It'll help keep you well in the winter. Here, take it." He came nearer. Hopper cautiously reached out, picking one of the root bits from the dirty hand. The old man nodded gratefully. He scratched a root bit with a long fingernail and held it near Hopper's nose.

Hopper cautiously inhaled and smiled. "Hey, I know that smell. That's . . . Cord, smell this." He took one of the bits from the old man's hand, scratched it, and held it out for Cord. At first, Cord frowned and shied back. "Come on, Cord, it won't hurt you. It's downright pleasant. See if you know what it is."

Cord craned forward, tentatively sampling the aroma. His eyebrows arched. "Well, I'll be damned. That's real familiar, alright. What is it?"

The old man nodded and gave a deep, earthy chuckle. "Sassafras." He put a fistful of root bits in Hopper's hand and held out a bunch for Cord, who stepped forward and took them.

The old man rubbed his soil-covered palms on his clothes. "I saw your truck and figured I'd gather some for you. I got plenty." He chuckled again, shaking a threadbare newspaper bag hanging from his shoulder. "Make tea. It'll keep you well." He looked past them at the water can in the pickup bed. "Maybe I could have a drink, like you said."

Hopper filled a cup and handed it to him. The old man took a long drink and shakily passed the cup back. "Could I have some more?" Hopper refilled the cup. The old man poured the contents over his hands. He removed a faded bandana from his coat and wiped his hands clean— sort of. He inspected his right hand. Apparently satisfied, he extended it to Hopper. "Thanks."

Hopper shook the damp, alarmingly cold hand. The old man reached out to Cord. "Thanks." Cord reluctantly accepted the gesture.

Though the old man continued to smile, Hopper saw tears moistening his eyelashes. "Use the sassafras to make tea. It'll be a blessing. Bye." He walked back toward the underbrush. After a few steps, he paused, looking over his shoulder. "I like your Rambler; always liked Ramblers."

He resumed his walk toward the trees. Hopper yelled, "Hey, were you at the shop watching us this morning?" The old man didn't reply. The cracking of dry branches continued long after he disappeared. Hopper and Cord stared at the soil-covered sassafras root in their hands.

Three

Hopper struggled to explain why he suddenly felt high, real high—Turkish hash high. He stood motionless in the grip of the moment as the old man carried the sounds of cracking twigs, incomprehensible muttering, and his bag of sassafras into the bush. Hopper let out a full-throated, intoxicated laugh. It was the only thing he could do to restore some element of reality to the moment. He imagined meetings like this in medieval times inspired tales of encounters with woodland wizards.

At first, Cord, his head cocked to one side, studied his friend. He looked into the bush, then back to Hopper, and then he, too, fell into a fit of laughter. Cord hopped on the tailgate, wiped his eyes, and smiled at the sassafras in his hand. "What the hell was that all about?"

Hopper raised a piece of root to his nose and drew in the earthy root-beer aroma. At that moment, he was sure he had never smelled anything so righteous. "I'm not sure. But if I felt more stoned, I'd think we ought to offer some acorns or feathers or something to the spirits of these woods."

He hopped onto the tailgate next to Cord. "You got to admit, Vernon, this is the most interesting first day on any job you ever had." After a few minutes of quiet reflection, complimented by renewed bird song and an oddly warm change in the wind's temperature, practicality levered its way back into his thinking. "What do you reckon Buntz will say when we tell him we met the ghost of the haunted forty?"

Cord scratched the back of his neck. "I don't think he'll be amused. He seemed awful touchy about the whole deal."

Hopper nodded. "Yeah, he probably won't have the same high, happy feeling we're enjoying. Podd will get a kick out of it, though. No telling how scary it'll be by the time he's through putting air into it." They laughed again. Hopper, feeling the moment's magic dwindling, drew a deep sigh. He opened the lunch pail and dropped the root inside. "Well, guess we better get back to work."

Cord dropped his bits of sassafras into the pail and hopped off the tailgate. "Right." He rummaged around in the truck bed. "Hey, Hopper, ain't this the cup the old-timer drank out of?"

"Yep."

"Where's mine? I'm thirsty."

"Oh, that one's yours. Got mine in my pocket. You don't think I'd let him drink out of my cup, do you?" He grinned. "It's okay, though. I'm sure the old spook didn't have nothing contagious." He shouldered his shovel and headed back into the trees, whistling. Cord, mumbling, rinsed the cup, inspected it, rinsed it again, and gave it a good wiping with his bandana. Mumbling still, he joined Hopper at the trunk of another hackberry.

It was a little past noon, and they nearly had the sixth and largest hackberry down. They decided not to break until it was out of the ground and loaded. The sun was high above the trees when the taproot yielded to the ax with a loud crack. Hopper, proud that he and Cord were turning out to be such competent hackberry bare-rooters, wiped sweat from his forehead. They heaved the heavy tree out of its hole and sat on the ground panting, their legs propped on the tree trunk.

Just as they were about to get to their feet and carry the tree to the truck, Cord squinted at the earth-covered roots twining their way to the thick trunk. "Wait a minute, Hopper. What's this?" When Cord reached toward the roots of the fallen hackberry, something flushed a covey of quail behind them. On reflex, they whirled to see what it was. Nothing. When they turned back to the tree, the sweat on Hopper's forehead turned cold. There, bound in the rootlets of the hackberry, was a child-sized boot.

The fragile leather threatened to tear when Cord made his first effort to pull it free. They used clippers to cut around it. When the boot finally came loose, Cord cradled it in cupped hands like a baby bird. Hopper scratched his head and watched his friend carrying the little boot, knowing he'd never have the guy figured out. One minute, Cord could be like this, all sentimental and thoughtful about something trivial like this beat-up little boot. The next minute, he could fly and jump into a bar fight that wasn't none of his business. Hopper admired Cord's fidelity to his code. He wasn't sure what it was, but whatever it was, Cord lived by it.

Cord deposited the boot on the tailgate and stepped back, studying. Hopper let him think for a minute and then asked, "What do you reckon the story is?"

Cord shook his head. "I don't know. Could be trash, could be mischief, could be nothing. But I got a twitchy feeling when I saw that little boot gripped by them dirty, woody roots."

"Well, don't think about it too much. We only got an hour for lunch, and I'm hungry. What do you want to do with it?"

"Let's ask him." Cord nodded toward the dirt road leading from the zoo. Buntz's golf cart kicked up busy clouds of red dust as it raced in their direction.

They waited with their hands in their pockets. Buntz smiled under his watch cap as he pulled the golf cart behind the pickup. "Looks like you guys been busy. How many you got?"

Hopper answered, proud and cheerful. "We got five loaded and one more ready." He thrust a thumb over his left shoulder.

Buntz beamed. "That's great, fellas. Right on schedule." His smile vanished. "What the hell is that?" he asked, pointing at the boot on the tailgate.

"It's sort of weird, Les. See, when that last tree came down, we found this little boot—"

"Get rid of it."

Hopper was caught off-guard by the abrupt finality of the order. "You want us to throw it away?"

"Get rid of it. If the pencil pushers in the head office hear about this, they're liable to think it's an artifact or something. They'll slow us down 'til historians or professors come over here, find some more rotten shit, and shut us down. Even if they don't find any more rotten shit, they'll have us standing around until they're sure there ain't any to be found. Either way, the dozers will be pushing down every tree in sight before we know it. Stuff like this happened before. We can't stand the headache right now. Get rid of it."

Cord frowned. "I don't get it. It's just a little boot."

Buntz sputtered, red-faced, and then took a breath and calmed himself. "Look, you two don't have no idea how hard I had to fight to get a chance to get as many good trees out of here as I can." He started walking in circles, kicking at clumps of brown grass.

"I had to do up a whole goddam written budget to prove I could save money if they let me have some men to work in here before the dozers show up. These bean-counting bastards got no idea how to value trees, shrubs, vines, and stuff. So I had to give 'em black-and-white figures. They still didn't get the big picture."

He stopped his circles and stared toward the zoo premises. "Neyland . . . Mr. Neyland didn't want to waste any man hours over here. He damn sure didn't want to hire the four guys I asked for." He resumed his pacing in ever-smaller circles, speaking mostly to himself.

"If they doze and burn everything in here, it's all the same to that hard-hearted prick. Hell, by the tantrum he threw before he finally agreed to give me two men and three months, you'd have thought I asked him to get his damn self circumcised or something."

He moved to the nose of the pickup, motioning Hopper and Cord to follow. He waved his arm at the thick brush on the west forty. "Look, there's hackberries, persimmons, hazels, mulberries, red buds, pines, plums, jasmine, honey locust . . . all kinds of good stuff in here."

He turned and looked at the men behind him as if searching for hints of sympathy. "You got to understand, there's valuable plants getting cut down, pushed over, piled up, and burned all over the damn world, and there ain't a thing I can do about it."

He stepped closer, staring at their faces with intense earnestness. "Look, boys, I can't explain it right now, but I got to save as much of this as I can. I ain't about to let a little rotten boot be the cause of me losing one single tree. I don't expect you guys to agree or anything, but we got a responsibility here. There's stuff right in front of us that we can—you know . . . " The sentence and his thought disappeared into the underbrush.

After some awkward seconds, he cleared his throat and stepped toward his golf cart, speaking over his shoulder. "You boys work with me, and you'll profit by it. Get rid of that damn boot and don't say nothing to nobody about it, okay?"

Hopper and Cord followed Buntz to his cart. He paused, offering a weak smile. "Look, fellas, there's going to be trees growing tall in this zoo, offering shade and nourishment for generations, and it'll be because of the work you're doing. That's something you can be proud of for the rest of your lives. Surely you can see that."

He pulled a shop rag from his pocket and wiped his face. "I'm over a barrel here." He was obviously pained to make the confession. "I really need you boys to promise me you won't say nothing about this crappy little boot. Keep it to yourself. Do this for me, and I promise you won't be sorry." With the same weak smile, he stepped forward, his hand extended. "Deal?"

Hopper shrugged and took his hand. "Sure. It's a deal. Far as I'm concerned, there never was any little boot."

Buntz's smile bordered on the radiant. "You're a pal, Hopper. How about it, Cord?"

"Can I keep the boot?"

Buntz's eyes widened, and his mouth hung open. "Keep it? What the hell for?"

"Because it might be an artifact or something, and I want it."

Buntz's jaws slammed shut. He sputtered, "Goddammit, Cord, why can't you just throw it away and pretend you never saw it?"

Cord fixed him with a narrow-eyed stare. "'Cause I did see it, and I want it. You got my word I won't say nothing about it. But I ain't throwing it away. That's the deal, and that's final. Take it or leave it."

Buntz stepped close and looked up into the eyes of the man towering over him. Cord gave no indication of being intimidated. Without taking his eyes off Cord's face, Buntz addressed Hopper. "What do you think, Hopper?"

"Hell, let him have the boot. It's just a piece of decayed leather. Not worth you having to explain why you fired us on the first day. That might start a lot of gossip about the forty and lead to embarrassing questions. Course, we'd have to tell our side of it." Buntz, still staring up at Cord, gulped hard.

Hopper went on. "Seems like I heard somebody say this might be a bad time to draw attention to any hiccups around the workings of the ground crew." Buntz gulped again. "You can trust Cord. If he says he won't say nothing, he won't say nothing."

"What about you?"

"Hell, my lips are sealed. I like sharing secrets with the boss."

Buntz stepped back, clearing his throat and extending his hand to Cord again. "Okay, you can keep the junk. You don't mention anything about it, which means I never knew anything about it. Okay?"

Cord took the outstretched hand. "Okay. I keep the boot; nobody says anything about it."

Buntz grinned. "You boys are Animal Tech Two material if I ever saw it." The men concluded their handshakes, and Buntz mounted his golf cart. "You fellas are making good progress here. Keep up the good work. I need guys around like you two."

As he started to pull away, Hopper yelled, "Wait a minute, Les. There's one more thing."

Buntz paused. "What?"

"See, there was a weird old guy that came walking up out of the woods. At first we thought he might be a spook, but then—"

"I don't want to hear about anything weird walking out of the woods. There was no old guy. It was your imagination running away with you. Keep quiet. Be cheerful and stay together. I'll see you back at the shop."

Hopper watched his new-made pal disappear down the dirt road in a cloud of red dust. He winked at Cord. "It's about time we found a way to turn that stubbornness of yours into a profit. Something tells me the next three months just got a lot easier." He eyed the small decayed boot sagging on the tailgate. "I got no idea what the story is, but this little boot turning up like it did seems like a piece of luck to me."

For the rest of that day, they took turns imagining how the little boot came to be a captive in those roots:

Hopper: "On some nearby homestead, a pioneer woman scolded her little boy for tracking mud into the house. He left his boots on the porch, and a playful dog snatched one and carried it down here."

Cord: "A tornado hit a nearby house and scattered some family's possessions all over the county. One of the kids' boots blew into these woods."

Hopper: "Thieves stole a shipment thinking it was valuable goods and discovered it was only a load of kids' footwear. Not seeing a profit, they threw some away."

Cord: "This was a freight route. A transport wagon hit a bump and lost a crate of boots, all sizes. The drivers didn't know about it until they reached their destination."

Hopper: "Some poor little fella got lost, and this is all that's left of him."

Cord: "This is an old family cemetery, and we accidentally dug into one of the graves."

Their speculations made the work speed by. At 4:45, they l[
their tools, secured the hackberries to the truck, and headed to the shop,
careful not to bounce any trees off the pickup. They parked next to the
Rambler. Cord carried the lunch pail and boot to the car and put them
on the backseat. Hopper noticed Podd straining to see what Cord was
doing.

"Hey, Cord," Hopper spoke over the Rambler's roof, nodding toward Podd, who was walking their way with a broad, lopsided grin.

"Did you boys see or hear anything—you know—unusual over
there?"

Hopper faked a terrified expression. "We sure did. We dug up a
couple of headless corpses that rose out of their graves and stumbled
around bumping into the pickup, feeling all over the bed with their long
bony fingers, looking for their lost skulls." He formed his fingers into
claws, crouched, and started stumbling toward Podd, who backed up as
Hopper drew nearer. "We could hear their heads off in the bush wailing,
'Podd, Podd . . . bring us Podd.'" He dropped his hands and grinned at
Podd's pale face. "Scared the shit out of us, didn't it, Cord?"

Podd stood rigid, a look of horror on his leathery face. He blushed
and released a nervous giggle. Then he got purple and scowled. "Okay,
you guys have your fun. But you let yourself get separated over there,
and something bad will happen for sure." He squinted into the Rambler.
"What's that you tossed onto the seat?"

Buntz, approaching on his golf cart, sped up when he saw Podd
hanging around the new men. "Podd," he shouted as he got near. "I'm
dang sure the shop is spotless, and all the equipment is oiled and put
away or you wouldn't be here in the parking lot jawboning."

Podd stammered, "I . . . uhh, I just came out to see if these fellas
needed any help unloading—"

Buntz cut him off. "I'll help these guys if they need it. You just take
care of your tools and the shop."

Podd tossed another glance at the earth-encrusted boot on the Rambler's backseat. He shuffled back to the shop, grumbling. Buntz motioned Hopper and Cord to step closer. "You boys didn't say nothing about . . . nothing, did you?"

Cord snorted, and Hopper spoke up. "Not a word, Buntz. A deal's a deal."

Buntz showered them with a relieved smile. "Come on, boys, let's get some wet burlap on these hackberries' roots so they'll rest easy 'til we get them replanted."

Four

Their budget didn't allow for steaks, but Carla worked the register at the Sizzlin' Sirloin steakhouse. She could be counted on for a discount if no manager was over her shoulder. To keep those discounts ringing up, they needed to play "Honky Tonk Women" when Carla danced through the door of the Blue Buzzard Saloon.

Hopper and Cord went through the line ordering steaks, salads, baked potatoes, and Cokes. Carla rang up grilled cheese sandwiches. The casual observer would never notice the quick winks and knowing smiles passing between them.

Settling into a booth, they smothered their steaks with Heinz 57 and dug in. As Cord put butter on a thick slice of Texas toast, Hopper studied his friend's face and then decided to raise the subject. "Hey, Cord, why the heck did you decide to make such a big deal outta that dirty old boot? I've been trying to figure what's on your mind, but I can't come up with nothing."

Cord seemed embarrassed, staring at his baked potato. "I got no logical answer, Hopper. There's just something about it that makes me—I don't know—sentimental or something."

Hopper mopped his plate with the remains of his toast. "Must be an emotional infection from your childhood. You probably lost something as a kid, and you been looking for it ever since. This will wear off when you figure out this boot ain't what you lost. It'll wind up in the trash in a day or two."

Cord nodded. "You're probably right. These days, I can't figure out why I do most of the stuff I do. It just strikes me as disloyal or hard-hearted to toss it in the garbage."

"We'll give it a good going over when we get home. You'll see there's nothing to it. You'll feel better, and that will be that." They finished their steaks and stood by the booth until Carla looked up from the register. They gave her a smile and a nod and headed back to the Rambler.

The house they rented backed up to a north/south rail line. A train was passing when they stepped through the front door. Nozetape, their roommate, was in his usual spot on the sofa carving totems on the bois d'arc rod he used as a cane. They exchanged greetings, but the train's rumbling drowned out their words.

Cord carried the boot to the kitchen, spread some newspapers on the table, gingerly positioned the boot in the center of things, and stood staring. Hopper retrieved some brushes from his shoeshine kit and put them on the table. Cord chose a soft-bristled brush and set about carefully cleaning the clumps of dirt from the tiny boot.

Nozetape blew wood dust from a carved owl's wing, laid the cane aside, and hobbled from the living room to the kitchen, taking a seat to watch what was happening. Hopper hated to see Nozetape's pained expression as he moved from place to place. He remembered what an able soldier Nozetape was before a "bouncing Betty" shredded his legs with shrapnel in Nam.

Once the train passed, Hopper filled Nozetape in on the events surrounding the boot's discovery. Cord alternated between the shoeshine brush and a toothbrush, gently removing the soil. Hopper wound up the recap by telling Nozetape about Cord's emotional attachment to the child-sized bit of decayed leather.

Nozetape nodded. "Cord may be emotional because he senses something important about this boot. It may have meaning for him—a message, you know, like the ring in *The Hobbit*." Nozetape was a Seminole half-breed. He claimed to possess credentials through the Cloud clan of his mother's people that would, by tradition, make him *Ishatahullo*, a warrior with magical powers. Hopper and Cord were in no position to contradict him.

Still, Hopper had a problem with this message stuff. Cord was too earth-bound in his thinking to pick up on mystic transmissions. Some correction was in order. "I disagree, Nozetape. I can see a guy being curious. I get that, but let's just put it in perspective. We get this ordinary job that happens to include clearing ground that has a creepy reputation. By coincidence, we turn up a kid's boot that got lost years ago. Naturally, anybody's imagination might get triggered. It hit one of Cord's emotional nerves. End of story. If I was to get all dreamy over something like this, you guys would wink, smile, and say, 'Ah, hell, that's just Hopper being Hopper.'"

Cord, concentrating on the boot, mumbled, "Don't forget the old man."

Nozetape perked up. "Old man?"

"Yeah, I almost forgot." Hopper told him about the old wood spirit stumbling out of the forest.

Nozetape toyed with his beard, speaking with a faraway look in his eyes. "I'm sure of it. These are messages. They're not separate deals. Something's binding them together and pointing to a path. If you can figure out how they're tied, you'll see what to do." He watched Cord working over the boot. "This thing on the table may belong to one of the little people."

Hopper studied Nozetape's face for evidence of a gag. "What do you mean 'little people'?"

"The Choctaws called them *Kawnuasha*; to the Cherokees, they were *Yunwi Tsunsdi*. My people called them *Este-lopocke*. There are stories about their power, what they could do for good or for bad. Sometimes they're friendly. Other times, they're like little demons. There were lots of them around here before white people came."

Hopper scratched his head. "You're shitting us, Nozetape. I've lived in Oklahoma my whole life except when I was in Vietnam, and I never heard anything about *Consh Unmi* or whatever." He pulled up a chair, put his right elbow on the table, and divided his attention between Cord's efforts and Nozetape's fantastic speculations.

Nozetape went to the refrigerator, retrieved a bottle of Boone's Farm apple wine, untwisted the lid, took a drink, and passed it to Hopper. "For real, Hopper. There are some old-timers that traded with the little people. You never heard of them because the people don't talk about them when white folks are around. There's lots of stuff the people talk about that would amaze you if you overheard." The only sound in the room was Cord lightly brushing the boot.

Nozetape took another drink. "Keep an open mind, Hopper. These little people are real. Hell, they could be all around us, and nobody sees them because we don't know how."

Hopper's first reaction was to utter a resounding "Bullshit. No way. Little people living around us in the shadows? No way." But he checked himself. Nozetape had to be dead wrong, but he wasn't sure enough to argue about it. He wouldn't argue about alien probes either, though he was pretty damn sure the odds were against it.

Hopper took the bottle. "So you're saying these little people, if they're out there, wear boots, and we just happened to find one?"

Nozetape took the bottle back and handed it to Cord, who seemed oblivious to the conversation. Nozetape scratched his beard. "Well, I never heard anything about what they wear."

Cord spoke up. "Bet a hundred dollars they didn't wear gold buckles."

At first, Hopper thought Cord was trying to add humor to their out-in-orbit-with-little-people conversation. How would a gold buckle figure into their speculations about Indian leprechauns? Then he saw a metallic glint shining against the little boot's soil and leather.

He pushed his chair back and hurried to stand next to Cord, who stepped aside, allowing Hopper a clear view. They stood together staring at the metal buckle, freed now from earth and decay. Nozetape shouldered between them, leaning forward, closely inspecting the mystery metal.

Hopper snorted. "That ain't gold; couldn't be. Got to be brass . . . doesn't it?"

Nozetape, mumbling, spun and limped off to his bedroom. Hopper spoke without taking his eyes off the shiny metal buckle. "Where you going, Nozetape?"

"Back in a minute."

Hopper put a hand on Cord's shoulder. "It's got to be brass, doesn't it? What would a boot with a gold buckle be doing buried in the Oklahoma County Zoo?"

Nozetape reappeared with a magnifying glass and a metal rod. "Let me take a look." Hopper and Cord stepped aside. Nozetape inspected the buckle with the glass. "There are nicks on the buckle, and the color inside the nicks is the same on the outside."

"Which means what?" Cord asked.

"Which means it don't look to be plated. Whatever metal this is, it's solid all the way through."

Hopper took the glass and studied the buckle as Nozetape opened a pocket knife. "So how do we know it ain't solid brass?"

Nozetape pressed the blade of the knife against the buckle. "It's soft, like gold." He touched the buckle with the metal rod. He looked at his two friends and nodded. "I think this is gold, fellas."

Cord took the rod from Nozetape's hand. "What kind of hocus pocus did you do with this deal?"

"No hocus pocus, buddy. It's science. The rod's a magnet from an old electric motor. Gold don't answer a magnet. I didn't feel any attraction between these two."

Cord put the rod to the buckle, drawing it away slowly. He shook his head. "I can't feel nothing either."

It was Hopper's turn. He tried the rod and looked at the other two, smiling. "Boys, this might be honest-to-God gold. How about it, Nozetape? What do we have to do to be sure?"

Nozetape scratched his right eyelid. "There is another trick I know, but we'd have to cut the buckle off."

Hopper slapped him on the shoulder. "What are we waiting for? Use that pocketknife, and let's get on with it."

Cord raised his hand. "Just a minute. I'm not sure we ought to damage this thing. It might be important to keep it just like it is."

Hopper laughed. "Oh, yeah, we wouldn't want to damage such a perfect historical specimen." He laughed again. "Don't you reckon they could repair the strap if it was important? What do you say, Nozetape?"

Nozetape cleared his throat. "I see what Cord is getting at. I know you can hurt the value of an old coin if you try to fool around with it too much. We ought to be certain before we go cutting pieces off this thing."

Hopper licked his thumb and cleaned more dirt off the buckle. He held the boot near his eyes. "Well, I'll tell you one thing. Gold is a downright beautiful metal, ain't it, boys?"

Nozetape nodded. "Gold's had an almost hypnotic beauty for thousands of years. It's precious for lots of reasons, one of which is its beauty don't get corrupted by rust." He studied the buckle, speaking in a dreamy voice. "There's been more people ruined, killed, betrayed, misguided, and destroyed by the lust for gold than was ever made rich by the stuff. Even fewer was ever made happy by it, that's for damn sure. You ask me, gold is a kind of emotional poison. It's fine in little bits—rings and bracelets and such. But in big doses, it causes a kinda spiritual infection that brings out the worst in people. There's no way to calculate the number of physical and spiritual deaths and collapses caused by this shiny metal."

Cord took the boot from Hopper and turned it round in his hands. "There's a story here, guys. Assuming this is real gold, what kind of kid would be wearing a boot like this? How did it come to be bound up in the roots of a hackberry tree?"

"Where's the other one?" Hopper added. "There ought to be another one unless this boot came off a one-legged kid." They all stood quiet in the presence of a small, fragile, decayed boot with a gold buckle reflecting the light.

Hopper snapped out of his reverie. "Hey, I almost forgot something." He opened the lunch pail and picked out some bits of sassafras root. He handed one to Nozetape.

Nozetape rarely smiled, but his eyes sparkled as he examined the root. He held it to his nose. "Know what this is?"

"Damn right," Hopper answered proudly. "That there's sassafras root."

Nozetape nodded and walked to the kitchen cabinet, speaking over his shoulder. "You guys want some sassafras tea?"

Hopper watched Cord continue to clean the boot while Nozetape put a pan of water on to boil and pared slivers off the root. "How about it, Cord? If this is gold, how much do you think it's worth?"

"I don't know. Could be the boot, if it stays the way we found it, is worth more than the buckle by itself."

"So how do we find out what we can squeeze out of it?"

Cord took a long drink from the Boone's Farm. "Now, before you disagree, I need you to hear me out. We probably ought to turn this over to Buntz."

Hopper blinked, caught in a powerful backwash of disbelief. "Hold on just a damn minute, Cord."

"Just let me finish. You gotta admit it ain't ours. We found it on somebody else's property. If we try to sell it, we don't know what kind of laws we might be breaking. Hell, some of them might even be federal, like destroying an important historical site or something. I don't know about you, buddy, but I already spent enough time in the stockade. I don't want nothing like a jail cell or probation to get between me and California."

"Federal? How could it be federal?"

"I don't know, Hopper. Fact is, we don't know what we might be into. Let's just stick to the plan. Earn some money, get the bus fixed, and hit the road in April."

Hopper rubbed his eyes. He resisted the temptation to say what was really on his mind, which was "Cord, we gotta tighten your screws, buddy. You're talking crazy. Gold just got dropped into our lap, and you're worried about whether this gift horse has federal teeth." Instead, he ad-opted a cool, reasoned tone. "Listen, Cord, we might be able to get a couple hundred bucks out of that old boot. That would go a long way toward shortening the days between Oklahoma winter and California sunshine. You heard the rules all your life. Finders keepers, possession is nine-tenths . . . all that stuff. Before we lose our heads and make an error that'll give us heartburn for the rest of our lives, we ought to find out what we can get for this thing."

Cord kept his focus on the boot. "There's too much we don't know, Hopper. You're right, we might kick our own ass if we give it up, but we'll sure as hell kick our own ass if we do something foolish and wind up squared off against the law again. Every time that happens, we're out-numbered and on the losing team. Let's just play it safe and give it up. Hell, there might be a reward in this someplace. That would put some worry-free, no-strings-attached cash in our jeans."

Hopper groaned. He knew Cord's mind was made up, and once that happened, he was a hard man to redirect. On top of that, Cord had great hazard-detecting instincts. His nose for trouble got them out of many a tight spot in combat and elsewhere. Hopper would never live it down if he talked Cord into something that landed them in the soup. Whether he liked it or not, Cord was probably right. This wasn't like finding a coin or nugget you could just walk into a pawn shop and sell. An antique gold buckle might set off alarms they couldn't hear until somebody showed up with a warrant. He decided, though it was damn painful, to play it safe—this time.

"You're right, Cord. I'd rather lose a thumb than let go of something like this. But I guess we ought to turn it over to Buntz in the morning."

Cord grinned and clapped him on the shoulder. "Let's keep our fin-gers crossed and hope there's a reward. If there is, the first drink comes out of my share."

The moment he uttered those words, the house filled with the rich, earthy aroma of sassafras. Cord fetched another bottle of Boone's Farm from the fridge. They left the boot on the table and went into the living room to drink chilled wine, watch *All in the Family*, and contemplate the pleasures of having gold in the kitchen, even if it was temporary.

A few minutes later, Nozetape brought cups of steamy sassafras tea sweetened with pure Sapulpa, Oklahoma, honey. Hopper put his feet on the coffee table, savoring the warm, homey atmosphere enriched by the smell of sassafras. The gentle lift provided by the Boone's Farm was a bonus. He marveled at the day's closing delights and smiled, thinking how all life's tragedies, regrets, and uncertainties could dissolve in an unfamiliar combination of sensory pleasures at the end of an unusual workday. "I just wish every home in Oklahoma could share in the blessings of gold buckles, Boone's Farm wine, and the smell of boiled sassafras."

Five

Wednesday, January 24, 1973

On the way to work, Buntz listened to news broadcasters covering President Nixon's announcement. The Vietnam War was officially over—for America anyway. Buntz really didn't care one way or the other. Vietnam was a long way off, and none of his emotional vines stretched that far. It was more his nature to be moved by problems he could fix: not enough water here, too much there, too much shade, roots planted too close together, leaf blight, aphids. There was nothing he could do about planes dropping chemicals from the sky with the cruel aim of destroying plants . . . and people, of course.

Enemy offensives, ambushes, village relocations, bribes, and executions—none of this had anything to do with the orderly cycles of Lester Buntz's life and had no effect on the secret heartbeat of the Oklahoma County Zoo. The military had no interest in Lester Leroy Buntz. Fallen arches. The feeling was mutual. He had nothing against the guys that went and did their duty. He just didn't want them bringing anything toxic into his garden. It was part of his job to see that the men on the grounds crew didn't spill any of their poisonous emotional byproducts onto his precious plants.

The only interest Buntz had in Vietnam was orchids, particularly his specimen of the Medusa's Head variety, which he coaxed into blooming in the greenhouse just after the first of the year. He toyed with the idea it chose this time to bloom because it sensed the war was ending. Maybe it takes that kind of rotation in the universal vibe, along with the proper light exposure, water, and fertilizer mixture, to persuade a timid, exotic blossom to show itself after years of care.

As he pulled into the parking lot, he waited to hear the end of the weather reports. Heavy snow and ice expected tonight and tomorrow. Good news, bad news. Good because snow cover with a slow melt provides his soil with a refreshing bath preparing for spring's up-shoots. Plus, snow is a nitrogen source. His plant roots loved nitrogen. Bad news because snow may be an excuse for somebody to not show up for work. If the weather got bad enough, Mr. Neyland might even close the zoo. Not likely, though. Mr. Neyland lived in the director's residence on the hill overlooking the zoo premises. Getting to and from work is no problem for him. Other people's headaches are no skin off his aristocratic nose—bastard.

Buntz unlocked the shop, unplugged his golf cart, and rode the electric hum to the north gate. He unlocked it, let himself in, locked it back, and drove into the darkened zoo. He needed, as usual, to take heed this morning. He pulled his watch cap over his ears and thrilled at the cold signals of coming snow.

He paused at the lake to marvel at the near-perfect equipment nature built into the ducks and geese. No matter how cold it got, these birds were prepared to handle it. He sat in the predawn light, admiring the birds and listening to the rise and fall of the north wind. Cold. He looked at his watch, sighed, and pointed the cart toward the shop. He needed to get some extra out of the crew today in case somebody couldn't get to work tomorrow.

As he rounded the turn coming into the grazing animal area, he saw Big Ned standing near his fenced enclosure as if he was waiting for Buntz to come along. Buntz was always reverent in the presence of the largest ox in the world, a gaur. This was one of the last breeds of oxen on earth that refused to get domesticated. Buntz knew what the Bible said about God giving man dominion over all the animals. But deep in his heart, he admired Ned and his tribe for refusing to submit to the yoke. He hoped it wasn't a sin to respect Big Ned for not yielding to man's dominance like a tamed poodle. Gaur cows would die before they'd stand still and let themselves get milked. And these big bulls were liable to stomp a guy to death for trying to get involved in delivering a gaur calf. Gaurs were proud and stubborn. They just couldn't get it through their big, undomesticated heads that all earth's animals were created for mankind's pleasure.

Ned's ancestral home was the tropical jungles of Asia. He didn't usually leave the warmth of his barn on cold mornings. Come to think of it, Ned wasn't usually out this early, no matter what. Buntz braked the cart to pay some heed to this curiosity.

Ned was a truly intimidating animal, seven feet high at his massively muscled shoulder. He weighed more than a ton and a half. His great curving horns, each over three feet long, were thicker at the gnarled base than a man's neck. Ned studied Buntz, who sat shivering in the golf cart. The huge gaur shook his head from side to side, a gesture Buntz interpreted as a warning. Buntz tried to open a mental receiver to understand what the giant ox was thinking: an animal from the steamy Asian tropics penned up like a passive domestic cow in the freezing Oklahoman dawn. Nothing.

Ned turned his enormous body and strolled with slow majesty into the protection of his barn.

Buntz watched the dark door where Ned disappeared, until the cold closed all peripheral avenues of thought. Teeth chattering, he pointed the cart toward the warmth of the shop. Still, the question needed an answer. Why would a giant, untamed ox leave the protection of his barn at dawn and stand by the fence waiting for him? What was he supposed to heed from this?

He was so preoccupied with this puzzle that he almost rolled over the peahen's remains. He jammed on the cart's brakes, veering off the sidewalk. He groaned at the sight of bloody feathers. Reflexively, he glanced across the lake at the director's residence, wondering if Mr. Neyland was standing at his tall window, watching. He hoped not, but you never could be sure about that prick.

Buntz prayed every day that things on the grounds would operate with smooth predictability. He needed the grounds crew to be running with unnoticed reliability—like the sun rising every day. But they needed to operate in a state of virtual invisibility like a subterranean water table. If nobody could think of any good reasons for a shakeup, he, Lester Buntz, might step quietly into the head groundskeeper position when Junior Willy retired in April.

But here he was, staring at the sad remains of a savaged peahen. Mrs. Kroneson, the chairman's wife, had a special attachment to these peafowl. If one of them got tore up and she found out about it, there would be questions. With questions, there's always instructions. When instructions drift outside the ordinary course of things, there are too many possibilities for screw-up somewhere.

He wasn't sure why, but the grounds crew was the first line of zoo security. It didn't make sense. After all, how did plant management qualify anybody to serve on a security detail? But this was no time to argue about it.

If it could be done safely, better to eliminate all trace of this crime than get bogged down in inconvenient questions.

As far as he knew, nobody had an accurate count of how many peafowl lived in the zoo. Mrs. Kroneson insisted they be allowed to wander wherever they wanted, so they weren't confined to an enclosure. If he could quickly dispose of the remains of this poor peahen, maybe nobody above him on the food chain would know anything about it.

He bounded off the cart and shielded the carcass from the view of the director's residence. He closed his eyes and tried to decipher the clues. The peahen was roosting in this black gum tree. Most of the carcass was carried off to be stashed someplace. He looked up into the bare limbs. These peafowl are light sleepers, quick to raise an alarm. Mrs. Kroneson said eastern potentates sometimes used them for watchdogs.

The killer had to be up there waiting when she flew up to roost for the night. Must've been a bobcat or feral house cat.

He knew the crew was assembling in the shop and getting limbered up for the workday. With luck, he'd get the mess cleaned up before any outsiders got tripped up by bloody feathers on the sidewalk.

Back on the cart, he raced for the shop as fast as his electric motor would take him. His preoccupation with the dead peahen completely closed the mental door on the Big Ned question.

Six

Hopper and Cord sat in the Rambler, listening to the news about the end of the war, when Buntz high-balled into the parking lot. Hopper knew it was useless but decided to make one last try. "Look, Cord, maybe we should think about it one more day, you know, find out what this thing is worth, get all the facts before we do anything rash."

Cord opened the driver's door and stepped into the January wind. He leaned down and spoke to Hopper through the open door, allowing the wind to blow directly into Hopper's earnest face. "You think it would be easier if we found out it's worth a thousand dollars? Face it, buddy, the more it's worth, the more heartburn it'll cause you when we turn it over. Do yourself a favor and let's get this over with."

Hopper groaned and hung on to his door as the hard wind tried to wrench it from his grip. He opened the back door and wrestled the lunch pail and thermos. Cord trotted across the parking lot to stop Buntz before he got into the shop. As Hopper straightened, Cord ran back to the Rambler. Buntz disappeared behind the shop's metal door.

Cord looked puzzled. "He don't want to hear nothing about that boot—ever. I told him I thought it might have gold in it. He said he didn't care if it had the map to the holy treasure o' Zion. He says the deal is settled for all time. We just need to keep quiet and get to work."

Hopper instantly felt as if the north wind was caressing him with a loving hand. No need to restrain his broad grin. "Well, you got to admire a man like Buntz. When his mind's made up, by God, it's made up. Now we got the green light to find out how much the dingus is worth and get some coins into the highway kitty. Hell, if we get enough out of that buckle, we might cut our work sentence short for smart behavior. We could be heading for California before next month's rent's due." Cord nodded, his expression unchanging.

They double-timed toward the shop. "I'd sure rather spend the winter in California than here freezing my ass off manhandling trees." Cord mumbled something that sounded like agreement, his words lost in the north wind.

Buntz motioned them to the coffeepot, where everyone on the grounds crew was assembled. "Podd, something got one of our peahens last night. I need you to get over to the big black gum tree north of the grazing animal area and clean it up. Take a hose and be sure to wash the blood off the sidewalk. We probably won't have a bunch of visitors today, but, still, we don't want nobody getting queasy because of a gory sidewalk. Don't leave it wet. It's cold enough to freeze. Take a bucket of sawdust and a broom."

A clean-cut guy who looked about twenty sat casually astride a red compressor. "Hey, Buntz, you going to introduce us to the new men?"

Buntz glared. "Oh, sorry, Clary. I mistook you for an adult who can introduce his damn self if he wants to. But if you need me to do it, I will. Podd, you already been introduced, so get on with that carcass clean-up."

Podd muttered, lowered the earflaps on his oily plaid ball cap, and stepped out of the shop with a hose under his arm and a bucket of sawdust in his hand. Buntz waited for the sound of Podd's pickup to dwindle and then turned his attention back to the crew.

"Okay, men, this big guy here is Vernon Cord. This here is Dale Hopper. The curly-headed kid here that needs to be introduced is Terry Clary." Hopper thought he detected a sneer on Clary's milk-fed face. No effort to shake hands from that guy.

Buntz continued. "This stoop-shouldered fella is Sid Phillips." A gaunt man with a naturally sad expression and prematurely graying beard extended his hand.

"Nuh . . . nuh . . . nice to muh . . . meet you ffffellas."

Hopper's eyebrows arched. "Pleasure's mine." He smiled as he shook the offered hand.

Cord shook his hand next. "Howdy."

"This fat black guy here is Charlie Antoine."

Charlie chirped happily, as if the line was rehearsed, "Welcome to the can-do-zoo crew, getting the work done with fo' dull shovels and one sharp spade. Nice to have two new men around to be confused, amused, and abused like the rest of us."

Buntz interrupted the handshaking. "Okay, everybody knows everybody, so let's get to work. There's a snowstorm coming, and we need to be sure we're ready. Charlie, you and Clary drive down to the yard and load up some sand and salt. I'll call and tell them you're on your way. Sid—"

Charlie butted in. "Sorry, Buntz, but would you mind if I take Sid? Clary here ain't got a sense of humor, and I get hypochondria if I'm stuck in a truck with him more than a couple minutes."

Buntz squinted back and forth from Charlie to Clary. "What you do say, Terry?"

The kid flushed. "Fine by me. I can't understand most of Charlie's gibberish anyway."

"Okay. Sid, you go with Charlie. Clary, you catch up with Podd. When he's done with the carcass clean-up, you guys meet me at the sable barn. The big horns on those antelopes are banging on their steel roof. We need to dig some of the dirt out and lower the floor in that barn."

Clary frowned. "Just the three of us? That'll take all day. We can finish by noon if these new guys give us a hand."

An exaggerated smile appeared on Buntz's freckled face. "Great idea, Clary. I think I'll just put you in charge so you can run the grounds crew like it oughta be run. Hell, while we're at it, we ought to go ahead and put you in charge of the whole damn zoo." His smile disappeared, and

Buntz stepped close to the younger man, who scooted backward on the compressor, a scowl on his face.

"I got news for you, youngster. Just because your mama is a distant relative of the Kronesons don't mean you was born with management skills. And no, it won't take the three of us all day; it'll take you two all day. I got other stuff to do. So get with it."

Clary turned a deeper red and swelled. "Then I change my mind. I'll go in the truck with Charlie."

"I don't have time for this, Clary. Go get Podd and meet me at the sable barn like I said."

Clary slammed the shop door on his way out. Buntz mumbled, "Lord, give me a good excuse to fire that kid so I can hire a hand that's worth something." He shook his head, sighed, and got back to business. "Okay, Charlie and Sid, let's move. Hopper and Cord, come with me."

They stepped into the parking lot, where the pickup waited. "You boys get me a dozen more hackberries today—fifteen if you can. If the snow's as heavy as they say, we may not be able to get to the forty tomorrow, and we don't need to fall behind." He clapped Hopper on the shoulder. "Remember our deal. Concentrate on the work, do me a good job, and all three of us will be drinking peach nectar and counting our money. Now, let's work."

Hopper tried to get a handle on his runaway excitement. All lights were green. The gold was theirs. And, of course, there was bound to be another boot somewhere with a beautiful golden buckle attached. Floating above that dazzling, hypnotic fact was his ironclad confidence they would find it. He shot a playful elbow into Cord's ribs and sang, in his best Beach Boy imitation, "We'll have fun, fun, fun when we find the gold and haul it away."

Cord grumbled, "We ain't there yet, and there's cold, hard work to do before we are."

The smile on Hopper's face was almost enough to warm the cab even with the engine shut off. "Just look at it like this, Cord. We were looking at just as many cold, hard days yesterday, but there wasn't any gold to warm us up like there is today. Depending on what that little boot is worth, and depending on how long it takes to find the other one, hell, we could be on our way in a couple of weeks." He squeezed his hands into a pair of wool glove liners and wrestled his leather gloves on over them. He clapped his muffled hands and pulled his collar over his ears. "Let's do some prospecting."

Hopper pushed open the truck door, and the damp wind reminded him they were racing a snowstorm. Soon, all this woodland would be covered in a thick white frozen blanket, adding another layer of complication to any effort to locate that other boot.

They stepped onto the brown brittle grass, assembled their tools, and headed for the nearest gray-barked hackberry. Before they got down to business, Hopper looked over his shoulder at the depression where they found the boot. He spoke over the wind. "What do you reckon the odds are the other boot's under this tree?"

Cord rammed his shovel into the cold soil. "You're lucky, Hopper, but you ain't that lucky."

Hopper set to work, pushing his shovel blade into the yielding earth. "Well, Cord, my friend, you never know."

Seven

They really didn't expect to find the other boot conveniently packaged in the roots of the day's first hackberry. Sure enough, it wasn't. It wasn't in the second, third, or fourth either. Electric anticipation somewhat neutralized the cold for the first hour. They took a coffee break in the pickup and agreed this whole deal would be a source of chuckles when they were enjoying cold beers after a long day of surfing in California.

Heavy gray clouds and increasingly bitter north wind sent the unmistakable signal. Something disruptive and powerful was on the march, coming their way.

The nature of Hopper's anticipation began to shift without his notice. Though he continued to be on the lookout for the boot, his main focus turned gradually toward the lunch hour. The lure of the warm heater in the pickup began to dominate his thinking. Conversation trailed off as it was just too hard to catch the words before they blew south on the wind.

When the fifth tree came down, Hopper shivered as he stepped out of the depression left by its falling. When he saw the piercing eyes staring at them, he stumbled backward, almost tripping over the tree. Cord, busy collecting tools, didn't see the old man at first.

Hopper shouted over the wind, "Cord . . . Cord, we got company." Cord, startled, stepped out of the depression, positioning the downed tree between him and the old man.

Yesterday, their visitor looked like some bewildered but kindly wood spirit. Today, with threatening clouds looming overhead, he appeared the very soul of warfare and winter severity. His long gray-black hair streamed behind him. His beard, driven by the wind, whipped over his right shoulder. His bloodshot eyes, stung by the north wind, watered with an abundance that might be tears of sorrow. His faded military fatigue jacket seemed to be shedding leaves and twigs in the gusts. He regarded them with an expression that might be the prelude to an all-out attack.

Once he recognized the old man, Hopper shouted, "Hey, brother, you got to be freezing out here. We have a thermos of hot coffee in the truck. Let's go warm our bones." He walked past the old-timer, glancing over his shoulder. Cord followed, rolling his eyes. The old man stumbled along behind like some man-shaped forest debris being blown along by the wind.

Hopper climbed in the passenger side and scooted over to make room. Cord slid under the wheel, started the engine, and glared at his friend. The old man stood by the open passenger door for an uncertain moment. Cord shouted through the open door, "Climb on in, fella. It'll never get warm in here if we don't close that damn door."

The visitor hesitated. Then, mumbling something incomprehensible, climbed in beside Hopper, leaving the door open. Hopper looked from the old man to the open door and back again. As he reached across the old man's body to pull the door closed, a gust of wind slammed it shut without being touched by human hand.

For a few seconds, Hopper and Cord sat wordless, staring at the otherworldly figure sitting beside them. He, also wordless, stared back. In the closed pickup, their visitor gave off an aroma like the underside of a log rolled over after years of forest decomposition—not obnoxious but old and earthy.

Hopper broke the silence. "Okay, then, let's hope this thermos managed to hold in some heat." He poured coffee into the thermos lid, handing it to Cord. Then he rummaged in the lunch pail and found a

Styrofoam cup. He filled it and handed it to the old-timer. Cord watched the process with an exasperated expression. "What are you going to drink out of?"

Hopper grinned. "I'll just drink mine right out of the spigot." He sipped black coffee directly from the thermos. Cord groaned.

"Got any honey?" The old man asked in a gravelly voice.

Cord's mouth hung open. "Do we got any honey?"

"Yeah, honey. To sweeten the coffee."

Hopper's head rolled back, and his laugh rocked the truck. "Sorry, buddy, I'll check again. But Cord here loaded the lunch pail, and I'm pretty damn sure he neglected to put the honey in again." He clapped Cord on the shoulder. "How about it, Cord? You forgot the honey again, didn't you?"

Cord mumbled through clenched teeth, "Well, silly damn me. I went off and forgot the honey—again."

Hopper's laugh collapsed when the old man fished around in the pocket of his fatigue jacket and produced a plastic squeeze bottle in the shape of a little bear. "It's okay. I got some." As Cord and Hopper watched, amazed, the old man squeezed thick golden liquid into the Styrofoam cup. He extended the bear to Hopper. "Honey?"

Hopper grinned and nodded. "Don't mind if I do, Mr. . . . by the way, what's your name?"

"Finn."

Hopper took the plastic bear and squeezed honey into the thermos. Cord groaned again. Hopper offered Cord the bear. "How about you, Cord? Honey?"

Cord shook his big woolly head and growled. "Maybe next time."

The three of them sat drinking coffee, listening to the wind buffet the truck. In time, Finn said, "You boys are digging up trees. Why?"

Cord stared out the side window as Hopper explained. "It's like this, Finn. This is part of the zoo, and they're going to put a big cat exhibit in here. You know, lions, tigers, leopards, mountain lions, stuff like that.

Our boss wants to get as many trees out of here as we can before the dozers show up. All the stuff we can't get out will get pushed over."

"You're not taking them out to burn?"

"Hell, no, Finn. We're digging them up so we can replant them someplace else."

The old man nodded. "Glad to hear it." After another brief silence, Finn spoke again. "So there's going to be dozers in here later?"

"Yep."

"When?"

"Well, me and Cord was hired 'til April. Guess the dozers will show up sometime about then."

The old man nodded again and began to fidget in his pockets. He came up with a handful of leathery pods and handed them to Hopper. "These are for you."

Hopper politely took the pods. Finn produced another handful and reached across to Cord. "No, thanks, Finn. I got plenty of those things at home."

Hopper elbowed him in the ribs. "Take 'em, Cord. You never can have too much . . . what are these, Finn?"

"Coffee . . . from the coffee tree. It's not as good as this." He raised the Styrofoam cup. "But it's good if you make it right and put enough honey in it. They come from trees right over there." He gestured vaguely to the northwest. "Be sure to boil it first, or it'll make you sick."

"Great," Cord muttered as he dropped the pods into the lunch pail.

Hopper grinned and dropped his into the pail. "Obliged, Finn. And thanks for the sassafras you gave us yesterday. Made good tea."

The old man peered into the open lunch pail. "Is that an orange? I love oranges, but they don't grow here. It's been a long time since I had an orange."

Hopper picked up one of the two oranges and handed it to Finn. He was amused to see Cord's jaw muscles working. "Here, take it. Fair trade for the sassafras, the honey, and these coffee pods."

The orange disappeared into one of Finn's frayed pockets. He abruptly opened the truck door. He stepped out without a word, slammed the door, and walked northwest toward the woods.

Hopper bounded out of the truck. "Hey, Finn, there's a bad storm blowing up, buddy. You have someplace you can go stay warm? If you don't find some shelter, you'll freeze. Maybe we can take you somewhere." Hopper couldn't tell whether the old man didn't hear or ignored him. "Hey, wait a minute, Finn, let me ask you something." Finn stopped but didn't look back.

Hopper sprinted over and spoke to him briefly. Then the old man disappeared into the woods. Hopper, hunkered against the wind, ran back to the truck. He crawled into the cab and took a drink from the thermos.

Cord asked, "Well, does he have someplace to stay? I sure as hell don't want to show up here tomorrow or the next day and find the old fella."

"He says not to worry, he knows how to stay warm. But listen to this. I asked him if he knew anything about the little boot we found. He said yes. I asked if he knew where the other one was. He said yes. I asked him where it was. He said, "'Here.' Then he walked off."

Cord frowned. "Well, that was some big help." They looked at the woods where Finn disappeared. Hopper reached into the lunch pail and unwrapped a bologna sandwich. He handed the other sandwich to Cord. "How about it, Cord? You want half my orange?"

Eight

Ollie Oleg appraised the threatening gray skies crowded with heavy south-blowing clouds. This time, the weatherman had it right. There would be snow and ice. No way to tell how much, but he couldn't afford to take a chance. Prudence required him to assume the storm would be severe enough to shut down everything. Maybe not, but there were thousands of dollars at stake, and Ollie Oleg was a man that never took unnecessary chances where his money was concerned.

He kept a close eye on the rearview mirror as he meandered around the streets of Southtown, Oklahoma City. He pulled into the stockyards and made a couple of slow circuits, being sure no one was following.

Satisfied, he took Northwest 10th west to Piedmont Road. He parked on the northwest corner of the intersection and sat smoking a cigar, watching the traffic. When the cigar was down to a nub, he drove four miles north to the county road. Turning west, he eased his Bronco onto an abandoned oil lease road. He rumbled over the cattle guard, made a U-turn, and waited, watching. He almost decided to go back home. There was always a chance someone with skills was tailing him without his notice. But his concern for his dollars helped him master his paranoia. He pulled the Bronco back onto the county road and crept the last two miles to the widow's abandoned farm.

He pulled the Bronco onto the grass behind the vacant widow's house and watched, listening. A vehicle approached from the west. He narrowed his eyes and focused on the gravel road, his right hand on the .357 Magnum on the seat beside him. A nondescript old pickup, a load of hay on the bed, motored past without slowing.

Ollie waited a few more minutes with the Bronco's window down— listening. The only sound disturbing the eerie quiet of the abandoned farmstead was north wind. He got out of the Bronco and walked to the cellar door, his eyes constantly scanning all approaches. He knelt his great bulk to examine the two massive industrial locks securing the heavy metal door to the cellar's cement frame. Seeing no evidence of efforts to force the locks, he walked to the back of the house and disarmed the two double-barreled shotguns, which were rigged inside the cellar's dark entry to blast four barrels of twelve-gauge double-aught buckshot into the face and chest of anyone who opened that door without knowing how to bypass the boobytrap.

He pulled the thick door open and grinned at the big shotgun bores staring lustfully at his face and belly like homicidal metal eyes. "Morning, lads. Glad to see you're wide awake and on the job."

Though the steep concrete steps descending into the cellar's bowels were dark, the underground complex itself was well-lighted, warmed, and humid. The primal smell of reptile wrapped around him as he stepped into the steaming humidity. He was sweating before he reached the concrete floor. The cellar was crowded with wire cages of various sizes. They were filled with a large, colorful array of exotic reptiles and amphibians. Huge constrictors flicked blue-black tongues, tasting the air. Brilliantly colored frogs from Amazonian rain forests offered bright contrast to the cellar's drab concrete-metallic environment. Crates of freeze-dried crickets, meal worms, rats, and mice were stacked in the middle of the floor.

Ollie strolled from cage to cage, feeding the captives and cooing lovingly to the scaly serpents and smooth-skinned amphibians. He paused at the cage containing the massive seven-foot diamondback rattler. Other than an occasional lazy flick of the tongue, the snake gave no indication of being aware of Ollie's presence. The fat man jostled the cage.

The viper became alert and rattled in threatening response. Ollie smiled. "You'd love to put a fang in ole Ollie, wouldn't you, Big-eye? Forget it. There's smarter snakes than you trying to find a way to get to me. They don't have no better chance than you. See, you don't have the thumbs nor knowhow to get out of this cage. And them other snakes ain't got the brains nor guts to work their traps."

Ollie shook the cage again, setting off another noisy chorus of rattles. "Difference between you and me, Big-eye, is when I want to put a fang in somebody, they never hear the rattle."

He stepped back and spoke to the entire menagerie as he might speak to an attentive audience. "You ignorant, cold-blooded darlings won't understand, but I feel like tellin' you something. Wheels are turning that make it necessary for ole Ollie to move you all out. I know how bad you're all gonna hate to leave the comfy shelter of my hospitality." He chuckled. "But it'll do you no good to bitch about it. After all, if you're stuck with a snake's brain, life's tough wherever you are. Ain't that what the good Lord said would be payback for the mischief y'all did in the garden of Eden?" He whistled "Springtime in Alaska" as he continued with his feeding chores.

From the large wire cage against the north wall, a ghostly white king cobra raised three feet of its nine-foot body to stare directly into Ollie Oleg's eyes. Ollie knew the legends about the hypnotic power of certain snakes. And though he told himself he didn't believe in such lore, he shivered reflexively and averted his eyes from the snake's gaze. He moved on to tend to his other business.

He walked to the rear of the cellar, where a massive steel door was cut into the concrete wall. He reached under his sweat-stained shirt and pulled a string over his fat neck and bald head. With the key hanging on the string, he unlocked a huge bolted device on the door. This room was dark on the other side of the bolt until Ollie found the lights.

Piled up around the room were sacks of gold and silver coins and bouillon along with thick bundles of cash. Ollie smiled appreciatively at the riches assembled in his vault. He was enjoying the literal golden age for the black-market trade of exotic reptiles and amphibians. Pet shops, collectors, and even prestigious zoos lined up to pay big money for unusual specimens. Albinos of any species were worth their weight in gold; ball pythons, Burmese pythons, monocled cobras all created a frenzy in the exotic reptile world. And thanks to the foresight and ruthlessness of Ollie Oleg, the early '70s found Oklahoma City one of the major hubs in this lucrative trade.

Though Ollie made good money in the drug business, the main source of his cash (and easy cash it was) slithered into his pockets via the reptile business. Hell, if he'd known how things were when he decided to branch out from petty theft, he might have bypassed the perils of the drug business altogether. Every G-man in the world wanted to lock up drug dealers, but nobody gets medals for locking up a guy who peddles pets.

Ollie made his ponderous way to a noisy electric refrigerator and got a cold Coors to counter the effects of the steamy subterranean tropical environment. He took a deep pull on the bottle and pondered his next move.

Things were changing. The golden age was ending for the Oleg brothers. The feds were closing in. They didn't have enough evidence to make a case, but without some skillful misdirection, it was just going to be a matter of time. Even if he could sidestep the drug snares, his sources told him Congress was bound to pass the Endangered Species Act by the end of the year.

Across the country, there was a growing determination to stop the capture, transportation, and sale of rare animals, just when demand was at its highest. Somebody powerful intended to get serious about shutting down and prosecuting black-marketeers like Ollie. So before the rains came, Ollie needed an ark.

It was time to send another camouflage south with a portion of his treasures. These shipments grew in size and frequency as the federal authorities telegraphed their tightening grip. It was a race. Ollie felt sure he could string the investigators along until he could get the bulk of

his riches south, stashed in clunkers or random collections of recondi-
tioned auto parts. For the moment, the G-men weren't concerned with
chopped cars, exotic pets, and the occasional transaction in low-value
hot merchandise. They were zeroed in on more tempting targets: drugs
and homicide. He was confident they had taken the bait, believing that
Ollie might be persuaded to help apprehend the real culprits. In return,
the feds suggested there might be some reduction in their prosecutori-
al zeal where his small-time mischief was concerned. For the moment,
they had no idea just how extensive his empire really was.

Ollie had loose ends to tie up. Bogus cases implicating dummy culprits had to be carefully constructed. Evidence had to be findable but
not too easy. And when he made his move, the authorities had to think
he was dead—not that it really mattered. Where he was going, he didn't
need to worry about extradition. But still, if the feds were convinced he
was dead and disposed of—without a trace—they might just file him
away in the "case closed" drawer. Hell, after a few years, when everything
got all unwrinkled, he might even be able to sneak back home.

Ollie filled his overalls pockets with gold coins and cash. He checked
his .357 Magnum just to make sure there was a 158-grain hollow-point
bullet in every chamber. He tossed a longing glance at his precious
hoard before turning out the light, backing out of his vault, and locking
the bolt.

As he made his final walk-through, admiring his inventory, he
stopped by a large tank in the cellar's northwest corner. This tank served
as home to his most remarkable specimen, Snowflake, the monstrous
albino gator. There wasn't another like him in the world. In a market
with an unquenchable thirst for albinos, Snowflake was a legend. "Are
you hungry already, you gluttonous bastard? How does another snack
sound to you?" Ollie went to the freezer in the cellar's northeast corner
and removed a stiff, pale human arm. "Here you go, you man-eating son
of a bitch. Enjoy." He threw the limb into the tank. The huge, colorless
reptile launched a savage attack on the frozen arm, splashing water on
Ollie, who stumbled back, laughing.

"You got no manners at all, Snowflake. Just the same, you're welcome." He watched the gator with a mixture of repulsion, fascination,
and admiration. He spoke with a sure confidence that comes so easy
when the albino monster is in his cage. "Any dreams you may have about
taking a bite out of ole Ollie, well, you can just forget 'em. Someday, no
matter how much money you're worth, I just might be wearing your ass
for boots."

Nine

When Hopper and Cord got home that night, they left the premature darkness, bitter cold, and howling wind behind and stepped into a house unusually bright, infused with the pleasing smell of sassafras. The chorus of Steely Dan's "Do It Again" played on Nozetape's reel-to-reel. Nozetape beamed an uncharacteristic grin as he hobbled to the door to meet them.

Before Hopper could compliment Nozetape on this outpouring of joyful vibes on this threatening winter night, Nozetape grabbed his shoulder, pulling him toward the kitchen table, chattering as they made their halting way.

"Hold on to your pump-jacks, boys. Have I got news!"

Cord stood in the doorway scratching his jaw. "You been doubling up on your pain pills again, Nozetape?"

Hopper struggled to shed gloves and coat as Nozetape towed him toward their wobbly wooden kitchen table. The table's scratched surface was completely covered with pages in clear plastic sleeves, copies of maps, old newspapers, documents, and reproductions of grainy antique photographs.

Nozetape was breathless. "My aunt's a curator at the Western States Historical Museum. I had lunch with her today and spent all afternoon at the museum trying to get a line on where that little boot came from. I think we might be onto something really big."

Hopper's coat and gloves fell in a pile on the floor. Cord tossed his onto the couch. Nozetape stood beside the table, an artist triumphant, displaying his creation. Hopper's head whipped to and fro over the confusing assortment arranged according to some order Nozetape was eager to explain. "Okay, Nozetape, what's all this got to do with the boot?"

Cord clumped over to the table and looked over Hopper's shoulder, chewing his lower lip. "I don't suppose it would do any good to ask for the short version."

Nozetape drew a deep satisfied breath. "Okay, let's start from the beginning." He handed Hopper a copy of a barely discernible old photograph of two men. Hopper could make out thick black whiskers, bushy eyebrows, and dark suits. The men could've been twins.

Nozetape pointed. "This is Gustaf Alimony and his brother, Wilhelm. They had a gun-manufacturing business in Prussia. They moved to England, where Wilhelm died. Gustaf married an English lady named Margaret Bodine." He handed Hopper another photograph of slightly better quality. One of the whiskered men, apparently wearing the same suit, sat in a chair with a bowler hat on his right knee. A lady in a high-collared white dress stood behind him. The dress might have been a wedding dress, but there was nothing joyful in the expression on either face.

Nozetape went on. "They had one child, Lawrence, who was a dwarf. Here's a family picture."

Hopper studied the stern old Gustaf Alimony, same suit, same hat; Margaret, wearing darker clothes this time, had one hand on Gustaf's shoulder and one on the shoulder of a tiny boy, dressed in a frilly shirt and knee pants. He looked more like a porcelain doll than a little kid.

Cord mumbled, "It never occurred to me that boot might belong to a dwarf." He poked the picture in Hopper's hand. "So this is the little fella it belongs to?"

"I'll get to that in a minute," Nozetape said, taking the picture from Hopper's fingers. "Margaret died, and Gustaf brought Lawrence into the gun-making business. Evidently, the little guy had an aptitude for manufacturing and design. He helped old Gustaf get some patents on firing mechanisms. Alimony Firearms was doing real well, when Lawrence got interested in underwater salvage."

Hopper scratched his beard. "That's an odd combination—firearms and underwater salvage."

"There's a lot about this story nobody knows. We do know that Alimony Firearms and Alimony Marine Salvage operated as different companies. Evidently, Gustaf or Lawrence got a lead on a Viking treasure ship full of gold and silver that sunk at a point on the Thames estuary called the Black Deep. My aunt says over the years, the Anglo-Saxon kings sent more than eighteen thousand pounds of silver and some huge quantities of gold to keep the Vikings from raiding England. These payments were called the Danegeld."

"Wait, wait . . . Danegeld?" Nozetape, impatient, slowed the story down for a brief tutorial on the history of English/Viking commerce.

"Anyway, the Alimonys developed a diving bell that allowed the old man to have air pumped to him so he could get down to the wreck and haul up a fantastic treasure."

Hopper gulped audibly. "Treasure. You mean there might be more to this than a couple of little gold buckles?"

Nozetape arched his eyebrows and nodded. "Could be. Could be a lot more. My aunt says this story pops up every five years or so. It's one of the most famous lost treasures on earth. It's the only great Viking treasure with bona fide links to Oklahoma. They got a whole exhibit at the museum. These are copies of some of the stuff in that exhibit."

Hopper rolled up his sleeves and made a beeline for the fridge. "Hold on a second, Nozetape. Don't say another word. My head's spinning. I got a get us a beverage to help focus our attention."

Cord studied the picture of the tiny boy who appeared to be looking at his father's big hat. "Got any pictures of Lawrence after he grew up?" Nozetape handed him a copy of a grainy photograph of Lawrence Alimony peering sadly into the camera, dressed in the dignified finery of a proper Victorian gentleman, only in miniature.

Hopper came back opening a bottle of Boone's Farm apple wine. He took a drink and handed the bottle to Cord, who took a long drink without taking his eyes off the picture. The grown-up Lawrence looked a lot like a scaled-down version his father, complete with whiskers and eyebrows.

Hopper recovered the bottle. "Come on, Nozetape. Let's hear more about the treasure."

"The old man went down in dangerous waters with equipment Lawrence designed and patented. They pulled up thousands of gold and silver coins. It was one of the most famous treasure recoveries in English history. It's called the Hogge Hoard. There was enough treasure to give Queen Victoria her share with plenty left over to make Alimony and son two of the richest guys in England.

"The Queen was so grateful, she awarded Gustaf the title of baronet. Since that's a hereditary honor, when Gustaf keeled over with a heart attack, little Lawrence, who was seventeen at the time, became the new Sir Alimony. Without old Gustaf looking out for him, Lawrence was a sitting duck for a gold-bricking high-class actress named Charlotte Selden." Nozetape unfolded a copy of an English newspaper dated July 1891. "Here's her picture. Not exactly the proper Victorian lady, is she?"

The photograph showed an attractive but pudgy young woman, teenager maybe, dressed in tights, reclining seductively on a couch, wearing a skirt way too short to satisfy the standards of Victorian modesty. She wore a Robin Hood hat and pointed a fencing sword in the air.

Nozetape, clearly enjoying the exercise, went on. "Miss Selden swept Lawrence off his little feet and lured him into a quick, scandalous marriage. Right away, she and some of her show business buddies got busy trying to clean him out."

Cord, still looking at the newspaper, snorted. "She may be cute by their standards, but she'd have a damn hard time getting her hooks into any treasure of mine."

Hopper chuckled. "Might not be hard if you was a rich orphan dwarf and this was the prettiest dancer in town who'd let you look at her legs backstage. Go on, Nozetape."

"It took Lawrence a couple of years, but he wised up. He gathered the bulk of his treasure, loaded it in a big trunk, and slipped out of London while Mrs. Alimony was out of town. He jumped on an American-bound ship in Liverpool and headed for California. When Mrs. Alimony got back from her frolic and found him lit out with all them riches, she went into an almighty fury, madder than a bee-stung skunk. She hired detectives and ruffians to spread out all over England and track him down so she could get her hands back on that booty. It didn't take them long to figure out he'd headed for the American territories."

Hopper nodded. "It would've been real hard for a dwarf with an English accent and a trunkful of treasure to blend in if he was headed across the American West."

Nozetape smoothed out a reproduction of an old map showing rail lines. He traced a solid colored line from New York to Chicago to St. Louis. He pointed to a dotted line running southwest from St. Louis. "This is the Missouri, Kansas, and Texas rail line, the MKT. We know Lawrence took this train from St. Louis all the way to McAlester, Oklahoma."

Cord interrupted. "How are we so sure about that?"

Nozetape flashed another uncharacteristic grin. "I'll get to that juicy tidbit in a minute. Anyway, he changed trains at McAlester and headed west on the Choctaw, Oklahoma, and Gulf line. He and Pete McGuire, the guy traveling with him, got off in Wewoka and fitted out with a wagon and team. They continued west from there."

Hopper scratched his head. "If they could ride the rail all the way to California, why get off in Wewoka and bump along in a wagon?"

Nozetape shrugged. "No one knows, but somewhere along the way, they picked up a tail. Four outlaws out of Texas caught up with them in what's now eastern Oklahoma County. There's lots of speculation about what got these outlaws interested in Alimony and McGuire. Could've been Mrs. Alimony's doing, but we'll never know."

Hopper handed Nozetape the bottle. "How come the outlaws left the little guy's boot? Was there some reason they didn't care about gold buckles?"

Nozetape took a drink, handed the bottle to Cord, and folded the railroad map. "Be patient just a little more, fellas. We're almost there. A detail of troopers from Fort Reno was in the area and heard shooting. By the time they got to the scene, Pete and Lawrence were goners. The four outlaws opened up on the troopers, and all four of them got killed in the shootout. The treasure was never found."

Cord chimed in again. "Okay, Nozetape, how do we know Alimony even had the treasure with him after he left New York or Chicago or St. Louis? Hell, he could've hid it or shipped it anywhere along the way."

Nozetape clapped his hands. "Presto! We know he had the treasure because he says so."

Hopper shook his head. "What you mean he says so?"

"Lawrence kept journals. He wrote the whole story from Liverpool to Wewoka, all the way up to a few hours before he got killed."

"No shit." Hopper was almost breathless. "So nobody found the treasure, and Lawrence had a journal. Surely that journal said where the treasure was."

"Afraid not, Hopper. If the journal told where the treasure was, somebody would've found it. People have been over these journals hundreds of times since Lawrence Alimony's trail ended and the Hogge Hoard disappeared."

Hopper couldn't contain his impatience. "So where's the damn treasure?"

Nozetape eased himself onto one of their creaky chairs. "The last three pages Lawrence Alimony wrote in his last journal were torn out. Everybody assumes if there are clues about where the treasure is, they're in those three lost pages."

"So where could those missing pages be?"

Nozetape rubbed his damaged legs. "Nobody knows."

Hopper plopped heavily onto the chair next to him. Cord peered over the documents as if someone overlooked the X marking the spot

Nozetape produced a copy of an inventory of Alimony's goods. "Lawrence's possessions were collected and carried to Fort Smith. Mrs.

Alimony's agents examined everything with magnifying glasses. They never found anything. Every single article that might have a map hidden in it or on it was shipped back to England, where Mrs. Alimony could inspect it herself. We're lucky the last journal was copied before the original was sent to the widow."

"You reckon somebody could've already found the treasure and just kept their mouth shut?"

Nozetape shook his head. "There was coins in the Hogge Hoard that came from the treasuries of Anglo-Saxon kings. If anybody found that stuff, some of it would've turned up."

Hopper scratched his head. "What about that other guy—Pete? Did anybody go over his stuff? Maybe he had the map."

Nozetape looked troubled. "Now that you mention it, I didn't see anything about McGuire's possessions."

Hopper eyed Nozetape with disbelief. "Well, hell, Nozetape, don't that seem like a logical place for them lost pages to be?"

"You're right, Hopper. I'll look into it."

Cord pulled up a chair and joined them. "With all the treasure hunters on the trail, how come no one found the boot?"

Nozetape shrugged. "Could be they were wrong about where Pete and Lawrence died. They surely combed and recombed the likely locations of Alimony's last stand with metal detectors, flashlights, and tweezers."

They sat quiet until Hopper lurched from his chair and stomped to the window. A mixture of rain and sleet began to fall. "Wouldn't it be great to find that treasure, boys, to be really rich?"

Cord went to the kitchen and started opening cans of chicken noodle soup. "Cheer up, Hopper. Yesterday you were all giddy about a chance at getting a couple hundred bucks out of the buckle."

"Yeah, but that was yesterday, before Nozetape pointed us to the yellow brick road."

The same realization jolted all three of them at the same time. Hopper whirled and shouted "The map!"

Cord was already on his way to the boot, which was sitting on a lamp table. Nozetape stuttered, "The boot . . . the map's in the boot. They went over everything except the boot. They didn't have it."

Cord carried the boot to the kitchen table and held it close to his eyes, examining every stitch that secured the sole to the upper. Hopper and Nozetape stood on tiptoe, trying to make their own inspection. Cord licked his thumb and rubbed the boot's sole, straining to see if there were markings. He showed it to Hopper. "I can't see anything except scuff marks. Do you see something?"

Hopper held the boot close to his own eyes. "Nothing. You, Nozetape?"

Nozetape went through the same operation. "Maybe it's someplace inside." He turned the boot upside down and shook. Dirt and a few small rootlets dropped onto the table. "Just a minute." He handed the boot to Cord, who went on with a careful inspection. Nozetape returned with a flashlight. "Let me see."

He shined the flashlight beam into the boot's throat. "Shit, I can't see a thing."

Hopper took the flashlight. "Hold it up so I can get a good look inside." He shined the light into the boot and squinted hard. Cord shook the boot again. Nothing came out this time. "Maybe we ought to disassemble this thing."

Cord shook his head. "You can tell by looking at the stitching nobody took it apart to hide a map and then restitched it." He twisted the heel to see if it might show a willingness to shift. Nothing.

They sat at the same time. No one spoke until Hopper said, "Boys, there's a treasure map in that other boot. Has to be. We got to find it."

Cord cleared his throat. "Don't get your hopes up, Hopper. We only got 'til April to look for it. There's no guarantee it's anywhere near the place we found this one. Even if we find it, there may not be a map."

"Yeah, but think about it, fellas. If we find that treasure, we'd be on easy street for the rest of our well-fed lives." Hopper slammed his fist down on the table. "Whatever it takes, I'm going to find that boot."

Cord and Nozetape exchanged glances. Cord spoke up. "Dale, just listen to what I'm about to say, and sleep on it. Yesterday, that little buckle, all by itself, was cause for celebration. Now, you got two hundred and twenty volts running through your hundred-ten wiring, and that ain't healthy. Hell, we might not be able to keep any part of the treasure even if we find it. Let's not let this treasure deal take our thinking down the wrong path."

Nozetape put Rare Earth on the reel-to-reel, and the opening riff to "Born to Wander" seemed appropriate for the moment. "You guys remember that movie *The Treasure of the Sierra Madre*?"

Hopper plopped onto their living room chair, dangling his leg over the arm. "Nice one, Nozetape. Three guys that are best pals set out to look for treasure, and one of them ends up getting greedy and trying to kill the other two. Nobody winds up with a goddam thing. But that's got nothing to do with us. We ain't that way."

"They wasn't that way to start."

Hopper lurched out of the chair and went back to the window. "What are you guys saying? You think we ought to just sell the one buckle and forget about the whole treasure?"

Cord carried the Boone's Farm to the window and stood beside his friend. Outside, nature was winding up for a real blast-everything-in-sight pitch. Slivers of sleet pattered against the window, mixed with drops of driving rain. Flashes of lightning gave brief form to the trees lining the street outside, which whipped back and forth, mindlessly obeying the confused and powerful switches in wind direction. He handed Hopper the bottle. "Here's what I'm saying, buddy. Let's see if we can find the treasure. No harm in looking. If we do, it's an even three-way split on everything we get out of it."

Hopper looked at him with a hurt expression on his face. "Of course that's right. How else would it be?"

Nozetape shook his head. "Leave me out of the split. I don't want any part of that treasure."

Hopper blinked in disbelief. "My ears must be playing tricks on me. I thought I just heard you say you want no part of the treasure."

"That's what I said."

"Well, brother, you got to explain 'cause I'm missing something. You put us on the trail and then say you're not interested in finding it."

"I didn't say that. I'm real interested in finding it. It's a mystery I'd love to solve. But if we find it, the only thing I want is a souvenir."

Hopper was struck by an emotional cocktail that whipped from amusement to sorrow to confusion and maybe even a touch of envy. Cord seemed lost in his own thoughts. Hopper shook his head. "You got to help me get a handle on this, Nozetape. What's the deal?"

Nozetape rubbed his ruined legs and shrugged. "I can't explain it. I just know for sure that if I take a share of that treasure, it would cost me a lot more than I'd make out of it." In the room's awkward silence, he sat looking at his hands. After a minute, he looked at his friends as if he needed some sign of understanding. "When I found out about the treasure, I got real excited. It was like a tidal wave washed over me. For a few minutes, I never wanted anything in my life as much as I wanted that treasure. But then it was like I heard a warning from somewhere. Maybe it wouldn't be bad for you guys, but I know for damn sure it would be bad for me."

Cord laughed. "Living with you guys is more entertaining than living in Disneyland. Hell, with you two around every day, who needs LSD?"

Hopper snorted. "Look who's talking. This is the guy that gets all sentimental and spooky about a trashy little boot."

"Right. Turns out it's a good thing I did, wouldn't you say?"

Hopper stood and stretched. "Just the same, we'll see how you feel when we actually get our hands on it. It'll be a lot harder to say, 'I can't take it 'cause I got a supernatural warning' when gold's piled on the floor in front of us."

Nozetape shrugged again. "Maybe."

After a second or two of private thought, Cord rejoined the conversation. "And if we don't find it, sounds like we got good reasons not to get busted up and bitter about it. Let's just chalk it up to the way the cards was dealt and concentrate on making the most of our move to California. Deal?"

"But there's treasure out there, Cord."

"I hope we find it, but find it or not, we can't let it crowd everything else out of our thinking. Like Nozetape says, remember *Treasure of the Sierra Madre.*"

Hopper took a long drink. "We ain't like that and never would be. Hell, we just don't have the seeds of that kinda greed in us—do we?"

Cord took the bottle back. "Well, just sleep on this question. Would you want to find the treasure if you knew it would ruin your life?"

The lights flickered as a strong thunderclap shook the house. With the next lightning strike, the lights went off, and the reel-to-reel went silent just as Quicksilver Messenger Service encouraged them to "have another hit of fresh air." Hopper spoke in the dark. "It's going to be a miserable night out there tonight, isn't it, boys?" No one answered. "I sure hope that old-timer out on the forty can find someplace warm to stay."

Ten

Bennie Wilkes stomped snow off his boots as he knocked on the door of the nondescript shotgun shack deep in the neighborhood known as the Flats. The houses here were built cheap and fast to provide residence for the flood of laborers who invaded Oklahoma City in the 1920s. They came by the thousands seeking employment in the metallic forests of oil rigs springing up everywhere as wildcatters and big oil companies sought to exploit the seemingly endless petroleum reserves directly under the city streets.

On a night like this, when snow blanketed the dilapidated car bodies, sagging carports, and bare yards, the oppressive air of decay accumulating over the last four and a half decades was temporarily disguised.

The residents down here in the Flats were well aware of their lowly status. They were doomed to live the bluest of blue-collar lives, which they faced with hopeless resentment and grim humor.

When no one answered his first knock, Bennie considered hurrying off the porch, hoping his "I tried" explanation would buy him some time. Just as he was turning to leave, the door opened. Big Pat never smiled, and when he spoke, his words always bore a poisonous undertone. He growled. "Evenin', Bennie. What brings you out on a night so full of danger and treachery?"

"Hi, Pat." He stood at the door, looking at the rubber mat that said "Welcome." "I meant to come earlier, but we had a shipment down to the yard that we had to get out before the roads—"

"Shut up," Pat thundered. "You didn't answer my question, so I'll answer it for you. You're out tonight because I told your deadbeat ass to be here tonight. Lucky you're on time because it would've gone hard if I'd had to come looking for you."

Bennie blushed and mumbled an elaboration on his pipe yard excuse, when a loud, calm voice drifted over Pat's head. "Hey, Pat, where the hell are your manners, son? It's cold out there. Ask Bennie to come in and have some coffee. It's rude to make a man stand on the porch and freeze when it's so warm and toasty inside."

Pat stepped aside, and Bennie squeezed by, eyes still downcast. The big, calm voice spoke again. "Take your coat off, Bennie. Come on in here and sit down. Get him a cup, Hub."

Bennie obediently removed his coat and looked around for somewhere to put it. After an awkward moment, Pat snatched it from his hand. Bennie gulped and walked the ten paces that separated the front door from the kitchen. Ollie Oleg sat at the table, the fingers of his massive hands laced over the bulging overall-clad belly.

Hub, one of Ollie's giant henchmen, solemnly offered Bennie a cup of black coffee. Ollie's smile displayed all the outward indications of real affection. "What was it you wanted to see me about, Bennie?"

Bennie stammered, "I'm really sorry, Ollie. I really was . . . you know . . ."

Ollie spoke soothingly. "Relax, Bennie. Sit down. I know you'd never welch on a debt you owed your ole pal Ollie. Really, sit down. We'll work it out."

Bennie looked over his shoulder. Pat stood behind him, hands deep in his overalls pockets. Bennie shuddered at the thought of the menacing objects concealed in the depths of those pockets. He moved, tentatively, to the vinyl kitchen chair across from Ollie's walrus-like bulk.

Ollie leaned forward, peering into Bennie's eyes. His smile, rich with that old Ollie charm, was contradicted by something cold and threatening in the eyes. "Believe me, Bennie, I understand. You took the long odds on Frazier hoping he'd find a way to stay out of Foreman's reach until the later rounds. If he'd done that, he might be heavyweight champeen of the world, and you would've had the biggest payday in your life, right?"

Bennie nodded.

"But the smart money knew that Frazier couldn't do that. He couldn't lay back. He had to take the fight to Foreman. He had to punch it out. The smart money knew Frazier didn't have a chance. What did you put on the fight, five hundred?"

Bennie nodded again.

"You got that much, Bennie? Can you settle up . . . tonight?"

"Look, Ollie, I—"

The smile was still there, but the voice lost all pretext of friendliness. "Goddammit, Bennie, it's a yes-or-no answer. Can you settle up tonight?"

Bennie shook his head. The friendly concern returned to the voice. "I'm sorry to hear that, Bennie, real sorry." Ollie leaned back in the creaky chair. "Any idea about how we can handle this? I mean, you know what happens if you can't get this mess straightened out."

Bennie gulped, hard. "Listen, Ollie, in a few days—"

Ollie's meaty fist crashed on the table, and Bennie started to his feet. Big Pat's hand forced him back into the chair. A sinister change transformed Ollie Oleg. He became a fearsome ogre clenching and unclenching his fists as he spoke through gritted teeth. "See, Bennie, if you'd have talked to me about time when you made the bet, I could've helped you. If you'd talked about time, I would've said, 'Bennie, boy, if time is a factor in this deal, don't make the bet. Time don't have no place in the equation. You win the bet, I pay you now—*now*, Bennie. You lose, you pay—*now*. See? If I owe somebody something, they never have to come looking for me. I pay my debts—on time. You follow me, Bennie?"

Bennie looked over his shoulder at Pat, standing between him and the door. Hub and Tiny, Ollie's other giant henchman, leaned against the refrigerator like grotesque bookends, their big arms crossed over their chests.

"Yeah, I get you, Ollie. What are you going to do to me?"

Ollie pulled a chair up next to him, hefted his big leg, and settled a heavy lug-soled Wolverine boot on the seat. "I'm going to give you a way out, Bennie."

Bennie began to shake, and his eyes started to water. "Thanks, Ollie. I'll do whatever you say, and I'll never put you in this position again. You just tell me what you want me to do. Anything, Ollie—really, anything."

Ollie's charming smile warmed the room. "I knew that's how you'd feel about it, Bennie. And now that I think of it, there is something you can do for me." He thrust a thumb over his right shoulder. "Go get 'em, Tiny."

Tiny heaved his big body off the refrigerator and disappeared down the narrow hall. Ollie spoke to Bennie without looking at him. "That Chevy C-10 of yours is four-wheel drive, ain't it?"

Bennie nodded eagerly, reflexively casting a glance over his shoulder as if he could see his pickup parked outside on the street.

"Good, because they're talking about closing the airport tonight, and I got some cargo that needs to be in Los Angeles tomorrow. In order for me to be sure I'm on time, somebody's got to drive this cargo to Dallas tonight so it'll be sure to make a morning flight."

Bennie blinked. "You mean if I drive something to Dallas tonight, we're square?"

Ollie's laugh shook the table. "Of course not, you dumbass. You think it's worth eight hundred dollars for you to drive to Dallas?"

Bennie's mouth hung open. "But Ollie, the bet I made was only for five hundred dollars."

Ollie's laugh dwindled to a chuckle. "Let me explain how it works, Bennie. You make a five-hundred-dollar bet. You lose, you owe five hundred. If I have to come looking for you, you owe six hundred or more, depending on your attitude. I come looking for you, and you can't pay—well, in a situation like that, there really ain't no cap on what you owe. In your case, you owe eight hundred dollars and a trip to Dallas. But I ain't unreasonable. You got a week to come up with the money. This Dallas thing, well, that's your down payment."

Tiny came back into the room and placed a plastic tube on the table in front of Bennie. The tube contained four small white snakes flicking tiny pink tongues. Again, Bennie's reflexes caused him to push his chair back and raise off the seat. Again, Tiny's big hand forced him back down.

Ollie laughed again. "Snakes bother you, Bennie?"

"I don't know, Ollie. I just . . . you know."

"Don't be embarrassed, Bennie. It's called ophidiophobia, fear of snakes. Did you know ophidiophobia is the most common diagnosable mental illness in the world? Yeah. About one-third of the people in the world are ophidiophobic. Funny, ain't it?"

Bennie tried to laugh, but the mechanism failed.

Ollie pulled a large pocketknife from his overalls pocket, opened the blade, and began to scrape grime from beneath his nails. Bennie stared at the snakes, wondering what they had to do with his problem.

Ollie cleared his throat. "Then, of course, there's some people that are fascinated by snakes—love the bastards. Bennie, did you know that there are people that would pay close to five thousand each for them little fellas in that tube in front of you?"

Bennie eyed the tube with renewed interest. Ollie continued. "Ball pythons is what they are. That, all by itself, makes 'em a hot item. But, as you see, these are albinos. That means there's people that would do almost anything to get their hands on one. People all over the world are trying to find a way to breed albinos, and they can't figure it out. Guess who figured it out, Bennie. Guess who figured out how to breed albinos of almost any species of snake."

"Must have been you, huh, Ollie?"

Ollie laughed. "Better. I didn't have to waste the time and put up with the hassle of doing it. All that got figured out by people I own. They do it for me, and if they try to fuck me—well, even if you ain't ophidiophobic, nobody wants to be snake food, do they, Bennie?" Ollie, Pat, and the giant henchmen all laughed.

Ollie fixed Bennie with a meaningful stare. "Here's what I need you to do. Cousin Mabel is waiting for you at the Skyline truck stop. Go pick her up and drive her to Dallas. She knows what to do with these cuties."

He nodded to the small white snakes in the plastic tube. Then he continued. "Mabel has the cash to check you guys into a hotel room near Love Field. Tomorrow morning, you see to it she gets on a plane for Los Angeles. Understand?" He waited for a response.

"Well, Ollie, the roads are getting real bad. What if I can't get through?"

Ollie's benign smile was again contradicted by the tone of his voice. "Get through, Bennie. Make sure Mabel gets on that plane. It's real important to me that these little guys get delivered to the buyer in Los Angeles tomorrow. But for me, it's only money at stake. For you, there's more—a lot more." He snapped the knife's blade closed and replaced it in his pocket. "I don't need to go into details about that, do I, Bennie?"

Bennie gulped and shook his head.

"Good. Now you go get Mabel, take care of this for me, and you'll buy yourself some time to sort out this other deal. Okay?"

Bennie nodded again.

Ollie waved his big hand, indicating the audience was concluded. He walked Bennie to the door, his arm around the man's shoulders in a gesture that any outside observer would take for tender friendship. "And, Bennie, next time you get the idea of betting on a long shot, talk to me first, will you? I hate to see a decent fella like you blundering into situations like this." They paused at the door. There was a tone of genuine concern in Ollie's voice. "Drive careful, Bennie."

Eleven

Hopper sensed someone in the corner of his room. He was surprised but not alarmed; had to be Cord or Nozetape. Had he overslept? "What time is it?" he mumbled, rolling over to see his bedside clock. It was flashing as it did when the power got knocked out and came back on: 12:00 . . . 12:00 . . . 12:00. "What's going on?" He tried to make out which of his roommates was sitting in the darkened corner.

"Cord, is that you? Nozetape?" No answer. Whoever it was sat in the dark without speaking or moving. Hopper turned the switch on his lamp. Nothing happened. He sat up and squinted into the dark, trying to see a face. "What's the matter over there? Speak up."

The visitor remained silent and motionless. The hair on the back of Hopper's neck tingled as a dull chill passed over him like the fog from a block of dry ice.

"Wake up over there, goddammit, and tell me what's going on." A lightning flash briefly illuminated his visitor's face. When Hopper saw who it was, he clenched his teeth and tried to push back through his headboard. It was a man, barely four feet tall, standing in the dark corner of his room. He had a full beard and bushy sideburns. His face was pale as boiled chicken. It was Lawrence Alimony, wearing the same sad expression as his picture. He was dressed in small-scale formal clothes covered in dust. He pointed the tiny finger of his right hand at Hopper. With his left, he motioned for Hopper to follow. Hopper's legs cycled as he tried to push himself as far away from the creepy little guy as possible.

Hopper summoned his most threatening snarl. "What do you want? Speak up now, or by God I'll thrash some information out of you."

In the eerie silver of another lightning flash, the little man pointed down at his feet. He was barefooted.

"What do you want?" Hopper tried not to sound alarmed, but it's hard to sound bold when you wake up to find a mute goblin loitering in the corner of your bedroom. The pale visitor shook his head and looked down at his bone-white feet and back at Hopper, his sad expression never changing. Without making a sound, the little man walked across the bedroom to the door, paused to point at his feet again, and backed into the hallway.

Hopper threw off the covers, mumbling "Shit" as he cracked his knuckles on the side table, reaching again for his lamp. This time, the light came on. The clock no longer flashed at 12:00; it was 5:11 a.m. He snatched up his blanket, wrapped it around himself, and stumbled across the bedroom.

He stood by the door, listening for the sound of bare feet in the hallway. Nothing. When he opened the door, he gagged, stumbling backward. Alimony stood there holding the boot out—offering it to him. Hopper shook his head. "No thanks, pal. It's your boot. You keep it."

A sad smile crossed the whiskered face. Then Lawrence winked. Hopper was seized with chills. The little man pointed again at Hopper with his right index finger while holding the boot in his left hand. In a grim, slow-motion gesture, he grasped the bedroom doorknob and pulled it closed.

Hopper shook off the chill, hesitated a moment, and threw the door open, flipping on the hall light. No one there. "Hey!" As soon as he shouted, he didn't know why.

The light came on in Nozetape's room. A second later, Nozetape's bushy head emerged through his bedroom door. He brought a hand up to brush long hair from his bleary eyes. "What the hell's going on, Dale? Who you hollering at?"

Hopper gulped hard. He knew exactly how this was going to sound. "Lawrence Alimony was in my room just now. He looked just like in the picture, except the little bastard was barefoot. Scared the shit out of me."

Nozetape looked up and down the hall and then peered at Hopper, frowning. "You're dreaming, Dale—or having one of your spells. There ain't no little barefooted guy here."

"I know, Nozetape. He ain't here now, but he was a second ago. He pointed at me, then he pointed at his feet, then he went and got the boot and showed it to me. Now he's gone."

The light came on in Cord's room. He stepped into the hall wearing plaid boxers, scratching his backside. "I sure hope a pipe busted or a burglar broke in. If this ain't serious, I'm going to be pissed off about you guys hollering so loud in the middle of the damn night."

Hopper mumbled, "It ain't the middle of the night. It's five o'clock in the morning."

Cord cocked his head to one side, started to say something, and then looked at Nozetape. Nozetape shrugged. "Dale said he saw Alimony standing in his room. He says the little fella was barefooted."

Cord leaned against his bedroom door. "Barefooted, huh? You sure?"

Hopper blushed. "Come on, you guys. There was a flash of lightning, and I saw him in the corner of the bedroom plain as I see you two now."

Cord yawned and rubbed his eyes. "Well, what do you reckon he wanted, Hopper?"

Hopper stepped past them headed for the kitchen. Nozetape watched him go. "Where you going, Dale?"

"The little fella brought the boot in here for me to look at. He wants us to know something."

Cord walked back into his bedroom and switched off the light. "Wake me up at six-thirty. And if the little fella shows up again, try not to holler about it."

Nozetape limped to the kitchen, where Hopper sat staring at the boot. Nozetape sat beside him. "You know, this is how Hamlet's troubles got started. He saw a ghost at night, and it wound up screwing up his whole life."

Hopper peered into Nozetape's sleepy eyes. "What the hell are you talking about, Nozetape? Unless it sheds light on what just happened, I got no interest in hearing about Hamlet and his troubles."

"Okay, Dale."

After a few minutes, Hopper got up, went to the kitchen drawer, and got a butter knife. He began to work the blade between the heel and the sole. Slowly, the heel began to loosen.

"You sure you ought to do this, Dale? You're going to damage it."

"I'm telling you, Nozetape, that little guy was trying to tell me something about this boot. I think the treasure map is in here somewhere, and he wants us to find it."

The heel dislodged and thunked onto the tabletop, a black lump of hard, old leather. Hopper picked it up, turning it over and over in his hands. With a look of frustration, he dropped it back on the table and went to the counter, where he started making coffee, grumbling under his breath.

Nozetape picked up the heel and started squeezing, twisting, and pulling in different directions. Hopper had just turned on the electric pot, when Nozetape shouted, "Holy shit, Dale, it's open. You were right—the heel's hollow. It's like a Chinese trick box. You got to push in one direction and pull in the other at the same time."

Hopper dashed to the table as Nozetape gingerly retrieved some folded papers from the boot heel's exposed hollow. He yelled, "Cord, get your ass in here, you lazy bastard. We're rich. We're all rich. We found the map."

As he charged out of his bedroom, Cord jammed a toe on the doorframe and bellowed a round of loud curses.

Hopper and Cord watched, wide-eyed, as Nozetape gently unfolded two pieces of remarkably preserved paper. Hopper frowned. "Turn them over, Nozetape. I don't see a map on this side."

Nozetape turned over both pages. They were filled with cursive writing but no map. "Well, just read what they say. Surely it will tell us where the treasure's hid."

Nozetape studied the pages, turning them over and upside down. He looked up, disappointed. "I can't read this, fellas."

Hopper pulled up a chair and slid the sheets over for his own inspection. He leaned over the paper, squinting. "What the hell is this? I can't make a thing out of it neither."

Cord took his turn. He shook his head. "Whatever this is, it ain't English. Even if you account for this old cursive, I can't read a single word."

Hopper sent Nozetape for his magnifying glass. They inspected the writing line by line. None of it made sense. Hopper stared at the paper, chin resting on the palm of his left hand. "Code. The little fella wrote in code. Smart. Even if somebody found this stuff, if they didn't know his code, they'd never get their hands on his treasure."

"It ain't code," Cord said. He tossed the magnifying glass clattering onto the table. "It's German." He addressed Nozetape without taking his eyes from the paper. "Didn't you say the old man was German?"

Nozetape nodded. "Yep. How do you know this is German, Vernon?"

"Look at all the *ders* and *das* he uses in here. I'm pretty sure this is German."

"Great." Hopper poured three cups of coffee. "We got the key to the treasure right here on our table, and none of us can unlock it." He brought coffee to Cord and Nozetape and went back for his own. "Do we know anybody that reads German?"

Nozetape scratched his head. "Bennie lived in Germany 'til he was eleven. I don't know if he remembers how to read it—or if he ever knew how."

Hopper groaned. "You mean our Bennie, who works at the pipe yard?"

Nozetape nodded. "Yeah. His dad was stationed in Germany after the war. His mom's German."

"Ain't there anybody else? Bennie . . . well, he's not the kind of fella we need in our business. I mean, he works at the pipe yard. Ollie Oleg's pipe yard. If Bennie deciphered this, no telling how big a cut he'd want. And if he got greedy, he'd peddle the deal to Ollie, and you know where that would lead."

Cord shook his head. "I suppose we can try to get our hands on a German dictionary and do our best to figure it out ourselves."

"What about you, Nozetape? Anybody else you can think of?"

Nozetape shook his head.

"I don't like the dictionary idea. That would take too long. I want somebody to read this today."

Cord picked up the magnifying glass and continued to inspect the old pages. "Well, that's the tradeoff. You want safety or speed? I don't think you're going to get both. If you let Bennie take a look at this, he'll know what's in it, and we'll have to rely on him to tell us the truth and keep his mouth shut—and that'll cost us plenty. He'll try to get up an auction between us and Ollie. And if I know Ollie Oleg, he'll wind up with everything."

Hopper got to his feet and paced to the living room window and back. "You're right, Cord. If something like this got out, no telling how many eyes, ears, and grubby fingers might start getting in the way." He came back to the table and put a hand on Nozetape's shoulder. "I don't know how the roads will be this morning, and I don't even know if the bookstore will be open. But if you can, get over to the mall and get your hands on a German-English dictionary and try to decipher this stuff." He pounded Nozetape on the back. "We need us a translation, Nozetape, and we need it yesterday. You got to figure it out."

Nozetape nodded. "There's one more thing we need to think about."

Hopper and Cord spoke at the same time. "What?"

"According to my aunt, there was three pages missing from Alimony's journal. We only got two here."

Hopper stammered, "The other boot. The third page has to be in the other boot. We got to find that boot, Cord."

Cord nodded. "Looks like we only got two-thirds of the secret." He took a drink of his coffee and stared at the unreadable documents before him.

Hopper's voice had a firm, cold edge to it. "We'll find that other boot if I have to uproot every goddam thing growing on the forty." They all sat quiet, entertaining their private visions of what the treasure might look like, what it might do. They all sighed at the same time.

Hopper went back to the coffeepot. "No use trying to get back to sleep now. Guess I'll just get ready for work."

Cord spoke up. "One more thing, Hopper. Did you really see the little man? Was it a dream, a hallucination, a flashback . . . what?"

Hopper blushed. "It must've been a dream. Guess my mind was wrestling with the facts, and my imagination just manufactured the little guy to get me on the right track."

Nozetape sat looking at his hands. Hopper noticed. "What, Nozetape? Had to be a dream or hallucination, right?"

Nozetape didn't look up. "Might've been. But if it was, how do you account for them little wet footprints leading out the back door?"

Twelve

The sanders did a good job preparing 36th for morning traffic. Cord relaxed a little. "I don't know, Hopper. What makes you think it's reincarnation? Why do you think any of this has to make sense?"

Hopper held his fingers over the vents as the air began to warm. "It's that ink-blot test, buddy. The way you're looking at it, everything is just an accidental stain. To me, it looks like a picture of gold coins and rose petals. Everything that happened to us, every decision we made, was all linked up in a karma chain pullin' us to this minute."

He studied his friend's face in the dash lights to see if anything was getting through. He couldn't tell. He continued to talk, as much to himself as to Cord. "It's like that little boot was waiting for us all these years. Think about it. Suppose it was Podd that found the boot. What do you reckon would have happened?"

"It would've got tossed in the trash."

"Exactly. Now, let's say me and you find it, but we don't have Nozetape for a roommate. Do you think we would ever have connected that boot with the treasure?"

"Nope."

"Okay. You starting to see? Let's take it a step further. Me and you find the boot, Nozetape is our roommate, but his aunt is a schoolteacher and has no connection to the museum. We still have the boot, we still have the buckle, but we wouldn't know a thing about the treasure. And how about this? You think that little Alimony guy would have showed up to give us a hand if you hadn't been so respectful of his boot? I'll tell you, Cord, there's more to this than just coincidence. There's a hand guiding us. If it isn't karma, it's something else. But it's something, and it makes sense."

Cord's laugh was so loud and sudden, it made Hopper jerk. "Yeah, like a guardian angel or the ghost of Shambhala."

Hopper frowned. "Cut it out, Cord. If it ain't reincarnation, what do you think it is?"

"It's coincidence, Hopper. Pure and simple. Blind coincidence."

Hopper shook his head. "Just can't be, Cord. Coincidences don't just pile up the minute you're nearing the crossroads. Too much is getting crammed into the narrow window opening for us. On the emotional satisfaction scale, calling this a bunch of lucky accidents hits about a two."

The Rambler felt warm and quiet. Cord broke the silence. "Hopper, what do you think the chances are a fella could flip a coin and have it turn up heads ten times in a row?"

"Well, if that fella ain't cheating, I'd say that's pretty long damn odds."

"It happens, Hopper. It's like in a sidewalk crap game. Sometimes a guy can roll seven on eight or nine straight passes. Long odds, but a guy can hit a streak of good luck—or bad, depending."

Cord turned right onto the Interstate 35 on-ramp. Traffic flew by as if there were no snow piled on the highway shoulders. Cord gave the signal and eased onto the roadway. "Hopper, my friend, you're setting yourself up for lifelong disappointment. There ain't any guiding hand behind any of this. Maybe we've hit a stretch of smooth road for a change. Maybe not. The odds of us finding some treasure are too long to calculate. The odds of us being able to keep something if we do find it are longer still. Whatever happens, buddy, it's nothing more than the way the cards are dealt. And there's a hell of a lot more than fifty-two cards in the deck we're playing."

Hopper unbuttoned his coat and struggled to get his hand into his jeans pocket. Cord glanced over. "What are you doing over there?"

"Trying to get a quarter out of my pocket."

"What for?"

"Just wait . . . you'll see." He came up with the coin. "Okay, Cord, I got this quarter. It's a plain, ordinary quarter, heads on one side, tails on the other. Call it."

"What for?"

"I'm just going to test something out. Call it."

"Whatever you have in mind, Hopper, it won't prove nothing, no matter how it comes out."

"I ain't trying to prove nothing to you, Cord. This is for me. Call it."

"Okay, if it makes you happy, heads."

Hopper flipped the coin. "Tails." He flipped again. "Tails." Again. "Tails." He slipped the coin into his coat pocket and crossed his arms. "Just like I figured. Reincarnation."

Thirteen

When they got to the shop, Hopper was surprised to see most of the crew loading tools and gear as if the snowy day was nothing unusual. Buntz saw them as soon as they stepped through the door. "You two know where the PR office is?"

Cord glanced at Hopper. "We know where the PR office is?" Hopper shook his head.

Buntz was putting on his gloves. "That's okay. Follow me. You guys will be working there this morning. There's a bunch of pamphlets and stuff about the new exhibits that need to be unloaded and organized."

Hopper stiffened. "I thought we was hired to clear the forty."

Without slowing down, Buntz slid one of the bay doors open to allow a pickup to back out. "That's exactly why you was hired. But in case you didn't notice, there's a foot of snow on the ground. Anyway, Mr. Neyland told me to have you two go to the PR office and lend a hand. So that's where you're going. Back this truck out and follow me."

He hopped on his golf cart and shot outside into the blustery cold. Hopper and Cord exchanged a look and then piled into the truck. Cord backed the pickup out and followed Buntz across the access road.

When Buntz stopped to unlock the north gate, Hopper said, "How the hell are we supposed to find that other boot if we're dickin' around in the PR office?"

"We're just going to have to be careful and patient. Look at it this way. Maybe by being good soldiers and helping out in the PR office, we can add some more to our karma deposits."

"Funny, Cord."

Buntz motioned them through. Once he locked the gate behind them, he shot past and drove into the zoo. West of the lake, between the primate building and the aquatic mammal exhibit, Buntz pointed to a two-story building with a small parking lot behind. He drove off on the sidewalk toward the grazing animal area.

Hopper and Cord sat in the parking lot for a brief discussion. "You think we'll be here all day, Cord?"

"You heard the man. We'll be here 'til they're done with us."

Hopper sighed. "Well, he says report to the PR office. Here we are, so I guess we better report."

Cord opened his door. "There is a bright side, buddy. At least we won't be outdoors stomping around snow, freezing our feet all day. The treasure's been lost about a hundred years. It'll be just fine with me if it waits to get discovered on a warmer day."

Fourteen

When they opened the PR office door, they were surprised by the delicious aroma of strawberry incense. Hopper closed his eyes and savored the moment. He tugged on the back of Cord's coat. "Smell that?"

Cord took a deep breath. "Strawberries."

Hopper grinned. "This just puts an exclamation point on what I've been saying. With everything else lining up so good, smelling strawberries like this on a winter day is a bonus. I'm telling you, Cord, all the signs are pointing to glory."

Hopper closed the door behind them. From somewhere, he heard classical music. He jabbed Cord in the ribs. Cord rolled his eyes. "Yeah, I know, Hopper: swell music, good sign." They stood in the doorway, looking around. To Hopper's eye, the PR office looked more like an artist's studio than a corporate brain center. In the middle of the room, a long rustic wooden table was surrounded by eight sturdy slat-back Quaker chairs. At the table's center was a large, highly polished wooden bowl filled with different-colored apples.

Hopper instinctively wiped his feet, crossed the waxed wooden floor, and picked up an apple. After a cursory inspection, he whispered over his shoulder, "These ain't plastic, buddy. They're real apples." Scattered around the table's polished surface were realistic renderings of animals in their natural habitat: zebras in tall grass, snakes on desert outcroppings, horses in clover-covered meadows, leopards lounging on tree branches, birds wading in shallow water.

The morning sun shining across the lake filled the room with gold-toned light. The view of the lake and the director's elegant residence on the hilltop above it were . . . perfect. Hopper soaked it all up, the aroma, the apples, the music, the view. He regarded everything cascading through his senses as proof he was standing on the threshold of a new day bound to open onto the yellow brick highway leading to California and a life of leisure and warm sun.

Cord wiped his feet and followed Hopper to the table. He picked up a vivid drawing of a group of Emperor penguins standing together in a pose suggesting familial intimacy. Their dark bodies, with hints of yellow on their white breasts, stood in contrast to a frozen, blue-ice background. He dropped the drawing and shifted his weight from foot to foot. "What are we supposed to do, Hopper?"

"I say we stand here like good soldiers at our duty station until somebody shows up to give us our orders. For now, let's me and you sponge up the feeling of being in a warm room, showered by soothing music and smelling strawberries."

Cord walked to the window and stared at the lake while Hopper examined a portrait of a big-horn ram perched majestically on a high snow-covered rock. His absorption with the artwork was interrupted when he heard a door open. For the first time, he noticed the stairway at the rear of the office. She was looking down on them from the landing on the second-floor loft, like a goddess waiting for them to kneel in adoration.

Her long brown hair, tied into a ponytail with a tan-colored ribbon, was slightly unruly, as if she'd just stepped out of a brisk wind. From this distance, her eyes seemed a curious tawny color that reminded Hopper of the breast feathers of a mourning dove.

"You must be here to help me with the promotional materials." Her voice was deep for a woman's, but Hopper suspected she could purr if she wanted. When she started down the stairs, he watched as he might watch some exotic, beautifully colored fish gracefully swimming toward him in an aquarium.

Her smile was lethal. Hopper thought, *Man, a smile like that could pull a fella head over boot laces right off the straight and narrow path of gainful employment and tumble him directly through the gates of perdition and get his ass fired.* She purred, as he knew she could, "I hope it's not too cold in here. I turned the heat on about an hour ago."

Hopper leaned against the table and watched her continue down the stairs. She was tall, maybe tall as him—maybe taller. She wore a thick sweater, the color of Wild Turkey Bourbon spun into a warm fabric. He never saw anyone make walking down stairs looks so much like ballet. Her stylishly faded jeans were just tight enough to give evidence of impressive athletic potential.

Hopper had a natural weakness for women in boots. Hers were high-quality tan leather with high heels, laced to the knees. He was about to say something charming, when the office door opened. A tall man looking like he stepped off the cover of *GQ* magazine stood eyeing him and Cord with an expression of hard appraisal. Hopper sensed there was more to this inspection than a big man simply taking the measure of a couple of new hires. It was more like an undertaker sizing up a pair of newly arrived corpses to be sure he could fit them in the right box.

"So you're the new men Junior sent over . . . Mr. Hopper and Mr. Cord?" His voice was deep and commanding.

Hopper answered, "No, Mr. Buntz sent us over."

"I'm Julian Neyland. Buntz works for Junior Willie. Junior Willie works for me." He closed the door, thoroughly wiped his fancy snakeskin boots on the mat, and strolled into the office like it was his home. He smiled a Hollywood smile and spoke to the lady with that executive voice of his. "Good morning, Audrey."

Hopper couldn't tell whether her smile was bona fide or just part of the wardrobe. Whatever it was, it was splendid. "Good morning, Julian. I have coffee brewing. Would you like some?" She turned those dove-colored eyes to Hopper. "Coffee for you two?"

Neyland spoke before Hopper or Cord could answer. "We probably should let these men get busy. I know we're taking them away from
other chores that they need to get to. Anyway, they have coffee in the
shop, and I'm sure they had some before they came over, right, boys?"
He said it in a way that indicated there was only one permissible answer.
"The van in the parking lot is loaded with boxes. I need you men to bring
those in and stack them on this table. Let's go."

Her voice was frothy with charm. "Just a minute, Julian." She walked
to Hopper and smiled at him, eye to eye, extending her long, graceful
hand. "I'm Audrey."

He took her hand. Her skin felt like the union of classical music and
strawberry incense. "It's a real pleasure to meet you, Audrey. I'm Dale
Hopper. You can call me 'sweetheart.' And, of course, me and my friend,
Cord, would love to have a cup of your delicious coffee before we start
hauling in those boxes."

Her hand lingered in his for a couple of beats longer than the normal
handshake. Was this something special just for him, or was it just her
way? She looked at their clasped hands and smiled before they separated. She walked to Cord. He took her hand, stammering, "Vernon . . .
Vernon Cord."

Hopper noted a cloud crossing Neyland's handsome features. He
knew that expression. This was a jealous guy trying to control a deep
boil. There was a venomous tone not very well concealed when he
spoke. "Hopper, you should know this lady you've just been so familiar
with is Mr. Kroneson's daughter."

He heard Cord release a faint groan. Audrey looked over her shoulder, watching, obviously curious about his response. "Well, I don't know
your dad, Audrey, and I sure hope I didn't offend you by being so familiar. You really don't have to call me 'sweetheart' if you don't want to. And
to keep from being too familiar in the future, I promise I won't call you
'sweetheart' until you say it's okay."

Audrey covered her mouth with both hands, obviously attempting
to stifle a laugh. Neyland took a step in Hopper's direction and looked
down on the shorter man. "Listen, mister, if you value your job—"

Audrey interrupted him. "How do you like your coffee . . . Dale?"

"If I can't have it on the beach with Irish whiskey and whipped cream, I'll take it black."

This time, she couldn't restrain a throaty laugh. "I'm fresh out of beaches and whipped cream. It'll have to be black, I'm afraid. How about you, Vernon?"

"Black's fine, Miss Kroneson."

"You take yours black, don't you, Julian?"

Neyland was furious and pouting. "Yes, black." Hopper enjoyed an inward chuckle. A scowl like the one darkening Neyland's features might cause him some heartburn if Neyland wore a uniform with chevrons and rockers on his sleeve. But he couldn't get too worked up by a guy that smelled like lilacs.

Audrey glided toward the back corner of the office. She spoke over her shoulder. "You all just take a seat. I'll be right back. We can get to work as soon as we've had our eye-opener."

When she returned with their coffees, Hopper could tell Neyland was about to say something, so he made a preemptive maneuver. "I know I'm showing off my ignorance, but who wrote the music we're listening to?"

Neyland's scowl deepened and reddened, but the rich warmth of Audrey's voice dominated the atmosphere. "This is Edvard Greig. It's the London Philharmonic rendition of the Peer Gynt suite. Do you like classical music?" She leaned back in her chair, cradling her coffee cup with both hands. Hopper thought, *I'd like to be that coffee cup for about ten minutes.*

"Some classical music I like—this you're playing now, for example. But some I've heard is boring."

She turned her attention to Neyland. "What about you, Julian? Who is your favorite composer?"

"Easy," he said, casting a glance that reminded Hopper of a bad card player holding aces. "Wagner. I love the depth and power of Wagner's work. I'm a great admirer of *The Ring Cycle.* I doubt anyone in the world could have done such a good job of capturing, in musical form, the archetypical appeal of these ancient stories. How about it, Mr. Hopper? Do you like Wagner's music? Or is he one of the composers you find boring?"

That was clumsy, Hopper thought, but just the same, he felt like he'd just received the conversational equivalent of a body slam. "I . . . uhh, I'm not sure I've ever heard anything by Vogner."

Neyland's eyes had a malevolent sparkle as he peered over the rim of his coffee cup. "Well, you should listen sometime."

Cord cleared his throat. "Wagner, huh? Wasn't he Hitler's favorite composer? Jew hater, wasn't he?"

Hopper heard Neyland's teeth clink on the cup. He wanted to yell, "Touché! Nice thrust, Cord." He sure hoped Cord knew what he was talking about. If he did, in one slick maneuver, he changed Neyland from a refined music expert to a guy that had the same musical taste as Nazis.

If Audrey appreciated Cord's ambush, she gave no sign. She just casually picked up the thread. "I agree Wagner was a genius. But don't you think his work is a little . . . ponderous?" Neyland was obviously preparing to come to Wagner's defense, but Audrey refocused the conversation. "And you, Mr. Cord, who is your favorite classical composer?"

At first, Hopper wasn't sure whether Cord didn't hear the question or was just ignoring her. He stood looking thoughtfully at the lake. Then he spoke without elaboration. "Rimsky-Korsakov." He looked at Hopper and winked. Again, Hopper found himself bewildered. He'd known Cord his whole life. How did Cord become educated about classical composers without Hopper knowing about it?

Neyland abruptly pushed back from the table. "Well, I'm sure we could discuss music all day, but we have work to do." He gestured at Hopper and Cord with his coffee cup. "I've unlocked the van. You men hop to now and unload those boxes." Hopper tossed a glance Audrey's way. She offered a resigned smile and shrugged. They drained their coffee cups as Neyland tapped the toe of his fancy boot and looked at his watch.

As Hopper and Cord made trips in and out of the office hauling boxes, Audrey and Neyland were head to head, examining diagrams and graphs. On the surface, Neyland and Audrey were working together on the opening of the big cat exhibit. But deep down, there was an antimagnetic tension. Were they on the upward arc of a romance? Were they in a static orbit? Were they in the process of disconnection? Whatever was going on, Hopper decided to find a way to squeeze himself into the dynamic.

Even though she seemed thoroughly engaged in their business, Hopper could tell she was watching him. Good sign. Neyland was oblivious, perfectly absorbed in the outward appearance of the business of arranging zoo affairs. Hopper pegged Neyland as the type of dandy who was certain, with his pressed shirt, creased britches, exotic boots, and manly aftershave, no woman could resist him.

Hopper overheard Neyland suggest, "Maybe you'd like to come to the residence today and join me for a working lunch. I cook up a pretty impressive pot of chili, if I say so myself. It's been simmering since early this morning. Should be perfect by lunchtime."

Hopper slowed the process of stacking boxes to eavesdrop. He couldn't read her reaction. Was she amused, irritated—what? She examined a brochure with a magnifying glass. "Is it vegetarian?"

Neyland blinked. "Vegetarian?"

"Your chili, is it vegetarian?"

Neyland frowned at the brochure in his hand. "I didn't know there was such a thing as vegetarian chili."

Hopper was sure her smile was for him. They were sharing a joke at Neyland's expense. "Sure, it's really very good if you make it right. I think I have a recipe around here somewhere. I'll see if I can find it for you."

Neyland ran his fingers through his thick black hair. When he glanced up, he appeared to become aware that Hopper overheard his offer of chili luncheon go haywire. A red tint crept over Neyland's complexion. "If you have all the boxes out of the van and stacked where they belong, you two can get back to the shop and see if Junior has some work for you."

Hopper's heart took a nosedive. He thought their PR duties might last until lunchtime. He wanted to find a way to compare notes on the pleasures of vegetarian chili with the beautiful Audrey Kroneson. With a little time, he might charm this enchanted princess who reigned over this realm of magic apples and strawberries. He didn't feel too disadvantaged in this reach for Audrey's affections. What he lacked in cash, education, exotic footwear, and classical music expertise, he made up for in humor and confidence. He glanced at Cord, who shrugged, put his gloves on, and walked toward the door.

Words tumbled out of Hopper's mouth like a recording of someone else's speech. "Glad to, boss. Me and Cord would be happy to rush right back over to the shop and see if there's some breezy outdoor work we can do. It's way too nice and warm in here for a couple of hardworking, winter-lovin' men like us."

Audrey laughed. "Well, before I release you to the charms of your outside winter labors, I may have some additional warm chores to burden you with."

Neyland blinked like a man caught off guard by a photo flash. "What more do you need from these guys, Audrey? They've unloaded all the boxes."

"There are a few things upstairs they could bring down for me."

Neyland, defeated, seemed to shrink. "Well, I suppose I could bring some invoices over from the office and reconcile them here."

Hopper couldn't help but appreciate how perfectly her beautiful smile concealed a ladylike kick in the seat of Neyland's pants. "Oh, you don't have to do that, Julian. We can manage here."

"But . . ."

"Seriously, with everything you have to do, I'm grateful you were able to take as much time as you have to help me. I can't let your willingness to lend a hand interfere with overall zoo operations. We'll be fine."

"But . . ."

"And I'll find that recipe for vegetarian chili for you. Maybe you can make it for us sometime."

His practiced confidence melted into a weak smile. "Sure . . . sure. I'll make us some vegetarian chili."

She opened the office door. "I really appreciate your help, Julian. It was very thoughtful of you. And I really like your boots." Hopper thought he detected the faintest note of sarcasm.

Neyland glanced down absently at his highly polished snakeskin footwear. Hopper leaned on the fireplace mantle, where Cord was studying photographs. Neyland ran his fingers through his hair again, recovered his confident air, and frowned at Hopper. "You get finished here as soon as you can and get back to the shop. Junior must have a million things for you to do." There was something in the way he said it that sounded like a threat.

Hopper beamed. "That'll be fine, boss. We'll be here working like a couple of soldier ants 'til Audrey says we're finished."

Neyland's face reddened again. "I'd rather you didn't call me 'boss.' 'Mr. Neyland' will do."

Hopper offered a lazy salute. "Whatever you say . . . Mr. Neyland."

Hopper heard him mumbling as he stepped out into the snow. "Vegetarian chili, my ass."

When Neyland was gone, Hopper noticed Cord still staring at the photograph on the mantle. He stepped over to see what his friend found so fascinating. He couldn't believe his eyes. Hopper spoke over his shoulder. "Is this who I think it is?"

Audrey crossed the room and picked up the photograph. She held it like she might hold a fragile leaf on the verge of decay. "Yes, that's Mother and Dad with Uncle Lyn." She handed it to Hopper for closer inspection.

"So you're related to the former president?"

"No, he and Dad were good friends. We always called him Uncle Lyn. Dad and Mother are attending his funeral now."

Hopper put the photograph back on the mantle. He was surprised when she turned away just as a tear rolled down her cheek. He couldn't figure why he felt awkward and a little guilty. He looked at Cord, who shrugged and continued to lean on the mantle.

Hopper restrained the urge to apologize but couldn't think what he'd be apologizing for. He cleared his throat. "Well . . . uhhh, Audrey, maybe you should tell us what you'd like us to do now."

At that moment, she could have been the perfect model for a painting. He would call it *Beautiful Lady Remembering a Loved One on a Winter Day—by a Lake.*

She was the first person he'd ever known who actually touched a president of the United States. She was the first really rich person he'd ever met except Ollie Oleg, the king of the Flats. There was no way to know whether Ollie was in her league where money was concerned, but he damn sure wasn't anywhere near in the class and beauty department. *Funny,* he thought, watching her there by the window, *I never thought of rich people crying about anything.*

When she spoke, she sounded far away. "Do you think he was a good president?" Cord didn't react. He stood like a statue there at the mantle, staring at the lake.

Hopper wailed internally. *Can't we go back to discussing Vogner? Why does this have to stray into politics?* "Well, to tell you the truth, Audrey, I don't mean to step on anybody's toes, but I'd prefer any president that didn't send Americans off to war unless it's self-defense—like World War Two."

Hopper could barely hear when she spoke again. "If it wasn't for Vietnam, he would have been . . . great."

Hopper hoped she didn't hear Cord mumble, "A lot of people would've been a lot of things if it wasn't for Vietnam."

Hopper cleared his throat again. "About the work, Audrey."

She turned from the lake and looked at them, closely for the first time. "You were both soldiers, weren't you?"

Before Hopper could answer, Cord spoke up. "Yes, both of us. We both enlisted. And yes, we both did two tours in Vietnam."

She brushed a renegade strand of hair behind her ear. "I'd like to hear about it."

Oh, no, Hopper thought. *Here we go.* He glanced at Cord and noted the telltale flexing of his jaw muscles. He decided, for the protection of the feelings of all concerned, to channel the conversation away from potentially dangerous waters. "Let me ask you something. Your dad was never in the service, was he?"

"No, he wasn't."

"Anybody in your family ever been in the military?"

"Daddy's older brother, Uncle Phineas, fought in the Pacific theater in World War Two."

"He ever talk about it?"

"I don't remember ever talking to Uncle Phineas at all. He's estranged from the family. No one's seen him in years."

"Well, some guys that's been in combat like to talk about it, and some don't. See, I can talk about it for hours. But Vernon there, he don't like to talk about it at all. So about the work . . . "

She nodded. "Vernon, would you bring that open box to the table? And, Dale, if you look in that drawer," she pointed to a nearby desk as she started upstairs, "you'll find a box of black ink pens. I'll be right back."

Hopper found himself comparing her fluid motions to those of a swan in flight as she drifted up the stairs. "Get that out of your head and get the pens like she said," Cord muttered, strolling to the stack of boxes.

Gone only a few seconds, she bounded down the stairs carrying a thick notebook. She instructed them to take a seat at the table. Hopper knew sitting on his butt making notes in black ink was nowhere in his job description. Just the same, at that moment, she was the boss. He nudged Cord. "You heard the lady. Take a seat."

Hopper settled onto one of the well-cushioned chairs. After a moment's hesitation, Cord took a seat across the table.

Audrey opened the notebook and handed them each two sheets of paper filled with names and addresses. "We're going to address some of these brochures." She opened the box of pens and handed one to each of them. "While we're doing it, you can tell me about yourselves."

Hopper didn't mind. He reeled it off: Born in Buffalo, Oklahoma. Father was an oilfield truck driver. Moved to Oklahoma City when he was five. Attended Chisholm Oaks Schools from kindergarten to graduation. Knew he was going to be drafted but was told if he enlisted he could join under the buddy system. He and Vernon signed up together, went through basic and AIT at Ft. Polk, got orders for Nam, assigned to the 25th Infantry Division, did their tours, got discharged, came home. "And here we are."

As he spouted off the broad outlines of his bio, Audrey addressed one brochure after another. She spoke without looking up. "What about you, Vernon? What's your story?"

"I was born in Oklahoma City. Other than that, if you heard Dale's story, you heard mine."

"So tell me about Vietnam."

Cord dropped his pen on the table. The tension in his voice and body bordered on the dangerous. He looked at Audrey hard, unblinking. The only part of his body that moved was his lips. "Miss Kroneson, you must not have heard what Hopper just told you. I'm giving you the benefit of the doubt, because to blunder into an area that you was asked, real nice, to stay out of would be rude. I'm really sorry about the death of your Uncle Lyn. I don't mean to hurt your feelings or offend you, but I'm working overtime to forget Vietnam. I'm happy to chat about the weather, the heavyweight champ of the world, or Lightnin' Hopkins's music. But there's really nothing I have to say about Vietnam that you'd want to hear." He recovered the pen and resumed addressing brochures. "Hopper can tell you anything he wants and probably will. Just spare me the pleasure, will you?"

Audrey didn't look up, and her expression didn't change. But Hopper noticed a tremor in her lower lip and a discreet brush of her eyes with her left hand. He wanted to kick Cord's butt. Cord could be real crotchety sometimes, but he could also keep his mouth shut. Hopper's natural inclination was to touch Audrey's shoulder, try to comfort her to make amends for Cord's inconsiderate honesty. But this was unknown territory. She was way higher on the employment food chain than he was, and she was rich. Probably, in her life, nobody ever talked to her as harsh as Cord just did. So he kept his hands to himself. Still, he couldn't keep his mouth shut.

"Never mind Cord, Audrey. You're sort of catching him at his worst. He don't do well so early in the morning, and his penmanship is lousy. But I know how to cheer him up. You think you might be able to feed some rock 'n' roll into your stereo?"

Her fingers brushed her eyes again. "Sure. The Stones alright? I usually only listen to them when I'm here alone."

Hopper leaned back and clapped his hands. "How about that, Cord? The lady is reading our minds. Put on the Stones, Audrey. If you don't have any Vogner, the Stones will do fine. That'll cheer up this sour bastard, pardon my language. "Sympathy for the Devil" if you got it."

Fifteen

Neyland paced before the tall windows overlooking the lake, his binoculars around his neck. He paused every few seconds to raise the glasses, trying to see what was happening in the PR office. The grounds crew pickup was still there, so those two clowns must still be with her. The shorter of the two, Hopper, was obviously an insolent, smart-ass. Neyland released the binoculars and resumed pacing. Maybe he should call the PR office. He could pretend to call to see if tomorrow would be a good day to try that vegetarian chili.

He didn't like the way that Hopper prick acted so chummy with Audrey. What steamed him most was the fact Audrey seemed amused by the clown's foolishness. Neyland trained the binoculars on the PR office again. Maybe he should just go back and order these stooges to report to the shop. Better yet, maybe he should fire them. No, that was out of the question. Ollie made it clear he wanted them to remain zoo employees until further notice. But Neyland, the blueblood, didn't like taking orders from southside trash like Ollie Oleg.

Goddammit, he was a Notre Dame grad. So what would Ollie do if he just defied the fat turd and fired them both? Neyland shivered. He didn't know what Ollie would do. There was something scary about the guy—really scary. Neyland hated the idea that Ollie had something on him. A devious schemer like that could destroy his career. That would be awful, of course. But Ollie also had the capacity to do worse—much worse. Until Neyland figured a way to slip out from under Ollie's greasy thumb, he couldn't take a chance by defying the villain.

He resumed his pacing. *Vegetarian chili!* How was it he didn't know she was a vegetarian? He plopped into the plush easy chair by the blazing fireplace. His plans had gone so wrong. He was hauling in loads of black-market money like Ollie promised, but the cash had heavy chains around it. Now his plans to sweep Audrey Kroneson off her feet and move into Zack Kroneson's inner circle were experiencing a hiccup.

He couldn't believe a long-haired, no-prospects, army grunt, ignorant pawn in Ollie's game could be any real competition in his scheme to win the hand of a prize like Audrey. He was just going to have to use his position as zoo director to keep the hippie freak out of his private preserve. Neyland's determination to charm the beautiful Audrey had obviously stalled. Even so, he was certain she was attracted to him. Why wouldn't she be? He was handsome, athletic, well-bred, charismatic, possessed of good taste and a quality education. It was plain to see he was a comer. Still, she was going to be a tougher nut to crack than he thought. But he was smart, and he was patient. He was a man who always got what he wanted, and he wanted to be Zack Kroneson's son-in-law. And no lowly Animal Tech One was going to derail his plans.

Sixteen

With the Rolling Stones playing in the background, Audrey unrolled a large plat on the table and stood admiring it like an artist lingering over her masterpiece. She walked slowly around the table, deliberately smoothing corners. Hopper was surprised at the tenderness of the gesture. She might have been caressing a treasured family Bible.

She drew her finger along an irregular red line near the center of the plat. "This line is the original Kroneson Park Grandpa Caleb planned when he developed this land. He envisioned a housing addition with gardens and walkways as an attraction to potential homeowners."

She brushed unseen particles from the park's outline. "We have some wonderful old pictures of how it looked back then. If you're interested, I'll show them to you sometime." A delightful hammer blow rang on Hopper's heart: *I'll show them to you sometime.* If she was serious, this meant there would be another time, another opportunity—bonus.

"One of Grandpa Caleb's friends rescued a fawn from a barbed-wire tangle. Granddad believed neighborhood children would enjoy seeing the baby deer while they were out for a walk, so he built a pen. That was the beginning of the zoo. People in the surrounding countryside began contributing rabbits, raccoons, ponies, birds, sheep—all kinds of animals. Homeowners liked the idea of children growing up in the city having the opportunity to see animals up close."

Next, she traced the yellow line extending to the southeast. "This is the outline of the park at the end of World War One. The citizens of Oklahoma County were very proud to have a park like this. It helped take their minds off the terrible hardships of the war."

She seemed lost in a private meditation as she walked around the plat, tracing each expansion: the flood of 1923 that left part of the southeast section underwater, the massive improvement that left the zoo closed for a year but reopened and thriving at the end of the 1920s.

"During the Depression, the zoo was credited with bringing more happiness to Oklahoma's local citizens, especially the children, than any other feature in the county. Kroneson Park became the Kroneson Park Zoo in the forties. When Grandpa Caleb died, he left a whole half section to his three sons: Dad, Uncle Hez, and Uncle Phineas. No one knows why, or they won't say why, but the part Grandpa Caleb left to Uncle Phineas is mostly underwater from the flood. Before he died, Grandpa Caleb built his house on the tallest hill in the neighborhood so he could look out his window and see the zoo. Now it's the zoo director's residence."

Audrey went decade by decade, telling the trials and triumphs of the zoo. She described the important people who contributed to its growth. She listed, with pride, the roster of notables who visited the zoo through the years: Will Rogers, Senator Bob Kerr, President Eisenhower, John Wayne, Bob Hope, President Kennedy and Jackie, Charlton Heston. She spoke of the zoo as if it were something alive, something with a mind, with affections, with a will to grow and change.

Hopper felt bewitched by the sound of her voice, the grace of her motions, the drift of her enthusiasm. He forgot the snow outside, the job; he even forgot about the treasure.

This spell broke when Cord coughed. "Excuse me, Miss Kroneson, but there are lots of animals locked up in this zoo, right?"

She looked at him quizzically before she spoke. "Yes, we have quite a collection here now. When we're through with the planned expansions, we expect the Oklahoma County Zoo will be one of the largest in the world."

"You have animals from all over the planet locked up here, don't you? Desert animals, mountain animals, arctic animals, plains animals, jungle animals, animals from everywhere."

Audrey frowned. "Yes, our collection includes animals from everywhere."

"They're all captives here, aren't they? I mean you, me, and Hopper, we can walk out whenever we want. But once an animal gets locked in here, this is where it stays until it dies or gets traded off." Audrey started to protest, but Cord went on. "The only animal I ever heard of busting out of here got killed, right? Made a real splash in the news. They couldn't catch it, so they killed it, right?"

Audrey blinked at Cord, a stunned look on her face. "You sound like you don't approve of what we're doing here, Mr. Cord."

Cord scratched his jaw. "I don't know, Ms. Kroneson. What *are* you doing here?"

Her face colored. "This zoo is a great source of pride to the people of Oklahoma County. We do research that's beneficial to animals everywhere. We're taking an important lead in providing our animals with the most natural surroundings possible." She stammered slightly. "We have a long way to go, of course. But we're learning. By the time we're through, this will be one of the most advanced zoological parks in the world with every possible consideration given to the comfort and well-being of our animals. And yes, in the fifties, a leopard escaped and was killed in the efforts to recapture. It was an accident. They . . . we were trying to tranquilize it and . . . " There was something of a plea in her voice as her sentence trailed off, unfinished.

Cord nodded. "I heard you all have that leopard stuffed around here someplace so people can still look at it. No sense letting a good attraction go to waste."

For a second, Audrey seemed on the barely contained side of an eruption. She drew a deep breath in an obvious effort to speak calmly. "Let me give you some insight into the importance of our work here. Take our male lions, for example. Do you know what would most likely happen to them if they were left in the wild?"

"Apart from living like free lions, I don't know."

"Well, for your information, the number-one cause of death among male lions in the wild is other male lions. They hardly ever die a natural death, and when they do, it's through the terrible ordeal of starvation because they're too old or injured to hunt. Here, they have the opportunity to live a comfortable life for a lot more years than they could expect in the wild." She stopped her rapid exposition long enough to catch a breath. "And when we finish the big cat exhibit—which I believe is providing you with a job, Mr. Cord—our cats will enjoy the nearest thing to their natural habitat more than any exhibit in America, maybe the world."

Hopper felt it was time for a referee. "No need to let Vernon get you all worked up, Audrey. He loves lions. Hell, he's a Leo himself. He's just got this thing about cages, jails, and stockades. I'll bet if Vernon had to choose between getting mauled to bits by a male lion or living in a nice, grassy big-cat exhibit where all his dietary and entertainment needs was satisfied, why, he'd march right in that exhibit and invite you to throw away the key, right, Cord?"

Cord mumbled something incomprehensible. Audrey rerolled the plat. "Obviously, since Mr. Cord is temporary, he has no real interest in the history or long-term plans for this zoo." Hopper grimaced by the way she hit that *temporary* pretty hard.

Hopper threw Cord a do-you-have-to-say-every-damn-thing-that-comes-into-your-thick-head look. Cord shrugged and returned his gaze to the lake.

Audrey went through the motions of clearing materials off the table. Hopper knew she was formulating the precise blend of control, courtesy, and authority that would get them out of her office and back to the shop, where their misguided opinions about the merits of the Oklahoma County Zoo wouldn't annoy anybody.

Hopper would be sorry to go. He liked almost everything about her: the way she absently tucked those runaway strands behind her ear, the way she pushed out her upper lip when she was concentrating, the creamy color and smoothness of her skin, the way she walked, dressed—almost everything. What he didn't like was her apparent reluctance to grant that Cord's point of view could have some merit. How could you not consider the possibility there might be something sad about locking animals up for life, even if you were cocksure it was for their own good? He decided to make it easy for her. "Well, Audrey, guess you're done with us here. So we'll get back to the shop."

She seemed relieved not to have to issue the dismissal order. Without an exchange of goodbyes, they struggled back into their heavy coats and stepped back into the cold. It was like stepping out of a sweet dream of paradise and waking up in your cold blue-collar world.

Cord mumbled as they drove back to the shop. Hopper studied him for a minute, hoping Cord would decide to get whatever was eating him off his chest. But Hopper was too impatient to wait.

"I'm not trying to step on your toes or nothing, Cord. But why did you feel like you had to pick a fight with that gal? What the hell difference does it make that they got a stuffed leopard around here someplace? Look at it from the leopard's point of view. At least he died on the outside, fighting for his freedom. There was still something in him that made him take his chance and break out." Cord growled something about rich people and zookeepers.

"You know what your problem is, Cord? If you're talking to bankers, you're pissed off at bankers. If you're talking to insurance men, you're pissed off at insurance men. If you're talking to preachers, you're pissed off at them. Are you just naturally pissed off at everybody, or does everybody just naturally piss you off?"

"Musicians, Hopper. I'm not pissed off at musicians or strippers, and I'm not pissed off at folks that know what's right and mind their own business."

"Well, it's comforting that you always know what's right. Makes it easier to know who to be pissed off at."

They arrived at the north gate just as another zoo employee opened it for a delivery truck. Cord turned left onto the access road. After a few seconds, he admitted, "I was out of line."

Hopper knew Cord could be counted on to own up when he was

guilty of bad manners. "I get your point, Cord. But there's just some scraps you can't win, and there's some that ain't worth winning if you can. You know I don't like to give advice when it ain't been asked, but I want to give you some. There's a difference between being on assault and being on ambush. The way I see it, we're here on ambush. We're trying to stay out of sight, keep a low profile, draw our pay, find us a treasure, and get the hell out of here with as few cuts and bruises as possible. Sure, I'd like to unlock every cage in the place and set all the captives free." Cord nodded, indicating that he was listening and the message was getting through. Hopper went on. "But there ain't no advantage in ruffling feathers when we'll be leaving this joint in a few weeks. Am I wrong?"

Cord rolled the window down and drew a deep breath of cold air. "Of course you're right. I don't need to snap at every shiny minnow that gets dangled in front of me." He scratched his jaw. "You reckon I owe that gal an apology?"

Hopper thought about the pros and cons and decided maybe it was best to let it go. "I'm not sure we'll ever see her again. But if we do, let's pretend this deal never happened. Let's just be polite, keep our mouth shut, and do our job."

As Cord approached the shop parking lot, he flipped on the right-turn signal. "Let me ask you a question. Would you take her deal?"

"What deal, Cord?"

"The one where you get a longer life. You get all your food paid for, you get free living quarters, all your medical expenses are taken care of. Hell, they'll even throw in a hand-picked lady or two for your enjoyment. You'll never worry again about paying bills or getting fired. All you got to do is live in a comfortable exhibit for the rest of your pampered goddam life, existing for the pleasure of the paying goddam public. Will you take that deal?"

"Well, damn, Cord, if you put it like that, of course the answer's no." He spoke with the confidence of one who knows he'd never get such an offer.

Cord pulled into the shop parking lot. "Maybe Buntz will figure we can dig through the snow and get some more hackberries out. Over there by ourselves is probably the only place in this whole zoo where we belong."

Hopper nodded. They climbed out of the pickup and headed for the shop just as Buntz pulled up in his golf cart. He motioned them to follow. He moved with his typical speed and focus to the coffeepot and whirled, waiting impatiently for them to catch up.

When they were close enough, he spoke just above a whisper, even though no one else was in the shop. "What happened in the PR office, boys?"

Hopper related the highlights.

"What did you do to piss off Neyland?"

Hopper and Cord traded glances. "Hell, not that much, Buntz. We traded views on classical music, he told me not to call him 'boss.' I said okay. What's up?"

"If I'd known he was going to show up, I would've warned you guys to keep your mouths shut. That guy's touchier than high-octane nitro. Any little thing can set the bastard off—don't ever tell anybody I called him a bastard. Anyway, I suspect he's trying to compensate for having a tiny dick—don't ever tell anybody I said that either. Whatever happened over there, Neyland's on the warpath. He's drawn a target on you guys, especially you, Hopper. So you're going to have to weather a storm for a while."

Hopper frowned. "What storm?"

Buntz made a circle on the floor with the toe of his boot. "He's probably going to make things tough for you. Don't worry, though, it won't last long. He'll forget all about it in a day or two. Probably because his attention span's as short as his dick—forget I said that. So you guys are gonna need to hunker down until he gets pissed off at somebody else and starts making life tough for another victim."

He made earnest eye contact with them, one at a time. "Just hang in there with me, fellas. I promise, whatever headaches you have to put up with in the short term, I'll cure 'em up later."

Cord squinted down at Buntz, who didn't return his gaze. "Like what, exactly, are we going to have to put up with?" Hopper could tell the answer to that question might be an important pivot in Cord's longevity as a zoo employee. Cord could handle the work fine. But the people were wearing him slick—like a tire running a long time on hot pavement with too much air pressure.

Buntz sighed. "For the rest of the afternoon, Neyland wants you helping out in the snake house."

Hopper and Cord shook their heads at the same time. "Now hold on, Buntz," Cord said, frowning. "I don't work in snake houses. They're usually full of snakes, ain't they?"

Buntz nodded. "I can't lie, that place is full of snakes, salamanders, frogs, newts—all kinds of creepy stuff. But you won't have to touch 'em or anything. All you got to do is go inside, collect the soup, and bring it out to the dump truck. That's all."

"Soup?" Hopper and Cord said it at the same time.

"That's what we call it."

"That's what we call what?" Cord asked with a snarl.

"Snake shit. The snake guys bag it up, and usually all we do is drive the truck to the back door. They haul it out. But one of the guys didn't show up today, so you guys have to do it."

Hopper laughed. "Oh, no, we don't. We don't have to do nothing with soup. We was hired to work with trees. Nobody said anything about us having to fool around with snakes or their soup."

Buntz was pleading. "Look, if you guys buck up on this, Neyland will fire you in a hummingbird's heartbeat. If that happens, the chances of me getting new men in time to do any good on the forty is a big fat zero." He wiped his nose with his sleeve. "I really need you guys to hang in there. You got to have faith. You got to wade through the tough time . . . I mean not literally *wade*, but you got to handle this. If you do, everything will be fine."

"How?" Cord asked. "How would you make it up to us for having to throw bags full of snake soup onto a dump truck?"

Buntz clasped his hands behind his back and walked in small circles. "I don't know. I'll come up with something." He brightened. "How about this for starters? You guys had lunch yet?"

Cord looked at his watch. "Not yet, Buntz. It ain't quite lunchtime."

"Tell you what. You guys be good sports, grit your teeth, roll up your sleeves, hold your noses, and go handle the soup—not literally handle, but you know what I mean. Do that, and I'll buy you lunch. Tonight, I'll figure some way to see you both come out on the good side of sticking with me. What do you say? Hungry?"

Hopper asked, "Can I talk to Cord in private for a second?"

Buntz looked disappointed. "Well, okay, you guys talk it over. I got a couple of things to do in the office anyway." He stomped off to his office at the back of the shop.

"What do you think, Cord?"

"I hate snakes."

"Me too. But that's beside the point. If we lose this job, we got no chance to find the treasure. Plus, even if we don't find the treasure, we need these wages to pay our way out of town. I say we stick it out and make damn sure Buntz knows we're doing him another favor."

Cord drew a deep breath. "Okay, but who knows what Neyland will do next to make our lives miserable?"

"Let's hope Buntz is right about him having a short dick with matching attention span."

Buntz came charging out of his office. "Well?"

Hopper put a hand on the smaller man's shoulder. "We like you, Buntz. We think you're the kind of fella that can be trusted to keep his word. We'll stick by you for as long as we can. We'll hold our noses and load that soup, just like you said."

Buntz enthusiastically shook hands with both men. "This is going to work out great, boys. Let's go eat."

Seventeen

They piled into Buntz's Dodge pickup and navigated the icy streets for the three miles to Love's Country Store, where Buntz promised they could get great sandwiches. All the way there, Buntz talked nonstop about the pleasures and marvels of working at the zoo.

"Every month has its own special personality. Take January, for example. Did you know the great horned owl lays her eggs in January? She picks the toughest time of the year to hatch her young. Know why? Because January is her best hunting season. When it snows like this, it's a smorgasbord of rabbits, voles, mice, squirrels, and other little edibles. Tell you something else: she don't build her own nest. She'll find a nest built by crows or hawks and kick their butts out of their own nest. Know why? Because she's tough enough to do it, that's why. And I'll tell you something else . . . ."

Even while he was chewing his grilled cheese sandwich, he sang the praises of the honey locust tree that bears its fruit in winter when grazing animals, like deer and bison, need all the help they can get to keep from starving. He talked about the Great Purple Hairstreak butterfly that lays her eggs where the larvae can feed on the mistletoe.

When Buntz just about exhausted the charms of January and was launching into the glories of February, they got back to the shop. Buntz jumped out of the Dodge and motioned them to follow. "Can one of you boys drive this dump truck and operate the PTO?" He pointed to a big gray 1970 Ford F-600 dump truck.

"Cord can," Hopper volunteered

"That right, Cord? Can you drive this thing?"

"Yep."

"Okay, you know where the snake house is?"

"Nope."

"Follow me. When you get there, park at the back door. Go inside and talk to Feeney. He'll tell you what to do. Be careful what you say to that maggot. Anything he hears will go straight to Neyland." He mounted his golf cart and spoke as Hopper and Cord made their slow walk to the dump truck. "This may be a tough afternoon, boys. It ain't because the work's hard; it's just . . . well, keep your mind on the future. I'll have you back in the fresh air on the forty quick as I can."

He sped off as Cord fired up the Ford and lumbered after him. Buntz waited at the north gate and locked it behind them when they passed through. Then he hummed by on his electric motor and led them to the snake house. He didn't slow down, as he indicated the place with a wave of his left hand, and disappeared toward the nocturnal animal exhibit.

Hopper guided Cord as he backed the Ford close enough to the rear door to cut down the number of steps they'd have to haul the soup.

They stood at the back door of the snake house, looking at each other and shivering.

"Cold out here, ain't it?" Cord asked

"Yep. It'll be warm in the snake house."

Cord nodded. "Yeah, they have to keep it warm for the snakes. Cold-blooded bastards."

To Hopper, the snake house door looked like the door to the slaughterhouse in the stockyards. He clapped his hands. "Well, the sooner we get through loading soup, the sooner we can leave the snake house behind."

Cord sighed. "Okay, let's get this over with."

Inside, the first thing they noticed was the smell. Hopper tried to think of something to compare it with. Nothing came to mind. It wasn't an overpowering stench, like a feed lot. It damn sure didn't have any chemical smells like a garage or hospital. It was just strong—and it was just bad.

They stood in a large room lit by a single bare bulb hanging from the ceiling. There were maybe fifteen large black plastic trash bags near the door. Hopper shuddered when he speculated on the contents of those bags. In addition to the soup bags, there were bags of sawdust and wood chips, gravel and other material Hopper couldn't identify. He examined one. "Holy shit. Know what's in this bag, Cord? Freeze-dried crickets."

"You're lying."

"No, take a look. This is a twenty-five-pound bag of freeze-dried crickets. What do you reckon they do with freeze-dried crickets?"

Cord snorted. "Oh, I don't know. Mix 'em up with popcorn and eat 'em for a snack. You know damn well what they do with freeze-dried crickets. But I don't care to pollute my mind thinking about it, thank you."

Then there were cages of live chicks, mice, and rabbits and glass boxes crawling with live crickets. Hopper recoiled at the thought of the fate awaiting these little animals. He'd seen a snake unhinge its jaws, opening its nightmarish mouth impossibly wide to swallow a fish he had on a stringer. A sight like that, reflected in the pale beam of a flashlight on a dark creek bank, hit something primal and terrible in Hopper's psyche. In Vietnam, they'd been warned to be on the lookout for flying snakes—*flying snakes,* for crying out loud—that glided out of trees and latched onto your damn neck.

He swore to himself he'd quit and give up all hope of finding the treasure before he'd watch some scaly snake eat a baby chick or mouse, even though he had no particular affinity for mice.

From somewhere in the dark interior, he heard a voice. "Close the damn door. We have to keep it warm in here." Hopper tried to locate the voice. Cord pulled the door shut. With the fresh air cut off, the room darkened, and the smell grew stronger as it prowled out of the darkness and tightened its grip on their senses.

Hopper spoke to the darkness. "We're here to see Feeney."

"That's me."

"Well, maybe we can hear you, Feeney, but we can't see you. Where are you?"

A refrigerator door opened at the northeast corner of the room. They saw Feeney silhouetted in the fridge's light. He held a couple of containers that looked like something you might buy at a bait shop. He spoke without looking at them. "So you guys are the new men Buntz sent over to load the soup."

Hopper didn't like talking to Feeney's back. "Buntz told us to drive the truck over. That's all he told us to do."

Feeney closed the refrigerator door. The snake house grew dark again. "Well, Grassley got snowed in. He's my helper; lives over in Jones. You two will need to load the soup while I feed Cyclops."

Hopper cleared his throat. "We were told all we had to do was bring the truck."

Feeney walked toward them, limping. "Afraid you'll have to do more than that." He stepped into the glow of the weak halo cast by the light bulb. He might have been tall, but he was stooped. "I've been doing the work of two men all morning, so I'm behind. You two will have to take up some of the slack."

Feeney's thin dark hair was parted down the middle like Alfalfa of *The Little Rascals*. Hopper couldn't figure why a guy old enough to make decisions for himself chose to part his dang hair like that. The oddball hairstyle made Feeney's ears look big and loopy. A thin mustache and a scraggly excuse for a beard littered his angular chin.

Cord spoke to the creep. "What the hell is Cyclops?"

Feeney offered a crooked smile. "Cyclops is a phenomenon. He's a twenty-three-foot-long rock python, weighs nearly two hundred pounds. He's one of the biggest snakes on the planet. Watching him eat is a marvel few people have the pleasure of witnessing. Want to watch?"

Hopper shook his head. "Not unless you're going to feed him a motorcycle."

Cord asked, "What do you feed a snake that size? Surely it wouldn't be satisfied with freeze-dried crickets."

Feeney responded with his lopsided grin. "Pigs. He likes pigs. He prefers goats, but pigs are more fun."

Hopper winced. "Fun?"

"Sure. Goats go into shock. They just go limp. But pigs put up a fight. They make Cyclops do a little work to earn his grub. Know how he got his name? When he was being shipped from Africa, somebody fed him a big male Colobus monkey; threw it right into the crate with him. Must have been a hell of a fight in that crate. Cyclops won, of course, but the monkey got one of his eyes before it became dinner."

Hopper couldn't stand it. "Spare us the exploits of the monkey-eatin' python and tell us what we need to do to get out of here."

Feeney cocked his head to one side. "You two found something over on the forty, didn't you? What was it?"

Alarm bells clanged in Hopper's head.

"What are you talking about?" Cord asked

"Podd said you carried something away from the forty and put it in the back of your car. What was it?"

Hopper frowned. "Podd's full of shit. All we put in the car was our lunch pail."

Feeney shook his head. "No, you found something."

Cord took a step closer to Feeney, who took a corresponding step back. "What do you think there is to find, Feeney? Hell, there ain't anything over there but animal bones and thorny plants."

Feeney's crooked smile disappeared. "Load these soup bags on the dump truck." He indicated the black plastic bags lined on the floor. "When you're done, come and find me."

"Why can't you just wait here? We won't be more than ten minutes loading this stuff."

"Because I'm doing the work of two men, and I can't stand around watching you guys do mule work." He wheeled and limped away, disappearing through a metal door.

Hopper and Cord dragged the first two bags to the truck. Cord whispered just loud enough to be heard over the wind, "What the hell do you suppose this ghoul knows?"

Hopper shook his head. "All Podd could've seen was a trashy little boot. This creep can't know anything."

"How come he acts like he knows something, then?"

"Hell, you saw him. Working around snakes all day probably makes him dippy in his thinking."

They heaved the foul-smelling bags over the dump truck rails and went back for another installment. They had all the soup bags loaded in less than ten minutes. For a second, they considered just firing up the F-600 and taking it back to the shop.

After a short discussion, Cord shook his head. "The ghoul told us to come and find him. I guess we'd better."

Hopper, grumbling, followed Cord to the metal door where Feeney disappeared. Cord pulled it open.

"Feeney," he shouted. "We're through. Anything else before we split?"

They heard Sinatra singing "My Way" on shitty speakers from somewhere in the snake house. Cord boosted his volume. "Hey, Feeney, we're through. We're leaving."

Feeney's high-pitched, oily voice drifted faintly above Sinatra and through the aroma. "Come in here for a minute. I need your help."

"Doing what?" Hopper threw it back like an insult.

"Just come in here."

They looked at each other and sullenly followed the voice. They found Feeney sitting on a folding chair, peering into a glass exhibit illuminated by red light. Inside the cage, four white mice scrambled over a miniature landscape of tree limbs, dried leaves, scattered bark, and stone.

"Okay, Feeney, we're here. What do you want?" Cord's tone was sharp and impatient.

Feeney didn't look at them. His attention was focused on the mice exploring the limits of the exhibit. "I don't suppose you two have ever heard of Alimony's treasure." Feeney glanced at them from the corner of his eye. Hopper concentrated on controlling his reaction. He knew Cord was playing it cool too.

Hopper spoke. "The Alimony treasure is the cash a gal gets in the divorce when her old man gets caught fooling around, ain't it?"

Feeney's lip curled in a faint smile. "You two have no idea what's happening, do you? You see these mice running around the exhibit, all aimless and unsuspecting. They don't see, and you don't see, the danger under their feet. Look."

An arrangement Hopper mistook for a collection of random rocks stirred. The mice also detected the motion. At first, they scattered around the enclosure, panicked, looking for a place to hide. Finding their instinctive defenses to this lethal peril perfectly useless, they wound up pawing at the glass. The snake lazily raised its head to observe their hopeless escape efforts. Hopper wanted to look away but couldn't.

Cord growled, "Look, Feeney, if you're done with us, we got better things to do than watch your buddy size up his lunch."

Feeney didn't look up. "These dumb mice don't know the snake is watching every move they make. By the time they realize the awful truth, it's too late. If a mouse was smart enough to figure out how to reason with the snake, it might talk the snake into making a deal. But mice ain't smart. They wind up the same way every time—lunch."

The snake's head moved so fast, it was a blur to Hopper's eye. One of the mice collapsed onto its side, convulsing. Feeney *tsk-tsked.* "Too bad for that mouse." He looked at them and smiled his crooked smile. "If you two was to come across something valuable, surely you're smarter than a stupid mouse. You're smart enough to know you're being watched by a big bad snake you can't see." He turned his attention back to the exhibit, where the doomed mice dashed around in aimless panic while their stricken comrade succumbed to the venom. "Smart fellas that get their hands on something valuable might need help getting it off zoo premises. Smart fellas would know how to make a deal with the big snake and avoid getting swallowed up."

The snake began its slow, creepy approach toward the doomed mouse, barely spasming now.

Without warning, Cord kicked the legs of the folding chair, causing Feeney to collapse on the floor. Feeney stared up with cold reptilian hatred. Cord smiled. He spoke in a calm, threatening voice. "Feeney, I have some advice for you. Ask your pal Cyclops whether he'd prefer a helpless goat or the kind of fella that would chew his fuckin' eye out. Even if you're the biggest, baddest goddam snake in the world, there's always the danger you might bite off a shitload more than you can chew."

As Cord steered the dump truck with its load of snake soup back toward the shop, they realized they were trapped. They didn't have a key to the north gate, so they couldn't drive out of the zoo. They had no choice but to wait at the gate until someone came along to let them pass. As they waited, they kicked around these new complications. Feeney obviously knew about the treasure and suspected they were on to something.

"One good thing is Feeney won't say or do anything to get us fired. He needs us to be where he can keep an eye on us."

Cord nodded. "You reckon Podd shot his mouth off to anybody else?"

Hopper gave him an are-you-kidding look. "As I recall, Buntz told us Podd's still Animal Tech One because he can't keep his big yap shut."

Cord growled. "Maybe we ought to warn him about the dangers of spreading gossip."

Hopper glanced at the side mirror and noticed Buntz's golf cart, followed by a pickup with Podd at the wheel. "Here they come. For now, let's just rock along until we can figure the angles."

"Right," Cord said as Buntz pulled the golf cart up to the passenger side of the dump truck. Hopper rolled down the window. Buntz yelled across to Cord, "You did say you knew how to work the PTO, right?"

"Yep."

"You know where the city dump is?"

"Yep."

"Okay, drive this truck to the shop. There's a tarp and tie-downs behind the seat. Be sure the tarp is secure. If some innocent member of the motoring public gets a load of soup blown onto her windshield, somebody's liable to get sued. Then a whole bunch of somebodies is liable to get fired. Okay?"

Hopper gave a salute. "Got it, Buntz."

"This truck has a county permit, so you won't need to pay no fees. By the time you get back, it'll be about quitting time. See you back at the shop." He unlocked the gate and waited as the dump truck and pickup passed through.

In the parking lot, they battled the high wind to secure the tarp. Cord spoke above the gusts. "Look who's coming." Hopper saw Podd approaching the dump truck with a big smile on his hawkish face.

"You guys want me to show you the easy way to do that? I know most of the shortcuts around here."

Hopper answered, "Podd, you could do us a favor by minding your own damn business. But what's more important, you'd be doing yourself a favor. Long noses like yours that get stuck in other folks' doings sometimes gets doors slammed on them."

Podd's face contorted into an exaggerated expression of hurt feelings. "Gee, fellas, I'm just trying to be helpful. I don't know what I done to get you so touchy. If you don't want none of my help, fine. I just thought maybe if we all work together, friendly like, things would be easier for everyone."

Hopper moved further back on the truck rails and continued securing the tarp. "Your pal Feeney somehow got the notion our lunch pail was something special. He says he got that idea from you."

"Oh, well, see, I know a lunch pail when I see one, and—"

"Well, here's how it is, Podd. Me and Cord say it was our lunch pail. We ain't going to argue about something foolish like that. So if you got nothing better to do than gossip about our lunch, knock yourself out."

Podd's smile devolved into a sly grin. "Sure, fellas. If you say so. But if later you see the advantage of having someone friendly to talk to—you know, to make things easier—me and Feeney are the ones you want to tell your secrets to."

Cord fixed Podd with a cold stare. "Maybe you better take a walk, Podd. Otherwise, you may accidentally find yourself taking a ride in the dump truck under the tarp with a load of snake soup."

Podd shrugged and walked away, grinning. "Suit yourself, boys."

With the tarp secured, Hopper and Cord piled into the F-600 and bumped their way along the icy road leading to the dump. Cord operated the PTO without incident. They dumped the soup and headed back to the shop.

When they got back, everyone was busy cleaning muddy tools and hosing debris out of pickup beds. Buntz led them back to the dump truck, loudly announcing that he wanted to be sure the tarp was properly rolled and stowed. He motioned for them to climb into the cab.

Keeping an eye on the shop door, he asked what happened at the snake house. When Hopper gave him the rundown, Buntz gritted his teeth. "Goddam Podd. It's bad enough he's got a mouth the size of a truck tire and a brain the size of a butterfly's asshole, but he's got no control on his cockeyed imagination. He and that wormy Feeney are working themselves up about that Alimony treasure again. Every three or four years, somebody gets a fever, and they go crawling all over the 40 looking for clues. But everybody knows the treasure can't be there. Even if Alimony and that other fella got killed over there, the treasure has to be someplace else. Dumb shits."

There was urgency in Buntz's whisper. "We can't have anybody thinking there's some profit crawling around over there."

Hopper and Cord nodded.

"No matter what anybody says, you guys didn't find nothing in there except pinecones and sassafras, right?"

Hopper and Cord nodded.

"Okay, I'll figure a way to handle Feeney and Podd. And thanks for being good sports over that snake house deal. That was good work. See you tomorrow." He bounded out of the truck and stomped back through the shop door.

Eighteen

Hopper's excitement climbed as Cord handily steered the Rambler over the frozen muddy streets back to their rented house. Hopper knew it was too much to hope Nozetape had both pages of the Alimony journal deciphered. But it would be nice if the only problem left after tonight was how to dig up the treasure and spirit the boodle off the zoo premises without getting forced to cough it up to somebody.

They found Nozetape sitting at the kitchen table with Alimony's journal pages in front of him, an open notebook to his right, and a German/English dictionary to his left. Nozetape looked up bleary-eyed, and Hopper knew they wouldn't have the answer tonight.

There were no "hello, how you doing?" formalities. Hopper blurted, "What did you find out, Nozetape?"

"It's like we thought. Alimony wrote in German, but he wrote in something else too. I think it's French."

Hopper stood in the doorway with his mouth open. Cord stepped past him, shedding his hat, coat, and gloves. He strolled over to the table and looked over Nozetape's shoulder at the scribbling on his notebook.

"French?" Hopper almost whined. "You mean the little guy spoke English but wrote in some mixed-up German/French hodgepodge? Great. Can you make sense out of any of it?"

Nozetape shrugged and shook his head. "I've been going over and over this. I can pick out a word here and there, but most of it's a blur. He was a pretty smart fella. Even if somebody found his boot, they might not look close enough at the heel to figure out it was hollow. Then if they did find these pages, they'd never uncode his writing unless they could read German and French. I think he even threw in some English here and there just to up the confusion index." He dropped his pencil on the notebook. "I can pick out a snippet here and there, but if you add it all up, It's like trying to decipher Elfish if all you speak is dwarf."

Hopper stood in the door sputtering, "Elfish . . . what the hell does Elfish have to do with this?"

Nozetape grunted. "It's a figure of speech, Dale."

Hopper closed the door, frowning. "I need a drink. How about you fellas?" They passed the Boone's Farm and took counsel on their next move. Nozetape moaned when he heard about the conversations with Feeney and Podd. "So everybody in the damn world has suspicions we're on to something."

Cord peeled the label off the bottle. "I ain't that worried about Feeney and Podd. We can handle those two. I just hope they ain't a pipeline to some sombitch that might be a bigger problem. Feeney said something about some big snake watching us. Hope it was just a figure of speech."

"Like who?" Nozetape asked. "Who could be a big snake out there that knows about us?"

Cord sounded impatient. "Like anybody. Even if we didn't have to worry about some kind of legal problem, we might be looking at a health issue if there's somebody that figures to strong-arm us after we do all the brain work and heavy lifting."

Hopper laughed. "We wouldn't be interesting to anybody if they knew how roadblocked we are right this minute." He took a drink. "We've got to figure out how to unravel these Elfish pages."

Nozetape groaned. "Looks like I'm picking up a French/English dictionary to go with this one." He patted the German/English volume on the table. "Hell, by the time I'm through here, I ought to be able to hire myself out as a goddam codebreaker."

Hopper walked into the kitchen and opened a cabinet door. "We got a couple cans of chili left. That ought to do for tonight. Who wants chili—the beef and bean kind?"

Nineteen

The next morning, Buntz stopped his golf cart at the gate to the west 40. He sat listening to the wind blowing through the mixed population of bare trees and evergreens. The sun rising behind him caused the snow covering the ground and branches to sparkle like gold. The ice on the grass and limbs made everything look like it had a dressing of dazzling jewels.

He tried to imagine how all this would look when the dozers were done. All this earth would be turned over. The secret little pockets of jasmine, the hollies, the lilacs, the sweetgum and sassafras trees, the persimmons, the pines, the cedars, the sage . . . all these wild plants holding onto their little bit of soil would be ripped up when the topsoil got busted and churned.

Tree roots would be sticking up like ruined arms and legs. Next year, the owls, uncos, finches, sparrows, and nuthatches nesting in here would come, expecting to reoccupy their nests or build new ones. They'd find a plowed-up nightmare instead.

He knew no matter how many trees, herbs, vines, and flowers he saved, he was going to feel like shit about the ones he lost.

A pair of white-throated sparrows bobbed briefly on a scrub oak branch, swaying in the winter breeze before winging off to the South.

Buntz sighed and watched them disappear. "See, that's the problem with all of us that's got roots," he said out loud. "You feathered critters can move on whenever it suits you. Somebody pushes down your nesting tree, you just fly off and find another. Once the rest of us get rooted in, that's where we stay till somebody uproots us or we die."

He pulled his right glove off with his teeth and wrestled his coat sleeve back from his wristwatch. Time to get back to the shop. He wanted to be there when Hopper and Cord showed up.

Twenty

Buntz was waiting for them when they pulled into the parking lot. He motioned from the shop door. Cord chuckled. Hopper asked, "What's so funny?" as they stepped out of the Rambler.

"I wonder if Buntz slept a wink last night trying to figure out how to make up to us for having to load that snake soup."

"Don't laugh too hard," Hopper said, sending Buntz a friendly wave. "Something tells me that ain't the last trip we'll make to the damn snake house."

They followed Buntz to his tiny office at the rear of the shop. The other members of the crew didn't slow their morning preparations, but Hopper could tell they watched with curious eyes. Evidently, Buntz didn't often bring underlings into his sanctum.

"Shut the door. I want to show you something." He plopped into a creaky antique office chair and slid across the floor on noisy casters. There was no room for other chairs in the office, so Hopper and Cord stood waiting for Buntz to rummage around in the bottom drawer of a metal file cabinet. He produced an ancient book that looked like it might fall apart in his hands.

"Know what this is?" The twinkle in his eye suggested he regarded this gesture as a very pleasing gift.

Hopper grinned. "Hell, Buntz, looks like a book to me. What do you say, Cord?"

Cord scratched his jaw. "Yeah, I'd say it's a book alright."

Buntz frowned. "Well, this ain't just any book. I had to save up for years to get it. This was written in 1895 by a world-famous scholar, Dr. Matthew Edgemere Reynolds." He opened the book with the same care he might use to handle one of the original gospels. He ran his hand across the yellowed page and spoke without looking up. "Dr. Reynolds studied plants like nobody ever studied them before. He didn't just look at them under microscopes and stuff. He did plenty of that, of course. But he really watched them—watched them grow, sprout, bloom, and die; watched them do everything. He read every book he could find that had anything to do with plants. He talked to all the important botanists and horticulturists in Europe and America. He traveled all over Asia and Africa talking to scientists, holy men, healers, medicine men, and witch doctors. The scientists of his day thought he was off his rocker, obsessed or something." He sat for a moment with eyes closed and hands on the fragile page like a man in reverent prayer. "Let me show you something." He turned the book around so they could see.

The offered page exhibited a drawing of two men in quaint clothes— something the Pilgrims might wear—pouring water on the roots of a tree. As the tree trunk progressed up from the ground, its shape began to change until, just below the canopy of leaves, the trunk assumed the figure of a man. The tree-man's expression was familiar, but Hopper couldn't place it. He knew he should recognize it, and it bothered him that the answer was just out of his mental reach.

Buntz spoke in a low voice as if transmitting a deep secret. "This is Dr. Reynolds's drawing of a wood carving he found in Germany. He thinks somebody carved it around 1515. See, hundreds of years after Europeans became Christians, they still believed some trees was homes for spirits or maybe even had spirits themselves." He looked up at them, hopeful. "You guys think that's possible? Trees could have . . . you know, feelings or something?" He blushed and looked down at the book.

Cord rolled his eyes and elbowed Hopper in the ribs. Hopper cleared his throat. "To tell you the truth, I never really thought about it, Buntz. What do you think?"

Buntz ignored the question. "Listen to this." He turned another page and leaned over the book with his nose nearly touching the page. He read one word at a time—like a third-grader might. "'Ancient books by Buddhist scholars reveal that the earliest prac . . . practitioners of the discipline disputed on the question of whether trees had souls and, therefore, whether it was wrong to do them injury.'" He tapped the page lightly with his finger. "I want you to know I'm not an idolater or anything, but I can sort of see how people for thousands of years might think there was something, you know, special about trees. Dr. Reynolds says the word *tree* has the same origin as our words *truth* and *trust*. And look." He carefully turned more pages. "It wasn't just trees. They had beliefs about lots of plants . . . herbs and flowers and roots."

Cord sighed noisily. It was Hopper's turn to prod him with an elbow. "Look, Buntz, you won't take this wrong if I ask you a question, will you?"

Buntz blushed, shook his head, and closed the book carefully. "I just thought maybe . . . well, I guess we better get to work." He carefully replaced the book in the drawer, obviously disappointed about how the conversation had gone.

"Wait a minute, Buntz. Look, I'll make a confession here, but you have to promise it won't . . . uhh, affect the job." There was an uncomfortable silence in the office. Hopper glanced over his shoulder and noticed the crew throwing curious glances through the office window. "Look, Buntz. Something tells me you been keeping your thoughts on this to yourself because . . . well, you got your reasons. I just want to say I think I know exactly what you're talking about. I've actually talked to plants myself . . . really. And I've heard them talk back."

Buntz's mouth hung open, and his eyes seemed on the verge of watering. When he started to speak, Cord thundered, "Oh, for crying out loud, Hopper. The man said it's time to get to work, so let's get to work."

Buntz sat blinking at Hopper for a second and then, with an air of profound sorrow, rolled the chair back on its casters and got to his feet. "Right, let's get to work."

Cord opened the door and stepped onto the shop floor, mumbling.

Hopper followed. He felt Buntz's hand on his shoulder. "I'd like to talk to you about this more later, Hopper." Hopper nodded and took a step, but Buntz kept a grip on his shoulder. "One more thing. Miss Kroneson wants you and Cord to stop by the PR office about ten o'clock this morning. She promised she'd only keep you for a minute or two. And remember, if Neyland shows up, keep your mouth shut. Tell Cord to do the same. I'd like you to get at least fifteen hackberries out of there today. The ground's wet, so it should make easy digging. Maybe I'll catch up with you at lunchtime."

He released Hopper's shoulder and charged into the shop, barking instructions. Then it hit Hopper like a mule kick. The expression on the tree-man's face, he remembered where he saw it. It was in the movie where Charlton Heston played the painter—*The Agony and the Ecstasy.* It was the same expression on the painting of the guy looking at God at the moment of creation. He'd have to think about that later.

Hopper and Cord were in the pickup headed for the 40. Cord snorted, "Let me give you some good advice a fella gave me yesterday. Let's just keep our mouths shut, do our job, and collect our pay. Then we can get the hell out of Oklahoma in April."

Hopper gulped and nodded. "You're right, Cord. I . . . you're right."

Minutes later, dampness soaked through Hopper's boots and socks as he shoveled muddy soil from hackberry roots. As his feet and hands got wet, the cold marched like an infection through his arms and legs. Even though his winter work clothes provided a stout barrier against the wind, the damp chill used his hands and feet as a pathway to invade and freeze his whole body.

Hopper's mind kept rolling back to Buntz's old book with the picture of the man-tree. Even before this talk with Buntz, he wondered whether these hackberries felt discomfort when the ax blade severed the taproot. He knew for a fact the whole tree shivered when the root got hit, but he didn't know if it was just physics or maybe there was something more to it.

At 8:45, they crawled out of a muddy hole and trudged to the pickup to get warm. As Cord started the engine, Hopper poured them both a cup of coffee. Cord closed his eyes in ecstasy as he gripped the steaming cup in his frozen fingers.

For a few minutes, they spoke idly about the cold and their misfortunes in not having rubber boots and waterproof glove liners. After a short pause, Hopper couldn't stand it. "Okay, Cord, come out with it. What are you bottling up over there?"

Cord scratched his jaw and peered into his coffee. "I need you to be logical here, Hopper. I didn't make a big deal out of the little green man you saw in your bedroom pointing at his feet."

"I never said he was green, dammit. I said he was barefoot."

Cord looked at his friend sideways as he poured another cup of coffee. "I just want to know, do you think the little man was real?"

Hopper snorted. "Don't be a goof, Cord. I might get confused sometimes, but I'd never believe something so farfetched as a little guy coming back from the dead just so he can hang around in my bedroom and show me his feet. But let me ask you a question. How much of the knowable stuff in the university you reckon we know?"

Cord scratched his chin. "You mean just the two of us?"

"No, all of us. If you add up everything that everybody in the world knows, what percentage of the knowable stuff in the universe would that be?"

"Hell, I don't know. Say, ten percent."

"That means ninety percent of what's real and knowable out there none of us knows, right?"

"Meaning?"

"Meaning a lot stuff that goes on around us that we think we got a handle on might be out of our reach. Hell, for thousands of years, there was microbes in people's water, and nobody had a clue until somebody figured out a way to see 'em."

"So I guess you're saying the little guy might have been real, and Nozetape might have seen tiny wet footprints, and you and Buntz might be

communing with the spirits of cactus and trees and shit, and the re:
us just ain't using the right scope. Is that what you're saying?"

"Kiss my ass, Cord." Hopper looked at his watch. "We're supposed
to be at the PR office in about twenty minutes. We'll finish this conversation over a joint, and you'll see I'm right. In the meantime, let's see if
we can get that tree up and in the truck before we have to go over there."

As they put their gloves back on, Cord chuckled. "The whole time
we're working, I'm going to be cooking up a theory of my own. Could be
the zoo is the doorway to the twilight zone. That would explain all the
crazy stuff that's been going on since we came to work here: the boot,
the little guy in your room, a supervisor who thinks trees might have
souls." His chuckle turned into a full-blown laugh. "No telling what will
happen next. Hell, we might find out the 40 really is haunted."

The laugh stopped in his throat. He jerked up rigid when hard
knuckles rapped on the window next to his head. There, with acorns
and pinecones woven into his beard, stood Finn, smiling at them. "Oh,
yeah," Cord mumbled, "and I almost forgot about this guy."

Hopper jumped out of the truck. "Jesus Christ, Finn, man, am I glad
to see you. I was scared shitless we'd come over here and find you froze."

Finn pointed to the northwest. "I got a place over there. It's warm.
I'm fine. I looked for you yesterday. I was afraid you might be someplace
froze. I have something for you." He dug around in his bag and came up
with a peanut butter jar filled with something that looked like cloves. He
held them out in a dirty hand twisted by arthritis.

"What's this, Finn?"

"Pine nuts. I roasted them for you. They're good but a little hard
on your teeth. I can't eat them anymore. It's good to keep some in your
pocket. They help when you get tired. I get tired a lot these days."

Hopper took the jar. "Just a minute, Finn." He retrieved an orange
from the lunch pail.

"This time, it's your orange, by God," Cord mumbled.

"It's okay, buddy, I brought an extra one." Hopper handed Finn the orange. The old man stashed it in his pocket. Hopper tried to put a hand on Finn's shoulder, but he pulled away, giving Hopper a suspicious eye. "You don't mean to take me away, do you?" He bent over, covering his mouth, seized by a series of hard coughs.

Hopper shook his head. "No, Finn. I figure a fella ought to be where he wants to be. If you want to be here, that's okay with me. But that's a bad cough. How long has it been since you've seen a doctor? Maybe some medicine might help clear it up."

Finn frowned, trying to access a memory. He shrugged, coughed again, and shook his head. "I don't remember seeing a doctor since I got back from the Philippines."

"The Philippines? Are you a World War Two vet, Finn?"

"Yeah."

"Maybe we could get you over to the VA sometime."

"Thanks for the orange." He disappeared into the woods, his going accompanied by mumbling, twigs breaking, branches being pushed aside, and occasional violent coughing.

Hopper watched the old derelict disappear. He looked at the jar of pine nuts in his hand and felt their weight on his heart. Cord started the pickup. "Come on, Hopper. If he don't want to be helped, we got to leave him alone."

Hopper stood listening to the old man's departing noises. "Yep, I guess we better get to the PR office."

Twenty-one

Audrey leaned over a camera bag, arranging a collapsible tripod, when Hopper and Cord stepped into the PR office. Without straightening, she spoke over her shoulder. "Help yourselves to a cup of coffee. I'll be right with you."

Cord wiped his feet and marched directly to the coffeepot. Hopper, enjoying the view, decided coffee could wait. Audrey, still bent over the bag, glanced at Cord. When she made eye contact with Hopper, he smiled benignly. "Be glad to lend you a, uhh, hand there, Miss Kroneson."

She frowned. "I can manage, thank you—Mr. Hopper." Without hurrying, she finished packing the tripod, stood up, and placed the bag on the table.

Hopper beamed boyishly and heaved a deep sigh. "Well, I guess I'll have coffee now." Without taking his eyes from her reddening face, he wiped his feet and joined Cord at the coffeepot.

She cleared her throat. "I guess Mr. Buntz told you I wanted to see you this morning."

Hopper, still smiling, said, "Yep, that's why we're here, Miss Kroneson. What can we do for you?"

"I wanted to apologize. I was rude and insensitive yesterday. I'm sorry."

Hopper and Cord exchanged a glance. Cord poured Hopper a cup. Hopper took a seat at the conference table as Cord stared at the water birds gliding on the lake. "That was thoughtful of you, Miss Kroneson. Cord can speak for himself, but as far as I'm concerned, apology accepted."

"Don't you want to know why I'm apologizing?"

"You already told us. You were rude and insensitive. That's a good reason."

There was nothing apologetic in her expression. "I thought you might like to know why I'm sorry for the way I acted."

Hopper leaned back in the chair. "Sounds like you have something you'd like to get off your chest, Miss Kroneson. Go ahead."

She yanked the gold ribbon in her hair, releasing her ponytail into a cascade of unbrushed brown hair. "I changed my mind. You can go."

"Fine." Hopper dropped his half-full Styrofoam cup into the wastebasket. "Let's go, Cord."

"Wait." They stopped at the door. "Look, I'm trying to . . . After yesterday, I looked at your personnel files. I didn't realize . . . " Her voice trailed off.

Cord walked back to the coffeepot and refilled his cup. "Okay, Ms. Kroneson, you looked at our personnel files and saw something that made you feel you should apologize. Let me see if I can help you. Maybe you're feeling guilty because your daddy and his rich oil buddies backed their pal, your Uncle Lyn, when he decided to escalate the war and send hundreds of thousands of American boys to fight in Vietnam. Is that it? Maybe you noticed that none of the guys you grew up with got killed or wounded. Most of them got college deferments, and the ones that went into the service didn't get combat duty. Maybe you feel bad because you and your blueblood college friends were okay with labeling combat vets who came home as baby killers. No?"

"Please, Vernon, we had no idea—"

"Just a minute, I'm trying to help you here. You're trying to say you're sorry, and I'm giving you some multiple-choice possibilities to pick from. Yesterday, you looked us in the eye and found out something about the kind of men we are. You looked at our personnel files and found out that we're famous war heroes who got a bunch of medals for getting shot up doing our duty. If I'm wrong, Ms. Kroneson, feel free to straighten me out. Then it'll be my turn to apologize."

Hopper moved to Cord's side. "Take it easy, Vernon. All she wants to do is apologize. She's got her reasons. Let's leave it at that, okay?"

Audrey's hand was over her mouth. She looked down, and her hair obscured her face. Cord stared past her, his eyes fixed on the calm waters of the lake.

The atmosphere in the PR office had grown cold and damp. Hopper let the moment last as long as it should. He couldn't resist the urge to put his hand on her shoulder. She didn't seem to mind. He spoke with his most reassuring voice. "You might find this funny, Audrey, but after we left yesterday, I had to stop Vernon from coming back to apologize to you. Seems like everybody felt like they was steppin' on everybody else's toes. Tell you what . . . let's start fresh. Do you like the blues?"

Audrey brushed a tissue across her nose. "Yes, I like the blues very much."

"Well, me and Cord here will be playing some real sweet blues tonight at the Blue Buzzard Saloon. There's nothing like good music and a cool beverage to make folks overlook everybody else's bad manners. Come by tonight, and we'll buy you a drink."

She blew her nose. "I'm not sure the Blue Buzzard Saloon is my kind of place."

Hopper broke into a hearty laugh. "Oh, I can tell you for damn sure it ain't your kind of place. But if you come, I'll make you a couple of promises. First, your apology will be accepted—in spades—by both of us." He shot Cord a stern look. "And next, I promise you'll have a good time."

Audrey reformed her ponytail and tied it up with the gold ribbon. "I'll think about it."

"You do that, Audrey. Now, me and Cord need to get back on the job. We got trees to move." As they stepped out of the PR office, Neyland raced up on his golf cart. As he bounded off, he self-consciously tucked a comb back into his hip pocket.

"What are you two men doing here? I thought you got everything done yesterday."

Cord ignored him and went to the pickup. Hopper flashed his brightest smile. "Mr. Buntz told us there was a thing or two we needed to attend to in there." He thrust his thumb toward the office door. "So we did. Now, we're headed back to the west 40." He winked. "You take care, Mr. Neyland." He whistled happily as he joined Cord in the pickup. Neyland scowled watching them drive away. When he stepped into the office, Audrey was bent over the conference table, examining a phone book.

"What were those two doing here?"

"Oh, I just wanted to thank them again for their help yesterday. Julian, do you, by any chance, know anything about a place called the Blue Buzzard Saloon?"

Twenty-two

Hopper savored the wild, civilian smell of smoke and alcohol as he stepped into the welcoming darkness of the Blue Buzzard Saloon. Little Eva chirped cheerfully from behind the bar. "Hey, Pancho and Cisco, put down your tools and let me buy you something to get you through the night."

They set their guitar cases on the raised boards that served as the saloon's tiny stage. At the bar, Eva filled three shot glasses from the contents of the frozen bottle of Cuervo Gold tequila stashed in the icemaker. She handed them each a lemon slice and passed a salt shaker around. They each licked the skin between thumb and index finger and salted the wet spot. When the pre-shot ritual was perfected, she raised her glass. "Here's to Edward G. Robinson." She licked the salt, knocked back the tequila, and winced as she bit down on the lemon. Hopper and Cord did the same.

"Quick . . . " She filled the glasses again. "Before Big Pat gets here." She raised the shot glass as before. "Here's to Edward G." They repeated the salt-shot-lemon ritual.

Cord looked over his shoulder to the spot where Big Pat would be when he came in. Ollie Oleg, the godfather of Axel Flats, owned the saloon, but his brother, Pat, ran the place. Pat didn't care if the boys got drunk on the job. All they had to do to earn their pay was stay on their feet and play. But he'd fire Eva in the blink of a squirrel's eye if he caught her taking a nip. After all, part of her job was handling his money, and as Big Pat was overhead to say, "A tight woman is a careless woman." Cord took the bottle from Eva's hand. "This one's on me." He refilled the glasses. "Here's to Edward G. Robinson." They licked, drank, and bit, slamming their shot glasses on the bar. Eva, coughing slightly, stored the Cuervo back in the icemaker.

Hopper ordered a beer. "So what's up, Eva? How come we're drinking to Edward G. Robinson tonight?"

She eyeballed two glasses against the dim overhead light to make sure they were clean and drew two beers from the Coors tap.

"I don't know if you fellas realize it, but this week is one of the most important in American history. The war ended officially. We got our asses kicked for the first time—officially. LBJ died. The Supreme Court decided that abortion case, which is going to tear the country apart, in my opinion. And Edward G. Robinson died. Take my word for it, something cracked in this country's foundation this week. The America we were raised in is about to decompose before our eyes."

Hopper and Cord exchanged glances as Eva pulled a bar towel from the hip pocket of her tight jeans and went to work drying glasses. Cord walked behind the bar and retrieved the tequila bottle. "Come on, Eva, surely it ain't that bad. I mean, look, the country went through the Civil War, didn't it? After a generation or two, we got over that, didn't we?" He poured three more shots. "Anyway, no matter what might be going on outside that door, tonight we're going to get drunk and sing the blues. Cheer up, goddammit, and drink up. Edward G. would want it that way."

Eva put the towel back into her pocket and raised her glass. "To Edward G. Robinson."

Hopper and Cord took the stage at eight o'clock. Hopper leaned his ear close to his precious Martin guitar and reveled in the wonderful woody tones as he manipulated the tuning keys. The strings, one by one, fell into that magic realm where, in the hands of a capable musician, they work the magic we call music. Hopper believed everything in the universe made sense if you could figure out how to tune your mental strings. That thought, and the rosy glow that comes with a beer/tequila combo, made him happy.

Forget the war. Forget dead ex-presidents. Forget Supreme Court decisions that might bust up the country. Hats off to Edward G. Robinson, and let's play the blues.

The rowdy patrons of the Blue Buzzard had more in common than love of music and appreciation of cold beer. Most of them were born and raised in southeast Oklahoma City—Southtown. Many of them were veterans, and those who'd never served had family members who had worn a uniform.

This crowd would be enthusiastic about Hopper and Cord because they were Southtown boys, and Southtown folk believed in loyalty. They would applaud any performer from the Flats, the bluest blue-collar district in Oklahoma City.

Once the boys were tuned, they opened with Bo Diddley's "Who Do You Love?" This was a surefire leadoff. All the patrons of the Blue Buzzard knew the lyrics or could belt out a passable fake. These drunk weekend partiers were always eager to join in with noisy enthusiasm. Hopper knew the quicker the crowd loosened up and started singing, the more fun everyone would have. There was another advantage to starting with this song. The Bo Diddly beat was the unofficial heartbeat of the Southtown crowd. Every Southtown kid that learned to play the guitar had it down.

Big Pat finally rolled through the door and perched like a giant spider on a bar stool where he could keep an eye on Daryl, who collected the cover charge—in cash. Hopper imagined there was a network of invisible sticky webs running from Big Pat's huge body, threading their way through the pockets of all the patrons in the place. These webs were remarkably efficient at snagging all the dollars and quarters customers might carry into the saloon.

The beer, the mixed drinks (bring your own bottle), the pool tables, the pinball machines, the cover charge, the jukebox, the cigarette machines were all separate threads in the web tickling dollars from the pockets of the Blue Buzzard patrons, transferring those dollars into the pockets of the Oleg brothers. Everyone knew there were certain unbreakable rules—no credit, no checks, no trouble, no cowboy hats. There seemed to be no good reason for that last rule, but there it was.

Every patron of the Blue Buzzard knew Pat was the blunt end of the Oleg family financial tool. If you had business with the Oleg brothers, you talked to Ollie. If you screwed up, you answered to Pat. Even though Pat appeared motionless on his perch, he was alert and tingling in response to every vibration of every strand of the web in his sticky, dollar-snagging network.

When Hopper was onstage, he forgot everything but the irrepressible power of music. Something almost hypnotic happened when these Southtown folks got together at the end of a workweek. He tuned them like he tuned his guitar. He teased them into a harmonious whole. When he performed, he wasn't just playing the guitar; he was playing the crowd. He could raise them to a state of near-frenzied energy—"Baby Please Don't Go." Or he could calm them into an attitude of quiet reverence—"St. James Infirmary."

Hopper spotted Tom Wharton, a long-haired long-haul driver, in the crowd. "Hey, Tom, come on up here and give us a hand." A roar of approval accompanied this summons, as it did each time Hopper invited someone to join them onstage, which he did at least once a night. The invitation was never refused. The guest performer was always enthusiastically cheered into singing "House of the Rising Sun." There was no danger of embarrassment as everybody in Southtown could belt out the lyrics almost as naturally as they could join in singing the national anthem.

Tom staggered to the stage, and the nearest patrons gave him a boost up. As soon as Cord went through the opening riff, everybody in the place got into the act, which was fortunate. It was better if nobody heard Tom. He just couldn't sing. But his head was in the right key, so nobody heard the notes he actually sang.

Hopper knew he was carrying these scruffy patrons away—away

from Southtown; away from hard damn work in oilfields, pipe yards, garages, and truck docks; away from regrets about bad choices, cheating spouses, and losses suffered in the war. He was carrying them to a place where everybody knows the words, everybody sings together, and nobody cares if you're off-key. Even Little Eva stopped in the middle of drawing a pitcher of beer to sing out, "Mothers, tell your children not to do what I have done." When the song ended, the place exploded in whistles and cheers. Tom performed an exaggerated bow and then threw his big arms around Cord before Cord could stumble out of the way. This drunken display of manly affection ignited another cheer.

Hopper, warmed by the tequila and the crowd-love feedback loop, was playing great. His voice was clear and strong. He knew he never had to worry about whether Cord would miss a note or forget a lyric. Yep, if there was anything that might keep him in Oklahoma, it was the Blue Buzzard Saloon.

But everyone knew the Blue Buzzard was doomed. Sooner or later, there would be a fire and an insurance claim. Sooner or later, the Oleg family machine would collect the check, leave the ashes of the Blue Buzzard behind, and move on to another enterprise.

Hopper refused to think about it now. Like Cord told little Eva, *Tonight, we're getting drunk and singing the blues.* He pulled a bandana from his jeans pocket and wiped sweat from his face. Something he saw in the back of the bar slammed his chest like a hay bale dropped from a loft. He shook his head, thinking it might be one of his hallucinations. He blinked and looked again. No, they were real and sitting at a table bathed in the halo created by a blinking pinball machine. It was two Audrey Kronesons sitting side by side, smiling at him.

Hopper elbowed Cord and nodded. One of the Audreys raised a glass in greeting. Cord squinted, shook his head, and squinted again. He said something, but Hopper couldn't hear above the raucous crowd. Since Big Pat would never spring for a microphone, Hopper had to quiet the crowd. "Thank you," he shouted. "Thank you all, but if you guys don't cheer up, me and Cord will have to go over to Northside, where they know how to party." There were cheers, jeers, and raspberries. "Okay, okay, we'll give you another chance. But, listen, I know we don't usually take a break until after nine, but Cord is plum overwhelmed by Wharton's shameless behavior up here. So we need to break for a minute. He needs to get himself composed." Jeers in unison. "Alright then, we need some tequila." Shouts of approval. "Don't go nowhere. We'll be right back."

Hopper unslung his guitar and tried to make his way to the back of the bar to unravel the mystery of the two Audreys. He was delayed every few feet by happy Southtowners offering to buy his tequila shot. Cord watched for a minute and then made his way to the bar, where Little Eva was busy drawing beer.

When Hopper reached the table, he had to shout in order to be heard. "Mind if I join you?" One of the Audreys nodded. They both smiled. "Glad you decided to come. What do you think? I was right, huh? Not your kind of place."

One of the Audreys leaned close to his ear. "This is my sister, Abbie."

Hopper fell back in his chair, laughing. "Twins . . . Jesus. Of course you are. Hi, Abbie," he extended his hand. "I'm Dale Hopper. My friend here . . . " He noticed, with a slight sense of betrayal, Cord wasn't with him. For the first time tonight, he was sorry he had so much tequila so early. He was a little ticked off at himself. The idea of twins, so obvious now, hadn't occurred to him. But she was here, and that fact added the cherry on top of his growing belief that he was poised on the glorious brink of the perfect night. "Anyway, I'm Dale Hopper."

Abbie extended her hand. He didn't know what he was expecting, but her hand was hard and calloused like a laborer's. Of course, twins can look identical, but Hopper didn't expect them to have the same voice, which they did. Maybe his sober mind wouldn't have found this so surprising. But he was drunk. Maybe there was something a little edgier about Abbie's voice, a little stronger. "Audrey tells me you and your friend have a low opinion of rich people. She thinks maybe we can change your minds."

"It's not that we have a low opinion of rich people. We have a low opinion of snooty rich people. You two have changed my mind already. In fact, I think I could grow to love rich people, snooty or not. What are you ladies drinking?"

"Coke," they said at exactly the same time in exactly the same voice.

Hopper shook his head, smiling. "You two don't have a prayer of getting yourselves seduced if all you're drinking is Coke. Even if you're not aiming to get seduced, you might enjoy the rest of the show a bit more if you added something with a touch of attitude to your beverage. Could I buy you some bourbon or rum or something?"

The twins put their heads together, laughed, and nodded, their eyes telegraphing something playful. Hopper hoped he was receiving the right message. "I'll be right back. I'll be disillusioned and tempted to become a devil worshiper if you disappear while I'm gone."

They laughed again. Audrey spoke up. "How could we live with ourselves with your disillusionment and eternal damnation on our conscience?"

He made his way through the crowd, pondering her comment. Did she say *our conscience*, in the singular, like they just got the one they share? Or did he misunderstand because of the fog and racket? What the hell difference does it make anyway? When he got to the bar, Eva glared at the twins. Hopper ordered two rums with Coke.

Cord leaned back with his elbows on the bar. "What's the story?"

"Twins, buddy. They're twins, and they came here to see us. What do you think about that?"

"I reckon they came here for the same reason folks go to visit their zoo—to get a look at the peculiar wildlife in its natural habitat."

"Well, let's give 'em their wish. Are you going to join us?"

Cord turned to the bar. "Guess not."

This was another of those cases where Hopper couldn't figure him out. But tonight, he wasn't going to waste valuable time trying. "Okay, buddy, suit yourself." Beverages in hand, Hopper made his unsteady way back to the enchanted table.

He was no stranger to intoxication. He'd been drunk, stoned, knocked out, speeded up, slowed down, bowled over, and passed out more than his share. But there was something about sitting here with these tall, beautiful, rich—yes, very, very rich—twins that had him in a state of mellow excitement he never experienced before. They were carrying on a conversation: "How did this place get its name?" "How long have you been playing here?" "How long have you and Mr. Cord—" "You can call him Vernon." "How long have you and Vernon been playing music together?"

He heard the questions; he answered when spoken to. But he was so lost in their eyes, their smiles, that magical voice they shared. It was like someone else doing the talking for him, someone else's mind processing the questions, someone else speaking with his voice. He was floating, an eavesdropper whose real purpose in being there was to worship.

He wondered if the twins were aware of the spell they were weaving. Were they doing it by design? Or was it just a mystical byproduct of them being who they were, like perfume drifting off a pair of roses? Each time he answered one of their questions, he surprised himself. His speech had nothing to do with his mind. It was automatic. He'd never been so supremely intoxicated and yet able to behave as if he had some control.

Something was waving in Audrey's hand, something delicate, beautiful, and exotic, colorful, almost transparent. He couldn't bring it into focus, but he knew there was something familiar about it. He was too far gone to make a connection. He slipped into a deeper enchantment, trying to put a name on the article she held. It was like hypnosis.

The saloon became eerily silent, though he could tell the background activities continued. Those beautiful mirror-image lips continued to move and smile. Those eyes became luminous, otherworldly. The article in Audrey's hand swayed back and forth before his eyes like a wand. His mind was a helpless captive of that strange article—what was it? He had the urge to reach out and touch it, but there was an emotional forcefield creating the conviction that such a gesture would be irreverent.

He watched the wand wave back and forth and wondered whether he might be undergoing a spiritual transformation. Was he becoming something finer, a higher life form, more spiritual? He would have been happy to spend the rest of his life waiting for the moment when the truth would dawn on him and he could put a name on that delicate article in Audrey's hand.

She reached across the table and brushed his nose with it. The world became real again. The twins laughed together. Even their same-sister laughter was lyrical and harmonious. "You're staring." Audrey smiled.

Hopper blinked, embarrassed. "What's that you're holding?"

She brushed his nose with it again. "Haven't you ever seen a peacock feather?"

He felt himself blushing. "Of course I have. Just never seen one in a saloon before." They laughed again, and he laughed with them. He was in danger of letting their echo laughter take over his universe again, when he became aware of a tapping on his shoulder.

It was Sandy, the waitress. "Can I get something for you from the bar before you start up again?"

"Tequila for me, another rum and Coke for the ladies." Sandy made notes on her pad and disappeared toward the bar. Hopper briefly glimpsed Eva glaring in his direction, tapping her watch. He sensed Pat glowering from the door. But why waste a glance on fat Pat when Audrey and Abbie, the divine Kroneson twins, were right across the table?

Audrey was gently blowing the peacock feather. Her breath caused it to flutter. Hopper could only imagine what a pleasure it would be to flutter in the warmth of the whisper-breath springing from those lips. "Do you like stories, Dale?"

He leaned forward, elbows on the table. "There's probably no one alive that loves stories like I do."

"Should we tell him the one about the feather, Abbie?"

The other Audrey, the one named Abbie, smiled and gave a coy nod.

Audrey leaned close and brushed the back of his hand with the feather. "Once upon a time, there was a young girl named Io. She was so beautiful, she captured the heart of Zeus. Do you know who that was?"

"He was an ancient god or something, wasn't he?"

"He was king of all the Greek gods. His wife, Hera, was jealous and wanted to kill Io. Hera was very fierce and known to take terrible revenge on her rivals. So to prevent Hera from destroying Io, Zeus turned Io into a lovely white cow. He intended the cow disguise to be temporary. Someday, he hoped to restore her to her human form and beauty."

Hopper shook his head. "I'm guessing things got a little tricky for poor Io."

Audrey nodded. "Yes, Hera captured Io and tied her to an olive tree. She planned to keep Io tied there, where she would remain a cow forever."

The story began to materialize in Hopper's mind like a movie, as if Audrey and Abbie were communicating pictures telepathically. He saw Zeus, bearded, lustful, powerful, cast a spell on a beautiful young girl, cringing and fearful before him. A cloud of smoke envelops her, and when it vanishes, in Io's place he sees a cow. She tries to speak, but her vocal chords can only produce a mournful lowing. Zeus strokes her bovine nose and speaks reassuringly into her large floppy ear, "Patience, Io. This isn't forever. Your miseries on my account are temporary. When it's safe, everything will be as before. I promise." He sees Io wandering aimless across a grassy pasture, all the time under Hera's jealous, watchful eyes.

Io falls asleep, exhausted. When she wakes, she is chained to an olive tree. She tries to cry out for help, but she can't utter any sound but the sad mooing. As the sight was too painful for Hopper, he shook his head and willed himself to believe in rescue. He saw the story's arc and tried to predict the outcome.

Audrey continued. "Hera knew her unfaithful husband would try something. So she ordered her most loyal servant, the fierce giant Argus, to keep watch over Io to prevent Zeus from coming to her rescue."

Hopper, drawn fully into the story, felt his heart breaking. "Io didn't do anything to bring this on herself? All this happened just because she was beautiful, and Zeus wanted her?"

Audrey assumed a sad expression as if she herself was experiencing the pain of Io's misfortune. In a voice heavily freighted with sadness, she said, "She was innocent."

Hopper bristled at the notion of an innocent girl punished for the misbehavior of the adulterous big shot. "If Zeus was king of the gods, why didn't he just exercise his power and say, 'Look, Hera, if you have a problem with something I've done, take it up with me. But I'm not going to let you torture this girl'?"

Both women laughed. "Hera was unlike any woman you know. She was immortal, powerful, and capable of making Zeus's life wonderful or miserable as she chose. In fact, Hera's goodwill was important to Zeus's continued dominion. She was so powerful, as long as he had her support, no one would dare challenge his right to the Olympic throne. He'd have to humor her if he could. He wanted to help Io, but he couldn't do it in a way that openly offended Hera."

"I guess this Argus was a hard giant to steal from."

Audrey nodded. "Argus had a hundred eyes and could look in all directions all the time. No one could rescue Io without Argus seeing. A thief's identity would be instantly reported to Hera. Her revenge would be terrible. Argus, like everyone else, needed sleep. But he never slept with all his eyes closed at once. He had at least fifty eyes awake all the time."

Hopper was drawn back into the vision. Argus, the giant with a hundred eyes popping out all over his freakish head, blinking, peering in all directions, never stopping, alert to anyone approaching who might have a desire to rescue Io. Hopper winced when he noticed there was always at least one pair of eyes leering lustfully in Io's direction.

He rapped his knuckles on the table. "Zeus had to get her out. How did he do it?"

"Zeus had a servant who was the most talented musician and calming singer on earth. His name was Hermes. Hermes, disguised as a shepherd, sat near the olive tree where Io was tethered and began to play and sing. One by one, Argus's eyes fell asleep. Hermes kept playing until all hundred of Argus's eyes were sleeping. Then Hermes killed Argus and freed Io."

Hopper saw it all and thrilled at the realization that music played the key role in Io's rescue. Music. Damn straight. Audrey continued. "Hera was so distraught over Argus's death, she took his eyes and . . ." Audrey brushed Hopper's hand with the feather. "Placed them in the peacock's tail as decoration. See?" She took Hopper's hand in hers and gave him the peacock feather. He held it before his face and felt chills course through his body as he looked into the preserved eyes of the dead giant. His teeth clenched, and he felt he might pass out. *God damn, Hopper, get hold of yourself. It's just a story about why these feathers look like they got eyes on them.*

There it was, looking at him. Accusing. The dead eye of Argus the giant. Another casualty of Zeus's philandering whose only crime was that he was a faithful servant of a betrayed wife. Argus the guardian, who was murdered because he was charmed by music. In his mind, Hopper spoke to the eye in the feather. *Sorry, brother. You got a raw deal. But just for the record, I didn't like the way you leered at the cow.* He felt hands on his shoulders and jerked, startled. It was Sandy.

"Here's your tequila, Dale. Your drinks, girls." She frowned as she studied Hopper's face. "You okay, Dale?"

"Fine."

"Big Pat says it's about time for you guys to start up again."

"Okay, here I come." He knocked back the tequila and forced himself to get to his feet. He didn't trust his legs, so he leaned on the table. "Well, that's a hell of a story, ladies. One of these days, I'll tell you a story that'll blow your dress up—figuratively speaking, of course."

They laughed. "I'd like that," they said in unison. He tried to think of a logical follow-up but was lost in the fog. He was surprised to find he still had the feather in his hand. He offered it back to Audrey.

"Please keep it. We can't stay. But we enjoyed this. We really like your music. I want to talk to you Monday about maybe doing a performance for us. Do you do any old-time country music, like from the forties?"

He grinned. "You bet. We cut our teeth on Bob Wills and Hank Williams."

"Fine. Maybe I'll look you up at lunchtime Monday."

He straightened, found his legs reasonably steady, and tried to think of something charming and witty to say. Audrey rescued him. "We'll just finish our drinks before we go, and we'll say goodnight now."

"Goodnight." He didn't know whether to shake hands, offer a hug, or bow. While he thought it over, they both got to their feet and, at the same time, touched both his cheeks with those amazing lips of theirs. He turned, floating on a cloud, back toward the stage. But before he took two steps, he felt an anchor on his legs. He turned. "Whatever happened to Io?"

They laughed and raised their glasses. "That's a story for another time," Abbie said as she took a drink.

When he got to the stage, he placed the peacock feather carefully in his guitar case. Audrey and Abbie were already gone by the time he shouldered his guitar strap. At the bar, he saw Carla, from the Sizzlin' Sirloin. She waved. "Okay," he shouted. "This is where we do our Friday night salute to honky-tonk women." A cheer went up as Cord delivered the opening riff. As Hopper sang "I met a gin-soaked barroom queen in Memphis," he knew he and Cord could look forward to at least one steak dinner next week.

Twenty-three

Their gig lasted from eight o'clock to 11:30. They tried to time their breaks as close to nine, ten, and eleven as possible. At 10:30, they'd just finished Sonny Boy's "One Way Out," when Little Eva hurried to the stage and frantically motioned for Hopper to follow. He turned it over to Cord, who launched into a solo version of the Ledbelly classic "Midnight Special," another everybody-join-in favorite.

Eva bulldozed through the crowd toward the front door. Hopper followed, knowing whatever had her upset, he needed to concentrate on clearing the tequila fog or risk missing something important. As she passed, Big Pat grabbed her arm. "Where the hell are you going? There's people at the bar wanting beer."

"There's an emergency call for Hopper. Sandy can handle things for a minute. I'll get back as soon as I tell Hopper what's going on."

"What is going on?" He tightened his grip. Eva flashed a pleading glance over her shoulder.

Hopper put a firm, meaningful hand on Big Pat's shoulder. "She'll be right back." The two men locked eyes. Pat switched the stubby, well-chewed cigar from one side of his mouth to the other. "Make it snappy, goddammit. I'm losing money while you two are outside chewing the fat."

Eva hugged herself against the cold the instant they were outside. They stepped around the dark corner, where they had some privacy.

"What's up, Eva?"

"Nozetape called. Somebody broke into your place."

Hopper blinked at her, not comprehending. "Somebody broke into the house we live in?"

"Yes. Nozetape drove up as a couple of guys ran out your front door. He followed them to a house out by Jones. Then he called from a phone-booth."

"Where's Nozetape now?"

"He's at a gas station at Spencer Road and Twenty-third, waiting for your call. Here's the number." She handed him a napkin with a phone number on it.

"How long ago?"

"Just a couple of minutes."

"Okay, Eva, you better get back inside before you freeze or Pat has a stroke. I'll call Nozetape and get the details. Thanks, baby."

He trotted across the street to the payphone on the wall of the Quik-Mart. He dialed the number scribbled on the napkin. Nozetape answered on the first ring. "Nozetape, what's going on?"

"I was playing chess at Betty's. When I got home, I saw two guys hurrying out our front door carrying stuff. I think they got my reel-to-reel. I don't know what they hauled out before I got there. I drove by and turned right on the dead end, where I could watch them. They jumped in their pickup and took off. I guess I should have tried to stop them, but I wasn't thinking. So I just followed 'em."

"There were two of them?"

"Yeah."

"Did you see anybody waiting in the pickup?"

"No."

"So you followed them to Jones?"

"Yeah, they drove out in the country and pulled onto a long drive-way at a farmhouse. I passed by and doubled back to call the Buzzard."

"Could you tell if there was anybody else in the house?"

"Couldn't tell."

"So you're at Twenty-third and Spencer Road now?"

"Yeah, at a 7-Eleven."

"Okay, I'll get Cord, and we'll be there in about thirty minutes."

"Right, I'll be here. What do you think we ought to do?"

"Sit tight. Me and Cord will take care of this." He wasn't really surprised. Burglary was a fact of life along the tracks. Usually, no one had much worth stealing. But Nozetape's reel-to-reel stereo was legendary. Locks on doors in the neighborhood were mostly cosmetic. At best, they might pose a minor obstacle to the casual criminal. The best security was to be at home. He wasn't surprised. But he was pissed off. As he ran back to the Blue Buzzard, dodging the Friday-night Classen Boulevard traffic, he felt a tingling of gratitude. He knew where to find the guys who did this. If the assholes made their exit ten minutes earlier, he and Cord would've been straitjacketed by pointless rage with no hope of a rational outlet. No telling where such unsatisfied fury might spill over. Any bad-mannered patron of the Blue Buzzard could wind up paying the price—fat lips, black eyes, bloody noses—for somebody else's transgression. But Nozetape knew where the sleazebags were, so Hopper would be able to direct his thirst for judgment directly onto the thieving stooges that had it coming.

When he passed Daryl at the door, he stopped at Big Pat's stool. "Sorry, Pat, we're going to have to shut down early. Somebody just broke into our house and stole all our shit."

Before he could move toward the stage, he felt Pat's hand on his shoulder. "Afraid you're gonna have to tend to that after your shift. You can't leave yet. People are still drinking."

Hopper looked at the brisket-sized hand on his shoulder. It didn't move. He took a deep breath and met the big man's heavy-lidded stare. "It's like this, Pat; we can't wait. Nozetape followed the bad guys to their hideout, and he's waiting for us."

"Well, he's just going to have to sit on it 'til you're through working."

Hopper put a grip on Pat's thick wrist. "This doesn't have to get ugly, Pat. I got to go, and I got to go now—and that's that."

Pat released Hopper's shoulder and removed the stubby cigar from his mouth. "Look, kid, far as your music is concerned, I can take it or leave it. This weekend crowd likes you guys, so I keep you around. But if you and your friend leave before eleven-thirty, don't bother to come back. Third-rate potheads that think they can sing are thick as flies on a cow pie down here. Do yourselves a favor. Shut up and get to work."

Hopper studied the thick lips, heavy jowls, and vacant eyes. This was the face of a man that didn't make idle threats, a man that never forgot a slight. Hopper knew if he crossed the line he was straddling at this moment, he could never expect to get a square deal from Pat or Ollie for the rest of his life. But there was the loyalty factor. Nozetape was their friend, and some punks stole his stereo. Steal from one of us, and by God, you steal from us all. Nozetape was waiting.

"Sorry, Pat, Nozetape's got 'em spotted, and if we don't move now, we might lose our goods and the culprits. I like working here, and I need the money, but we gotta go, and, like I said, we gotta go now."

"It won't wait?"

"Don't know but can't risk it."

Pat dropped his cigar on the floor and mashed it out with the lugged sole of his Wolverine boot. "Suit yourself."

Hopper got to the stage just as Cord wound up the song. He spoke loud enough for Cord to hear over the cheers and whistles. "We got an emergency. Somebody busted into our place and stole Nozetape's reel-to-reel. Not sure what else they got. Nozetape followed them, and they're planted at a place in Jones. He's waiting for us. He'll guide us in."

Cord studied Hopper's face for the space of a heartbeat, unslung his guitar, and growled as he put it in the case. "Sons of bitches must pay for their goddam sins."

Hopper put a hand on Cord's arm. They could barely hear each other for the cries of protest rising from the crowd as it became apparent to everyone they were shutting down for the night.

"Pat says if we leave, we're fired."

Cord shook his head. "He don't mean it. He ain't that much of a dirt bag. If somebody busted into his damn house, and he knew where to find them, the only thing that would beat his big ass to their hideout would be the headlights on his Jeep."

"He says we're fired, and that's final." Cord looked over Hopper's shoulder at the fat man on the bar stool and shrugged.

They stepped off the stage to cries of "Encore!" and a chorus of good-natured catcalls. Hopper shouted above the noise. "Hey, settle down. We know it's early, but something's up. We got to tend to it right now. Believe me, we'd love to stay and party with you guys 'til the sun comes up. But you all know how it is. Sometimes you get the call and can't say no. You're all a bunch of losers, and we'll see you all later."

Cord stopped at Pat's stool as the walrus-sized man lit another cigar. "Hopper says if we leave we're fired. That right?"

"Yep."

"Ain't that a little harsh, Pat? I mean I can see docking us some money. But if you was in our shoes, you'd chase the creeps down and tend to 'em—pronto."

"True, but it wasn't my place got busted into, was it? It was yours. And it ain't my job on the line; it's yours. So, like I told Dale, suit yourself."

Cord took the cigar out of Pat's mouth. The walrus's eyes widened, and he tried to get to his feet, but Cord shoved him back onto his stool. Cord dropped the cigar on the floor and stepped on it. "You know, Pat, this is just the kinda inconsiderate stubbornness that's going to wind up being bad for your health."

Pat's lids lowered a degree. His deep voice rumbled. "What's that supposed to mean?"

Cord backed toward the door as Hopper kept a close eye on Daryl. "It means what you think it means. It's like Hopper's been saying, if karma boomerangs on you, it's your own shitty behavior that winds up knocking your damn teeth out. See you, Pat."

On their brisk walk to the Rambler, they discussed options. Calling the police was out. Nozetape wasn't sure whether his possession of the reel-to-reel was strictly legit. A friend with a reputation for questionable ethics gave him the stereo as payment for a debt. With cops out of the equation, that left the self-help solution: fast, effective, and satisfying. But there's always the opportunity for things to go wrong when you kick a man's door down and charge into his house unarmed. They didn't carry firearms in the Rambler, and tonight they didn't have time to remedy that oversight. They decided to postpone discussion of the plan until they did some recon.

When they pulled into the 7-Eleven parking lot, they saw Nozetape's Karmann Ghia. He hobbled out of the store leaning on his bois d'arc cane, carrying a coffee cup. He tossed the cup into the trash before sliding into the Rambler's backseat.

"What's the plan, fellas?"

Cord put the Rambler in reverse. "Show us where these guys are, and we'll take a look. Then we'll figure the best way to get your stereo back."

Nozetape guided them to the farmhouse. There was a long gravel drive leading up to a small house sitting on a hilltop. A '69 Chevy pickup and '71 Ford Mustang were parked in the driveway.

They drove past the house, careful not to alert the occupants that the place was being scoped. A quarter-mile north, they found a dirt road to an oil lease. Satisfied no one was watching, they pulled onto the lease road.

Nozetape fidgeted in the backseat. "You guys ain't planning on going all Charles Bronson on these guys, are you?"

Cord answered, "Wait here, Nozetape. You can't move too fast, and we might need to do some high-steppin'. We'll take a look. If it's too dangerous, we'll come back and figure some way to even things up. We'll be back directly."

They crawled through a barbed-wire fence to approach the house from the adjoining pasture.

Hopper mumbled as they neared the house, "I hope they don't have a dog. A big, noisy dog with sharp teeth and a bad attitude could complicate stuff."

There was frost on Cord's breath. "We'll stay flexible. We might have to call it off for tonight if we can't get a good look at the situation."

Approaching the house from the north, they saw lights in every room. Cord hung back. Hopper, the smaller man, crept to the nearest window, taking advantage of the trees and brush growing in the unfenced yard. He listened for barking dogs. It was quiet. Good.

He crept from window to window, peering into each room. Cord waited against the trunk of a tall tree. In a few minutes, Hopper returned. "Two guys, look like druggies. They're trying to figure out how to operate Nozetape's reel-to-reel. One is wearing a red stocking cap; the other has a long ponytail. I didn't see any weapons, but there's lots of stuff in the living room that could be grabbed and turned into trouble."

Cord nodded. "How do you see the play?"

"Not sure whether the front door is locked. If it is, not sure how strong the lock is."

"We could knock on the door and see what happens."

Hopper thought it over. "I say we go all Charles Bronson, bust in the door, and kick some ass. You take Stocking Cap. I'll take Ponytail."

"Let's go."

They eased their way to the front door. Inside, they heard Iron Butterfly's "In-A-Gadda-Da-Vida" playing loud. Good. Hopper pulled open the screen door. There was the slightest squeak in the unoiled hinges. Cord leaned back, Hopper mouthed the count: *one-two-three.* Cord kicked the front door into splinters. As Hopper and Cord charged through, both men inside leapt to their feet, tripping over their coffee table trying to run for the back door. The one in the stocking cap rolled on the floor moaning, grasping his right shin. The other hurdled the overturned coffee table and whirled, assuming a martial arts stance. After momentary eye contact with Hopper, he apparently decided hand-to-hand combat was a bad move. He dropped his karate pose and headed for the rear exit. Hopper bounded over the overturned coffee table and caught the guy by his ponytail, jerking backward with all his might. The fugitive fell flat on his back, noisily losing all the air in his lungs. Hopper pulled his limp weight back to the living room and released him lying face up, gasping, next to his whimpering friend.

Hopper looked around the room and spied a golf club. He picked it up and approached the two men, whose eyes may never have been wider in their lives.

"Evenin', boys. We're here to tell you something important, so pay real close attention. You two dumb shits picked the wrong damn house to burgle. See, we might not have got so pissed off if you'd stole the TV. We don't watch it much anyway. But we're music lovers. And any son of a bitches that busts into our house and takes our music, well, them sons of bitches have to give us back our stereo and pay a goddam penalty."

Ponytail propped himself up on his elbows. "Now wait a minute. We don't know what you're talking about. We never—"

Cord growled, "Shut up, stooge. Don't make things worse by lying to us. When we went to work tonight, that reel-to-reel was in our house. Now it's in your house."

"You got this wrong. We bought it. We got a receipt. It's in the bedroom. I'll go get it and show you."

Hopper raised the golf club. "You do that, buddy. You just get up off your ass and see if you can make it to the bedroom and find that receipt before I bust your shoulder blade. I'll bet you five hundred dollars you don't make it. But feel free to try."

Ponytail lowered himself back on the floor. "What are you going to do?"

Cord asked Stocking Cap, who was still groaning, "Your leg broke?"

"I think so."

"Roll up your jeans so I can see."

"I can't."

"I'm pretty sure you'd be a lot gentler than I will if I have to do it. Roll it up."

Stocking Cap winced and groaned as he rolled up his pant leg. Cord squinted at the blue-red gash on his shin. Blood oozed from the wound. "Don't look broke to me—but it might be. We ought to break lotsa bones on both you guys. Maybe we will. In the meantime, who's got the keys to the pickup?"

Neither of them spoke. Cord growled again, "Look, boys, I'm a frog's hair away from cracking both your stupid skulls as a lesson to chicken-shit thieves everywhere. So if I was you, I'd start trying real hard to get on my good side. Who's got the truck keys?"

The two men looked at each other and said nothing. Cord shrugged. "Okay, have it your way. They're all yours, buddy. Break something and keep on breakin' stuff 'til these mental wizards remember their man-ners." He stepped out of the way to give Hopper plenty of room for a wide-arc swing with the golf club.

"Wait," Stocking Cap yelled as Hopper put all his weight into the club. There was a meaty thud when the club impacted Ponytail's shin as he tried to scramble out of danger. He wailed and clutched his injured right leg.

Hopper grinned. "Looks like I'm a shitty golfer. But, you know what they say at the country club: practice makes perfect. I'll do better next time."

"Who's got the goddam keys?" Cord asked with deadly calm.

"Give 'em the fuckin' keys, Feeney," Ponytail wailed. "They'll kill us both."

"Fuck you. Give 'em the keys to your Mustang."

Hopper raised the club and stepped close. "Your name Feeney?" Stocking Cap nodded. "You know who we are?"

"Cord and Hopper."

"So the Feeney that works at the zoo, he your brother?"

Stocking Cap nodded.

"He put you boys up to stealing our stereo?"

"He didn't know nothing about the stereo."

Hopper scratched the back of his head with the golf club. "So why did he want you guys to bust into our place?"

"He just told us to look around. He said you took something from the zoo. He didn't know what it was. He just said it was something un-usual. All we could find, though, was the stereo."

"Unusual like what?"

"He didn't know," Stocking Cap whined. "He just said you guys found something that might be valuable. He didn't know what it was. He just told us to look."

"So all you took was the stereo?"

Feeney nodded toward his accomplice. "He wanted to take the TV, but I talked him out of it."

Ponytail blubbered, "Liar . . . you're a goddam liar. He's the one that wanted to clean you guys out. He even wanted to take your toaster. I just wanted to get the stereo and haul ass."

"Shut up," Cord thundered. "Give me the keys, Feeney."

"What are you gonna do?"

"Give me the keys, or we'll break your other leg."

Feeney whimpered as he struggled to get his hand into his pocket. He held the keys out. Cord snatched them and headed for the door. He spoke over his shoulder. "Keep these geniuses where they are for a cou-ple minutes. I'll be right back."

Hopper rested the golf club on his shoulder. "Just relax for now, fel-las. We're getting close to winding up your excitement for the night, un-less you figure a visit to the emergency room might be exciting." He sat in a rocking chair and leaned forward, smiling at the cowering thieves. "Nice of you boys to have us over."

In a few minutes, Cord and Nozetape pulled up in the Rambler. Hopper handed Nozetape the golf club. "These boys got one good leg apiece. If they get inconvenient, give them both a matching pair."

Hopper and Cord loaded the reel-to-reel, the amplifier, and speak-ers into the Rambler's trunk. When they were done, Cord pulled the phone cord out of the farmhouse wall. He took the golf club from Nozetape and pointed it at the two men on the floor. "We're letting you dimwits off easy. We ought to beat the shit out of you and steal your ratty RCA record player. Now I'm making you a promise. If we have any more trouble out of you, we'll leave you with scars, limps, amputations, or speech impediments you'll be dealing with for the rest of your thieving lives. Am I clear?"

They both nodded emphatic understanding. Cord continued, "Your pickup's about a quarter-mile down the road north of here, parked on the lease road. Keys are in the ignition. I let the air out of the Mustang's tires. I should've slashed them all the way around. That would serve you right. Now, you boys do yourselves a favor. You're too dumb to be outlaws. Get a job bussing tables or something. And one more thing. Tell your brother we'll be taking this up with him later."

Cord carried the golf club to the front door and threw it across the pasture with all his might. Hopper said, "If you're done speechmaking, let's hit the road." Hopper, Cord, and Nozetape hurried to the Rambler, which was pointed west toward the county road, motor running. Cord hit the gas, and they sped down the driveway, throwing gravel against the house.

Nozetape asked as they fishtailed left onto the county road, "You think they got a gun in there?"

"Maybe more than one," Hopper said, looking out the back windshield. "Kill the lights, Cord. One of them just limped out on the porch with something in his hands. If it's a shotgun, no worries. But if it's something else, no need to give him a chance for a lucky shot."

Cord killed the lights and slammed on the brakes in case someone might be calculating the Rambler's trajectory. After a couple of seconds, he hit the gas again. Nozetape gasped, "Can you see the road, Cord? I can't."

Cord responded grimly, "Can't see it, but I think I know where it is." They topped a hill, putting some real estate between them and anyone who might be trying to get a bead on them. When Cord switched on the lights, they were left of center but still on the roadway. He slammed on the brakes again, nearly launching Nozetape into the front seat. An Angus calf stood in the middle of the road, head lowered, staring into the Rambler's headlights.

Hopper laughed. "And the desperados' escape was blocked by a wide-eyed baby." He opened the door, stepped out, and walked up to the little bull. The calf bobbed his head. Hopper put a hand toward the calf's ear, but it turned and made two clumsy bounding movements, continuing to amble down the middle of the road. Cord rolled down his window. "Get him off the road, Hopper. We need to make tracks."

Hopper shouted and waved his arms, but the little bull faced him, shook his head, and pawed the pavement. Hopper mumbled, "Love to play with you, Ferdinand, but you need to get home to Mama. The next car rolling over that hill's liable to make hamburger meat out of you." With a quick grab, Hopper reached an ear. He scooped up the calf's forelegs and walked the struggling little bull off the road. Cord and Nozetape laughed as Hopper and the calf seemed to be waltzing into the weeds. Cord drove past. Hopper released the calf and trotted toward the Rambler, the calf in pursuit. Hopper jumped into the car. "Let's go, Cord. I think he means to follow us home."

The humor of Hopper's roadside dance dissolved when they turned right onto Northeast 23rd. When they pulled into the 7-Eleven where Nozetape's Karmann Ghia waited, they filled him in on the constellation of headaches gathering in their lives. Feeney at the zoo was turning out to be a menace. It was too early to judge just how serious it was. They lost their job at the Blue Buzzard, which threw their finances into a state of painful uncertainty.

"Things ain't all bad," Nozetape chimed in. "I'm starting to make my way through the notes and piece together Alimony's last night."

Hopper perked up. "We're all ears, Nozetape."

"Alimony says the guy he was traveling with, Pete McGuire, had experience with the army and some law enforcement. Pete figured out that somebody was on Alimony's trail. The night before they got killed,

Alimony spent some time writing about how sorry he felt for himself, cursed because he was a dwarf, cursed because he was an orphan, cursed because he was married to a gold-bricking harpy, cursed because he was forced to be a fugitive in this barbarian wilderness, blah blah blah.

"Anyway, Pete convinced him to hide the treasure. I guess Pete's saddle horse died. They buried the treasure under the horse's carcass, thinking nobody would bother turning over a dead horse carcass to look under it. They wrapped the treasure trunk in some extra harness they had in the wagon. They planned to get up the next morning and make a run for it."

Hopper asked, "Did he say what happened to the third page of his journal?"

"It's like we thought. It must be in the other boot. We'll talk about it more when we get home."

As Nozetape got out of the backseat and limped toward his Karmann Ghia, Hopper asked, "Suppose we never find the other boot. Is there enough in what we got to lead us to the treasure?"

Nozetape paused at the open car door. "I don't know. I haven't worked it all out. We'll talk at home."

As they drove home, they kicked around the possibilities on where, discounting the treasure, their California money might come from. Hopper thought for a minute. "One thing that might help in the short term is the deal Audrey wants to talk to me about Monday."

Cord's eyebrows arched. "You didn't mention it. What's the deal?"

"She said she may want to hire us to do a performance."

Cord snorted. "Probably wants a freebie."

Hopper shrugged. "Maybe. But for sure if we lose the zoo gig, we're screwed."

Hopper could never tell when Cord was down in his spirits. He seemed always to be running in the same gear no matter how good or how bad things went. Tonight, he seemed down. This whole deal about someone breaking into their house and then losing their job was hitting him harder than Hopper expected.

"Tell you what. Let's get Eva to give us a joint. Let's get high and kick things around. That'll make us feel better."

Cord nodded. "Good idea. All the glow from the tequila, beer, and music got drained off by that greaseball Feeney and his chickenshit buddy." After a second, Cord said, "Know what we forgot? We didn't check the ID on the other asshole. We know who Feeney is, but we don't know who the other guy is."

"Chalk it up to the fact we're drunk. If we'd been sober, we would've thought of that." He took a deep breath. "Too late now."

They stopped at the Blue Buzzard. Daryl looked uncomfortable. "Look, boys, since you aren't employed anymore, I got to collect the cover."

"No, you don't," Cord growled. "We're coming in to pick up something we forgot."

"But—"

"We'll take it up with Pat."

Pat saw them coming. He took the cigar out of his mouth, hitching his pants up over his big belly as he got off the stool. "What are you two doing here?"

Hopper chirped, "Hell, Pat, we came to finish up our shift."

Even in the Blue Buzzard's dark interior, they could see his face redden. "Well, your damn shift is over for good. Make it easy on us all and hit the road."

Hopper flashed his boyish smile. "Just relax a minute, Pat. We forgot something at the bar. After we pick it up, we'll be on our way."

"Whatever you forgot at the bar belongs to the bar. Beat it."

Hopper was still smiling. "Sorry, Pat, we need it."

Pat's right hand moved toward his back pocket. Hopper was still smiling. "Don't do that, Pat. You're a tough guy, but you're fat and slow. I'll put your fucking lights out before you finish the thought."

Pat glared at him but didn't move. "Are you crazy? You got a death wish or something? You know who I am? You got any idea what happened to the last guy that threatened me?"

"No idea, Pat. But I know this. We didn't pick a fight here. We were in the right, and you decided to be an asshole about it. If you'd tried just a little bit to be a decent human being, we'd still be friends. Hell, we can be friends again if you're a big enough man to apologize."

Cord was at the bar, talking to Eva. She put her arm around his neck and kissed him on the cheek. Hopper watched her right hand brush Cord's coat pocket.

Pat, still glaring at Hopper, hissed, "I wouldn't apologize to a couple of losers like you if my nuts was in a vice."

Hopper laughed. "I bet I could change your mind, but I'll probably never get the chance to put your little nuts in a vice to prove it. I can always dream, though."

Cord hurried by without stopping. "Let's go."

Hopper winked at Pat. "Night, Pat. Always a pleasure talking to a genuine humanitarian." He felt Pat's malevolent stare on the back of his neck. No doubt the toad was trying to manufacture some telepathic misfortune.

Back at the house, they found Nozetape limping back and forth in short bursts across the living room. Before they could ask, he looked up with an expression of near panic. "The boot's gone."

Hopper and Cord stood at the door, stunned.

"Shit!" Hopper exploded. "It never occurred to me they'd take a trashy piece of old leather."

Cord collapsed on the couch. "If we wasn't drunk when we found out it was Feeney, it might have occurred to us."

"Shit." Hopper sat on the couch next to Cord as Nozetape continued to hobble around the living room. "The journal pages are here, ain't they?"

Nozetape stopped pacing and blinked. "Yes. They're in the pocket of my notebook." His voice was tentative. "Should we go back for the boot?"

Cord shook his head. "Too dangerous tonight. Too many things can go wrong. We'll have to sleep on it and figure our next move in the morning."

Nozetape stammered, "Sorry, fellas. I feel like this is my fault. If I'd been home, maybe they wouldn't take the chance to steal anything."

Hopper got up and clapped Nozetape on the shoulder. "Don't beat yourself up, buddy. You ever heard of Argus?"

Nozetape blinked. "No."

"Well, Cord has a joint in his pocket. Let's fire it up, and I'll tell you a story about Argus, the most qualified guard that ever lived. Even Argus got his pocket picked. Let me tell you all about it."

Twenty-four

Saturday, January 27, 1973

Hopper was dreaming of a white calf, dancing in a beautiful green meadow, when the phone jolted him awake. He looked at the clock: 8:59. They'd stayed up late eating ice cream and fantasizing about life as a rich philosopher rock star.

The phone kept ringing. He considered letting it ring until the caller gave up or somebody else answered. But it might be important, and the other two may not give a shit. He made his bleary-eyed way to the hall and picked up the receiver.

"Hello."

"Who is this?"

"This is Hopper. Who's the hard-hearted bastard calling a nest of night owls at this hour?"

"This is Ollie Oleg. Hope I didn't wake you. You boys need to get in the habit of getting up early. How do you expect to get ahead in life?"

Hopper became instantly alert. Whatever was going on, Ollie wasn't calling just to give them advice about the advantages of early rising. "Well, to tell you the truth, Ollie, we never figured to get ahead. We was just hoping to keep on treading water."

There was a genuinely mirthful laugh on the other end of the line. "Treading water? I like the image. But you might be able to do better for yourselves. You busy right now?"

Hopper didn't like playing word games with Ollie, especially when he was fuzzy-headed from last night's indulgences. "Well, Ollie, we're looking for part-time work today. We got fired from our weekend job last night."

"Yeah, I heard." The note of sympathy in his voice was almost convincing. "In fact, that's one reason I'm calling. There's an opening at the Blue Buzzard. Suppose you boys stop by the yard this morning and fill out an application? Maybe I'll put in a good word for you. I got some influence over there. Come by and see me at ten o'clock. I'll buy you a cup of coffee. We'll talk some business."

There was something about the call that stimulated Hopper's danger-sensing antenna. "Let me check with Cord."

"You do that. Check with Cord. Then you two come by the salvage yard at ten o'clock. See? I won't take no for an answer. You boys come on down. I think you'll find it in your interests. See you at ten." Click.

Hopper rubbed his eyes, trying to figure the angles. Maybe Ollie wanted to offer their job back. Possible but not likely. Maybe he figured they had some form of discipline coming for bucking up to Pat. Again, possible but not likely. If there had been some real harm done, maybe.

He rolled over the possibilities as he got the Folgers on to brew. He knocked on Cord's bedroom door. "Hey, pothead, wake up. We got an appointment with Ollie Oleg in an hour. I got coffee brewing. I'm getting in the shower. If we're going to be there at ten o'clock like Ollie says, we'll have to leave in thirty minutes. Get a move on."

He heard sleepy grumbling. "What's the big rush? Why do we have to bust our ass just because Ollie Oleg says jump?"

"I'm thinking there's more to this summons than his desire to have an early-morning chat. Something important's happening, and we need to know what it is."

"Maybe he wants to get us over there so he can beat the shit out of us 'cause you had the gall to put your hands on Pat last night."

"Maybe, but I don't think so. Anyway, my curiosity's burning rubber. Let's go see what that fat bastard has in mind."

Thirty minutes later, they were showered, coffeed, and headed for the Southside Salvage Yard. The business looked like a '70s version of an Iron Age war chieftain's stronghold. The yard was surrounded by weathered chain-link fencing topped with four strands of rusted, heavily barbed wire. The array of hubcaps covering the fence facing South Robinson Ave. looked like trophies won in centuries of "loser dies" demolition derby tournaments.

When the big man was in residence, the heavy metal gate at the entrance, equipped with oversized chains and pulleys, yawned open to allow access to those who had deals to make with Ollie Oleg.

At night, the heavy gates clanged shut, and four massive mongrels roamed through the car bodies piled up in various stages of cannibalization or decomposition. The animals were on eager watch for any trespasser foolish enough to try to steal from Ollie. During the day, the dogs paced like caged lions in a smallish wire kennel next to the battered metal building that served as the yard's office.

There were some who shivered every time they drove by this metallic graveyard. Some because of what they'd heard, some because of what they knew.

During business hours—7 a.m. to 9 p.m. every day but Sunday— Ollie was in the building conducting mysterious transactions with shady people from both sides of the Mexican border. Everything he did produced money. Not quarters, halves, fives, and tens—the usual currency in the Flats—but money, the kind people have in mind when they refer to someone as "having money." Money enough to buy whatever you want whenever you want. No one knew how rich Ollie was. But to all outward appearances, he was no better off than any other small-time business operator in the Flats.

Some of his enterprises operated in plain sight: the salvage yard, the Old London Flea Market (the largest in the state), the Magic Cue Pool Hall, the Blue Buzzard Saloon, the Southside Liquor Store, Ace's Garage, the O.K. Pipe Yard. Then there were rumors about other concerns where Ollie's big fingers pulled invisible strings: the Victory Funeral

Home, Acme Plating. Then there were those other nefarious doings that careful people didn't know about and didn't want to know.

Just as the huge dogs were on guard at night, Ollie's two oversized minions, Hub and Tiny, were always nearby when the heavy gate was open.

When Cord pulled the Rambler through the gates—at ten o'clock sharp—Hopper saw Hub's big head in the office window. The Rambler's tires crunched on pea gravel covering the driveway. The thick-muscled dogs set up a chorus of loud barks and low growls. The office door opened, and Ollie stepped onto the unpainted wooden steps. He held a short, well-chewed cigar in his teeth, part of the family uniform. His thumbs were hooked into the bib of his overalls, which covered a sweat-stained T-shirt stretched tight over his big belly. Ollie smiled his wide, friendly smile. He removed his cigar, spat on the gravel, and waved.

Hopper was fascinated by Ollie Oleg. It was part of Ollie's creepiness that everyone liked him even though they had no illusions about who he was and what he did. *Maybe it's like smoking,* Hopper thought. *People keep doing it even though they may die for their pleasures.*

When Hopper and Cord got out of the Rambler, Ollie spoke in his deep elephantine voice. "Mornin', boys. What can I do you out of today?"

"We need a starter solenoid for our bus."

The cigar wagged in Ollie's mouth as he spoke. "Chevy, ain't it? 'Fifty-five?"

"'Fifty-nine."

Ollie spoke over his shoulder. "Hub, we got a starter solenoid that'll go on a 'fifty-nine Chevy school bus?"

Hub mumbled something from inside. Ollie scratched a bushy eyebrow. "When do you need it, Vernon?"

"Anytime in the next couple of months."

Ollie nodded. "We can get it for you. You boys come on in for a cup of coffee." He stepped aside to allow them to walk past. Hopper and

Cord lingered on the steps. "After you, Ollie," Hopper said with a wide smile.

Ollie returned the smile. "Sure, fellas, come on in."

When they stepped inside, Hub kicked the door shut behind them. Sitting on Ollie's beat-up wooden coffee table was Sir Alimony's boot. Across from the boot sat the two guys who stole it. They were a lot more beat up this morning than they were when Hopper and Cord left them moaning on their dirty farmhouse floor.

Hopper looked over his shoulder. Hub and Tiny, both armed with brass knuckles and a short length of lead pipe, barred the door. Ollie sprawled on a cracked Naugahyde couch, the stuffing held in here and there by duct tape. "First off," he said, putting a match to his cigar. "I want to thank you boys for being so prompt. See, that's a sign of reliability. And that's something I like to see in young folks like you." He shook the flame from the match and dropped it in an overflowing ashtray. "Next, I think Feeney and Biscuit here have something they want to say to you."

The two roughed-up burglars mumbled something without looking up. Ollie thundered, "Can't hear you boys. Speak up."

Feeney rubbed a blackening eye. "Sorry we broke into your place and stole your shit."

The other one, Biscuit, eyed Hub and Tiny ruefully. Then he spoke to Hopper and Cord without looking. "Yeah, sorry."

Ollie waved his beefy left hand at two vinyl chairs across the coffee table from the two burglars. "Have a seat." Hopper didn't like sitting with his back to men like Hub and Tiny, but Ollie obviously had something on his mind. Hopper and Cord were safe until some cards were showing.

"Tiny, get these fellas some coffee." He grinned. "It'll have to be black. We don't do nothing to doctor up our coffee 'til after lunch. Then we sweeten it with a squirt of Old Grandad. Right, boys?" Tiny and Hub mumbled agreement as Tiny brought two cups of coffee in chipped Phillips 66 mugs.

"Now, before we get down to business, I think Feeney and Biscuit have to be somewhere, don't you, boys?"

They both rose sullenly and limped around the coffee table toward the door. "Am I right, boys? You two got someplace you need to be?"

They spoke in unison. "Yes, Mr. Oleg."

As Hub and Tiny stepped away from the door, Ollie called out cheerfully, "Glad you two could stop by this morning. I enjoyed our talk." His voice took on a more threatening tone. "Next time, don't wait so long to look up your ole uncle Ollie. You got my meaning?" They nodded without looking back. Hub closed the door behind them.

"Now," Ollie said, smiling cheerfully. "Let's talk about this little boot." He propped his own big, lug-soled boots on the coffee table. "To show you my heart's in the right place, let me start by telling you a few things you may not know. I'm assuming you know about the treasure, right?"

Cord looked at Hopper and shrugged. Hopper said, as convincingly as he could, "What treasure you talking about, Ollie?"

There was no change in his expression when Ollie reached into his back pocket and produced a long, folding pocketknife with what appeared to be bone-handled scales and a saber-toothed tiger scrimshawed on the handle. He tossed it to Cord. "Ever seen a knife with finer workmanship, Vernon? Highest-quality German-made steel, and those handles look like bone, don't they? Well, they ain't. That's mammoth ivory. Mammoths are extinct, you know. Know how they got extinct? They couldn't adapt when shit was changing around them. They couldn't appreciate the trouble they was in, and even if they could, they was too stupid to figure out how to survive.

"Now you fellas are sort of in the same situation as mammoths was in. Your surroundings is getting a lot more dangerous than they used to be. If you two are smart as I think you are, you'll make the right move: you'll adapt; you'll survive."

Hopper leaned forward and looked Ollie directly in his fishy blue eyes. "What the hell are you talking about, Ollie? If you got something on your mind, spell it out. If you're wanting a reward for getting back a trashy little boot we was going to throw away anyway, you can kiss our ass. What's this about?"

Ollie's face got frighteningly red. The smile was still there, but there was something venomous in his tone. "Toss me back my knife, Vernon."

Cord tossed it back. Ollie unfolded the blade. "Let's start again. And you boys fuck with me one more time this morning, I'll close that gate, and I'll have somebody's digits on this table, and they damn sure won't be none of ours." He pointed the blade to himself, Hub, and Tiny. "You boys know something about the Alimony treasure, don't you?"

Hopper, being partial to every digit he had, and knowing Cord felt the same, decided to see what he could do with the cards he was dealt. "Okay, Ollie, we heard a rumor about some treasure."

The couch squeaked as Ollie leaned back. "There, now, I knew you boys could adapt. You just increased your chances of survival. Let me give you an example of what I'm talking about. Know what a hemophobe is?"

Hopper was getting tired of the verbal dance. "I don't know, Ollie. A parasitic worm?"

Ollie's thunderous laugh shook the office. "Hear that, Hub? Hopper here just called you a parasitic worm. What are you going to do about it?"

Hub started a slow walk in Hopper's direction. "I'm gonna choke him 'til he passes out."

Ollie laughed again. "Don't do that, Hub. He was just making a joke. We don't want him passed out just yet." Hub hovered over Hopper, clenching and unclenching his meaty fists before he backed off. "No, Hopper, a hemophobe is a guy that can't stand the sight of blood. Hub here is a hemophobe. Know how he found out? You want to tell him, Hub, or you want me to?"

Hub growled, "I'd like you to drop it, Ollie."

"I don't mean to rile you, Hub, but I need to make a point." Ollie's eyes sparkled over the rim of his coffee cup as he took a long, slow drink.

"See, Hub had no idea he was a hemophobe. He was a grown man and saw blood all his life, just like the rest of us. Then one day, I gave him a job to do. The details ain't important. Anyway, there was blood, lots of blood. And Hub faints." Ollie laughed and slapped his big thigh. Hub seethed. "That's right, fainted dead away . . . sure did." The laugh faded. "Here's the point. Even though Hub is a hemophobe, he does his job. He tries to avoid doing stuff in the slaughterhouse—don't you, Hub?—but he does what he has to. He adapts; he survives." He took another drink of his coffee.

"Now, back to you guys. About the treasure, what did you hear—exactly?"

"We heard a little Englishman was hauling a treasure across Oklahoma when he and his partner got jumped and killed. They didn't have the treasure with them, and nobody ever found it."

Ollie leaned forward and studied Hopper's face with scary intensity. "That's it?"

"That's pretty much it."

"Any idea what this little boot has to do with it?" he asked, pointing his blade at the artifact.

"We guessed this was one of the boots the little fella was wearing when he got killed."

"Where'd you find it?"

"We found it bound up in the roots of the tree at the zoo."

"Where's the other one?"

"Don't know."

"You looking for it?"

"Yeah."

"Why?"

"I figure you know the answer. That little buckle is gold."

Ollie squinted at it. "That the only reason? You ain't looking for it because you figure it'll point you to the treasure?"

"If it was to point us to the treasure, that would be great. But we figure that's a long shot."

Ollie smashed the knife blade deep into the coffee table. Hopper and Cord both jerked reflexively at the violence of the gesture.

"Well, here's the deal, boys. You two wouldn't know what to do with that treasure if you found it. That land you're working on is a public trust, which means it belongs to the state government, which means if you find something, the trust and the law would jerk it through your fingers quicker than you can say 'wooden nickel.' I know what to do to protect it and move it so we keep every dollar that can be squeezed out of it. You boys be smart, adapt to the situation, face the fact." He worked the blade out of the table and smiled as he inspected the edge with his thumb. "We're partners. That's what that dumb sombitch Feeney forgot. He figured to bypass his old benefactor and pocket everything for himself." Ollie closed the blade and put the knife back in his hip pocket. "Feeney's regretting his greed today. Just like you boys will if you try to cut me out."

Ollie heaved his massive body off the Naugahyde and walked around behind them, putting a hubcap-sized hand on each of their shoulders. "You two are smart. Real smart. You're going to find us that treasure. And everybody's going to make out alright. Share and share alike. Let me show you what a good partner I am. I'm gonna buy that boot from you." He reached into his pocket and extracted a wad of money. He peeled off five hundred-dollar bills. "Which of you boys is the banker?" Cord nodded to Hopper. Ollie shoved the cash into Hopper's shirt pocket. "You fellas ain't gonna make the same mistake as Feeney. I got eyes everywhere. Now, you go on over to the Buzzard and see Pat. He wants a word."

Hub and Tiny moved away from the door, allowing them room to leave. Hopper patted Hub's thick shoulder. "See you around, Hub. Sorry about your hemophobia deal." Hub glowered.

On the way out, Cord hesitated and looked into Tiny's doughy, emotionless face. "How is your mom, Tiny?"

"She's got the cancer."

"I heard. How she doing?"

"She's gonna die pretty soon."

"Sorry, Tiny. Tell her I said hi."

"Thanks, Vernon."

Hopper paused at the door. "Hey, Ollie, mind if I ask you something?"

"You can ask."

"How did you know those guys broke into our place?"

"You boys don't need to be concerned about how I know the stuff I know. You just need to be clear in your thinking. I find out the things I need to find out. I knew Feeney and Biscuit was up to something. When I asked them about it, they tried to bullshit me, but I got a built-in bullshit-o-meter." The office shook with the thunder of his high-volume laugh. "Me and Hub and Tiny had the pleasure of teaching them one of life's most surprising and important lessons. When you go to hatchin' plots, you gotta assume the world is a hell of a lot smaller place than most people think—ain't it?"

Hopper looked at Cord and nodded. "Yep, and seems to be getting smaller by the hour."

"Well, like my old daddy used to say, no matter how small it gets, it'll always be bigger than a coffin."

As they walked to the Rambler, Ollie waved a merry goodbye with a big smile on his wide face. "You boys drive careful. I don't want nothin' to happen to my favorite partners."

On their way to the Blue Buzzard, they tried to triangulate the situation. Podd told Feeney they found something. Feeney was interested in the treasure, but he had other mysterious business dealings with Ollie. By Ollie's lights, he was entitled to a piece of everything *extracurricular* Feeney had his hand in. Feeney looked up their address and sent his brother to look for something. Somebody got their wires crossed; maybe the brother was pulling a double-cross. Somehow the whole deal registered on Ollie's radar.

Hopper shook his head. "It fits, Cord. But there's pieces missing. Something ain't right."

"Any idea what these missing pieces might look like?"

"Not yet, but I think we can identify the big snake Feeney was talking about."

———

Eva's Chevy Nova and Pat's Jeep were in the Blue Buzzard parking lot. When they stepped into the bar, Pat, on one knee, contended with his big belly as he collected quarters from the pool table. When he saw them, he straightened and poured quarters into a canvas bag. He dropped the bag on the table's worn green surface, clenched his fists, and eyed them with volcanic hostility.

"Hey, Pat," Hopper shouted cheerfully. "We just talked to Ollie, and he told us to come over here to see you. He said you wanted to apologize for your asshole behavior last night. And we didn't have to put your nuts in a vice or nothing. It's a big man that knows when he's been a heartless donkey dick. You're a hell of a man, Pat—a hell of a man."

Pat's face took on the same dangerous redness they recently saw on Ollie's. "Oh, you're a clown, Hopper, a real wiseass. Someday I'll get a chance to stomp some humility onto that clown face of yours."

"Let me see if I got things figured out. Ollie wants you to offer us our jobs back, and he wants you to give us a raise."

Pat sputtered, "He didn't say nothing about no raise."

"Well, I'm sure if you check with him, he'll okay it. It'll be two twenty-five a weekend instead of two hundred. Right?

"I'll call Ollie."

Twenty-five

Buntz showed up about ten o'clock Saturday morning, even though it was his day off. He wanted to be sure there was no snow or ice on the walkways. No matter how discouraging the weather might be, if the doors were open, somebody always showed up. He'd seen people wearing rain gear leaning into a storm to peer into empty exhibits. He'd seen mothers struggling to push baby strollers through deep snow. There may be only one or two visitors all day, but somebody always came.

Buntz felt unusually happy. The storm hadn't disrupted much. The rapid warming was causing snow and ice to disappear in all the right places. He was pleased to see the sun shining and the pedestrian walkways clear.

Everything changed when he rounded the turn from the aquatic mammal exhibit toward the main entrance. Just off the sidewalk, in the shade of a tall oak, he saw the bloody fluff and feathers. Something had killed another peahen. He turned off the golf cart and walked, sadly, to the scene. He probably ought to go ahead and report this second incident. He knew for sure there would be more mischief if the culprit wasn't apprehended. Sighing, he returned to the golf cart. He hurried to the shop to load some sawdust and the tools he needed to bag the bloody feathers.

As he drove to the shop, Feeney ran him off the sidewalk, racing away from the snake house on his own golf cart. Buntz came to a sliding sideways stop. Feeney's stop was maddeningly slow and controlled. Buntz jumped off his cart, working hard to resist the urge to pound Feeney into a mess of gator chow. "What the hell's wrong with you, Feeney? Even on Saturday morning, you go racing around here like a maniac? You're liable to run somebody down."

The bill of Feeney's ball cap obscured his face. He didn't look up when he spoke. "Sorry, Buntz, I was . . . you know, in a hurry."

"In a hurry for what?"

"I . . . uhh . . . I gotta go, Buntz."

Something wasn't right. "What are you up to, Feeney?"

When Feeney looked up, Buntz could see he looked as if he'd gone a couple of rounds with a capable heavyweight. He had a fat lip, a knot on his head, and a purple, nearly closed left eye. "Jesus, Feeney. What happened to you?"

"Uhh, I had an accident. Yeah . . . an accident. That's why I was in a hurry. I got to see a doctor."

"Holy cow, did one of them snakes bite you or whip your ass or something?"

"No, no, nothing like that."

"What, Feeney? What's going on? If you hurt yourself on the job, we gotta file a report."

"No, it wasn't on the job. I . . . well, I got a little liquored up last night and . . . fell down. No need for any reports. I'll just go have a doctor take a look."

"Okay, Feeney. You go see a doctor. But there's no excuse for driving dangerous around here. If I hadn't swerved, we might both be headed for the doctor's office."

"Sorry, Buntz. I'll be more careful. I'd appreciate it if you didn't mention this."

"Sure, Feeney. I'll keep this to myself, but maybe this deal ain't the biggest worry on our list."

Feeney rubbed the knot on his head. "Whaddaya mean?"

"I hear you and Podd been trying to talk our new men into looking for that Alimony deal. Seems you're looking to sell them on the idea of finding and stealing it."

Feeney stuttered, "That's just bullshit, Buntz. I never said nothing like that."

"You know, mischief like that might cost a fella his job."

Feeney gave him a sly grin. "Don't worry yourself about that, Buntz. I won't ever be talkin' to those guys about stuff like that."

"See that you don't, or I might have to fill out reports about all this."

"Sure, Buntz, sure."

Buntz watched him drive away, slow and careful. Something was off center. He shrugged and got on his cart. Whatever mischief Feeney was up to, it wasn't his concern.

He was concerned, however, by the fact Mrs. Kroneson loved these peafowl. If he couldn't put a stop to the bloodshed, that might be all the proof Neyland needed to veto Buntz's promotion to head groundskeeper. He mumbled a prayer as he headed to the shop. "Lord, whether this peahen-killin' scoundrel be bobcat or feral housecat, lead the varmint into the racoon trap I'm about to set. Help me catch this critter, Lord, and I'll be the best dang grounds crew guy you ever created. Amen."

Twenty-six

Nozetape was pulling into the driveway when Hopper and Cord got home. Hopper grabbed his elbow. "Glad to see you up and around, Nozetape. Let's go over to Ruby's for lunch. We need to talk about how to keep us all from getting extinct like a herd of dumb mammoths."

At Ruby's Chicken Fried Steak Palace, Nozetape leaned across the table and spoke confidentially. "The troopers' report says they caught up with the outlaws not long after sunup. According to Alimony's journal, they planned to leave at first light."

Hopper nodded. "I gotcha. If they left at dawn and got caught just after sunup, they may not have got too far from where they left the treasure under the dead horse."

"Right. I'm guessing they got caught right where you found the boot."

"Any idea how far we need to backtrack to get to the treasure?"

"We know it's east of there because Alimony and Pete planned on heading west."

Cord was drawing circles on a napkin. "So the treasure could be a quarter-mile, half-mile, or mile east of where we found the boot?"

Nozetape nodded. "I'd be surprised if it was more than a mile."

"How far east does the Kroneson empire extend?"

"Far enough. The treasure's either on property belonging to the Kronesons or land they gave to the zoo trust."

Cord turned the napkin over and penciled an N at the top. He made a dot on the right edge. "Let's say the boot marks the spot; here's where Alimony died." From the dot, he drew a diagonal line to the southeast corner and another to the northeast corner. He made a dotted line about a third of the way east of the dot. "The notes tell us they buried the treasure, tied it up in a harness under a horse carcass." Nozetape nodded. "Is there any way we could find it without the map that's supposedly in that other boot?"

Nozetape cleared his throat. "Well, it's a long shot." He poured sugar into his tea as Hopper and Cord waited.

Finally, Hopper couldn't stand it. "Speak up, Nozetape. Tell us about the long shot."

"We could try to use hazel."

Hopper's mouth hung open for an instant. "Who the hell is Hazel?"

"It's not who; it's what. Hazel is a kind of tree."

Hopper shook his head. "You're making this too damn hard, Nozetape. Spell it out."

"Okay, look at this." Nozetape pulled a page from his notebook with an illustration of a man holding a Y-shaped stick while two other men dug stones from the ground.

Cord studied the drawing. "What is this?"

"It's an illustration from a German book on mining published in 1555. According to this book, these old German miners used divining rods made from hazel wood to find precious metals buried in the ground."

Hopper threw his head back and laughed. "So you're saying we use some witchcraft hocus pocus, go marching around the zoo with a divining rod sticking out in front of us, hoping it'll point to the treasure?" He reached across the table and pulled a lock of Nozetape's long hair. "I love the resourcefulness of it, Nozetape. And introducing voodoo into the deal appeals to my natural love of adventure. But it ain't practical."

Nozetape sat red-faced, frowning. "You want me to finish, or is your mind made up?"

"No, brother, I got nothing else at the moment. I'd love to be persuaded this hazel idea might produce something."

"Look at this." He produced a 1970 article from a newspaper in Wiltshire, England, reporting that a local lady successfully—again—located water using a hazel divining rod.

"Great, Nozetape, you might be getting my attention if we were looking for water. But I got no problem finding water. There's a whole damn lake full of it."

"Would you let me finish? I just wanted to show you that people are using hazel as recently as a couple years ago to find stuff."

"Go on, Nozetape. I'm sorry," Hopper said, restraining a smile.

"Here's a piece from *The Agricultural Survey of the County of Cornwall* published in 1797. See here? These miners claim they can find metal deposits from five to twenty fathoms deep. They call it *josing*. And look at this. You know who Linnaeus was?"

Hopper and Cord looked at each other and shook their heads in unison.

"He was an eighteenth-century scientist who laid the foundation for the scientific names of every plant and animal on earth. He heard about this belief in divining rods and set up a scientific experiment to prove it was a fake. He hid a bag of gold at the foot of a tree in a forest. But he forgot which tree it was. So guess how they found it."

"Somebody used a hazel stick?"

"Right."

Cord scratched his jaw. "If it's that easy, how come all the treasure in the world ain't already been dug up?"

Nozetape winked. "Because it isn't that simple. Apparently there's a formula you have to follow to get the wand ready. Listen to this." He pulled some sheets from his notebook and read the ritual for cutting a wand shaped like a Y, peeling the bark, drying it in moderate heat, and soaking it in the juice of either a wakerobin or nightshade plant. "Sharpen the lower end of the Y. If you're looking for gold, attach some gold to the forks with a hair. Use the wand when the moon is waxing. Then you'll find your gold."

Hopper laughed again. "Nozetape, I love you, brother, but this is just crazy. If we're going that route, why don't we just use a metal detector?"

Nozetape snorted. "You know what a metal detector's range is?"

"No."

"Suppose the treasure's in the middle of some exhibit. Do you think a metal detector can see that far?"

"I don't know, Nozetape, but—"

"Suppose it's a foot or two under a concrete sidewalk. How good is a metal detector for that?"

"Hell, I don't know, Nozetape. But people use metal detectors all the time, and before this morning, I never heard about anybody using hazel wood to look for treasure."

Nozetape stuffed his papers into his notebook. "Yeah, I guess you're right. It's crazy. We're better off going with your plan . . . Oh, right, you don't have a plan. How about you, Cord? You got a plan?"

"I was thinking about drafting Hopper to use the hazel wand to fig-ure out which animal cage we got to crawl into to find this treasure."

The waitress, Mandy, came by to refill their tea glasses. She put her hand on Cord's shoulder as she topped them off. Hopper leaned back in the booth. "Are you superstitious, Mandy?"

"I sure am. I'm real careful when salt gets spilled in here. I always throw a little over my left shoulder. And I got a spell to say if I ever break a mirror, and I never let nobody put a hat on my bed, and—"

"Have you ever heard of people finding treasure with a divining rod?"

She bit her lower lip as she considered. "Water, maybe, but never treasure."

"If some famous scientist said he lost some gold and somebody found it for him using a divining rod, would you believe it?"

"A scientist?"

"Yeah, a famous scientist."

"Sure, if a famous scientist said somebody did it, I'd believe it."

"Thanks, Mandy. You coming to the Buzzard tonight?"

"You asking for a date?"

"Can't tonight, Mandy."

"You two?" She used the pitcher to indicate Cord and Nozetape.

They said in unison, "Can't tonight."

She smiled. "Well, if you put it like that, maybe I'll come."

On the way home, Hopper was in good spirits. No hangover, they had their job back, Nozetape had reassembled the reel-to-reel, they had music, he'd enjoyed some good laughs at lunch, and he had $500 in his shirt pocket. It was a long shot, he knew, but there was a possibility that Audrey and Abbie might show up at the Blue Buzzard again tonight.

When he glanced at Cord, he could see his jaw muscles working. "What's on your mind, Hondo?"

"Something's fishy, Hopper."

As always, Hopper took Cord's trouble-sensing instincts as warranting serious consideration. "Spell it out, buddy. What are you thinking?"

"I don't like the Feeney/Oleg connection. There's something going on that had nothing to do with us. Somehow, we got tangled up in it. I've seen what happens when careless bugs get pulled into the middle of the spider's web. They never come out better off, and the spider always comes out fat."

Hopper mulled the facts. Cord was right. Whatever was going on between Ollie and Feeney, it was in their interest to know what it was. They needed to know where the web lines were. Hopper asked, "You reckon it has something to do with Feeney's work at the zoo?"

Cord shrugged. "Until today, I didn't know Ollie had any interest in mammoth ivory. Hell, for all we know, he could be the kingpin black-market mammoth-ivory trader of the world. Maybe he's got his hands into the black market for snakes and lizards. God knows there's cages full of that weird shit sitting all over the flea market: puppies, kittens, iguanas, baby chicks, little turtles—who knows what all? Feeney's greasy enough to sign on for any kind of backdoor business the Oleg brothers hatch. We ought to find out what's what."

Hopper nodded. "Now, about Nozetape's hazel idea. Does it make any sense to you?"

"No," Cord said without hesitation.

"Me neither. But until we come up with a map or a better plan, we ought to keep an open mind."

Cord grumbled, "I'm afraid this time an open mind could lead to a shitload of silliness."

When they walked into the Blue Buzzard that night, Little Eva motioned them to the bar. She was pouring tequila before they got there. "What are we drinking to tonight, angel?" Hopper asked cheerfully.

As she cut a lemon into sections, she said, "First off, we're celebrating you guys getting your job back. I was afraid it might have been my fault you got fired."

She passed them each a lemon wedge as Cord looked at her quizzically. "How could it be your fault? All you did was tell us about Nozetape's call."

"I could have waited until your shift ended."

"Yeah, but then we'd have been pissed at you for keeping important stuff from us." Cord arranged the lemon wedge next to his tequila shot.

She handed them the salt shaker, and they completed the ritual. "True, but I was telling myself all night last night that if I'd kept my big mouth shut, you'd be pissed, but you'd still have a job. You'd have got over it. So here's to your continued employment at the Blue Buzzard." They slammed down the tequila, licked the salt, and winced as they bit into their lemons.

Hopper reached over the bar and put his hand on her cheek. "Hey, Eva, you did the right thing. Far as me and Cord are concerned, losin' a job is a small price to pay for doing what's right. Pour another, and we'll drink to doing what's right."

She withdrew her cheek from his palm and pretended to do something at the register. Cord spoke up. "Hey, Eva, like Hopper said, everything turned out right. No need to fret anymore."

Hopper sensed she might be crying. "Come on, Eva, do like me and Cord. Put it behind you, and let's make the most of the night in front of us."

She spoke with her back to them. "I just wish . . . there's something . . ."

Hopper could tell there was more to the deal than she was saying. "What is it, Eva?"

"I don't know. Maybe I secretly wanted you to get fired. Maybe I wanted to get you guys out of this place."

Hopper and Cord exchanged a glance. Hopper laughed. "Hell, we love you too much to ever leave, Eva. You got to get this under control. It's Saturday night in Southtown, sweetheart. Pour us some more tequila and let's have fun."

She turned back to the bar, obviously trying to muster a smile, but it was weak. "Tell you what we can drink to. We can raise a glass in honor of my thirtieth birthday; how's that?"

Hopper slapped the bar. "Great, I'll drink to that." He reached for the tequila bottle. "Let me buy the last round. Here's to us getting our job back, and here's wishing Eva McMurphy a great goddam Saturday night birthday bash."

Cord offered a hearty "Amen," and they all made the most of the moment.

They started their set by announcing that it was Eva's birthday and they expected to see everyone in the place being unusually generous with their tips.

They opened with a song dedicated to the lady of the hour. It wasn't the blues, but it was met with wild enthusiasm: "You Are My Sunshine." Hopper noticed Eva frequently wiping her eyes with a bar towel. It wasn't like her to be so emotional. He couldn't figure it out. All efforts to do so came to a tire-screeching halt when he spotted Audrey and Abbie paying the cover at the door. They both declined to have their hands stamped. Hopper wasn't surprised; nobody's brand on those gals.

They had their own bottle of Bacardi rum, which told Hopper they intended to stay awhile and fully participate in the spirit of the evening. Several times, Hopper saw hopeful Southside drunks stumble to their table. He was amused each time the disappointed suitors limped off.

At each break, Hopper beelined to their table, where they enjoyed light, superficial conversation, which he found unsatisfying. Cord spent his break time at the bar with Eva. Hopper felt he was in the emotional equivalent of a funhouse. Everything was recognizable but distorted. Cord was at the bar, but he should be here. The Kroneson twins were here, but they really didn't belong. Eva should have been happy, but she was suffering from concealed torments.

During one of the breaks, Audrey leaned near his ear and said, "Have we lost our charm? Last night, we had your undivided attention. Tonight, you seem distracted. Are you only interested in us when we're telling entertaining stories?"

Hopper tried to come up with an explanation that made sense, but the only possible rationale collecting in his funhouse brain was gibberish. From somewhere, words spilled out of his mouth, strange to him as they seemed surprising to the Kroneson twins. "Have you two ever been high?"

In a very unladylike response, Abbie choked, covering her nose as some of her beverage dripped out. Audrey's mouth hung open in an expression of surprise and amusement. She said in an affected British accent, "I say, Abigail, there appears to be rum coming out of your nose." The sisters put their heads together and nearly collapsed in unrestrained laughter.

Between spasms and after several attempts, Abbie added in her own pseudo-haughty affectation, "I believe that would be demon rum, my dear." Hopper couldn't help but fall into the laughter with them. All three laughed with such an obvious lack of normal control that it spilled over to the surrounding tables radiating outward. In less than a minute, every patron in the Blue Buzzard was laughing along with all the other laughers. Even Cord and Eva were laughing at each other. Only Pat seemed immune to the contagious mirth outbreak.

Audrey leaned near his ear again. "Ask us again on the next break."

Hopper, wiping his eyes, offered a weak salute and headed for the stage, motioning Cord, still laughing, to join him. He shouldered his guitar strap and raised his hands. "Come on, kids. You guys got to cheer up. This is getting depressing." The place exploded. Audrey and Abbie, their heads on their table, took turns shoving each other and slapping the tabletop.

Hopper shouted above the raucous laughter, "Okay, let's do this one." He and Cord broke into their guitar rendition of Ian Whitcomb's "You Turn Me On." As anticipated, when they got to the lyric "come on and do the jerk with me," most of the crowd joined in with their best imitation of the classic jerk motion.

When it was time for the last break, Hopper hurried back to the Kroneson table. Audrey, with a mock-haughty expression, asked, "I'm sorry, what was the question again?" Which sent the sisters into another gale of laughter. When they had it under control, Audrey asked, "Can we trust you, Dale?"

He sat back in mock astonishment. "Of course not. I'm a man."

Audrey became serious. "Really, Dale, if we were to share secrets with you, could you—would you keep them?"

Without hesitation, he leaned forward on his elbows. "Ladies, I'd do almost anything you asked me to. And if you asked me to keep a secret, I'd die before I'd let you down."

The women exchanged a glance. "When this place closes, would you like to come to our apartment?" Audrey asked.

His heart hammered against his chest so hard it nearly broke his breastbone. "Well, me and Cord was planning to attend the monthly meeting of our book club, but—sure, I can come over."

Abbie looked at the bar. "What about Vernon? Do you think he'll come?"

Hopper laughed. "I believe the answer to that question is—hell, yes, he'll come."

Audrey handed him a slip of paper with an address written on it. She asked, "What will you be driving?"

Hopper spoke, studying the address, trying to visualize the location, "A 'sixty-three Rambler, why?"

"We have to notify the guard."

His head snapped up on reflex. "Guard?"

"It's okay; he'll be looking for you. There won't be any trouble." Before he could say more, they were on their feet. Audrey spoke. "We have to go now." She bent and kissed his cheek. "We'll see you in a little while."

The softness of her lips banished every other sensation from his consciousness. He didn't see, hear, feel, or smell anything but Audrey Kroneson as she and her twin disappeared through the door.

He and Cord finished the night with their version of Howlin' Wolf's "Howlin' for My Baby," which justified every patron to close out the night's entertainment with their best wolf howl imitation. As the crowd showered them with raucous expressions of appreciation, Hopper and Cord cased their guitars and made their way to the barstool that served as Pat's perch. Hopper stepped up to the big man as Cord went outside to get the Rambler.

"That's two fifty, Pat," holding out his hand.

"Bullshit. It's one fifty, and you're lucky to get that. I'm docking your ass for leaving early last night." He held out three fifty-dollar bills.

Hopper took the money and stashed it in his shirt pocket. "Thanks, Pat. See you next Friday. And by the way, we decided to accept your apology."

Pat snarled, "Keep it up, wiseass. One of these days, we'll see who gets the last laugh." That statement echoed in Hopper's mind as he stepped into the cold and found Cord waiting in the Rambler.

"You know, Cord," he said as he slid into the warming interior, "that fat prick has something scary and dangerous up his sleeve. We're going to have to be on our toes, or some of our favorite body parts might get chopped off."

———

Cord turned left on South Robinson, headed north. Hopper was about to break the good news about their invitation to the Kroneson sisters' apartment, when Cord broke his first. "Listen, you're going to need to drive the Rambler home. I'm going over to Eva's."

Hopper stuttered, "But . . . but I got us a date with the Kroneson twins . . . the Kroneson twins, man."

"Sorry, Eva needs some cheering up. I guess it's something to do with turning thirty; I don't know."

"But, Cord, this is a dream come true, buddy. They're rich, they're beautiful, hell, who knows how a night like this might wind up."

Cord put the Rambler in park and looked at his friend. "Okay, I'll let you make the call. A couple of rich girls who own a zoo would like a couple of unusual specimens to come by so they can see how these creatures behave in strange surroundings. Or a friend who knows and likes us for who we are needs a helping hand. You decide."

"Jeez, Cord, if you put it like that, you know the answer. You need to go to Eva's."

Cord put his hand on his friend's shoulder. "Right. You need to drop me at the Skyline. Eva don't want Pat to know we're so chummy. She'll meet me there after she's done with closing chores."

At the Skyline truck stop, Cord got out, and Hopper took the wheel. Cord spoke through the Rambler's window. "Don't let them put a collar on you or neuter you or nothing like that. And don't let 'em teach you any tricks—like balancing a ball on your nose or jumping through flaming hoops."

"Kiss my ass, Cord. I don't think they got any interest in neutering me, and I already know them tricks. That collar deal, well, I might have to hear them out on that suggestion."

Cord waved from the parking lot as Hopper headed north for his adventure with the Kroneson twins. He drove to the intersection of

Northwest 63rd and May Avenue and turned west. He drove slow, looking on the right side of the road. Odd house numbers always on the north. He saw an entrance with a guard shack and figured this must be the place.

He stopped at the gate. The square-jawed, buzzcut guard was on the phone. He tossed Hopper a disinterested glance. Hopper waited while the guard took his time concluding the call. When his conversation ended, he slid open a glass window. "Help you?"

"Yeah, I'm here to see Miss Kroneson."

"Name?"

"Dale Hopper."

The guard looked down his nose at the Rambler. "Just a minute, I'll check." He closed the window, picked up a clipboard, and turned his back. Hopper waited—and waited. He gave the guy time enough to go back a week or two and then got out and rapped on the window with his knuckles.

The guard stepped back to the glass. "I need you to get back into your car, sir."

"What's the hold-up, Sarge?"

"Just checking to see if you're on the list. You're not."

Hopper could see his name right there on the clipboard. "Look, right there on the top of your list. That's me, Dale Hopper."

"Sorry, sir, you're not on the list. I'm going to have to ask you to leave."

"Look, buddy . . . "

"Leave now, or I'll call the police. It's really that simple."

Hopper considered pulling the guy through the little window and administering a good old-fashioned front-yard butt-kicking. But he really didn't need to revisit the jailhouse. No need to give Buzzcut the satisfaction.

"Okay, Sarge. Have it your way. Next time, I'll come in Miss Kroneson's car."

The guard gave him a triumphant smile. "Don't count on it, hoss."

Twenty-seven

Sunday, January 28, 1973

It was Sunday morning, and they drove to El Patio for their weekly serving of huevos rancheros with chili. On the way, Cord asked whether he learned any cute tricks from the Kroneson girls. Hopper related the story of his dismissal by the buzzcut gate guard.

"So you never got in?"

"Nope."

Cord laughed. "You're blaming the guard?"

Hopper frowned at the unspoken indictment of the Kroneson sisters. "Of course it was the guard. They gave him my name. I saw it on his list. The jerk just appointed himself chaperone and decided a guy in a Rambler wasn't suitable company for the princesses."

"You don't think the ladies were having a little fun at your expense?"

"No. Like I said, it was the guard."

"Okay."

"What about your night? How were things with Eva?"

It was Cord's turn to frown. He turned right on Classen Boulevard and drove a couple of blocks without speaking. Hopper waited. "There's something going on with her she won't talk about."

"Any ideas?"

"No. If she don't want to talk about it, why be a nuisance?" This was another point where Cord's code was firm.

Hopper hoped Little Eva's problems didn't have anything to do with them.

They went through the routine of greeting all the bleary-eyed regulars at El Patio and engaged in their obligatory flirtation with Nan, the waitress. Hopper spooned thick, peppery salsa onto the egg-centered chaos, nearly spilling over the sides of his plate. "Know what we ought to do today, Cord?"

"Yeah, nothing. Let's not do anything today. Let's lay around the house, listen to music, drink wine, and knock the Nerf ball around."

"Listen, Cord, I think we ought to go to the zoo and take a look around."

Cord stared at him with a shocked expression. "Correct me if I'm wrong here, but we work at the zoo, don't we?"

"Yeah, but—"

"We'll be at the zoo all day tomorrow—working. Am I wrong?"

"No, but—"

"So explain why the hell we want to take our day off and go out there to look around?"

"The main reason is there's a treasure buried there somewhere. It wouldn't hurt just to look over the ground. You never know what might be there to see if you just look. We got employee passes, so it won't cost us nothing."

After a short round of complaints and explanations, Cord agreed they ought to go to the zoo.

They parked in the main parking lot, which was on the west side of the zoo premises. They went through the gate to the west forty and looked east. Cord shook his head. "We won't be able to tell a thing. Probably none of the roads we see were here back then. If the treasure happens to be under the foundation of any of the buildings here now, there's no chance of us getting under it. And I'll tell you right now, if we find the other boot and it has a map that says the treasure's buried in the gator pit, it's just going to have to stay buried. No treasure is worth me getting chunks bit off my ass by alligators."

Hopper smiled at the mental image of Cord scaling the fence with a big reptile in hungry pursuit. "Don't worry about gators. They keep them in a warm bath through the winter. So we wouldn't have to dodge around them until it gets warm. By then, we'll have the treasure in the bus and be headed for sunny California. Far as I know, they don't allow gators on the beaches out there."

Before they started their eastward walk, Hopper scanned the woods, hoping to see Finn. *Hope the old guy's okay.* They headed toward the zoo's main entrance, looking around with no idea what they were looking for.

They showed their Animal Tech One IDs and went through the front gate, no questions asked. They followed the sidewalk south, pausing to admire a group of large white rabbits—tundra hares, according to the sign—crowding together at the base of a willow tree on the edge of a snowy bank. Their chubby cheeks operated like little machines as they nibbled fallen willow branches skillfully extracted from beneath the snow.

Hopper was disappointed so many exhibits were vacant. Even so, he stopped and read the placards. Cord questioned him about it. "We need to get familiar with which animals are dangerous. We don't know what pens we might have to crawl into. That one back there with the tundra hares, we could explore in there, no worries. We're not likely to get mauled by those fluffy little guys. But these fellas," he nodded to a collection of large, shaggy wolves watching them from the pen across the sidewalk, "look like they'd love to get their fangs into a couple of unarmed treasure hunters."

They followed the sidewalk to the southeast. Hopper nudged Cord. "Hey, look at that." He pointed to the pachyderm enclosure, where Abbie Kroneson was walking Daisy the elephant, the zoo's all-time favorite attraction. Abbie walked beside Daisy's big head with a hand behind the elephant's ear. Daisy walked slowly as if she didn't want to leave Abbie behind.

Hopper leaned on the rails surrounding the enclosure. He remembered the surprising strength and toughness in Abbie's hand. He guessed that's what happened when you worked with elephants. He and Cord watched in quiet admiration. Hopper spoke without taking his eyes from the woman who looked so small beside the great gray bulk of Daisy the elephant. "Amazing that an animal that could squash her like a bug seems to have real affection for her."

Cord mumbled, "That's the secret to big animal survival on a planet where humans are on the prowl. If you're going to get along with the most efficient killer that ever lived, you better act like you love 'em, whether you do or not. Even that might not save your ass."

Hopper studied his friend's face. "Jesus, Cord, if I'd known you were going to get so philosophical about the cold facts of survival of the lovable, I'd have kept your mind focused on the fuzzy bunnies." He turned his attention back to Abbie and shouted, "Hey, miss, how much you want for your elephant? I got a single male back home, and I need a breeding pair."

Abbie squinted in their direction. She frowned. "We waited for you two last night. Did anyone ever tell you it's rude to accept an invitation and then not show up?"

"Not guilty," Hopper shouted back. "Your guard wouldn't let us in. Said I wasn't on the list."

"Well, that's just nonsense. I heard Audrey give him your name and tell him you would be in a Rambler. I saw him write it down. You were on the list."

"I know," Hopper responded cheerfully. "I saw my name. But your guard threatened to call the police. Since I wasn't sure you guys would go my bail, I decided to keep the peace and go home, alone and disillusioned. For a second, I contemplated suicide but then realized I'd miss breakfast."

She studied him a moment with a skeptical look on her face. "Why didn't you call?"

"If I'd been thinking ahead, I'd have got your number."

She sighed. "I'll speak to the security supervisor."

Hopper laughed. "Forget it. If we can wrangle another invitation, it'll be a pleasure to see the look on that fella's face when he has to let us in. Far as I'm concerned, that'll settle the score."

She favored him with that dazzling smile. "You're a fair man, Dale Hopper." She cocked her head to one side as if a thought just occurred to her. "I didn't know you guys were part of the Sunday crew."

"We're not. Today we're civilians just looking things over like the paying public."

Abbie walked Daisy over to the rail where Hopper and Cord leaned. "Introduce us to your friend since we didn't meet this weekend."

"This is Vernon Cord; Vernon, this is Abbie Kroneson and her boss, Daisy. We were just discussing whether it was possible for an elephant to have any real affection for a human being or whether they only act like that to keep from being on the menu."

"Of course elephants can love people. They're very intelligent and emotionally complex, maybe more than some people. Daisy and I love each other." She put a hand on Daisy's lower jaw. "Don't we, Daisy?" Daisy nodded her big head and used the tip of her trunk to flip Abbie's ponytail.

Abbie turned her attention back to Hopper and Cord. "I'm happy to meet you, Vernon. Sometime, I'll bring you into the enclosure and formally introduce you to my friend Daisy. When I make the introduction, you'll know right away whether she likes you."

"Oh, yeah? How will I know?"

"Easy. If she dislikes you, she'll jump up and down on you until she turns you into a muddy puddle." Her lyrical laugh lost none of its charm in the sober daylight. She walked Daisy as near the rail as the moat surrounding the enclosure would allow. "Tell them good morning, Daisy."

The elephant raised her trunk and gave a squeaky, subdued elephant salute.

"Good morning to you, Miss Daisy." Hopper tipped an imaginary hat. He nudged Cord. "Be polite; say good morning."

Cord blushed. "Good morning, Daisy. I hope you're enjoying your walk with Miss Kroneson on this beautiful Sunday morning."

Daisy answered with another happy-sounding squeak. Abbie stroked Daisy's trunk lovingly. "Well, I have to take her inside for a bath now. See you." She and Daisy walked slowly toward the wide door opening into the pachyderm building. Abbie stopped and looked back over her shoulder. "Will you be playing at the Blue Buzzard this Friday?"

Hopper answered, "Yep."

"I really enjoyed your music. Maybe we'll come again."

"That would be great," Hopper shouted as the woman and the elephant disappeared into the building.

Cord mumbled as they continued their walk toward the lake. "Maybe working with elephants has its charms, but I don't think I'd ever get used to the smell."

They rounded the southeast corner of the zoo premises and saw a grounds crew pickup by the zebra enclosure. At the same moment, they heard Buntz. "Hey, Hopper and Cord, glad to see you boys. Come over for a minute."

They walked to the pickup and saw Buntz half concealed in chest-high dead brown grass. He leaned against a rusty pipe fence with a wire cage balanced on the top pipe. "It's muddier down here than I thought. I need you guys to lend me a hand."

Cord frowned. "What are you doing in there, Buntz?"

Buntz snapped back, "What's it look like I'm doing? I'm trying to get this damn trap over the fence. Now come on in here and make yourselves useful."

"It's our day off," Cord said as if Buntz didn't know.

"Hell, I know that, but this ain't no time for punching a time clock."

Hopper took a deep breath. "Okay, Buntz, here we come." Cord followed as they slogged through the deep mud obscured by tall brown grass. He mumbled, "Whose bright idea was it to come out here on our day off?"

"Quit bellyaching. We're building up some family-sized deposits in our karma account. This will be another mark on our side when it's time to decide whether we find the treasure."

"I sure hope whoever's keeping these accounts is figuring things the same way you are."

When they reached Buntz, he ordered, "Hold this." They got a firm grip on the contraption balanced on the pipe. Buntz climbed over the fence and grasped the cage from the other side. "Okay, now I'll hold it while you fellas climb over." Cord grumbled unintelligibles as his muddy boots slipped on the rounded pipe surfaces.

Buntz ignored him and spoke cheerfully. "Lucky for me you boys showed up. I sure misjudged what a job this turned out to be."

Hopper asked, "Exactly what is the job, Buntz?"

"We got something killing peafowl, and these birds are Mrs. Kroneson's special darlings. If we can't put a stop to it, things might get complicated. So we got to bring a halt to the carnage."

Hopper started to mention the peacock story Audrey told him, but decided Buntz didn't need to know about enlisted men fraternizing with the Kroneson girls. Buntz climbed up the trunk of a thick elm to a place where the tree forked, creating a crotch. "Okay, boost her up."

They shouldered the trap high enough for Buntz to get a grip. "What do you reckon will wind up in the trap?" Cord asked.

"Bobcat or feral house cat most likely." Buntz unstrung a coil of rope attached to his belt and expertly knotted the trap to the tree. They hadn't noticed the bag hanging from his belt. He drew it up and removed the carcass of a good-sized turkey hen. As he put the remains in the trap, he chattered about how he found her dead on the road by his mailbox this morning and figured she'd be perfect marauder bait.

With the trap tied securely in the tree's fork, the dead turkey hen placed inside, and the trap's trigger set, Buntz shimmied down the trunk. "Okay, boys, let me buy you a cup of coffee."

As they waded through the mud back to the pickup, Cord said, "Might as well have some coffee. Looks like our sightseeing is over." He glanced at the gooey earth clinging to his jeans and boots.

Buntz didn't hesitate to slide into the pickup, muddy boots, clothes, and all. "Climb in, boys. We'll have the shop to ourselves. What are you fellas doing here on a Sunday morning? I'm glad you're here, of course, but what's up?"

"Well, Buntz, me and Cord decided that if we was to get on permanent, it would pay if we knew more about the zoo layout. So far, we know about the forty, the PR office, and the snake house. Guys that aim to get promoted to Animal Tech Two should know a whole lot more about the place where they work."

Cord groaned under his breath.

Buntz beamed. "You men will be running this place before you know it."

Back at the shop, Buntz bailed out of the pickup and strolled at his usual high-speed gait to the shop door, withdrawing his keyring. "Never mind the mud, fellas. I'll have the other guys hose things down tomorrow."

Inside the shop, Buntz switched on the fluorescent lights and made his rapid way to the coffeepot. Once he had coffee brewing, he motioned them to the wobbly card table surrounded by four metal folding chairs. "Let's have us a working man's heart to heart." He disappeared into his office and came out with a large black lunch pail. Hopper and Cord sat down. Buntz joined them. "I'm going to share something I've never shared with anybody." He opened the pail and removed a bottle of Bushmill's Irish whiskey. "Now I don't want you to get the wrong idea. We never, I repeat, never drink on the job." He poured three cups of coffee and added a dash of Bushmill's to each. "But we're off the clock, we put in some overtime, and I feel good about our chances of catching our raider in the trap. So here's to us in hopes that fortune smiles on our varmint-trappin' labors."

They each took a healthy pull on their Styrofoam cups. Buntz released a moderately restrained *whoopee*. He chattered as he refilled the cups and added another splash of Bushmill's. "I'm really glad you boys came along. Most of the other guys on the crew are okay, but to get the most out of your work, there's got to be more than money." He took another ample drink. "I know there's more to you two than meets the idea . . . I mean the eye. You're men I can trust. You see the bigger picture."

Hopper took another drink and leaned across the table, speaking in a confidential tone. "Buntz, can I ask you a question?"

Buntz leaned back in his chair with a satisfied smile on his face. "Fire away, Hopper. Ask me anything."

Cord looked edgy as Hopper leaned closer. "Are there any hazel trees over on the forty?"

Buntz's face broke into a broad grin. "You bet there are. There ain't as many hazels as hackberries, and they're harder to find, but they're in there." He gave Hopper a sly smile. "You know more about trees than you're letting on, don't you?"

"No, I just heard some interesting stories about hazel wood and thought maybe you could tell us something about them, maybe even show us one."

Buntz leaned forward, bringing his face closer to Hopper's. "I don't know what you heard, but try this one. You know who Jupiter was?"

Hopper felt a chill run through him. He felt like something important was about to be revealed. "Jupiter was some kind of ancient god, wasn't he?"

"He was the king of all the ancient gods."

Hopper sat stunned for a second, marveling at this puzzling echo from last Friday night's conversation with Audrey Kroneson. "I thought that was Zeus."

Buntz's eyes widened. "Damn, Hopper. There is more to you than meets the idea." He took another drink and refilled his cup. "Jupiter and Zeus are the same. 'Zeus' is his Greek name. He was 'Jupiter' to the Romans."

"So what does he have to do with hazel wood?"

"Jupiter had two sons, Apollo and Mercury. Apollo had the same name to the Greeks and Romans. But Mercury was 'Hermes' to the Greeks."

Hopper's eyes widened. "Holy shit, did you say 'Hermes'?"

Buntz nodded. "Yep, Hermes. Anyway, these brothers exchanged gifts. They each promised to use their gift to make life better for mankind. Mercury—Hermes—gave his brother, Apollo, a lyre made of tortoise shell. According to the legend, when Apollo played this instrument, it had the power to free up the artistic skills of anybody who heard the music. Guess what Apollo gave his brother."

Hopper whispered, "A hazel wood wand."

Buntz reached up with both strong, calloused hands and took Hopper's bearded face between them in a gesture of surprising affection. "Exactly! Apollo gave Hermes a hazel wood wand. Any person touched with that wand got the power to express his own thoughts better than ever before."

Cord finished his cup and poured another half full of coffee. "Can I see that bottle, Buntz?" Buntz nodded, still looking deep into Hopper's eyes. Hopper found himself gripped by a sense of pure wonder.

"What else, Buntz? What else about the hazel wand?"

Buntz released Hopper's head and stood unsteadily. He went into his office and returned with the old book he showed them before, the one with the picture of the man-tree. He flipped carefully through the yellowed pages until he found a chapter titled "The Hazelnut." On the chapter's title page, two men in togas sat together under a tree that appeared to have a shield, decorated by symbols, in the branches. One of the seated figures held a stringed instrument. The other held a staff with the bodies of two snakes intertwined, their heads near the top of the staff.

Hopper's eyes widened. "Cord, take a look at this."

Cord, rolling his eyes, got out of his chair and stood behind Hopper, looking at the picture. Hopper put his finger on the staff. "This staff, this is the one Apollo gave Mercury-Hermes?" Buntz nodded, smiling. "This is made of hazel wood?" Buntz nodded again. Hopper turned his wide eyes to Cord. "You recognize this, Cord?"

Cord leaned over the picture, squinting. "Holy shit, is that what I think it is?"

"Bet your ass. That's the insignia of the US Army Medical Corps. That's the shoulder patch on Nozetape's field jacket."

Cord stood upright, addressing Buntz while still staring at the book. "How old did you say this book is?"

"The book is almost one hundred years old. That wood carving is over four hundred years old, and the legend, well, hell, that's been around for thousands of years."

Cord started to say something but changed his mind. Hopper couldn't contain himself. "This is just too weird, Buntz. We got a friend who was a medic in Vietnam, and he was just telling us about some of these hazel wood legends. This is freaky stuff here, brother." He gulped and considered before he asked the next question. "Our friend says people use these hazel rods to find stuff, like water . . . and stuff. Is that true?"

Buntz nodded vigorously. "Right. People have been using hazel wands to find water, minerals, and lost treasure for hundreds, maybe thousands, of years."

Cord looked sideways. "Do you believe any of that stuff, Buntz?"

Buntz closed his book and rested his right hand on it as if he was about to take an oath. "I believe there's all kinds of power in plants that people don't know about. Almost every day, scientists discover healing power in roots, flowers, seeds, barks, and branches that ancient people knew ages ago. I don't know one way or the other whether a hazel rod can point somebody to water or minerals. But I wouldn't be surprised."

Hopper sat back down. "One more thing, Buntz. What do the snakes coiled around this wand have to do with anything?"

Buntz shrugged. "I tried to get to the bottom of that myself. All I can find is that snakes showed up on the hazel staff somewhere in prehistory. Nobody knows for sure when it happened or what it means. The book says people have been worshiping snakes for thousands of years, all the way back to Egyptian time. They were symbols of healing and immortality. As for what they have to do with this hazel wood story, who knows? All I can figure is snakes may be part of a message important thousands of years ago, but today, nobody remembers."

"So snakes are part of this symbol for pure decoration?"

Buntz shrugged again.

Cord snorted. "Well, whoever thought up that part could've skipped it."

When the emotional RPMs in the shop gradually recalibrated back to normal, Buntz slapped his knees with his wide, calloused hands. "Well, I'm glad you boys showed up, and I really enjoyed this little party. But now go home. See you back here in the morning."

They walked to the shop door with Buntz right behind him. As they stepped out, Buntz blushed. "I want to tell you guys that I appreciate having a couple of fellas around that—well, that know how to keep their mouth shut. It's . . . it's important, see? So . . . thanks." The door closed, and they heard the lock click.

Twenty-eight

On the way home, Cord shook his head. "I know it's piled pretty high, but like I keep saying, it's coincidence, that's all. You're reading too much voodoo into it."

"I'm not saying voodoo, Cord. Did I say a word about voodoo? But ever since we started to work at the zoo, things are getting laid out for us like outlines of a picture we're supposed to figure out. There's part of the story you don't know yet. Before today, did you ever hear of Hermes?"

"Nope."

"Mercury?"

"The planet and the metal but not the god/guy."

"I never heard of Hermes til Friday night. Listen to this." He related the Zeus-Io-Hera-Argus-Hermes story just as he got it from Audrey. Cord never interrupted; he just shot an occasional suspicious side glance. "So, see? She tells me this peacock feather story that's got Hermes right in the middle of it. Then Nozetape springs this hazel wood kink into the deal. We come to the zoo and get in the middle of a chore to catch a peacock killer—"

"Peahen."

"Goddammit, stay with me, Cord. This is all happening while we're mentally kicking around the hazel wood stuff."

"*You're* kicking around the hazel wood stuff."

"Me and Nozetape are kicking around the hazel wood stuff. Then right in the middle of all this, we find out this Hermes plays an important role in both stories—totally separate and running on parallel tracks at the very time we're trying to un-riddle this treasure deal."

Cord laughed and shook his wooly head.

"Come on, Cord. We got a ticket to ride here. Somebody or something's lining things up in our favor. You got to get onboard, broaden your perspective."

"Okay, how's this for another perspective? Nozetape says this treasure would be bad luck for him, right?"

"Yes, and . . . ?"

"He says he thinks it would be bad for us too, right?"

"Yeah."

"What if all this is bait? What if all this ain't being laid out by some good-hearted, fair-minded karma account-keeper that has our welfare in mind? What if we're overdrawn in our karma account and we're heading for a massive payback crack-up? What if we're nothing more than tiny-brained mice livin' it up without a clue that we're about to be lunch for some big, hungry, cold-blooded snake?" Cord got quiet and concentrated on the road.

Hopper let his comments sink in, then laughed. "This can't be a set-up to a bad end."

Cord snorted. "You a lot more sure than the facts justify."

"It's the vibe, Cord. All I'm picking up is good vibes." He crossed his arms and nodded. "This deal is bound to work out for us."

Cord restrained a smile. "*Vibes*, he says. It's all going to work out peachy because *I'm getting good vibes*." He shook his head, still battling the smile. "I swear, Hopper, if all this wasn't so goddam funny, it would be giving me a major case of the creeps."

Hopper leaned back and closed his eyes. "Just embrace the creep, my friend. Look at it like a rainbow with a pot of gold at the end of it 'cause that's damn sure what it'll turn out to be."

Back home, Hopper was eager to bring Nozetape up to date on what they learned about the mysteries of the hazel wand. But as soon as they stepped through the door, Nozetape met them with a worried look. "I'm not sure, fellas, but I think we may have more trouble."

Cord frowned. "What kind of trouble?"

"You know that big guy that works for Ollie—Tiny?"

"Sure, I've known Tiny since we were kids. What's up?"

"He called and told me to have you meet him at the Chisholm Oaks football stadium tonight at seven o'clock. He said it was important for your health."

Cord blinked. "For my health? What the hell does that mean?"

"I don't know, Vernon, but he didn't sound happy."

Cord turned to Hopper. "What do you reckon this is all about?"

Hopper plopped into the oversized yellow beanbag chair. "What happens if Ollie looked that boot over good and noticed the heel came off during a recent surgery? What if he figures we're holding out on him? If he wanted to be sure he knows everything we know, what would he do?"

Cord nodded. "He'd assign Pat, Tiny, and Hub to rough us up and squeeze the facts out of us—all the facts."

"So what's your suggestion? What do you think we ought to do?"

"Be at the stadium at seven o'clock. We can always play dumb about the boot heel. If we show up like curious lambs, that would add some weight to our story."

Hopper ran his fingers through his long blond hair. "Okay, we stick to the story. We know nothing about the missing boot heel. Play it cool. Right, fellas? Maybe that'll throw the suspicion spotlight on Biscuit and Feeney." They all nodded. "Right."

Cord shot him an accusing glance. "What kind of *vibe* are you getting from this deal, buddy?"

Twenty-nine

It was dark at seven o'clock when they pulled into the stadium parking lot. At first, they didn't see Tiny's pickup. He flashed his lights as they drove up. Cord pulled up next to Tiny's vehicle and rolled his window down. "What's up, Tiny?"

Tiny didn't look at them. "Get in."

Hopper was relieved to see Tiny was alone. The worst-case scenario would've involved Tiny, Hub, Ollie, and Pat all waiting with a combination of sharp and blunt instruments in their big hands and mayhem in their icy hearts.

When Hopper slid in next to Tiny, leaving Cord by the passenger door, he felt like a hamburger patty squeezed between two heavy buns. Cord leaned forward so he could see the big man behind the wheel. "Tell us what's going on, Tiny."

"Mom died this afternoon." He put a cigarette to his lips, inhaled, and then drank from the Coors can he held between his legs.

There was real emotion in Cord's voice. "Sorry, Tiny. I always liked your mom."

"I told her you said hello. She didn't understand much at the end. But she smiled when I said your name."

"Is there anything we can do?"

"Two things."

"Just tell us what."

"First, I want you to be a pallbearer at Mom's funeral. None of the other guys ever gave a shit about her. She always liked you. So I hope you'll do it."

"Sure, Tiny. I'd be proud. What else?"

He took another drink. "Watch your ass. Shit's about to get heavy, and I don't know if I can be much help when it drops."

He took another drag from his cigarette. They waited. He didn't say anything. Finally, Hopper took the initiative. "Can you tell us what's coming down, Tiny, and what it has to do with us?"

"You guys ever heard of RICO?"

Hopper and Cord exchanged a quizzical glance. Hopper answered, "I never heard of Rico. Who is he?"

"Not a *he*, a *it*. RICO is a law. It's some kind of federal deal they're using to put a noose around Ollie and Pat's fat necks. Mine too probably. The feds are developing an interest in you guys too."

That statement hit him like a jolt from a cattle prod. Hopper knew he and Cord had been careful about tiptoeing on the right side of the law, especially the federal law. Any talk about federal nooses was bound to cause serious heartburn. "How can that be, Tiny? We haven't done a thing to cause the feds a bit of concern since we left the army. They told us to stay out of sight, and that's what we're doing. We might do a joint now and then but no violations that would make it worth their while to put us in the headlines again. Why would the feds give a shit about us?"

"It's Ollie they're squeezin'. If Ollie tumbles, so does Pat. The Oleg brothers are looking for any door they can find to get out of."

Cord asked, "You got any more of that beer in the truck bed?"

"Yeah, grab yourself a couple and bring me one." Cord slipped out and came back with three cold cans of beer.

He handed one each to Tiny and Hopper and opened the third for himself. "Spell it out, Tiny. We need to know as much as you can tell us."

"Don't know much. Can't tell you everything I know, but you boys are being fitted for the striped britches."

"But like I said, Tiny, we ain't done nothing."

"Don't matter. Ollie's bank accounts are froze, but he hardly ever uses them anyway. He does almost everything in cash. They can keep them accounts froze 'til frogs grow fur coats, and that won't be nothing but a chigger bite on Ollie's ass. They're looking for ways to get him in a vice and squeeze the juice out of him. There are search warrants coming any day, and they'll be looking everywhere to see where Ollie hides his riches—and other stuff. But they don't know where to look, or even what they're looking for, unless Ollie leaves them a trail of breadcrumbs."

There was something dangerous and sinister in the "other stuff" part of that comment. But Hopper wanted to keep Tiny's focus on the most important point. "Help us out, Tiny. What's any of this got to do with us?"

"There's lots of drugs moving through the Blue Buzzard. Ollie and Pat never touch the stuff, but they're pulling the strings. Ollie's looking for somebody to lay it off on, somebody with a profile the feds will recognize."

Hopper's jaws clenched. "He's trying to find a way to hang the Blue Buzzard's drug traffic on me and Cord?"

"He's trying to find patsies for the chopped car parts moving through the yard, the stolen goods moving through the flea market, the unexplained bodies doubling up in the coffins planted by the Victory Funeral Home. There's leaks coming from somewhere, and Ollie's starting to feel the squeeze."

Cord snorted. "If he thinks he can hang anything on us, he's out of his twisted mind."

"Yeah?" Tiny's voice was thick with sarcasm. "What does he need to put you behind bars? Witnesses and evidence. You think he can't find scabs that would swear they buy their stuff from you guys? As for evidence, if I was you, I'd give that bus a real thorough going over—quick. Your house too."

The picture Tiny painted was clear, believable, and frightening. Once the enormity of the situation fully settled in, Cord asked, "Why are you telling us this, Tiny?"

"I guess 'cause Mom died today, and I been thinking. I wasn't much of a son. I done stuff, bad stuff. She hoped I'd make more of myself." He stubbed his cigarette on the palm of his calloused hand. "I could have got on as a driver at the truckyard where Uncle Don, Mom's brother, was a supervisor. I wouldn't have got rich, but I'd have made a good living." He fired up another cigarette. "I didn't get rich anyway." He rolled the window down and spat on the ground, speaking to the dark. "Guess I turned out to be a shitty husband, shitty father, shitty son. Maybe I can do something good here at the end."

"What do you mean by 'the end,' Tiny?" Hopper asked, afraid he knew the answer.

"You guys don't worry about me. I made my bed, now I'll sleep in it. So you fellas go home. Check your bus over good—real good. Check your house too. Be careful. I've done all I can." He rolled his window up and started his engine.

As Hopper and Cord got out, Hopper spoke. "Tiny, can you tell us anything about—"

"I can't tell you nothing about nothing. And I don't need to tell you guys we never had this talk. And, Vernon, Mom's funeral is Tuesday. Call Rhonda for the details." He shifted the truck into first. Hopper closed the door and stepped away. Tiny made a U-turn and stopped, rolling down his window. "Vernon, thanks." He rolled the window up. Hopper and Cord watched his taillights disappear.

Thirty

Hopper tried to untangle things as Cord battled to stay on the safe side of the speed limit. "You got any idea how this happened, Cord?"

Cord's eyes shifted nervously from the road ahead to the rearview mirror. "Just goes to show, if you're walking in the dark, you can step in cow shit no matter how careful you are."

"What the hell is that supposed to mean?"

"It's like you keep trying to make sense of stuff by using karma, re-incarnation, unseen hands, good vibes, and bullshit like that when the truth is life don't have to make sense. Any diagram you come up with that looks like it might explain the arc of things is as unreliable as a god-damn kaleidoscope. Turn it a couple of degrees, and the whole fuckin' thing gets rearranged and refocused. We didn't do nothing to earn it when we was riding high, and we didn't do nothing to bring this on. If we get pulled under, it ain't because we're bad guys, and if we get out, it ain't because we're good guys."

"Well, hell, if that's true, Cord, what's your hurry to get home?"

"We got to check the bus."

"See, that's what I mean. We might not have had a hand in getting ourselves into this jam, but we darn sure have a say in whether we get out of it."

"Well, let's not waste our time debating the ultimate mechanics of the cosmos. Let me hear your thoughts on our situation."

"First, you know Tiny better than I do. How much stock can you put in what he says?"

"Hundred percent. He may be a thug, but he ain't stupid, and he's got no reason to lie to me."

"If that's true, Ollie's behind the eight ball like Tiny says. The law's probably got him cold, and he knows it. So what can he give the badges that might loosen their grip around his throat? He can give them as many other felons as he can manufacture. That way, he looks good by comparison and gets points for helping sweep all the riffraff off the Oklahoma City streets. He'll own up to some piddlin' stuff like chopped car parts and persuade them he's helping them bag the real kingpins."

Cord glanced at the speedometer and eased his foot off the gas. "Meaning he's got to frame somebody else to play the role of kingpin. Meaning, when it comes to the drugs moving through the Blue Buzzard, we might be the kingpin."

They drove quiet, surrounded by the dark, almost empty Sunday-night streets. Hopper broke the silence. "We got no idea what kind of timetable we're looking at. Now we know why Ollie needs to keep us on the payroll at the Blue Buzzard."

"Yeah, and we know why we need to get out of the Blue Buzzard pronto."

"Not so fast, Cord. If we make any sudden moves, Ollie's liable to get nervous and pull a trigger before he intends and before we're ready."

"So what are you saying?"

"Let's do like Tiny said and make sure nothing is planted on the bus or in the house. Then let's dangle the treasure in Ollie's face. If he thinks we're getting close, he won't want us in trouble. He loses his chance to get the gold if we duck out of sight or get locked up. If I know Ollie, his lust for that treasure will throw a shadow over every other plan he has, at least until he's got no choice but to give it up."

Cord groaned. "This is a dangerous game, Hopper. Maybe we ought to just drop everything and break for California now."

Hopper shook his head. "We'd never make it. The bus ain't

roadworthy, and even if it was, we only got the five hundred Ollie gave us for the boot plus the one fifty we got for this week's wages. It ain't enough. If we bolt, we'd be looking over our shoulders for who knows how long. If Ollie makes us interesting enough, a hurry-up trip to California might be just what the feds need to go on a Hopper/Cord roundup. Let's not make anybody nervous 'til we have a plan. We need to figure out how to give ourselves the best chance of staying on the sunshine side of the bars."

Cord nodded. "You're right. Let's get home, give the bus a good looking over, and sleep on our problem."

"Okay. So let's stop at the Del Rancho and get us a couple of chili cheeseburgers. Trying to figure out how to stay a jump ahead of Ollie Oleg makes me hungry."

Thirty-one

The bus was parked in the driveway of a vacant house across the street from their house. They made a thorough inspection using a drop light to look under the hood, under the body, and in every possible hidey hole on the interior. Satisfied that, at least for tonight, no contraband was stashed onboard, they went inside and explained everything to Nozetape.

He ran his fingers through his scraggly beard. "This is bad, fellas. Looks like there's big, dangerous pieces getting moved all over the board, and we don't even know how we got in the game."

Hopper reassured him they'd find an escape hatch. "In the meantime, we could uncomplicate things if we could get our hands on that treasure."

Cord growled, "Sure, that's all we need—a bunch of unexplainable gold we dug up on somebody else's land without letting them know we was looking for it. And if we do find it, how are we going to convert it to dollars without landing us in the soup? And then there's Ollie. He'll be watching us with them snake eyes of his to be sure we don't cut him out. Finding the treasure might not help us at all."

Nozetape nodded. "That's what I been saying. Ever since that gold buckle came in this house, it's like there's a dangerous net being thrown over us. Maybe the first step in us finding a way through this maze is to forget we ever heard of the Alimony treasure."

Hopper laughed. "You couple of sourpusses. You're the only guys I know that can find the dark side of finding treasure. Tell you what. I'll find it, and if you two don't want any of it, no hard feelings."

Nozetape gave a vigorous nod. "Okay by me."

Cord gave a fake chuckle. "Yeah, right."

Hopper started down the hall toward the telephone. "You guys talk it over. I'm going to call Eva and see if there's anything she can tell us."

She sounded sleepy when she answered the phone. "Hello, who is this?"

"Eva, were you already in bed, baby? Sorry if I woke you."

"You can make it up to me by coming on over to keep me warm."

"I thought that was Cord's job."

"Bring him with you."

"Listen, Eva, not counting the deal with Pat on Friday night, have you noticed anything weird going on around the Blue Buzzard?"

There was an uncomfortable silence on the other end of the line. "Like what?"

"Anything, Eva, anything that might cause me and Cord to be on the lookout."

Another pause. "Who you been talking to?"

Hopper felt an alarm bell echoing somewhere. "Come on, Eva, be a pal. Just tell me if you know something that would give us a reason to be more on our toes than usual." For a second, Hopper thought the line went dead.

"Swear to God, Hopper, swear to God you won't repeat not one peep of what I'm about to tell you."

Hopper was disturbed by her uncharacteristic need for reassurance. "Jesus, Eva, you know you can trust me."

"Swear to it."

"Okay, I swear to God I won't repeat one word of what you tell me unless you say it's okay."

"There was a narc in the place just before Christmas."

"How do you know it was a narc?"

"Because they beat it out of him, that's how."

"Who did?"

"Don't ask me any questions. Just listen."

"Okay, Eva, go ahead."

"There was this narc buying stuff in the place just before Christmas. He turned up missing. Later, some suits with badges showed up to talk to Pat. He took them back to his office. They talked awhile and then left. After that, Pat told me to be damn sure I didn't know nothing about no narc. I told him not to worry. But then I got a visit from the same guys. They was at my house at the crack of dawn. I told them I didn't know nothing, but they didn't believe me. They told me if I changed my mind and decided to talk, they'd guarantee my protection. But if I knew something and didn't talk, I might be an accessory if it turned out there was crimes committed."

"Did you tell Pat about this visit?"

"Didn't have to. They told him they was going to talk to me." She lowered her voice to a degree barely audible. "Something's happening. Pat and Ollie are planning something big, and they're super-paranoid. It's just a feeling, Dale, but I think they're moving stuff, like they're getting ready to liquidate and split."

"You think they're going to leave town or something?"

"I don't know, Dale. I've already said more than I can back up. Take it for what it's worth."

"Can you think of any reason why Cord and me should be worried?"

"Pat hates your guts. I don't know why. I don't know how far he'd go to do you guys some damage. But if he had the chance and thought he could get away with it, he'd skin you both."

"Thanks for the lowdown, Eva. Now how much of this can I tell Cord and Nozetape?"

"Make sure they know to keep everything to their damn self. I don't know how thin the ice is I'm skating on."

"If you feel the ice crackin', Eva, let me know. I'll find a way to help. You got my word." Again he thought the line went dead. "Eva, you there?"

"There's something else."

"Okay, I'm listening." He heard her sniffing like she was crying. "What is it, Eva?"

"I'm afraid I might have done something to put you and Vernon in a jam. I could kick myself for not telling you before."

Hopper shifted the phone to his other ear. "You gotta tell me everything, Eva. We need to know exactly what's the score."

"I'm sorry, Dale. I didn't know . . . "

"Come on now, Eva. Get hold of yourself and tell me what you've done. It's going to be okay, I promise. But you have to spell it out."

She sobbed, then sighed, then cleared her throat. "Remember how you got the job at the zoo?"

"Sure, we answered a want ad."

"Remember where you got that want ad?"

"Yeah, you showed it to us."

"Pat told me to give it to you. He wanted you guys working there. He told me to persuade you to answer the ad."

"How did Pat know we'd get the job? There were other applicants."

"I don't know. He just told me to be sure you both applied for that job. It was like he knew you were going to get on."

Hopper's memory spun back through the chronology. Eva gave them the ad. They filled out an application. They got a call to set up the interview. They sat down with a guy from personnel. He called them the same day and told them they had the job and should report to work on Tuesday. If Pat had a hand in getting them hired, he must have contacts at the zoo higher on the food chain than Feeney.

Eva was whimpering. "I should have told you. You should have known that Pat had an interest in getting you on the zoo payroll."

Hopper controlled the urge to chew her out for keeping them in the dark about schemes that might involve them in Ollie's machine. Hell, they were supposed to be friends. "I guess Pat ordered you not to tell us."

"Yes."

"Did he threaten you, Eva?"

She moaned, "Yes."

"Listen, sweetie, don't worry about a thing. Me and Cord are big boys, and we was about to put two and two together anyway. We would have figured it out even if you didn't tell us. You go on back to sleep, and let's forget about this conversation."

"I'm afraid, Dale. You remember Bennie from the pipe yard?"

"Sure, why?"

"The day after that big snowstorm, he got picked up and questioned by the same guys that talked to me."

"Yeah?"

"That afternoon, the hydraulics on his forklift failed, and he got crushed by a load of pipe."

Hopper felt himself choking. "He's dead?"

"Yeah."

"Do you know what he was questioned about?"

"All I know is he mentioned your names."

"And you know this how?"

"'Cause those same two guys came back and tried to pressure me into telling them something more. They said it looked like somebody monkeyed with Bennie's forklift to fix it where the hydraulics wouldn't hold. They said something about . . . murder." She sobbed. "You don't think Pat and Ollie would go that far? They wouldn't . . . would they?" Before Hopper could think of something to say, she babbled on. "I don't know what they're up to. I don't know how I got so messed up in this quicksand."

"Leave it to us, Eva. We're gonna hogtie them fat bastards with their own goddam rope."

"I'm so sorry, Dale."

"Don't fret about it, darlin'. Go to sleep and leave it to us."

When he hung up, he drilled into Cord and Nozetape how critical it was for them to keep a tight lid on what he was about to tell them. It really wasn't necessary as neither man was apt to shoot off his mouth if a loose lip might land Eva in a tight spot. He related everything she told him.

Cord, frowning, rested his chin on his palm and concentrated on a spot on the living room wall. Nozetape hobbled back and forth across the shag carpet, his hands clasped behind him. Hopper let the facts sink in before he spoke.

"We're dangling over a pit, boys. The Oleg brothers want us at the zoo for a reason. We know now they want us at the Blue Buzzard so they can pin their drug doings to our ass. What possible reason could they have for getting us hired at the zoo? And who, besides Feeney, is their contact there? Got to be somebody with enough pull to get us hired."

Cord scratched his jaw. "The only reason they'd want us there is to pin some other illegal bullshit on us. Has to have something to do with Feeney's shenanigans and someone higher up's gotta be involved."

Nozetape stopped pacing. "So what do we do?"

Hopper answered, "We play our hand. We got eyes. We got ears. We got brains. And we're starting to get information. The monkey wrench in Ollie's works is the treasure. He'll string things out to the last possible minute as long as he thinks there's a chance he'll get his fat, greedy hands on that gold."

Cord grumbled, "I just hope we're still around when the curtain comes down on Ollie's play."

Thirty-two

Monday, January 29, 1973

On the way to work, Hopper and Cord ran through the list of problems piling up and kicked around the roster of possible solutions. Hopper asked, "What would be the downside of sitting down with Ollie and everybody putting their cards on the table?"

"You think he'd admit to scheming on how he can fit us out for the rap on his drug business? If we tell him we know, he's going to want to know how we found out. And if we don't come clean, we got no control over where his suspicions alight. He'll get around to focusing on Eva for sure."

Hopper nodded. "So we play dumb until he decides it's time to spring the trap?"

"Doesn't sound too smart, does it?"

"No, it doesn't."

"How will we know if things are getting out of control?"

"Hopefully, you can keep Tiny talking, and I think we can trust Eva to tell us as much as she can."

At the shop, Buntz was charging around like a mobile air compressor, barking orders and checking progress. Podd was hosing down the interior of the pickup that got muddy placing the trap. Hopper heard him asking Buntz, "What did you do this weekend to get this dang truck so dang muddy?"

Buntz answered on the move. "Don't have time to discuss it now, Podd. Just get that truck hosed off. It don't have to be spotless; just get it clean enough we won't be embarrassed if Mr. Neyland drives by." He signaled to Hopper and Cord. "You two come with me."

Hopper saw the resentful expression on Podd's face. He offered Podd a friendly wave as the three of them piled onto Buntz's golf cart and backed out. As they approached the north gate, Buntz unhooked his keyring and handed it to Hopper. "Unlock the gate and lock her back when we're through."

They rolled around the zoo's southeast corner, and Buntz jammed on the brakes. "You two guys wait here. If we spot our culprit, you can come and help me get him down. Then we'll take care of it."

He bounded off the cart and waded into the tall grass. He scurried over to the pipe fence and disappeared toward the trees. After a couple of minutes, he returned, shaking his head. "No takers. Hopefully, he's just not hungry. Maybe next mealtime he'll come by for an easy lunch. Now we got to get you guys over to the forty. This may be your last day on the hackberries. I'll flag some hazel trees. Maybe you can start bare-rooting them tomorrow. You can do them just like the hackberries. I think we only got a dozen or so, so we may be able to start moving some persimmons later in the week."

Buntz headed the golf cart back toward the shop. He was talking about the challenges of growing eucalyptus in the greenhouse when they pulled into the parking lot. He dropped them at their pickup and darted away—still talking.

Thirty-three

They'd been on the forty for about an hour when Hopper heard a rustling in the trees. The rustling was punctuated by an occasional deep cough. He stopped digging and watched Finn stride out of the forest surrounded, as usual, with an aura of something ancient, unpredictable, and incomprehensible. Hopper waved. "Hey, Finn, glad to see you, old-timer. I brought you an orange."

Finn marched up to them with a paper bag in his gnarly outstretched hand. Cord leaned on his shovel as Finn pushed the bag forward. "I brought these for you."

"What did you bring us this time, Finn?"

"Filberts."

Hopper took the sack and looked inside. He carried it back to Cord, a broad smile on his face. "Know what these are?"

Cord looked inside. "Sure, they're filberts."

"Know what else they're called?"

"No idea."

"These are hazelnuts, buddy. Hazelnuts. From the legendary hazel tree. That wonderful tree that gave Hermes his magic rod. That same tree that people have been using to find minerals and treasures for ages." He turned his bright smile to Finn. "Did you gather these filberts somewhere near here?"

The old man nodded and pointed back into the forest.

"Have you had these for a long time?"

"Gathered them last fall."

"What made you bring them to us today?"

"Because this is the day you're supposed to get them. Can I have the orange?"

Hopper reached out to slap Finn on the shoulder, but the old man recoiled. "You're not going to take me away, are you?"

Hopper dropped his hand. A sad envelope formed around his heart. "No, Finn. Like I said before, we wouldn't take you anyplace you didn't want to go."

"Okay. I'll take the orange now." He followed Hopper to the truck.

Hopper got the orange from the lunch pail and tossed it to Finn, who made a two-handed catch. Hopper leaned on the truck as Finn peeled the orange with a long, grimy thumbnail and put the rind in his coat pocket. "Hey, Finn, let me ask you something. When I asked you if you knew anything about a tiny boot out here, you sort of acted like you knew something."

Finn nodded as he bit into the juicy orange, his eyes closed in ecstasy.

"Tell us about it, Finn. What do you know?"

"It belongs to the little fella that lives out here with me."

The remark caught Hopper off guard. "What do you mean by that, Finn? Is there someone else living out here? What's that got to do with . . . with the little boot?"

The old man doubled over in a fit of severe coughing. Hopper hurried to his side and put a hand on his shoulder. This time, Finn didn't draw away. "Listen, Finn, you're burning up. You need to let us take you to the VA hospital. You got your military ID, discharge orders, or DD-214?"

The old man shook his head and stood up with his hand over his mouth. Droplets of orange juice and blood flecked his beard. With his hand over his mouth, he squinted to the east. "Who's that?"

Hopper saw Audrey park her Jaguar by the gate and begin a careful walk over the uneven ground in their direction. Hopper laughed. "That lady is discovering how hard it is to walk up here with high-heeled boots. That's Audrey Kroneson."

"Audrey?"

"Yeah, Audrey Kroneson."

Finn wiped his beard with his palms, looked at his hands, and wiped them on his coat. "I have to go now. Thanks for the orange." He spun and began his hurried march back into the woods.

Hopper yelled after him, "What about the boot, Finn?"

"It's here," and he was gone.

Cord, scratching his head, watched Finn disappear. Hopper left the pickup and went to meet Audrey. "What brings you into the wilderness amongst the savages?"

She smiled and waved a greeting that warmed Hopper like a ray of sunshine through a window pane. She shouted as she approached, "I came to apologize—again. Abbie told me about the unpleasantness with the guard. In a way, I'm relieved, though. I was afraid you just changed your mind and stood us up."

Hopper laughed. "I may be rough, Audrey, but I ain't rude. I'm willing to give the guard another chance to let us through. "

"I think I can guarantee you'll get that chance." She continued to make her awkward way over the uneven ground. Hopper was amused. Even her stumbling was a thing of beauty. As she drew nearer, she spoke again. "In addition to the apology, I wanted to ask you something. It's about Miss Christmas. Have you met her?"

"Nope."

"She is the curator for the greenhouse. She's been here at the zoo almost longer than anyone. We're having a birthday party for her Friday. She loves Bob Wills and Hank Williams. We thought maybe you wouldn't mind serenading her."

By then, Audrey was standing directly in front of him. The heels on her boots added enough height to bring them almost eye to eye. The south wind blew her ponytail over her right shoulder. He tried not to imagine what it would be like to touch the spot where her delicate jaw joined her graceful white neck. He cleared his throat. "We'd be honored to serenade Miss Christmas on her birthday."

She brushed the unruly ponytail away from her red lips. "Don't you need to check with Vernon?"

"No need. He may be unpredictable sometimes, but where playing music is concerned, he'll do it."

"Would a hundred dollars be enough? We only have an hour."

He laughed and shouted over his shoulder, "Hey, Cord, the lady says they'll pay us fifty dollars if we'll play some old-time country for an hour on Friday. What do you say?"

Cord shouted back, "Tell her to make it sixty."

Audrey put her long fingers over her mouth and restrained a girlish laugh. Then she shouted over Hopper's shoulder, "You drive a hard bargain, Vernon, but it's a deal." She favored Hopper with a flirtatious wink. "Come to the administration building a few minutes before noon. And thank you." She turned back toward her Jaguar. She waved as she walked away. "Bye."

He stood in awe, watching her go. He couldn't imagine a ballerina on earth with charms to match those of the Kroneson twins. "See you Friday," he shouted after her.

When Hopper rejoined Cord at the pickup, Cord was still scratching his head. "You think that old-timer really knows anything about that other boot? And what do you think he meant about some little fella living out here with him?"

"We'll just have to keep his attention focused long enough to get some straight answers."

"You think we ought to go see if we can find him and try to get to the bottom of it now?" Cord asked.

"No."

"Why not?"

"Because here comes Buntz." Hopper watched as Buntz's golf cart bumped along the rough ground leading up to the forty. He stopped the cart, locked the brake, and jumped off with a roll of orange tape in his hand. "You boys come with me. I'll mark the hazels. They're smaller than hackberries. I think there's only about a dozen in here, so you ought to be able to get them out in one day." He strode into the woods, Hopper and Cord a few steps behind.

Cord spoke to the back of Buntz's head. "I'm going to need to take a couple hours off tomorrow."

Buntz whirled. "What do you mean you need to take off? We don't have time for you to be taking off right now."

"I got to go to a funeral."

"Your mom died?"

"No."

"Then you don't need to be there." Buntz resumed his walk into the woods.

"Let me put it to you like this, Buntz. I promised to be there, so I'll be there. I expect I'll be back right after lunchtime."

Buntz stopped and took a deep breath. Without looking back, he said, "I suppose Hopper has to go to this funeral too."

Hopper walked up to his side and clapped him on the shoulder. "Nope. I'll be here on the job bright and early. They got all the pallbearers they need on this deal."

Buntz looked over his shoulder at Cord. "Why didn't you tell me you were a pallbearer?"

"Didn't think it made any difference."

"Well, it does. I'll cover for you. You get here as quick as you can."

"Okay, Buntz. And thanks for being, you know . . . so understanding."

Buntz cleared his throat. "Forget it. Come on, let's go. And you guys stay close to me, okay?"

Buntz put orange tape on ten hazelnut trees. Hopper was surprised. They looked more like overgrown shrubs than trees. Buntz chattered the whole time about the virtues of these trees, the value of the nuts, its importance in Norse mythology, its hardiness. By the time they were through, Hopper knew that, according to Norse and Teutonic myth, hazel wood was sacred to Thor, their thunder god. "Among the Irish, the hazel was respected as the tree of wisdom."

Hopper was fascinated. "So these ancient people believed plants had stories and magical powers?"

Buntz nodded. "People started worshiping the power of plants probably thousands of years before they invented writing."

"How come they stopped? I mean today you never hear anything about the stories behind plants."

"This is what happens when people get too far from the soil. They lose interest in old-fashioned stuff like moon phases, planting cycles, pollination, harvests, and fertilization. Ancient beliefs and stories run themselves through the soil you're standing on and up through the soles of your feet and into your brain. They can make you feel yourself drifting into a kind of worship, I guess you'd call it. You got to watch it when that happens." He mumbled under his breath, "That's probably the devil's doing."

On the way back to Buntz's golf cart, they paused long enough for him to point out a persimmon tree. They groaned as he began to extol the tree's marvels and importance to Japanese culture. "In ancient time, it was their symbol for victory."

Hopper asked, "Hey, Buntz, I don't mean to interrupt here, but did you ever get a chance to straighten out that Feeney character?"

Buntz gave them both a solemn eye and continued toward his cart. "I don't know, fellas. I ain't the gossiping kind. But there's something funny about that egg. I'm not sure what he's up to, but I'm damn sure it's got something to do with them snakes he loves so much. I'm okay with all the little green garden snakes and rat snakes. I'm even okay with an occasional bull snake. They cut down on the mouse and rat population. But, hell, in that damn snake house, they got an albino cobra that's sixteen feet long—sixteen feet. That bastard can raise enough of his body off the ground so he can look a fella in the eye." He shivered as they walked. "They got snakes in there that's so big they feed on whole goats.

And that Feeney, if I ever saw a guy that oughta be working in a snake house with big snakes and lizards, he's that guy. Anyway, he says he won't give you any more trouble about that treasure nonsense."

Hopper took a chance. "You ever heard of a guy named Ollie Oleg?"

Buntz shook his head. "Never heard of him. What's he got to do with anything?"

"He and Feeney got something going, and we don't know what it is."

Buntz nodded. "If you boys know what's good for you, you'll stay as far from Feeney's business as you can. I don't know who this Ollie fella is, but if he's got doings with Feeney, I've heard as much about him as I need to."

They were back at his golf cart. "Let's get back to work. See you guys at the shop this afternoon."

When Buntz was gone, they returned to one of the hazel trees and found a branch that had about three feet of smooth wood before it forked. They cut it, and Cord carried it to the pickup.

Hopper grinned, "Now that you know that hazel wood's got magical powers and can generate wisdom, how does it feel to be carrying a branch in your hand? You feeling smarter and better-looking?"

"That ain't exactly how I'd describe it. More like foolish and borderline desperate comes closer to it. Here, you take it."

When Cord threw him the hazel wand, Hopper knew it must be his imagination; all Nozetape's mumbo-jumbo bridged over to Buntz's "ancient" this and "mystery" that. He'd be surprised if his mind didn't play tricks on him when his hand touched the hazel wood.

He felt a smile spread across his face. "Cord, I believe this hazel wand is going to lead us to the treasure."

Thirty-four

Tuesday, January 30, 1973

Hopper drove the Rambler to work on Tuesday morning. They agreed Cord would drive Nozetape's Karmann Ghia to the funeral. Then Nozetape would bring him to the zoo.

It would be easier if Nozetape just went to the funeral with Cord. But Nozetape was real conscientious about skipping all funerals or any other rituals for the dead. After Vietnam, he was plagued by headaches, nightmares, and depression. The army doctors diagnosed him as suffering from "battle fatigue." But an old Seminole healer told him his problems sprang from his failure to purify himself after being in so much physical contact with death. The healer persuaded Nozetape to undergo a tribal purification ritual involving smoke, herbs, and all-night vigils— problem solved. But part of the cure required Nozetape to stay away from all dead people and rituals relating to the dead for five years.

Cord said it was all superstition. But as far as Hopper was concerned, the proof was in the curative pudding. If it made Nozetape well then it was great medicine.

So Nozetape loaned Cord his car.

As usual, Hopper was the last one in the shop. As he assembled the tools he needed to work on the forty, Buntz approached. "What are you doing?"

"Getting ready to get you some hazel trees out of the west forty."

"You ain't going over there by yourself. Anyway, I got a job I need you to do for me this morning." Disappointing news. Hopper hoped to find old Finn and maybe get more information in a one-on-one chat.

"Really, Buntz, these hazel woods are pretty small. It don't have to be a two-man job. I think I can make some good progress even without Cord."

"I'm sure you could, but Miss Christmas needs help in the greenhouse this morning."

Podd chirped up. "Why don't you let Hopper go on over to the forty all by himself? I'll be glad to give the old lady a hand."

"Why don't you go help Clary load that fertilizer like I told you? I want a good layer of that put on the hydrangea beds across from the bear enclosures."

Podd sulked. "I don't know why these two know-nothin's get all the clean, sweet-smelling jobs."

Clary grumbled, "Yeah, Buntz, what have these fellas got on you that makes you so sweet on them?"

Buntz stalked over to the pickup where Clary was loading bags of fertilizer. He stood inches from the taller, younger man, glaring up into his face. "I don't need to explain a goddamn thing to you, Clary. But I'm going to let you in on my decision-making process here. You're working with chickenshit today because I'm confident that's a job you can handle. Hopper here is helping Miss Christmas because he's got good manners and knows how to behave. I ain't that sure about you."

Clary tensed. Hopper could see there was real danger of this getting out of hand. "Hey, Buntz, I might be wrong, but I think Clary is using his conversation with the boss as an excuse to neglect his chickenshit duties."

Clary looked past Buntz and fixed his mirthless smile on Hopper. "I think the day will come when I get a chance to take this up with you somewhere off the job."

Hopper smiled back. "Can't wait, Clary. But I hope you clean up first so I don't get that chickenshit smell on my hands while I'm thrashing you around."

Clary's smile disappeared. Hopper laughed loud and happy. "Come on, Buntz, let's me and you go to the greenhouse."

Buntz, mumbling, led Hopper to the golf cart. On the way to the greenhouse just north of the administration building, Buntz started to rave about Miss Christmas's kindness, sensitivity, and knowledge of plants. "She's never been married. Worked here since the thirties, started as a teenager. She's a sweet old lady. You'll like her."

He stopped the cart in front of the massive, hangar-shaped green-house dominating the southwest corner of the zoo premises. Hopper followed as Buntz charged through the door. Buntz immediately re-moved his watch cap and stuffed it in his pocket. A white-haired lady that could have stepped out of a Norman Rockwell postcard looked up from the exotic flower she was bending over with an old-fashioned wa-ter can. "Good morning, Lester."

Buntz dropped his eyes like an embarrassed schoolboy. "Good morning, Miss Christmas. Dale here volunteered to help you out this morning."

Hopper stepped forward, extending his hand. "I'm Dale Hopper. Very pleased to meet you, Miss Christmas."

Her clear blue eyes sparkled as she raised her right hand swathed in bandages. "Sorry I can't shake your hand, Dale, but as you see, I've had a mishap."

Hopper blushed. "I'm sorry. I didn't notice."

"Think nothing of it, Dale. It's kind of you to offer your help today. I'm afraid I can't lift much anymore even if I don't have to contend with an injured paw." She regarded her bandaged hand and smiled.

Buntz cleared his throat. "Well, I got to get going, Miss Christmas. You keep Dale as long as you need him. I'll check back later to see how things are going."

"Thank you, Lester. I shouldn't think this would take very long."

Buntz donned his watch cap and headed for the door.

Miss Christmas patted Hopper's shoulder with her left hand. "Now, Dale, if you would put that bag of potting soil on this worktable, we can get started."

"Yes, ma'am." Hopper did as she instructed. At her direction, he opened plastic bags containing aromatic collections of beautiful flowers and colorful plants.

Miss Christmas prattled about the origin of each package as Hopper helped place the contents in pots containing plant food and rich soil. "These lovelies are proteas from the slopes of Haleakala in Hawaii; these are orchids from the rain forests of Uganda, and here we have . . . " She offered him a tumbler of iced tea, at least he thought it was tea of some kind, though the flavor was rich and exotic.

The greenhouse atmosphere reminded Hopper of the Vietnamese tropics. Occasionally, mist jetted from nozzles located throughout the building. The air was thick with tropical aromas. The translucent walls dripped condensation. The pleasant singsong quality of Miss Christmas's voice, the occasional hissing of the misters, the weight of the warm, constricting atmosphere lulled Hopper into a state of pleasant intoxication.

He moved around the greenhouse in a dream state, cheerful and robotic, complying with Miss Christmas's instructions and responding to her occasional questions with a serene detachment, like his perfectly obedient body was somehow separated from his curiously observing mind.

"Do you know what yesterday was, Dale?"

"Let's see . . . January twenty-ninth, wasn't it?"

"Yes. It was also the feast day of St. Fiacre. Do you know who he was?"

"No, ma'am."

"He's the patron saint of gardeners and those who grow medicinal plants."

"I didn't even know there was a patron saint for those folks."

She lit the area around her with a motherly laugh. "Oh my goodness, Dale, there's a patron saint for everyone."

"So how do you get to be the patron saint of gardeners?"

She asked him to hand her some garden shears and began to trim dead leaves from a collection of plants she called "money trees." "For centuries, the church was suspicious of those who used medicinal plants to cure disease. Such healers were suspected of dabbling in witchcraft. Saint Fiacre was a remarkable gardener who used his knowledge of healing plants to help cure the sick. He was so successful that he was accused of witchcraft. He might have been executed but for the intercession of St. Faro, his supervisory bishop."

"You mean a guy could get killed for using plants to cure people?"

"Surely. In fact, many women who relied on traditional medicine weren't as fortunate as St. Fiacre and didn't have the protection of a bishop. Large numbers of them were found guilty of witchcraft and executed." Her laugh was like the tinkling of bells. "Where are my manners? Could I get you something else to drink?"

She poured him another tumbler of tea. "Amazing how the mist and condensation in here furnishes almost all the moisture one needs. You'd be surprised how much nourishment we absorb through our skins."

Hopper shook his head and smiled. He liked getting his nourishment the regular way. He wondered if people who spend most of their time working with plants, like Buntz and Miss Christmas, just naturally believed there were powers and mysteries in green things.

"Did you know that plants enjoy music? They do. People don't realize that plants have preferences. Human beings are perfectly willing to grant that plants have needs like water and soil. But people find it hard to accept that plants may also have desires."

Hopper surveyed the array of exotic flowers, vines, leaves, and stalks and tried to imagine how a plant would express its desires if it had some. "Have you discussed this with Buntz?"

"Oh, most certainly. Lester has an uncanny ability to sympathize with plants. I'm afraid Lester Buntz would have been under grave suspicion if he'd lived during St. Fiacre's day. Well, speak of the angels. Here he is now."

Buntz stepped into the greenhouse, removing his watch cap. "Everything okay, Miss Christmas?"

"Everything is peachy, Lester. Thank you for lending Dale to me this morning. You can have him back now." She extended her left hand. "Would you remove my glove, please?" Hopper carefully removed the cotton work glove. She offered her pale, calloused, blue-veined hand. "Thank you, Dale. It was a pleasure working with you. I hope to see you again soon."

Hopper smiled. "Count on it, Miss Christmas."

Thirty-five

Cord showed up at Sooner Park Church of Christ at 9:50, just like Rhonda said. Two gray-faced employees of the Victory Funeral Home greeted him when he stepped into the sanctuary. Tiny's sister, Rhonda, huddled in a black-clad tearful trio with Beulah and Bertha, Mrs. Lucan's two sisters.

The bulging contours of Rhonda's big body stood out with unpleasant detail in the unnecessarily tight black dress. She started to cry half a dozen steps before she reached Cord. He braced for the soggy prolonged hug he knew was coming. She sobbed as she crushed against him, flinging her heavy arms around his neck.

"Mom is gone, Vernon. She's gone." He put his arms around her in an awkward hug. Rhonda sniffed. "At least her suffering's over. She's in a better place now."

Cord, trying to ignore the tobacco and beer fumes contending with her perfume, patted her big back. She sniffed some more. "Thank you for being here, Vernon. She always liked you."

"She was a good woman, Rhonda." He looked around the church. "Where's Tiny?"

She blinked and studied him with a confused look. "He ain't with you?"

"I haven't seen him since Sunday night."

"You sure?"

"I haven't seen him since Sunday night, Rhonda."

"Well, he ain't been home, and he ain't been with us. Where do you suppose he is?"

"How do you know he hasn't been home?"

"Because we been over there several times, and we keep calling, but he don't answer."

"Was his pickup in the drive?"

"No."

"When was the last time you talked to him?"

"He called me Sunday after he talked to you."

"You have any idea what Tiny's been up to, Rhonda?"

She shook her head, a shredded tissue pressed to her nose. "He's been really upset about Momma. You know Tiny; he don't show his emotions, but I could tell it was bothering him. He works six days a week over to the salvage yard from sunup to sundown, sometimes later."

Cord shook his head. "I don't get it, Rhonda. It's unlike Tiny to stay away from you and your aunts at a time like this." He scratched the back of his neck. "Look, I'm not trying to stick my nose in anybody's business, but do you know whether anything was bothering Tiny other than your mom's health?"

She bit her lower lip. "Not that I know of, Vernon."

On a whim, Cord asked, "Have you talked to Ollie lately?"

Sniffling, "Mr. Oleg called to offer his condolences. Those beautiful flowers behind Momma's casket are from Mr. Oleg and his brother."

"Has Ollie asked about Tiny?"

Rhonda blinked at him, red-eyed. "No, he hasn't."

"If he does, don't mention that I talked to Tiny Sunday night."

"But—"

"It's important. Just keep it to yourself, okay?"

"If you say so, Vernon."

Cord looked at his watch. "I got time, Rhonda. I think I'll run over to Tiny's and see if he's there."

Rhonda grabbed a handful of his shirt. "I wish you'd stay, Vernon. We really need a man to be with us."

"I'll be back in twenty minutes."

"Vernon . . . "

"I'll be right back."

He sped the three and a half miles to Tiny's rundown shack in Axel Flats. Tiny's GMC pickup wasn't in the driveway. Cord knocked on the front door and peered through the window. He saw no indication anyone was in the house. He tried the door. Locked. At the rear of the house, there was a disassembled motorcycle scattered in disarray under the dilapidated carport. He knocked at the back door. Nothing.

When he went back to the front, two men in suits were leaning against the Karmann Ghia. They grew tense when he walked to within arm's reach. They both straightened. The shorter man spoke. "Mind if we ask what you're doing here?"

"Looking for someone. What are you doing leaning on my friend's car?"

"Can we see some ID?"

"I answered your question, but you didn't answer mine. What are you doing leaning on my friend's car?"

"We're just resting, mister. Sorry if we upset you. Now can we see some ID?"

Cord reached into his back pocket. Both men reached into their coats. The tall one growled, "Nice and easy, if you please." Cord removed his wallet with two fingers and withdrew his driver's license. He handed it to the shorter man.

"Now how about if you two show me some ID?"

"So you're Vernon Cord. We've heard of you, Mr. Cord."

"I'm flattered. Now I'd like to know who you fellas are. Maybe I've heard of you. So let's see some ID."

"What are you doing here, Mr. Cord?"

With a blindingly fast move, Cord snatched his identification from the questioner's hand. The shorter man looked stunned. The taller man took a step in his direction.

Cord stepped forward to meet him. "Are we going to have a brawl out here because you stubborn sons of bitches are refusing to identify yourselves?"

"Who says we are?"

"Everybody in this goddam neighborhood will testify to it if it comes to that."

The tall man took another step as the shorter man spoke up. "Let's all calm down. Show him your identification, Smalley." They both produced FBI credentials. "Satisfied, Mr. Cord?"

"John Tillis and Edward Smalley. Never heard of you."

Smalley ground his teeth as he spoke. "Now we have to ask you, as part of an official federal investigation, what are you doing here?"

"I'm looking for Tiny Lucan. His mother's funeral is going to be starting in a few minutes. Me and his sister was hoping he'd be there."

The two agents looked at each other. Tillis spoke. "His sister doesn't know where he is?"

"You'll have to ask her."

"You don't know where he is?"

"Well now, Mr. FBI investigator guy, if I knew where he was, why would I be here looking for him?" Smalley's face reddened.

"How about if we take you downtown for a more detailed chat?" Smalley growled.

"Suppose you wait until after the funeral."

The big man growled again, "Suppose . . . "

Tillis put a hand on Smalley's shoulder. "Where can we reach you, Mr. Cord?" He took a notepad and pen from his inside jacket pocket. Cord gave his address and phone number. "Thank you, Mr. Cord. We'll be in touch."

Smalley stepped away from the Karmann Ghia door. "You run along to your funeral, Mr. Cord."

Cord crawled into the car and rolled the window down. "You got it wrong, Smalley. It ain't my funeral."

Smalley smiled. "Oh, yeah, my mistake."

Cord got back to the church ten minutes before the funeral started.

Thirty-six

Hopper bent over an ax blade, sharpening it with a metal file, when Cord stepped into the shop. The expression on Cord's face made the announcement. There was more trouble. He motioned Hopper to follow him to the coffeepot. Glancing furtively around the area, he asked, "Anyone here?"

"No, what's up?"

"Tiny's missing."

Hopper ran his fingers through his hair. "So he missed his mom's funeral?" Cord nodded. "What do you reckon the story is?"

"All I can say for sure is it's got to be bad. There's more." He related the details of his encounter with Smalley and Tillis.

Hopper exploded. "Shit. Benny talks to the feds and winds up dead. Tiny throws a scare into us and disappears. What the hell is going on, Cord?"

"I don't know, but while he was driving me over here, Nozetape says people are watching the house."

"He know who?"

"Could be the law, could be Ollie's bunch, could be paranoia. I don't know. But he's full speed ahead getting that hazel branch ready. He's got it stripped and dried. He's soaking it in his secret ointment. No telling what kind of hocus pocus he's whispering to it. He's checking on moon phases and figuring when's the best time to give it a try. He sees this treasure deal is the best shot we have at buying our way out of the quicksand we're wallowing around in."

"Well, it's a plan."

Cord asked, "You got a backup in case the branch don't work?"

"Working on it. Let's get our tools together and get over to the forty. Buntz wouldn't let me go over there without you to babysit."

Cord rubbed the back of his neck. "Everywhere we look, people are making maneuvers, and the only plan we're working on is a magic stick that might work if Nozetape does his voodoo right. Correct me if I'm wrong, Hopper, but if a grownup was to analyze our situation, he might say we're acting like desperate stooges."

Hopper laughed. "Well, we're new to the game, buddy. Let's let Nozetape work the magic stick angle, and we'll see if we can come up with plan B."

As they drove to the forty, they kicked around the possible reasons Tiny might miss his mom's funeral. Maybe he was drunk or stoned somewhere. Maybe he was in jail. Maybe he was in a hospital. Maybe he was hiding. Maybe he got hopeless and killed himself. Maybe somebody had him locked up somewhere. Maybe somebody took him out of the picture—permanent.

When they reached the forty, they saw Finn lying against a tall oak. At first, Hopper feared the old man crawled up against the tree and died. He bounded out of the truck and raced to Finn's side. Kneeling, he took the old soldier's hand to feel for a pulse. Finn's eyes fluttered open and darted around, a panicked expression on his weathered features. When he focused on Hopper, he grasped Hopper's collar. "I was afraid you weren't coming back. I have something for you."

Hopper patted the old man's gnarled hand. "Okay, old buddy. You about caused me to have a heart attack. I thought you'd cashed in your chips. You want an orange? I brought you one."

"You need to promise me."

"What is it, Finn? What do you need?"

"You have to promise not to forget me."

The simple, pathetic request caused a lump to form in Hopper's throat. "Hey, Finn, you don't need to worry about that. For the rest of my life when I smell sassafras or see oranges or hazelnuts, I'll think of my old pal Finn."

Cord knelt to look Finn over. "You need to get to a hospital, Finn. You're in bad shape."

Finn struggled to get to his feet, failed, and cast a pleading glance at Hopper and Cord. They grasped his bony arms and helped him to his feet. Finn opened his coat to reveal a wild assortment of rusty license plates, tin cans, twigs, and branches. Hopper felt the air go out of his lungs when he saw, dangling on the right side of Finn's coat, secured with a shoelace, a tiny boot.

Finn offered them a snaggle-toothed grin. "I told you it was here."

Hopper stammered, "Holy shit, Finn, you know what this is?"

Finn nodded. "You two have been real respectful, so I checked with my little pal. He says it's okay for me to give you this. I was afraid you'd never come back. I was afraid I missed my chance."

Hopper reached out to put his hand on Finn's shoulder. At first, the old man started to draw away, but he tentatively relaxed and allowed the contact. "Listen, Finn, you need to see a doctor, or you're not going to last much longer."

Finn stared at them with a blank expression. "Don't matter." He undid the shoelace securing the boot to his coat and handed it to Hopper. It was in much worse shape than the other. Hopper licked his thumb and cleaned the crusted soil from the buckle. He showed it to Cord.

"Finn, this buckle is gold. It's valuable. We can't take it from you; it wouldn't be right."

Finn shook his head. "Obliged. But I got no need for gold. I need a favor."

"What can we do?"

"I need a ride downtown."

Hopper beamed. "That's great, Finn. The University Hospital is down there. We could get them to give you a tune-up. We could hustle you down there right now."

"Skip the hospital. I need to be at the Colcorde building at ten o'clock in the morning."

Hopper and Cord exchanged glances. "No offense, Finn, but if you show up at a fancy office building, they're liable to run you off or lock you up."

Finn snarled. "It's a free country. I did my part to keep it that way. I can come and go where I want."

"Calm down, Finn. Of course you can."

Cord asked, "Why do you need to go there, Finn?"

"I got business. You want the boot or not?"

"Let me get your orange." Hopper went to the pickup and brought back an orange. "Look, Finn, if you want to go downtown, by God, we'll get you there. We'd do it for you boot or no boot. But ten o'clock might be a problem, see . . . "

"I got to be there at ten o'clock."

Hopper thought it over. "If me and Cord can't take you, would you ride with a friend of ours?"

"He won't take me someplace I don't want to go?"

"He'll be here at nine-fifteen tomorrow. Tell him where you want to go; he'll take you."

"Promise?"

"You got my word."

The old man stowed the orange in his pocket. "I like orange peel in my tea." He fumbled in his pocket and came out with a notepad and a pencil. "I don't know your names."

"I'm Dale, and this is Vernon."

Finn scribbled on his notepad. "I don't know your last names."

"Mine's Hopper. His is Cord."

"Hopper and Cord, c-o-r-d?"

"Yep, that's us."

"Thanks." He turned and made his unsteady way back into the woods. Then he stopped and spoke over his shoulder. "What did the girl want yesterday . . . Audrey?"

"She knows we're musicians. She wants us to play some music for her."

Finn nodded. "I'd like you to play for me sometime. I'll see you tomorrow."

Hopper shouted after him, "Think about making a stop at the hospital, okay?" No response.

When Finn was gone, Cord took the boot from Hopper's hand. The ancient leather almost came apart at his touch. He pushed and pulled on the heel. Nothing happened. Hopper held out his hand. "Here, let me try." His efforts to open the boot heel failed as well.

Cord took a thick-bladed folding knife from his hip pocket and began to work on the heel. "Hey, ain't you the one that was so all-fired determined not to do any harm to an artifact?"

"That was before people started disappearing and dying in workplace accidents and federal agents started leaning on Nozetape's car." With some effort, Cord managed to separate the heel from the sole. He mumbled, "They sure as hell built 'em good in Alimony's day." He continued to pry and probe until the heel was disassembled.

Hopper's excitement redlined when Cord removed a badly damaged, deeply soiled page from the boot's hollow heel. A breeze threatened to blow the fragile sheet to tatters. Cord shielded the page with his body and walked to the truck. Hopper gathered the boot's remains and followed.

When Hopper slid into the pickup, Cord was leaning over the old paper spread out on the seat. "It's a map, isn't it?" Hopper asked excitedly.

"It ain't shit, Hopper. It ain't shit." Cord sat up and looked out the driver's window at the brown prairie grass blowing in the north wind.

Hopper bent over the weathered paper. His heart sank. He could see no evidence of any writing or drawing on the aged brown surface—nothing. The paper threatened to disintegrate in his hands as he lifted it near his eyes for closer inspection. There might be a useless smudge here and there, but Hopper could find no trace of a map or any written instructions. He sat back against the seat. "Well, what now?"

Cord sighed. "I don't know. This sort of feels like a dead end. Any ideas?"

"Well, we still got the hazel wand."

Cord burst into mirthless laughter. "Jesus Christ, Hopper, putting our entire collection of fragile goddam eggs in the voodoo basket sounds crazy and dangerous to me."

"You're right, Cord. It's crazy and dangerous. So what basket do you propose we put our goddam fragile eggs in?"

Cord raised his hands in a gesture of defeat.

"Okay, how about we call Ollie tonight and tell him we found the other boot? Let's tell him we got a line on the treasure."

Cord nodded. "I think I see where you're going. Fill in the blanks."

"Let's do it on the move. Buntz deserves some work out of us."

Hopper explained his thinking as they set to work bare-rooting hazelnut trees. "We buy ourselves some time. If Ollie's waiting for us to find the treasure, he might hold off on his plans to dump us in the soup as long as we run a convincing stall."

Cord pulled the top branches of the hazel wood to give Hopper an angle on the tap root. "Ollie's a crafty old thug. Suppose he wants all the information we have so he can dig it up himself? Why does he need to keep us around?"

"You're right. That's a problem we got to solve. How can we stall him without causing him to suspect we're on to him?"

"Well, if we're going to call him tonight, we better have something to say."

Hopper jumped out of the depression left by the fallen hazelnut and squinted to the east. Cord released the tree and stepped to Hopper's side. "What is it?"

"Not sure. Just got the feeling somebody was watching us."

Cord scanned the fence and parking lot beyond. "I don't see anything."

"Me neither."

"Who do you reckon it was?"

"I could be wrong, but I'm guessing there's somebody in the neighborhood that's got ties to Ollie."

"Feeney."

———

At the end of the workday, Buntz motioned Hopper and Cord to follow him outside. "We got a problem."

Cord frowned. "Great. What's our problem this time?"

"The marauder ain't taking the bait. He's probably getting hungry, which means he might be on the prowl again. If he gets another peahen, it's bad for me, and it's bad for you. It cuts down my chances of getting you boys on permanent."

Cord asked, "So how do we solve our problem?"

Buntz didn't make eye contact. "I know it's asking a lot, but how would you fellas feel about doing a little night patrol?"

Cord's mouth hung open, but Hopper seized the opportunity. "We could probably help out for a while, Buntz. Is there any money in it?"

Buntz frowned at his feet. "Well, I'd have to pay you out of my pocket. I can't have Mr. Neyland knowing what's up, and I'd have to run extra wages through payroll. So I'd appreciate if you boys go easy on me."

Cord looked at Hopper with an expression of disbelief. Hopper ignored him. "We couldn't do it Friday or Saturday 'cause we got another job. But maybe we can work something out."

Cord grabbed Hopper by the arm. "Excuse us a minute, Buntz. I need to talk this over with my partner." The last two words dripped sarcasm. Cord pulled Hopper toward the Rambler. "What the hell are you thinking, you maniac? How are we going to spend all night prowling around the zoo looking for a serial peahen killer and still solve our other problems? If you remember, our house just got broke into, and we been warned that somebody might try to plant evidence on us. Why would you want to make things easier for the bad guys by being gone all night?"

Hopper grinned. "You're not seeing the big picture, buddy. If Buntz wants us to watch things at night, that means we get advantages. We get a key to the gate, so we can come and go when we want. We can roam around the zoo at night without anybody watching us. And night access adds some mustard to our pitch to Ollie."

Cord thought a minute. "We'll have to rely on Nozetape to keep the orcs out of our digs."

"Right." They walked back to Buntz, who was fidget-waiting. "One more question. Can we have a key to the shop so we can make coffee?"

Buntz clapped them both on the back. "I wouldn't expect you guys to patrol the zoo all night without coffee. Believe me, you won't be sorry for going beyond the call." He wrestled two keys from his massive keyring, glancing up occasionally to be sure no one was watching. He looked over Hopper's shoulder as he handed Cord the keys. "This one is to the north gate. This one's to the shop. I'll never forget what you're doing." He clapped them on the back again and strolled off, whistling.

Cord looked at the keys in his hand and shouted at Buntz's back, "Hey, Buntz, what are we supposed to do?"

Buntz answered without looking back. "Stop that peahen-killin' marauder."

———

The first thing Hopper did when he got home was call Eva at the Buzzard. He told her about Tiny not being at his mother's funeral and Cord's encounter with Tillis and Smalley. "Yeah, that's the same two that questioned me."

"Did the feds leave you a card?"

"Yeah, I'm supposed to call if I remember something."

"Give me the number."

"I don't have it here. It's at home."

"When you get home, call and leave the number with Nozetape."

"What's going on, Hopper? I'm afraid I'm going to flip out over all this."

"Just act normal. Me and Cord will get everything all sorted out. I got to go now. We'll talk soon."

"But—"

He hung up and looked at his watch: 6:15. Ollie would still be at the salvage yard. He dialed the number. Hub answered. "Is Ollie there?"

"Yeah, who's calling?"

"It's Dale Hopper."

"Now ain't that a coincidence? Me and Pat was going to drop by and see you guys tonight."

"Put him on the phone. I'll save you fellas a trip."

Ollie came on the line. "Hello, Dale." The voice was thick with friendliness. "I hear Vernon was at Mrs. Lucan's funeral today. Tiny wasn't there, I hear. He ain't showed up for work in a couple of days. Any idea where he might be?"

"Sure don't, Ollie. Odd that he wouldn't come to his own mom's funeral."

"Yeah, it is. But I thought Tiny might be developing a drug problem. He's been acting, you know, spacey lately, and you know how them druggies get."

"I heard he drank a bit, but I never heard he did any drugs. Maybe a little pot."

"See, that's what I mean. You start with a little pot, then you use a little more, then a little more. Next thing you know, you're missing your own mom's funeral. Say, when's the last time you saw Tiny?"

"At your place this weekend."

"You didn't see him after that?"

"No."

"He didn't come by your place, or you guys didn't meet up somewhere for a skull session?"

"No, Ollie, I didn't see him after we left your place."

"Did he call you up for a little chat?"

"No, we haven't seen or talked to Tiny since we saw him at your place on Saturday."

"How about Vernon? He see or talk to Tiny?"

"No, Ollie, neither of us has seen or talked to Tiny."

"How would you know whether Cord has?"

"Because we discussed the fact Tiny missed his mom's funeral, and Cord said he hadn't seen or talked to him."

"No idea where he is?"

"Goddam, Ollie, let's get this out of the way once and for all so we can get down to business. Me and Cord ain't seen Tiny, and we got no idea where he's at. Okay?"

"Okay, Dale, okay. We're just worried about him, that's all. So what is this business we need to discuss? Tell me you found the Alimony treasure and your wanting to get together to divvy up the boodle."

"Don't have it yet, Ollie, but we're closing in."

"You're shitting me. You really think you know where it's at?"

"We don't know exactly, but we think we know how to find it."

"You're shitting me. How you gonna find it?"

"We got a map."

A loud laugh exploded on the other end of the line. "A map. Hell, I got a map. I got three or four of them. I would have sold you one of mine for half what you paid for the one you got."

"The one we got was in the boot." The laughter ended so abruptly that Hopper thought the line went dead. "You there, Ollie?"

"There was a map in the boot you sold me?"

"There was a map hidden in the heel of that boot."

The voice was congenial, as usual, but there was something lethal in the undertone. "So you pulled a fast one on old Ollie, huh? You sold me a boot after you filched the map out of it and didn't say a word about it to your partner? That wasn't neighborly, Dale."

"Hey, Ollie, let's get something straight. Your little maggot buddies stole that boot. We had no intention of selling it. So don't go bellyaching about the fact we took something out of it before your thieves grabbed it. Fact is, we wasn't sure what it was we found in the boot until today."

"Goddammit, if you told me about it, I could've cleared up exactly what it was. They never found the last three pages of Alimony's diary. He hid them in his boot heel, didn't he? Clever little bastard. So where's the map now?"

"Safe."

"Oh, no, you don't. Don't . . . do not give me 'the map's safe' shit. I want that map."

"Well, you ain't getting it, so let's get down to business."

"Now listen, you little prick—"

"You're not being smart, Ollie. A smart guy wouldn't be calling me names and giving me a reason to hang up the phone and look for another partner."

"Bullshit, there ain't no other partners."

"Well, then, I guess we got nothing to talk about. Bye . . . "

"Wait, wait . . . Okay, I'm listening. Lay it out."

"We got this map, but the landmarks are all identified in a foreign language. We're about to get it translated—"

"I can get it translated for you."

"We're about to get it translated, and we managed to fix it so we can dig up the goods without anybody knowing."

"I'll send out a couple more guys to give you a hand."

"Will you just listen, Ollie? It's possible the treasure's under one of the buildings on the zoo grounds. If that turns out to be the case, we'll have to figure out how to get at it. But if it's someplace me and Cord can dig it up, we're gonna need your help getting the stuff converted to cash. We wouldn't know where to start."

"Fifty-fifty?"

"Don't you want to share?"

"Quit screwing around."

"I get a third, Cord gets a third, and you get a third."

"No dice. I get forty percent."

"You get a third. Deal?"

There was a deep, dangerous laugh on the other end of the line. "Okay, Dale, deal. You drive a shrewd bargain, boy. Maybe I got a job for you when this all gets sorted out. If Tiny don't show up, I got an opening."

"Don't hold your breath. Now we need something from you."

"What?"

"We need a metal detector."

"Sure, I'll bring it right over."

"Don't bother; we won't be here. We're working night shift at the zoo."

"There ain't no night shift."

"I don't have time to explain it now, Ollie. We'll be by the salvage yard this weekend to get the gizmo. By the way, how do you know there's no night shift at the zoo?"

He emitted a deep rumbling chuckle. "What I know and how I know it ain't none of your business. How long do you think it will take you to get the treasure?"

"Depends. Maybe a week, maybe two."

"Two weeks? Can't you get in any sooner?"

"We're trying, Ollie."

"Okay, get it fast as you can. See you Saturday."

"Right."

"Oh, Dale, you got any idea what that treasure's worth?"

"No."

"No one does. There was stuff in Alimony's trunk that nobody knows how to value. But I guarantee, you guys dig it up, and all three of us is richer than kings."

"We got to find it first, Ollie. See you Saturday." He hung up the phone and turned to Cord. "You get that?"

"So you think you bought a couple weeks?"

"No matter how much gold he has piled up, he'd sell his mom to add a few shekels to the pile. We're safe until he thinks we're pulling something or the squeeze gets too tight around his fat throat."

At home, Hopper filled Nozetape in on the other boot and the tattered, useless page they found in the heel. He relayed their agreement to get the old man to the Colcorde building by ten o'clock the next morning. "You come to the west parking lot by nine-fifteen. If Finn has it together enough to be there, we'll get him into the car."

Nozetape nodded. "You got that third page? I'd like to take a look." By then, it was in pieces. They assembled it on the kitchen table. Nozetape studied the frail remains with his magnifying glass. "Nothing. I can't make nothing out of this."

"Looks like we're going to have to rely on your magic hazel wand method."

Cord groaned.

"You got it all ready, Nozetape? Me and Cord have a chance to give it a try tonight."

Nozetape blinked. "You're going to break into the zoo and try the wand tonight?"

"Don't have to break in. We got a key. Buntz wants us to patrol the zoo to protect his peacocks."

"Peafowl," Cord corrected.

Hopper scowled. "Anyway, we might as well do a little prospecting while we're at it."

Nozetape got excited. "Great, I have the wand all prepared. I have two thin pieces of gold wire wrapped around the handles so the wand will know what you're looking for."

Cord groaned again, louder this time.

"Okay, we got to go. Eva's going to call you tonight with a phone number for some FBI guys. Write it down and tell Eva thanks."

Nozetape's mouth hung open. "FBI guys? Why do we need the phone numbers for FBI guys?"

"Because we might need to talk to them. We got to go, Nozetape. See you in the morning." They placed the hazel wand in a pillowcase and headed for the zoo.

Thirty-seven

It was dusk when they arrived at the zoo's north gate. Hopper felt like they were entering a parallel sinister zoo that didn't exist in daylight. His planning of this mission failed to consider that this unfamiliar experience might stimulate unexpected alarms. There were animals in here—big predators and snakes. They were all supposed to be caged, but . . .

As Cord drove the Rambler to the PR parking lot, Hopper noticed the tall lampposts erected at regular intervals throughout the park. He'd never paid attention to these lights before. Measured against the ponderous darkness, crowding in on everything in the zoo, the glowing halos at the tops of these posts seemed weak and shy.

The wind stirring the trees caused crazy shadows to bound, creep, and slither across the walkways. They sat quiet in the darkness.

Cord heaved a deep resigned sigh. "Well, here we are. What's your play, Butch?"

Hopper tried to sound confident. "Well, no matter how cold and scary it is out here, at least we don't have to worry about tripwires, punji sticks, and ambushes." As the Rambler's warmth dissipated, Hopper said, "You ready for this?"

Cord turned the Rambler's radio to KOMA. The Beach Boys sang a happy tribute to Barbara Ann. "I guess we have to be, huh?"

When the song ended, Hopper stepped from the car, took the hazel wand from the pillowcase, and stood in the PR parking lot. Cord walked to his side. Hopper looked from the wand to Cord and back to the wand. "You want to try it?"

"Do I look like an idiot? No, I don't want to try it. This harebrained scheme belongs to you and Nozetape. It's all yours."

Hopper turned the wand over in his hands. " Okay, how do you think we ought to do this?"

"Stick it up your ass and walk backwards, of course. How the hell am I supposed to know?"

"Big help, Cord, thanks." Hopper grasped the forks and pointed the long end at the walkway. He turned right and walked toward the grazing animals area. Cord watched, his hands in his pockets. "You coming?" Hopper shouted over his shoulder as he shuffled down the middle of the sidewalk, waving the wand side to side.

"You know this is ridiculous," Cord yelled as he hurried to catch up.

After a few more steps, Hopper came to an abrupt stop. When Cord stepped beside him, Hopper stared in astonishment at the long end of the wand. "Swear to God, Cord, it jerked. This thing almost jerked out of my hand."

"Bullshit."

"No, really, it jerked toward the lake." Hopper's shoulders twitched. "There, it did it again. Did you see that?"

"I saw a delusional guy stumbling over his own feet."

"Bite it, Cord. This wand jerked toward the lake."

"Well, if it did, you're forgetting an important part of the hocus po-cus. People use these things to find water too. Last time I looked, the lake's full of it."

Hopper cleared his throat. "Yeah, you're right. I got all excited for nothing. Of course the wand would take us to water if it could. We got to get away from the lake to get a clear signal to the gold."

Cord snickered. "Yeah, the lake's interfering with the wand's ability to pick up the gold vibe."

"Laugh it up, buddy; we'll see who's laughing when this wand leads us to the Hogge Hoard." Hopper walked through the grazing animals area, waving the wand. Cord followed, mumbling.

After about twenty minutes, Hopper called out, "Hey, Cord, my hands are cold. Come on up here and take a turn."

"I'm taking no part in this voodoo horseshit."

"Come on, Cord, be a pal. My hands are freezing."

"I'll do it on one condition."

"What?"

"You can never tell anybody I did anything so stupid as skulk around the zoo at night waving a forked stick, expecting it to lead me to a treasure."

"Deal. Now take your turn skulking." Hopper pushed the wand toward Cord, who looked at it in disgust. "Come on, Cord, do your duty."

Cord took the wand and muttered something about insanity. He walked through the wild canine area, waving the wand halfheartedly. As he approached the pachyderm enclosure, he dropped the wand and jumped backward. "Son of a bitch shocked me," he said, looking at his hands as if they might burst into flame.

"Let me see." Hopper shined the flashlight on Cord's palms. "Oh, I get it. This is a joke, right? You're having a little fun trying to get me all excited."

"No shit, Hopper, that thing shocked me."

Hopper picked up the wand and inspected the three ends. He grasped the handles and waved the wand in all four directions. "I don't feel a thing."

"You don't feel a thing because there ain't a thing to feel. I must have had a flashback or something." He looked quizzically at the palms of his hands.

"Yeah, probably a flashback. I'll take over for a while." Hopper continued toward the main entrance, waving the wand. He came to an abrupt stop, the wand pointing into the elephant enclosure. "Did you see that, Cord?" he whispered.

"I'm not sure. What happened?"

"This thing almost jumped out of my hand trying to get in there. Here, you take it and see if it'll do it again."

"No, sir, I've done my lunatic duties for the night."

Hopper propped the wand against the concrete barrier surrounding the enclosure. He leaned on the barrier and stared into the dark exhibit.

"It's in there, Cord," he whispered. "Alimony's treasure is buried in there somewhere. Right now we're standing a few feet from one of the greatest treasures on earth."

Cord leaned on the barrier next to him. "You don't think we let ourselves get all spooky so our imaginations played tricks on us?"

Hopper shook his head. "I don't know what you felt, but I know that stick jerked me toward that place right there." He pointed to the middle of the elephant's outdoor area. "It's pointing us to the treasure, Cord. We're going to be rich, buddy—rich. I was afraid the treasure might be someplace where we couldn't get to it, under a building or something. But all we got to do is get in there with Ollie's metal detector, find the goods, dig 'em up, and, California, here we come."

He put his hands on his hips and jigged expertly up and down the walkway as Cord looked on, a faint smile on his not-so-handsome features. "Gold. There's gold in there, Cord, and," singing, "we're gonna find it, we're gonna find it. We're going to fill our hands, our pockets, our hearts and brains with it." He spread his arms wide, looked up in the dark sky, and shouted, "Thank you, Lord, Shiva, Great Spirit, Buddha, Allah, Mescalito, Hermes, Zeus, or whoever. Whoever knitted all this together to bring us to this spot, we're too grateful for words. And whoever's listening, give our regards to Sir Alimony. Tell him thanks for doing his part to show us the way. Tell him we're real sorry how things ended up for him. But if it makes him feel any better, tell him we'll remember and be grateful as long as we live. Amen. Say 'amen,' Cord."

Cord responded with an embarrassed, "Amen."

"Let's go to the shop and brew some victory coffee."

They decided it was quicker to go around the main entrance and through the petting zoo than go back the way they came. Hopper didn't realize the gate to the petting zoo was locked at night. His elated heart sank a degree or two when he noticed their return to the PR office would take them past the snake house. If Cord gave any indication of being uncomfortable about being so close to that place, Hopper would happily backtrack the long way around.

As they neared the snake house, Cord stopped and gave the fisted combat sign to be still and quiet. Hopper froze. Through the snake house window, they saw flashlight beams darting furtively through the dark. Cord crouched, stepping under a nearby tree, where he was shaded from the overhead light. Hopper followed.

Keeping an eye on the flitting flashlight beam and being sensitive to movements near them, Hopper whispered, "What do you think's going on in there?"

"Something that can only be done in the dark. Let's take a look."

"What for? Jesus, Cord, that place is full of snakes and lizards and shit."

"If I'm right, we might learn something useful. Come on." Cord made good use of the natural cover as he warily approached the herpetarium. Hopper stayed close behind, making sure no one—or nothing—was creeping up behind or on either side.

While Hopper guarded their rear and flanks, Cord eased forward, peering through a window. After a few seconds, he motioned Hopper to follow. They made their careful way past the aquatic mammal exhibit. Safely away from the snake house, Hopper asked, "What's up, Cord?"

"Looks like Feeney is pilfering reptile food and eggs. I'll bet my ass he and Ollie are in the black-market snake and lizard business."

"Is there money in that? I mean who buys black-market snakes and lizards?"

"I got no idea. But for damn sure, if Ollie's got a finger in it, he's pulling money out of it." He squinted back toward the snake house. "There's got to be some way we can use this. Put your mind to it and come up with something slick and profitable."

"Can do. Now I'm freezing and feeling like there's snakes everywhere. Let's get to the Rambler and warm up."

Thirty-eight

Hopper dreamed he was rowing Audrey on a beautiful tropical river. The air was rich with fragrances of exotic flowers. Bright blossoms decorated the heavy canopy of vines and broad leaves on both banks. The black bikini she wore didn't do much to conceal her feminine charms. She smiled seductively from the shade of a broad-brimmed straw hat. She extended her graceful hand, and a gorgeous, delicately colored Vietnamese Mandarin swallowtail butterfly alighted on her palm. She laughed when the butterfly fluttered from her hand and brushed Hopper's nose with a whispery wing before flitting off into the jungle. She leaned forward and whispered, "Dale, I need to tell you something." He moved his ear near her gorgeous lips, hoping to hear her declaration of affection. "We're about to go over a waterfall."

He bolted up, rubbing his eyes, confused, disoriented. "Where the hell am I?" He saw Cord sitting in a folding chair at the card table, head back, snoring mightily. He smelled burnt coffee and realized they were in the shop. He glanced at his watch: 4:06. "Jesus, Cord, wake up. Shit. We got to go."

Cord came around gradually, snuffling as his eyelids fluttered. "What's going on?" His voice was thick. "What's burning?"

"We cooked the shit out of the coffee, buddy. We got to go."

"What's the rush?"

"If that peacock killer got another bird while we were asleep at the wheel, we gotta get rid of the evidence. If Buntz takes us off night patrol, we'll never get a chance to get into Daisy's yard and dig up the treasure."

Cord rubbed his eyes and looked at his watch. "Yeah, we better have a look around."

They hurried to the zebra area, where Buntz set up the trap. They walked around the edge of the lake, shining a flashlight along the ground, looking for signs the peahen stalker might have pounced again.

As they rounded the turn across from the PR office, their flashlight beams fell on a nightmare scene. A huge feral cat stared defiantly into the beam, his face covered with blood. One eye glowed, monstrous, in the beam. No light reflected from his other ruined socket. Fearless, the cat continued to chew on the feathered remains of his latest victim. Hopper charged toward the big cat, waving his arms. The predator stopped chewing the carcass, laid its ears back, crouched, arched his back, and uttered a low menacing growl. The wide feline face was crisscrossed with scars, and the nose was off center. This was an old cat that obviously survived hundreds of battles and seemed eager to survive another. Hopper stopped waving his arms and stood looking at the cat, who went back to his feast, continuing to utter threatening growls as it dined. Hopper walked back to Cord, who smiled.

"Well, I guess we know who's boss."

Hopper was not amused. "We got to do something about this, Cord."

Cord nodded, still smiling. "It would be nice if we could catch him. We could keep him under wraps until we get the treasure. That way, we control our excuse for being here at night."

"Okay. Let's catch him."

"Go ahead."

Hopper scratched his head, keeping an eye on the marauder. "How about this? Let's use our coats like nets. I'll come up on his right; you take the left. If he bolts, we take care of the carcass. If he stands, we throw our coats over him and bundle him up."

"Then what?"

"We'll cross that bridge if it comes to that. Let's go." They removed their coats and split up, coming at the cat from opposite directions. The big feline laid his ears back, displaying one impressive canine tooth. He'd lost the other somewhere along in his travels and struggles. As they approached, the cat ramped up his threats. When he seemed on the verge of attacking Cord, Hopper shouted and waved his coat like a matador. The cat accepted the challenge and made a threatening move on Hopper. Hopper prematurely threw his coat toward his bounding attacker. But the cat, though old and scarred, was nimble enough to dodge the clumsily tossed coat. Hopper scrambled backward as the crouching cat charged a few steps in his direction. Cord shouted and ran toward the cat, who turned his attention back to him. Hopper recovered his coat and made another effort to fling it over the snarling animal.

Abruptly, the cat bounded away, uttering loud, snarling complaints as it disappeared into the tall grass. Hopper shined his flashlight after the animal.

"Cord, we should have had a better plan. The last one was weak."

Cord nodded. "What are we going to do about this?" Pointing at the peahen's bloody carcass.

"I got an idea. Maybe that old boy just doesn't like turkey. Maybe he won't eat nothing but peacocks."

"Peahens."

"Right. Maybe, if we bait Buntz's trap with this peahen, we'll have better luck catching our varmint."

"I think you're onto something, Hopper. Let's get to the shop and get a trash bag so we can clean this up and save our bait."

They bagged the carcass, hastily cleaned up the kill site, baited the trap with the peahen's remains, and hurried home for an hour's sleep.

Thirty-nine

Wednesday, January 31, 1973

After a brief restless sleep, they were up and showered. On the way out, Cord found a note from Nozetape with the office numbers for Tillis and Smalley.

From the shop, Buntz followed them to the forty so they could talk privately. "Anything happen last night?"

Hopper spoke up. "We think we saw your culprit. It's a big-ass snaggle-toothed wildcat. He's on the prowl for sure."

Buntz rubbed his palms on his jeans. "What are we going to do?"

Hopper grinned. "We're going to catch him for you, Buntz."

"You're sure? You guys can catch him before he kills anything else?"

"We can get him for you. Everything's going to be fine."

Buntz seemed on the verge of giving Hopper a grateful hug, when a thought stopped him. "How long you reckon it'll take? I'm not sure how long I can keep you on my private payroll."

"Well, if we continue to keep him off the peacocks, he might put something else on the menu for a while. If he satisfies his appetite elsewhere, it'll take more doing to lure him into a trap. But we'll get him."

Buntz rubbed his coat sleeve across his nose. "Well, I guess you fellas know I'll never forget this."

"You already told us, Buntz."

They stood a few seconds in awkward silence as he obviously searched for more words to say. To unfreeze things, Hopper asked, "When we catch this old cat, what's going to happen to him?"

Buntz shrugged. "I guess I'll have to shoot him in the head."

Hopper didn't like the answer. "Is that necessary? I mean, this is a zoo. Isn't there something productive we can do with him?"

"Like what?"

"I don't know. It just seems a shame to execute the old boy for doing what comes natural."

Buntz frowned. "Shame or not, we can't just let him go. Hell, you could drive him a hundred miles off, and he might come back if this is his favorite restaurant. We'd be right back where we started. Neyland would laugh me off the premises if I told him I wanted the zoo to take care of a useless feral cat for the rest of his life. And I damn sure don't need to keep a killer cat caged up at my place. Course, if you guys want him for a pet—"

Cord spoke up. "No, we don't want him."

"Then that settles it. You just catch him and leave the dirty work to me."

Hopper tried to think of some way to keep the topic alive. But it seemed like a dead end, at least for now.

Buntz opened a new subject. "Okay, fellas, you been bare-rooting trees. Now I'll show you how to do a job that requires more skill. When we move over to the persimmons and pines, you'll need to leave a root ball so there's enough soil on the roots. If you make it too small, the tree will die. Let me show you."

He found a smallish persimmon tree and made a wider entry, allowing a deeper depression under it. "As you go, be careful about banging around on the roots. Cut them clean and gentle. If you're rough, you'll rattle the root ball, which causes soil to fall off. And the wood on these persimmons is harder than hackberries or hazel woods. You'll need to take care that your tools are sharp."

They watched him expertly trench around the tree with a sharp-edged spade, stopping to use clippers to sever the roots as he went. Where they might use an ax on a hackberry or hazel wood, he showed them how to use saws to put less stress on the root ball. "This takes longer, but these trees need more pampering."

Once the taproot was exposed, he carefully sawed through it and gently laid the persimmon on its side. He wrapped the root ball in burlap, using nails to secure the coarse material to the soil. He showed them how to make a sling with burlap to carry the tree to the truck.

"Remember this. The bigger the ball, the more likely the tree will live. But the bigger the ball, the heavier it is. So here's where judgment comes in. It'll take a little time to find the sweet spot. Start making the root ball bigger than you think you need. Keep trimming until you can move it. It needs to be heavy but not so heavy you mess up your back. You'll get the hang of it. Now, I got to get Sid and Charlie on the road in the dump truck to pick up a load of cotton hulls from the gin in Chickasha. We'll need that stuff for mulch. So go to work and be careful not to kill any of my persimmon trees."

As soon as Buntz was gone, a gangly figure crept from the trees. At first, Hopper didn't recognize Finn. He'd combed the debris out of his beard. His long gray-black hair was pulled back in a ponytail. He wore a wrinkled, oversized brown corduroy jacket. The white shirt appeared clean but unironed. The khaki pants, bunched at his skinny waist, were held by a belt with a long portion of leather dangling below the buckle. The pants were too short, revealing white socks, uneven, and a pair of scuffed black shoes.

"Finn, I almost forgot."

The old man doubled over in a fit of deep racking coughs. When he straightened, there were flecks of blood in his beard. "I have to be at the Colcorde building at ten o'clock."

"Yeah, here comes your ride now. Let me clean you up a little bit." Hopper poured water on a bandana and cleaned the blood from Finn's beard. He studied the old man's face. The eyes were yellow and bloodshot. He breathed with his mouth open, and his breath was rank. Some teeth were missing, and those remaining were obviously rotting. Hopper was stricken by an almost overwhelming protective instinct. He felt responsible for this old vagrant veteran.

"Finn, I got to tell you something, buddy. You're in real bad shape. You shouldn't be coughing up blood like this. I'm asking, as a favor, let my friend take you to the hospital. If you don't get some treatment, you won't be around much longer. Then who would eat all my extra oranges?"

Finn shook his head. "What happens now don't matter. When I'm done downtown, I'll be finished."

"Is there somebody we can call for you? You got family—brothers, sisters, kids?"

Finn shook his head. "Too late. They can't do nothing for me now. There's only my little pal, and he says it's time to go."

"I wish you'd let us help you, Finn."

The old man stepped close and put his hand on Hopper's shoulder. "Thank you, Dale. You done more than you know—you and Vernon. I gave up praying a long time ago." He started to say more, but an onslaught of violent coughing doubled him over. He went down on one knee and spat blood on the ground just as Nozetape drove up.

Hopper started to ask about this little pal, but Finn waved him off. Hopper helped him to his feet, cleaned his face again, and gave him the bandana. "Listen, Finn, Nozetape here is going to take you to the Colcorde building like I promised. But you really need medical attention, and you need it today. Just go to the hospital and let them give you a once-over. Do this for me, would you?"

Finn shook his head and stumbled toward the Karmann Ghia. Hopper and Cord each grasped an elbow and helped him to the car. Nozetape watched with a horrified expression.

"That old fella ain't going to die in my car, is he? I like this car, and if he dies in it, somebody's gonna have to buy me another one."

Hopper didn't respond. "Take him to the Colcorde building. Help him inside and do what you can. When he's done, try to talk him into going to the University Hospital. He's a vet, and they'll look after him for free."

"What do I do if he dies on me?" Nozetape whined.

"He ain't going to die." Hopper cast a sad, uncertain eye on the old man. "Just look after him until you drop him off at the hospital, and if he just won't go, bring him back here."

Nozetape nodded. "Have you called them FBI guys yet?"

"We'll call them at lunch."

"You guys be careful. There ain't nobody at the house, and somebody with skills could plant something where we'd never think to look. Our goose would be cooked."

"We may not need to worry about planted contraband just yet. Just take care of old Finn. We'll sort this other shit out directly."

As Nozetape drove away, Finn slumped in the backseat. Cord asked, "What do you think was so important for him to do downtown?"

Hopper shook his head. "No idea. But we ought to see if we can find where he stays. Maybe we can talk to this little pal of his or find something that would tell us where we can find his kinfolk. Somebody needs to talk him into getting some help."

"What about this persimmon tree?"

"It'll wait."

Since Finn previously indicated he had a place somewhere to the northwest, Hopper assumed his—what? Home? Hideout? Wherever he stays, it must be over there someplace. The woods grew thicker as they searched. They found it impossible to move in a straight line. Some places displayed evidence of Finn's comings and goings: a leather strap tied to a low branch with a tiny bell attached, a shallow hole in the ground with a pile of rocks in the center, an array of animal bones arranged in a rectangle around a horned skull.

Hopper stood on the edge of the rectangle, feeling it would be disrespectful to step inside that boundary. Cord stood beside him, scratching his head. "You reckon this means something that can be figured out, or is all this pointless as a baby scribbling with a crayon?"

An inexplicable impulse pushed Hopper to step into that bony rectangle. He stood by the skull and closed his eyes. Images flooded into his brain: piles of gold coins; a tiny boot gleaming with rich polish and bright buckles; white cows lying peaceably in green pastures; Audrey Kroneson wearing a leafy crown and a colorful butterfly on her outstretched palm; Daisy the elephant staring intently into his eyes; Cord kneeling over Finn, who was dressed in a white robe with his arms crossed over his chest, gold coins on his eyes. He saw a great tree uprooted and toppling over on its side, leaving a yawning pit where its roots should be. He felt himself falling, falling.

From far away, he heard Cord's voice. "Take it easy, buddy. Take it easy. You okay? Can you hear me?"

He forced himself to fly upward, dodging gnarly roots reaching out to keep him in the pit. "Come on, Hopper. Open your eyes, buddy. Can you walk? We got to get you to a doctor."

He opened his eyes to see Cord's face in the blurry foreground of a riotous mixture of bare brown branches and green pine needles. He moved his arms and legs, realizing he was stretched out on the ground within the rectangle of bones old Finn had arranged on the forest floor around a horned skull. The earth under him felt soft, cool, and restful.

"I'm okay. I just decided to take a little nap. Nothing to worry about." He blinked in an attempt to draw Cord's face into clearer focus. "Jesus, Cord, you look like you've just seen a headless spook. Help me up. We got to get out of here before you faint or something."

Cord snorted. "Hold on a second, Hopper. You sure you can stand up? You fell pretty hard. I don't want you to get on your feet if you're just going to do some more acrobatics."

"I'm fine. But we gotta get out of here. What time is it?"

Cord looked at his watch. "Quarter to eleven."

"Let's get to the pickup for some water. You look thirsty."

Cord snorted again as he helped Hopper to his feet. Hopper expected to feel dizzy or weak, but the second he stepped out of the bony rectangle, he was fine, as if nothing happened. He headed back toward the pickup.

Cord spoke behind him. "This way, Hopper."

"What?"

"The truck's this way. You're headed deeper into the woods."

***

Hopper felt Cord watching him as they resumed their work. "You sure you don't need to see a doctor?"

"I'm fine, Cord."

"What the hell happened over there? I mean you stepped over those bones, wavered a second, then—boom—down you went."

Hopper blushed. "Believe me, Cord, I just took an unscheduled vacation. It won't happen again."

"Well, that's a relief. Now I can stop worrying." He looked at his watch. "Lunchtime. Let's go make a call."

***

They drove to the Love's Country Store. Hopper made the call while Cord stood by to discourage eavesdroppers. Neither Smalley nor Tillis was in. "They'll know what it's about. Tell them we'll have a couple of hours after we get off work. Tell them to come by the house if they want to talk in person," Cord instructed. Hopper left the address and phone number.

They went back to the forty to have their lunch. Hopper took his orange from the lunch pail and noticed the extra orange. At that moment, he knew that for the rest of his life, whenever he saw, tasted, or smelled oranges, his memory would carry him back here, and old Finn would be in his mind, holding out a fistful of sassafras. Cord roused him from his reverie. "What are we going to offer the feds?"

"Nothing. We're just going to tell them we ain't drug dealers, and we know what Ollie's up to."

Cord laughed. "They'll be so relieved to know how spotless we are. What makes you think they give a shit whether we're innocent or guilty if they get a free ticket to a conviction? They're not going to care one way or the other, if we don't come up with something to make their life easier."

"You may be right, Cord. But the truth is we got nothing to give them but hearsay and suspicion. No doubt they know a shitload more about Ollie's doings than we do. I just want to look them in the eye and tell them the score."

"What good do you think that will do?"

"What harm will it do?"

Cord considered this for a minute. "It might make it harder if they believe we're innocent pawns in Ollie's game. But in my opinion, it won't make a shit. But you're right. If they get it in their head to nail us, innocent or not, talking to them won't hurt."

When their lunch hour was over, they went back to work. Their labors were interrupted by a chorus of sirens blaring across the zoo's west parking lot. It sounded like a convention of siren manufacturers. Cord squinted to the east as if he might see through the trees. "What the hell do you suppose is happening?"

"If them are fire trucks, the whole damn zoo may be burning."

"Come on, Hopper. We better get over there. They may need our help."

They were speeding along the access road toward the north gate, when Buntz, coming the other way, motioned them to follow him to the shop. He was off the cart and headed their way before they came to a complete stop. Cord rolled down his window. "What's up, Buntz?"

Words tumbled out so fast Hopper could barely follow. "It's bad, boys. Big Ned killed a guy."

"What happened?" they asked at the same time.

"I guess an electrician came to fix a short in one of the outside outlets in Ned's enclosure. The guys in charge of the grazing animals told him to stand by for a few minutes. They had to go help deliver a baby giraffe. But the electrician didn't wait. When Dwayne and Earl got back, they found him dead."

Cord got out of the pickup and leaned on the roof. "What's going to happen now?"

Buntz wiped his face with a shop rag. "First thing is I got to send everybody home. We're shutting everything down. I've already caught the rest of the crew, and they'll be here in a few minutes."

Hopper stepped out of the pickup. "Can we finish up the day on the forty?"

"If you're in the middle of something that can't wait, Neyland . . . Mr. Neyland says you can finish. But they want everybody out of here by four o'clock, period. So your Rambler has to be out of sight by four-oh-one."

Hopper and Cord nodded at the same time. Hopper asked, "Is this trouble going to spill over onto the grounds crew?"

Buntz shrugged. "Hope not. But it's more important than ever that you guys catch that peahen-killin' varmint. Somehow, Neyland found out about the peahen that Podd cleaned up."

Cord growled, "Wonder how that got out."

"Don't matter now." Buntz spoke as an Oklahoma County sheriff's prowler drove through the open north gate. "Mr. Neyland knows, and he pinned my ears back for not filing a report. He'll tattle to Mrs. Kroneson the first chance he gets. Anything else happens right now, and it's my ass." He wiped his face again. "You guys gotta catch that cat before he does any more mischief. That's all there is to it."

Hopper asked, "What about Big Ned?"

"Don't know. They haven't got around to deciding on that yet. But you guys don't need to worry about that. Just go for now. Come back tonight and get that cat."

They drove back to the forty to load the persimmon tree. When they got back to the shop, Buntz ordered Podd and Charlie to offload everything and water the tree's root ball before they left.

As they were leaving the parking lot, Nozetape skidded up next to the Rambler. He shouted through his open window, "Finn's in the hospital. When he finished his business at the Colcorde, I was bringing him back here. He had a coughing fit and passed out. I rushed him over to University Hospital and hung around for news. They told me I better round up his family, and I didn't know what to do, so I came for you guys."

Hopper yelled at Buntz, who was almost back in the shop, "Hey, Lester, we just found out we got a buddy in the hospital. We might be a little late getting here tonight."

Buntz waved. "Don't worry, I'll hold everything down until you get here."

Hopper turned back to Nozetape. "Who'd Finn see at the Colcorde building?"

"He went to see a lawyer."

"A lawyer? What for?"

"Don't know. I helped him up there and sat around in the waiting room until they finished. Took two hours. Then I helped him to the car."

"Well, hurry back down there. See if the lawyer's still there and tell him Finn's in the hospital."

"How come?"

"If Finn's got business with a lawyer, maybe somebody at that office knows how to contact his family. We sure as hell don't know nothing."

"Right." They started to race away from the parking lot, when Nozetape slammed on his brakes. Cord pulled up next to him. Nozetape rolled his window back down. "One more thing. The last thing Finn said as they wheeled him away was 'Tell Dale and Vernon to bring their guitars.'"

"Our guitars? What for?"

"I guess he wants you to play 'em." Nozetape sped away.

It was two miles out of their way to go home to get their instruments. When they pulled into their driveway, they saw a black sedan parked on the street. "Great," Cord muttered. "Here's Smalley and Tillis."

The agents were on the sidewalk leading to their porch before Cord got the front door unlocked. They followed Hopper and Cord into their living room. "Nice of you fellas to ask us over," Tillis said, smiling. "What can we do for you?"

Hopper extended his hand. "I'm Dale Hopper." Tillis looked at the outstretched hand, smiled, and clasped it.

"I'm Agent Tillis. This is my partner, Agent Smalley." Smalley reluctantly took Hopper's offered hand.

"Look, fellas, I know I said we could talk, but we just got word that a friend of ours is in the emergency room down at University Hospital. He's in real bad shape, and we need to get there, pronto."

Tillis was smiling, but there was something cold and threatening in his eyes. "So you stopped by here on your way to the hospital to tell us we're wasting our time waiting for you."

"No, we forgot all about you guys. We came for our guitars."

Tillis blinked. "You made a detour in your dash to the hospital to get your guitars."

"Yeah, our friend asked us to bring them."

Tillis took off his sunglasses and stowed them in his jacket pocket. "It wouldn't be that you guys are just having a little fun jerking us around, would it?"

"Not at all. We're not having a bit of fun jerking you boys around. We really want to talk to you. But this situation came up sudden-like, and we don't have time to discuss things right now."

There was real menace in Smalley's voice. "Oh, I think you have time. I think you want to talk to us about drug trafficking, black-market merchandise, and a disappeared federal agent. I think you might want to tell us about some hydraulics failure at a pipe yard that caused the death of a federal witness. I think you really want to talk to us. Because if we thought you didn't, we might get the idea you were keeping things from us. And if we thought you were keeping things from us, we'd be forced to ask ourselves what you're hiding. So I guess you have time to talk to us, right?"

Hopper felt heartsick. He wanted to answer their questions and do everything he could to prove he and Cord had nothing to do with anything. But there was a chance Finn might die while they were passing time with the FBI. At that moment, Finn had top priority.

"Look, we want to tell you guys everything we know about the Oleg brothers and the shit they might be doing with a character named Feeney, and . . . well, we just don't have time right now. We know you don't owe us one, but we really need you guys to give us a rain check this one time."

"We might if we had some idea what we're waiting for."

"I don't follow."

"Have you got something solid to give us in return for this rain check?"

Hopper, in an instinctive gesture, displayed the palms of his hands. "We got nothing solid to give you. The only thing we know for sure is that we ain't doing anything that would interest you."

Smalley growled through clenched teeth. "You brought us here to say you got nothing for us but your promise that you're a couple of lily-white lambs? Is that what you're saying?"

"I know it sounds squirrely, but that's the truth, and we really got to go."

Tillis looked at Cord, who was looking at the ceiling. "Your friend speaking for you too, Mr. Cord? You got nothing to give us?"

"Afraid he's telling it straight."

Smalley took his sunglasses out of his pocket. "Okay, boys, if that's the way you want to play it, that's the way we'll play it. But there's something you need to know. You can play any funny game you want, but we always—and I mean always—get the last laugh. Good evening, gentlemen."

As they opened the door, Tillis took a notepad from his pocket. "By the way, this friend that's in the hospital, what's his name?"

"Finn."

"First or last name?"

Hopper looked at Cord, who shrugged. Hopper cleared his throat. "Don't know."

Tillis flipped his notebook shut. "So you don't have time to talk to us because you're in a big hurry to pick up your guitars and rush to the hospital and see a friend, and you can't even tell us this friend's correct name. Is that it?"

"Believe me, Agent Tillis, I know how this looks and sounds. But we're on the level."

Tillis donned his own sunglasses. "Sure you are. Evening, gentlemen. We'll be seeing you."

Forty

The white-clad lady behind the desk eyed their guitar cases when they stepped into the emergency room admitting area. "Can I help you?"

Cord took a seat as Hopper attempted to get information on Finn's location and condition. "All I know is his name's Finn."

"Are you family?"

"Well, not really."

"I'm sorry. I wish I could help you. We're only authorized to give information to family members."

"We're not even sure he's got family. Far as we know, we're the closest he's got."

"I'm sorry. It would be against hospital regulations."

"He was in real bad shape, ma'am. It's very important that we see him."

"I really wish I could help you, but without more information, there's nothing I can do."

There was a prolonged exchange of near-desperate pleading and sympathetic but firm refusals. When it was clear the nurse could not be moved, Hopper considered ignoring the stubborn gatekeeper in angel-white and making an unauthorized inspection of the emergency room records. But he knew such a maneuver would draw the vigorous attention of hospital security. He plopped, dejected, into the seat next to Cord. "Short of tearing this place apart, I don't know what to do." He got up and began to pace. The door opened, and a distinguished, gray-haired gentleman in a striped navy suit stepped to the information desk.

"Excuse me, ma'am, my name is Jude Thorson. I'm an attorney. My client was admitted here this afternoon. Can you tell me what room he's in?"

"Of course. Name, please?"

"Alimony."

Hopper froze in his tracks and focused all his attention on the conversation taking place at the information desk.

"Felix Nathan Alimony?" she confirmed.

"Yes, Felix Nathan Alimony."

The truth hit Hopper like a lightning bolt. He charged up to the lawyer, almost bowling him over. "Sorry, but I just overheard you say you were here to see Mr. Alimony."

"Yes."

"He's a friend of ours. We just call him 'Finn.'"

"Yes?"

"We'd like to see him."

Thorson turned back to the desk. "You were about to tell me where he is."

"I'm afraid he's in intensive care, Mr. Thorson."

"Tell me how to get there, please." With directions to the ICU floor, Thorson turned back to Hopper. "I'm Jude Thorson."

"Yeah, I heard. I'm Dale Hopper. This is Vernon Cord." Thorson studied them carefully. "So you're friends of Mr. Alimony's?"

"No. We're friends of Finn's."

Thorson nodded. He eyed their guitar cases. "Mind telling me what this is about?"

"It was our friend Nozetape that brought Finn in. Finn wanted us to bring our guitars."

Thorson nodded again. "Okay, let's go see Mr. Alimony."

At the ICU desk, another firm but courteous nurse stopped them. Thorson produced a signed notarized power of attorney. The nurse said he could go in, but Hopper and Cord would have to stay in the waiting room.

Thorson said, "Wait here, boys. I'll get the lay of the land and get back to you." A door buzzed open, and he disappeared into the recesses of the intensive care unit.

Cord scratched his jaw. "How about that. Who would've figured that the old man was a relative of Sir Lawrence Alimony?"

Thorson came back into the waiting room. "It's bad, boys. He's got widespread cancer and pneumonia. They don't think he has much time."

"Are we going to be able to see him?"

"Don't think so."

"Have you notified his family?"

"He's the last of the Alimony line. There isn't anyone to notify." Thorson removed a card case from his pocket and gave Hopper and Cord each a richly engraved business card. "There's nothing you can do here. If you'll call me later, I'll give you an update. Better yet . . ." He removed a notepad and pen from his jacket pocket, "Give me a number where I can reach you, and I'll call with an update when I have more information."

Hopper balked. "All due respect, Mr. Thorson, but since he asked us to come, it seems real inconsiderate for us to leave without him knowing we're here."

Thorson nodded. "I understand. And I promise, if he's at all lucid, I'll be sure to tell him you came by."

Cord put a hand on his friend's shoulder. "Let's go, buddy. Mr. Thorson's right. We can't do any good here now. And we got some important stuff to tend to." Thorson wrote their number and address in his pad.

Hopper took a deep breath, turned, and followed Cord down the hospital corridor.

They were standing at the elevator when a nurse called out to them. She was hurrying down the hall. "Dr. Hepler asked if you would mind coming back for a minute."

"Dr. Hepler?" Hopper asked.

"He's taking care of Mr. Alimony."

"Oh, sure." They followed the fast-moving nurse back to the desk.

Thorson was speaking to a short, heavy doctor sporting a Fu Manchu mustache. The doctor looked at them and then looked at Thorson, who nodded. The doctor walked toward them, extending his hand. "I'm Dr. Hepler. I understand you're friends of Mr. Alimony. He's asking to see you. Ordinarily, in situations like this, only family can see a patient in ICU, and we usually don't allow more than one at a time. But Mr. Thorson thinks it might be important for Mr. Alimony to know you're here."

Hopper nodded. "Thanks, Doc."

"I'm afraid I can only allow about five minutes. I'm sure you understand."

"Sure."

"Follow me, please."

The nurses all looked puzzled as Hopper and Cord, carrying guitar cases, followed Dr. Hepler into the solemn sanitariness of the ICU.

Hopper fought the urge to gag when Dr. Hepler pulled a curtain aside. Finn, dressed in a hospital gown, had an oxygen mask on his face with tubes inserted in both arms and one running under the mask. He looked shrunken and dry in the bed, like something made of straw, twigs, and hair. Monitors beeped behind him like scavenger birds waiting for the signal to start the cleanup.

Finn's eyes fluttered open. Hopper imagined that somewhere behind the oxygen mask, he smiled. Finn raised a bony arthritic finger and pointed to the guitar cases.

Hopper spoke in a respectful whisper. "Hey, Finn, you look like a man that could use a hot cup of sassafras tea. It's supposed to help keep you well." Finn coughed. It might have been a laugh.

"You said you wanted us to play something, so here we are. Not sure what you'd like to hear, but—"

Finn pointed to the table by the bedside. There was a drawer. He directed a pleading look to the doctor. "Oh," Hepler said, "his things are in there."

"You want me to look in there?" Hopper asked. Finn responded with a weak nod. Finn's old notebook was there with an assortment of tobacco cans and other debris. None of it looked like it belonged in this sterile environment. Hopper held the notebook up. Finn nodded. Hopper thumbed through the pages filled with unreadable scribbles and symbols. There was also a faded yellow photograph of a young, handsome Felix Alimony in uniform with his arm around a beautiful Asian lady. "Was this your wife?" Finn nodded, tears glistening on his eyelashes. "She's real pretty, Finn. Is there someplace we can get hold of her?"

Thorson leaned near his ear and whispered, "She's been dead a long time, Mr. Hopper."

Hopper gulped hard and tried to think of something to say, but the well was dry. He turned his attention back to the notebook. Near the back, Hopper found where Finn had written the names *Dale Hopper* and *Vernon Cord*. Under their names were three words. *Red River Valley*. "Is this what you want us to play? 'Red River Valley'?"

The old man nodded.

They didn't waste much time tuning. They sang softly in their best Everly Brothers harmony:

From this valley they say you are going.
We will miss your bright eyes and sweet smile,
For they say you are taking the sunshine
That has brightened our pathway awhile.

Finn closed his eyes.

So come sit by my side if you love me.
Do not hasten to bid me adieu.
Just remember the Red River Valley,
And the cowboy who loved you so true.

They played the song once through without singing. Hopper played the melody with as much love as he could put into his strings. They sang it one more time, and the monitor signaled that the song, for Finn, was over once and for all.

The doctor pushed them out of the room, allowing just enough time for them to pick up their guitar cases.

Forty-one

They sat in the Rambler without speaking. Simon and Garfunkel's "Scarborough Fair" played on the radio. Hopper tried to analyze the messed-up alchemy of his emotions. He'd seen men die—plenty. But seeing old Finn give it up in the hospital's antiseptic environment hit a previously undiscovered emotional chord in his heart. No way this could be a tougher loss than seeing a buddy smoking a cigarette and making a joke one minute and blown to bits the next. But there was something inexplicably hard about this. There was no guilt like the pressure that followed some battlefield losses. But guilt was something, almost solid, like a rock. You could recognize it, name it, roll out your logic, and fight it. There was something different about this. The old man, a fighting man in his day, a man who loved and was loved, who wound up old, ruined, and alone. Hopper was surprised to recognize an element of fury in the aftermath of Finn's death. A stiff current of anger coursed through him, but there was no identifiable object to channel it toward. Who was responsible for the vacuum that closed in on Finn and left him starved for the company of someone who cares; alone and suffering from the pitiful desire to be … remembered?

The most surprising thing Hopper discovered in the Rambler's quiet front seat was a heavy overburden of self-pity. When he tried to focus the beam of his thinking on the possible reasons he might feel sorry for himself in the wake of the old soldier's death, the beam blinked off, and there was nothing but dark.

"Where to now?" Cord asked, rousing him from his mental fumblings.

"Let's get us a bottle of wine and then relieve Buntz at the zoo. We'll light up a joint, give ourselves over to the sounds and smells of zoo animals, and drink a toast to old Finn Alimony, our buddy."

"Right." Cord pulled the Rambler out of the hospital parking lot and headed for Byron's Liquor Store a few blocks away. They bought a couple of bottles of Mad Dog 20/20 wine because it was cheap and had a twenty percent alcohol content. Before they got to the zoo, Cord pulled into a Sinclair service station but didn't stop at the gas pump. Before Hopper could ask, he said, "Nozetape will want to know about the old man. I'll give him a call."

Hopper nodded, unscrewing one of the bottles. In the empty car, his mind tried to drift back into the confusing emotional landscape. He refused to go back there. He hit the Mad Dog bottle, hard, and turned the radio's right dial until he found the right song: "The Tennessee stud was long and lean, the color of the sun, and his eyes were green." He hit the bottle again and added his harmony to the song. As usual, concentration on the music was a temporary remedy for all troubling mental disturbances.

By the time the song ended, Cord was crawling back into the Rambler. "I got news."

"I'm listening."

Cord took the offered Mad Dog bottle. "Like Nozetape told us before, Sir Alimony's stuff was all shipped back to England, where Mrs. Alimony and her show business pals gave it a real thorough going-over. Far as we know, nobody found anything. A couple years later, Mrs. Alimony had a brainstorm. What if Sir Lawrence handed the map over to McGuire? Or what if McGuire made his own map? So they got busy trying to lay their hands on McGuire's stuff, hoping there might be a tipoff.

The troopers did an inventory. McGuire had a saddle, a bedroll, a Colt Lightning carbine .44-40 army rifle, and a Colt .45-caliber Peacemaker sidearm."

"What happened to that stuff?"

"The army made a half-assed effort to identify McGuire's next of kin, but nobody was real aggressive in the search. McGuire's stuff was stored in a stable at Fort Reno. By the time Mrs. Alimony tracked it down, somebody already claimed it."

"Who?"

Cord grinned. "The receipt was signed by Hubert Alimony."

A shockwave penetrated the wine fog. Hopper shook his head like a man with water in his ear. "So how do all these Alimonys line up?"

"We'll have to get the rest from Nozetape when we get home. But you know what occurs to me?"

Hopped nodded, smiling. "I can read your mind. There was a lot more to old Finn than we could see with our naked eyes. We never did find out where he lived. Maybe we can learn something if we locate his hideout."

It was dark when they got to the zoo. As they drove into the parking lot, Buntz raced up on his golf cart, waving frantically. Cord rolled down the Rambler window. Buntz spoke in a hoarse whisper. "Turn off your lights before somebody sees you. Drive to the north side of the shop. I'll be there in a minute to explain."

Cord switched off the Rambler's lights and drove to the north side of the building, invisible from the access road. In less than a minute, Buntz jogged up and slid into the backseat.

"What's going on, Buntz?" Hopper asked.

"They're having a trial in the administration office."

Cord scratched his jaw. "Trial? What kind of trial?"

"They're deciding whether Big Ned lives or dies."

Hopper snorted. "Of course he lives. If somebody got killed in there, it's 'cause they was careless. Ned's not domesticated, and everybody knows it. He can't be put to death for following his nature."

"Bet your ass they can put him to death. The Kroneson girls are saying like you did. It's the dead guy's fault. Everybody's waiting for Mr. Kroneson to show up and make the decision."

Hopper was almost pleading. "Surely Mr. Kroneson will listen to his daughters. If they want to save the big ox, their opinion ought to carry some weight."

Buntz shook his head. "I wouldn't bet on it. When it comes to running things, Mr. Kroneson's cold as an Arctic fish. He'll weigh everything up and make a decision based on dollars and cents. I ain't the sort to be telling tales, but there's gossip floating around that there might be trouble brewing between the old man and his daughters."

Hopper's antennae tingled. "What kind of gossip?"

Buntz shot him a sideways glance. "I don't usually trade in talk like this, but I've heard that old Zack is losing control—I mean really. Those girls are about to come into lots of money of their own, and I hear they're not just leaving everything up to Daddy. They're acting like they got their own ideas."

Cord took a deep breath and shrugged. "Millions of cattle get slaughtered every day to satisfy someone's appetite for a burger. If the decision goes against Ned, at least there'll be a better reason to his end than all of them others."

Buntz pulled his right sleeve across his nose. "Yeah, you're right. But I got a bad feeling about all this . . . real bad."

Hopper cleared his throat. "What do you want us to do?"

Buntz seemed shrunken and tired. He squinted at the shop's metal wall as if trying to see into the administration building. "I don't know how long they'll be arguing over whether the big ox lives or dies. But could you guys come back around nine o'clock? Be careful; if there's still lights on over there, lay low."

From the backseat, he leaned between them, extending his hand.

"You guys got to promise me you're going to catch that peahen-killing varmint. Something tells me our whole future depends on it."

Hopper didn't like to make promises he wasn't positive he could keep. But Buntz needed some sunshine right then. So he decided to put his word on the line. He gave the calloused hand a bigger-than-normal shake. "Okay, Buntz, you got our word. We'll catch him."

Cord repeated the handshake, without the promise. Buntz climbed out of the car, standing awkward for a second, and then headed for the shop, speaking over his shoulder. "You guys get lost and come back when the coast is clear."

They drove to the forty without headlights. With flashlights and extra batteries, they resumed their search of Finn's lodging. It sounded like moaning, but Hopper knew the eerie voices seeming to press in on them from all directions were wind blowing through the trees—at least that's what he hoped he knew. His flashlight beam scurried over uneven ground while Cord's light cast wider arcs, looking for any sign that might lead to Finn's shelter.

The dark around them was almost total. Their feet shuffling through the forest debris sounded loud and foreign. When Hopper spoke, he was surprised at the loudness of his own voice. "I don't suppose you brought a compass?"

The beam of Cord's light froze on the knot in the bark of an old oak that looked like a gargoyle's profile. "No, and you didn't either, I guess?"

They'd been stomping in zigzags, bypassing fallen trees and skirting gullies, for about twenty minutes. If they were walking in a straight line, they might have gone a mile to the northwest. Without the benefit of sun, moon, stars, or landmarks for reference, they might have reversed course or walked in a circle.

Hopper muttered, "Sure glad you're keeping track of where we're going."

"Wrong," Cord snorted. "This ain't my navigator night; this is my illuminator night. Keeping our bearings while we stumble around on the haunted forty is your job."

Hopper groaned. "Great, I been busy trying to keep us from falling in ditches and gullies, and you been sightseeing. Let's stop for a minute and see if we can get our bearings."

They shined their flashlights around, hoping something helpful might appear in one of the beams. It didn't. Hopper's heart hammered against his chest when a sound drifted out of the dark. "Did you hear that, Cord?" He wanted to check the expression on Cord's face but knew it was a bad idea to shine the light in his eyes. He waited.

"I don't hear nothing except the wind, Hopper. What was it?"

Hopper felt cold and even more disoriented. "Nothing, I guess it was nothing. Which way do you think is east?"

Cord cleared his throat and started to offer an opinion, when Hopper interrupted. "Jesus, Cord, surely you heard that, didn't you?"

"I didn't hear nothing, damn it. What do you think you're hearing?"

In spite of the chill, Hopper felt sweat beading on his forehead. "It's probably my imagination, but I thought I heard Finn over that way." He pointed his flashlight into the tangle of stunted cedars and leafless scrub oak.

Cord spoke in a gravelly whisper. "Snap out of it, Hopper. In case you forgot, the old guy died this afternoon. Whatever you heard, it couldn't be him."

"Well, whoever it was walking around in there, he was saying our names and using Finn's voice."

"Bullshit," Cord thundered, directing his flashlight beam in a rapid back and forth. He jumped when Hopper put a hand on his shoulder.

"Listen, Cord . . . over there." He directed his flashlight beam into the dark woods. "Hear him? It's Finn. He's calling us."

"Goddam, Hopper, we got to get out of here and come back when it's light. You're off your hinges, buddy."

Hopper grabbed Cord's coat sleeve. "Come on; he wants us to follow him." He crashed into the darkness, shining the beam steady in front of him. Cord hesitated for a second and then stumbled after his friend, who was running deeper into the woods.

After a few minutes, Hopper came to an abrupt stop. Cord almost tripped over him. Hopper raised his fist in the combat signal for still and quiet. Cord froze, listening. They stood on the edge of a clearing. At first, the beam of Hopper's light appeared to shine on the sad face of Lawrence Alimony. Cord gasped. Hopper rubbed his eyes and realized the flashlight beam was reflecting on the large yellow eyes of a great owl perched on a tree branch on the far side of the clearing. With slow majesty, the owl blinked, turned her big feathered head, unfolded her wings, and launched from the branch, flying away from them into the darkness. "Come on," Hopper shouted as he ran after the owl.

"What for, Hopper?" Cord asked in close pursuit. "Why the hell are we chasing a goddam owl?"

Hopper, pulling ahead, yelled over his shoulder, "Finn wants us to follow."

"Why the hell would Finn want us to run through the goddam dark following an owl?"

Like magic, Hopper and his flashlight beam disappeared. Cord skidded to a stop in the soft forest soil. "Hopper, where the hell are you? Hopper?"

"Down here."

Cord shined his light on the ground and saw an abrupt drop-off. Hopper sat on the ground below him.

"You okay? Tell me you didn't break nothing or cut yourself open."

"I'm fine; may have a bruise or two, but nothing's broke. Come on down here and see what I found."

Cord slipped, skidded, and stumbled down the hill and found Hopper on his feet, shining his light on a large bone. He knelt to take a closer look. "What the hell you reckon this is?"

"Not sure, Cord, but it looks like a bear skull."

Cord stood up and shined his light around. "There's another one over there."

Hopper followed his beam. "That one may be a lion or tiger."

Cord's light continued to search the area. "Holy cow, Hopper, look." Between the skulls, a stone walkway led to a door that, at first glance, appeared to be leaning against the hillside. Hopper made his way up the stone path, noticing other animal skulls and bones lining the way to the doorway. He turned the knob on the door and pushed. It opened. He started to step inside. Cord grabbed his collar.

"Wait a minute, buddy. This place may be booby-trapped."

Hopper paused in the doorway and considered. "It's okay, Cord. Finn wouldn't bring us here and lead us into a trap. Come on."

The first thing he noticed when he stepped inside was the temperature. It wasn't exactly warm, but it was warmer than the air outside. Then there was the aroma. The atmosphere was rich with a mixture of sassafras and juniper. The floor was planked with swept wooden boards. The walls were covered with crudely constructed cupboards. In the middle of the single room was a pot-bellied stove with a stovepipe disappearing into the boards overhead.

Deer antlers, animal skulls, and bones were positioned chaotically around the place. In the corner was a slatted bed covered by a thin pillow and threadbare blankets. A makeshift sawhorse with an old saddle sat in a niche cut into the wall. There were several rough wooden boxes around the room. An ancient rocking chair stood by the stove.

Hopper found himself lost in a sad trance as he imagined Finn sitting here alone, year after year, lost within his private world, waiting for . . . something.

Cord broke the spell. "How long you reckon old Finn lived here?"

"Long time, I'd say."

Cord began opening the crude cabinets. They were full of an odd mixture of bark, nuts, roots, rusted tin cans, and other debris. In one cabinet, they found a stack of old notebooks filled with scribbled notes, drawings, diagrams, and symbols.

Cord made a close inspection of one of the notebooks. "Take a look,

Hopper. Looks like Finn sometimes used the same mixture of German, French, and English as Sir Lawrence did."

One of the more carefully crafted drawings caught Hopper's attention. "Look at this, Cord. Know what it is?"

Cord turned the notebook sideways and upside down. "Nope."

"It's the underside of a saddle with the stirrups spread out."

In unison, they directed their flashlight beams to the old saddle perched on the sawhorse in the corner of Finn's underground shelter. Cord was the first to speak. "Hey, you reckon that's the saddle that belonged to that McGuire fella traveling with Sir Alimony?"

"Let's see the diagram again." Cord handed him the notebook. "Hey, Cord, looks like there are scribbles under the saddle."

Cord squinted at the notebook in the flashlight beam. "Let's take a look." They hoisted the saddle off the sawhorse and laid it on its back. A series of dark marks was burned into the saddle's underside. One looked like a lopsided M. Rising from the M was a series of dots leading to a triangle with three arrows coming out of it. The center arrow touched a symbol that looked like a skull. Cord traced the designs with his finger. "If this is McGuire's saddle, I'll bet these marks have something to do with where the treasure's buried."

Hopper shined his flashlight around. The wavering beam caused the collection of animal skulls to appear to bob up and down as if they were demonstrating their eerie agreement with Cord's assessment.

Cord made a close comparison between the notebook and the markings on the saddle and put the notebook in his shirt pocket. "Let's get out of here. I'd feel better doing this by daylight."

"There are no windows here, so it'll be dark no matter when we come. In daylight, it'll be easier for Ollie's eyeballs to keep a watch on us."

"Maybe so, but I'm getting claustrophobic, and I need a break." Cord opened the door and stepped outside. Hopper joined him. Cord scanned the sky overhead. "Well, there's nothing up there to show us the way. We'll have to climb back up there and hope our instincts take us east." He picked up a long elk antler Finn had placed along his stone pathway. "Every twenty feet or so, we'll dig a furrow with an arrow pointing this way. When we come back, it may take some time, and we may not come in a straight line, but we'll find our way back."

They scrambled up the hill and took the next hour struggling through the brush, marking their way as they went.

Forty-two

When they arrived at work the next morning, bleary-eyed and mentally numb, they found the grounds crew engaged in aimless tasks around the shop. Podd and Clary pretended to sweep the floor, their heads together, talking about something they obviously didn't want others to hear.

Sid and Charlie checked air pressure in pickup tires, tractors, and golf carts. Buntz was absent. Hopper asked, "Why is everybody running in low gear? Where's the boss?"

Podd shot Clary a knowing glance. "Buntz got called to administration first thing this morning. Our instructions is to stay busy in the shop 'til he gets back."

Hopper didn't like any of it. It wasn't so much that Podd was obviously holding back. There was a toxic undercurrent affecting the atmosphere. He attributed his lack of excitement about last night's discoveries to emotional heaviness, sorrow brought on by Finn's death, and fatigue. But there was something else, something creating the sensation of environmental constriction. He knew Ollie was closing in. He and Cord were vulnerable, not only because they were in the dark about the timing and details of Ollie's play, but they weren't at their best—and they sure as hell needed to be.

Cord whispered, "What are you thinking?"

"I think there's another ingredient we need to talk about. Let's load up and get over to the forty, where we can air it out."

They got busy assembling their tools. Clary snarled, "Maybe you didn't hear. We're supposed to wait in the shop 'til Buntz gets here."

Cord ignored him. Hopper assumed his cheeriest attitude. "Well, we ain't loitering around pretending to be busy when there's persimmon trees that need ballin' out. So if there's something we need to know, we can be found on the forty."

As they loaded the pickup, Clary walked to the box holding the grounds crew vehicle keys. He put the pickup keys in his pocket and went back to his mock-sweeping. Podd snickered.

Charlie, watching on one knee by a John Deere 112 tractor, with a tire gauge in his hand, cautioned, "Ain't none of my business, Clary, but if you don't put them keys back, you may be openin' a whole can of whoop-ass on your own self, brother."

Clary spat back, "Button it, Charlie."

Charlie shrugged. "Okay, man, suit yourself. But don't go hollerin' 'Charlie, save me' when one of them soldiers puts your ass in a torture hold."

Without looking at Clary, Cord spoke as he filled the water can. "Put the keys back, Clary." Clary ignored him.

Hopper said, smiling, "Clary just wanted to save us a trip to the box, didn't you, Clary?" He walked casually toward Clary, who stood tense, ready. Hopper stopped a few inches from his face. Clary refused to step back. Hopper held his hand out, speaking in a low, threatening tone. "No matter what happens now, Clary, you're going to get embarrassed. The only question for you is whether you get hurt in the process."

Clary looked down his nose at the shorter man. "You must think you're pretty—" Before he finished the sentence, Hopper's left leg swept Clary's right leg from under him. Hopper grabbed Clary's shirt at the same time and jerked him sideways. Clary's right arm went down to break his fall. Hopper grabbed the left wrist with his left hand and, with his right hand, seized Clary's left thumb, bending it toward the wrist.

Clary tried to get up, but Hopper cranked back on the thumb. "Relax, Clary, or you'll have this thumb in a cast at bedtime." Clary winced and whimpered. With a firm grip on the left wrist, Hopper eased the pressure. Clary glared at him with an expression of raw hatred.

Charlie spoke from across the shop. "Told you, Clary."

"Shut up, Charlie," Clary hissed. Hopper added a touch of pressure. Clary groaned and settled back.

Hopper's voice was calm and cheerful. "Now look at yourself, Clary. You had to go start something just to prove what a jackass you are—and not just a jackass, a dumb jackass to boot. Now do the polite and smart thing and give me the keys."

"Fuck you . . . okay, okay, okay." Hopper relaxed his hold on the thumb until Clary extracted the keys from his pocket. Cord stepped over Clary's supine body and took the keys from his hand. "Thanks, Clary," he mumbled as he walked to the pickup.

Hopper, retaining his grip on Clary's thumb, grabbed his shirt and pulled him to his feet. Clary took a swing across his body, which Hopper easily dodged. He cranked the thumb, and Clary went to his knees. "Now listen, Clary, you're getting off light. You're not going to have to explain missing teeth, black eyes, fat lips, broken bones, stuff like that. You got a cheap lesson in manners. I'm going to turn you loose now, and you're gonna go back to playing with your broom. But pay close attention. If I have to teach you any more lessons, they're gonna cost you, brother. So do yourself a favor. Let this go." He released Clary's thumb and stood relaxed in front of the taller man.

"You'll lose your job over this."

"Don't think so. All I did was give you a hand when you got tangled up in your own feet and fell down. That the way you saw it, Cord?"

"That's how I saw it."

"Bullshit. Everybody in here saw what happened. You jumped me when I wasn't looking. Right, Podd?"

"Uh . . . sure, Clary . . . yeah, Hopper jumped you when you wasn't looking."

"Charlie . . . Charlie, goddammit, you saw him jump me."

Charlie added air to the 112 tire. "I just think it's real nice the way Hopper helped you up after your clumsy ass went all Bozo the Clown and fell over your own big feet."

While Clary tried to sputter something at Charlie, Sid's voice drifted from behind a golf cart. "I dddin't ssee nnnothin'."

Hopper opened the bay door, and Cord backed the pickup out. Hopper made a production of counting fingers. "By my figuring, that's three to two—if you and Podd get a full vote each." He gave a cheerful wave. "Okay, boys, if anybody's looking for us, we'll be over on the forty . . . doing our job. Bye."

They barely had their tools unloaded when Cord nodded to the east. "Here comes Buntz." They perched on the tailgate and waited. Buntz skidded to a broadside stop just behind the pickup.

Hopper waved at the obviously agitated Buntz as he spilled off the cart. "Now I may have a tongue lashing coming, Buntz, but—"

"Forget it. That's small potatoes. I need you to tell me who you are so I might be able to figure out what to do."

Hopper blinked at Buntz's red face. "You know who we are. I'm Dale Hopper, and this is Vernon Cord."

"Of course I know that. And I've looked at your personnel files, so I know all that other stuff. But you guys got to tell me everything, or all of us could wind up bear chow."

Cord scratched his jaw. "I thought there was stuff you didn't ever want to hear about."

Buntz launched into a tirade about knowing when to shut up and when to speak up. Cord interrupted him. "Calm down, Buntz. Suppose you tell us what's happening. Then we'll be able to figure out what you need to know."

Buntz took a deep breath, nodded, and unfolded the situation. "First, there's a hydrogen explosion in the Kroneson family. It has something to do with Big Ned and you guys."

Hopper interrupted. "How do we get connected with Big Ned and the Kroneson family?"

Buntz regarded him with a narrow-eyed glare. "You guys know more about that than I do. The old man didn't go into details. He just said that was part of the breakdown around here—you guys and the girls. You should know better—"

Cord interrupted. "Follow the thread, Buntz. Tell us what this is all about."

"The old man rained thunder down on us all: the girls, Neyland, Dwayne, Earl, me, everybody."

Hopper jumped in again. "Why is he hot at you?"

"Why do you think? Podd told Neyland about cleaning up the pea-hen carcass. Neyland jumped me about it. I can't lie under pressure, so I told him everything. He tattled to the old man. Now he's all raged up over the butchering of Mrs. Kroneson's precious birds.

"Then Mr. Kroneson threatened to fire Dwayne and Earl over the dead guy. He didn't give a shit that they didn't know nothing about how it happened or how the guy got in there. But nobody could do anything to save Ned." He shook his head and wiped his nose with his sleeve. "Poor dumb ox don't know it, but he may be eating his last meal right now. The Kroneson girls pitched a fit about it. The old man tried to shut them up. He kept saying, 'That's enough. We'll discuss this later, in private,' blah, blah, blah. But they wouldn't let up. Finally, the old man slammed his fist on the table and said the issue was settled, and if he got any more guff about it, people was gonna get fired, no matter who they were."

Buntz started to walk in circles, his hands clasped behind him. "There's going to be a top-to-bottom overhaul of all zoo procedures with a whole mess of strict new rules. Hell, it'll be like we're all getting pushed into a goddam cage."

Hopper asked, "So where do we fit in?"

Buntz stopped circling. He looked at the toes of his boots. "See, that's the part that don't add up. The old man wanted you guys fired right now, off the premises pronto. But Neyland went to bat for you. He didn't lift a finger to save Ned, and he didn't say a word when everybody else was getting scalded. But when the old man told me to give you guys your walking papers, Neyland asked if he could discuss it in private for a minute. They stepped out, and when they came back, you guys wasn't mentioned again. After the meeting, Neyland told me he saved your jobs—temporarily, but he couldn't do a thing for you if you ever talk to them girls again. And get this, you're gonna get overtime pay for working at night. But this is what blows my skirts up: he wants me to put Podd on night detail with you."

Cord frowned. "He say why?"

"He just said it would be better if there were three of you." Buntz walked to the pickup and hopped up on the tailgate between them. "What's going on, fellas? I'm lost here. I've been at this zoo my whole working life. I feel like everything's coming to an end. I always believed the Lord watches over them that tend his gardens. But I don't know."

Hopper asked, "How much do you want to know, Buntz?"

He looked from one to the other, heaved a deep sigh, and said, "I guess you better tell me everything." So they did. He asked an occasional question: "So Alimony was actually right there in your room with you?" Sometimes he frowned or shook his head. Sometimes his mouth hung open. He blinked in disbelief when they related the coincidences about the hazel wood, the tale of the peacock's feather, and the discovery of Finn's underground shelter. He hopped off the tailgate and faced them with an amazed expression. "So this Ollie guy's got coils around us all— maybe even Mr. Kroneson?"

Cord spat. "He thinks he does. But we're going to give him the slip somehow."

Buntz almost whined. "Fine for you guys, but what about me? I got no moves to make and nowhere to go. Me and Big Ned are kinda on the same conveyor belt to the slaughterhouse."

Hopper jumped off the tailgate and put his hand on Buntz's shoulder. "Try to relax for a second, Buntz. Worry won't get us nowhere. Plans are what we need now." Buntz took a deep breath and nodded. "Tell me something, Buntz. What would make you happy?"

Buntz shoved his hands deep into his pockets. "I'd like to be head groundskeeper at the Oklahoma County Zoo for the rest of my working life. I'd like to have enough in the budget to buy all the stock, supplies, and equipment I need. I'd like to get you guys on permanent and get rid of Clary. Then we could make these the most beautiful grounds the world has seen since Eden." He wiped his nose with his sleeve again. "That's what I want."

Hopper felt a twinge of guilt. If this was Buntz's dream, he might as well forget part of it right now. It was never going to happen.

Cord cleared his throat. "Let's concentrate on the short term for now. We got to catch your critter, and we got to figure out how to stay ahead of Ollie."

Buntz nodded. "Yeah, for now, let's focus on the short term." He stood looking at the zoo's northwest woods. "I guess saving these trees just got real unimportant, huh? Now there's jobs and lives at stake." He walked, dejected, to his cart. "I'm supposed to tell you guys to stay away from the Kroneson girls. So, I told you." He switched on the electric cart and drove away.

When Buntz was gone, they briefly discussed the advisability of returning to Finn's shelter. As they were more certain than ever they were being watched, they decided not to go back until the dark. They shouldered their tools and headed into the woods.

"So it's Neyland," Cord muttered.

"We know it goes that high, but we don't know if it goes as high as Kroneson."

"Well, we know Neyland said something that stopped Kroneson cold when he wanted to fire us." Cord spoke over his shoulder. "Everything points to a connection between Ollie and Kroneson. I wouldn't be surprised if Ollie don't have his fat coils around Kroneson's throat."

They found a persimmon tree and set to work making a large enough trench around that they could leave a sizable root ball. As they worked,

Hopper said, "How do you reckon the old guy knew we'd been fraterniz-ing with the twins?"

"Not sure, but that explains the guard ignoring your name on the list. If Poppa says no entry, by God, that means no entry."

As they progressed deeper under the tree, Hopper was extra gentle severing the roots. He couldn't bear the thought of adding a dead per-simmon tree to Buntz's other woes. He paused to wipe sweat from his face. "Hey, Cord, you think there's anything we can do for Big Ned?"

"Like what, exactly?"

"Like bust him out, set him up in a pasture somewhere."

There was no real mirth in Cord's laugh. "Big Ned's done for, Hop-per. Hell, he may be gone already. But gone or not, we couldn't any more bust him out of here than we could land a chopper on a bicycle. And if we could sneak a stock trailer in here and if we could coax that giant ox to get in, where would we put him that somebody wouldn't notice? After all, he's only the biggest goddam bull on the planet."

When they were finished, the root ball was enormous. Hopper stood next to it, admiring. "Well, if a big root ball helps a tree survive, this one should live forever." It took all their strength and several tries to get the tree with its huge root ball onto the pickup. The next root ball was smaller but not much. They leaned on the tailgate, huffing and puff-ing from their exertions.

Cord poured himself a drink of water. "Next time, maybe we should try to make these root balls smaller."

Hopper nodded, watching a Jaguar automobile pull off the access road and stop by the gate leading up to the forty. Audrey got out and shaded her eyes. "Hey, Cord, look who came looking for us."

Cord nodded. "You better go see what she wants. And don't worry about being seen . . . Something tells me we couldn't get fired now if we wanted to."

"I'll be right back," Hopper said as he walked to meet Audrey. They didn't speak, even when they were standing less than a foot apart. Audrey's eyes were red from crying. Hopper felt a powerful emotion-al outpouring. He ached for her, for Finn, for Big Ned, for Buntz. He touched Audrey's cheek. Her hand touched his. Her eyes closed, and tears streamed down her face and flowed under Hopper's palm.

She pulled away, sighing. "Seems like I'm always apologizing," she whispered.

He resisted the urge to touch her again. "You look like a girl that could use some music."

She smiled through her tears. "That's just what I was thinking. You know anyone that can help me?"

"Well, ma'am, I believe that would be me."

"What time do you get off?"

"Five o'clock sharp."

"You know where Rocky's is?"

"Sure do."

"It would be nice if you and Vernon could meet us there at five-thirty."

"Perfect. That's about three miles from our place."

She started to walk away, a forced smile on her movie star face. She paused and turned. "Will you still come if it might cost you your job?"

"Audrey, I'd come if it might cost me my life."

Her melancholy expression made room for a genuine smile. Hopper watched until she got back in her car and drove west.

The main thing that appealed to Cord about meeting the Kroneson twins, he said, was they were ordered not to.

As they were leaving the zoo at five o'clock, Podd followed them to the Rambler. "Well, fellows, looks like we're going to be a team." There was a note of triumph in his voice. "So what's the plan?"

Cord growled as he put the Rambler in reverse. "Meet us here at eight o'clock tonight."

Podd looked stunned. "We really ought to get started. After all, we got a job to do, and I need to—"

"See you at eight."

Hopper would've preferred dropping by the house for a quick shower, but he figured being on time to meet the twins was more important.

Rocky's was a cross between a rock 'n' roll beer bar and a cocktail lounge. It didn't boast the ritziest clientele, but it was a notch or two above the Blue Buzzard. When Hopper stepped through the door, he sensed her presence even before he saw her. His Audrey-seeking radar led him straight to her table. Audrey and Abbie both stood as Hopper and Cord approached. Audrey was dressed in her PR clothes: green sweater, tan slacks, shiny boots. Abbie wore blue jeans and a blue work shirt with scuffed cowboy boots.

Both women extended a hand to Cord. He accepted with cool courtesy. Marvin Gaye's "I Heard It Through the Grapevine" played over the speakers. When the waitress took their order and Audrey said, "Put it on our tab." Hopper started to protest. This was a first. Throughout his life, it was understood that when drinks are ordered, the guys pay. Then it hit him. He really had crossed a threshold. In the company of these women, he was in a different world. There were a lot of things about this world he couldn't grasp. Some of these mysteries he liked, some he didn't. The part where the ladies picked up the tab made him feel awkward, but he liked it.

Uncharacteristically, Cord kicked off the conversation. "From what I hear, you two had a pretty noisy dust-up with your dad this morning."

Abbie smiled. "Yes, that's one reason we wanted to see you."

The waitress brought back bourbon shots with water. Cord reached for the shot. "Not sure what to think about it. Maybe you'll clear up our curiosity. "

Abbie spoke, still smiling. "The main reason we asked you here is to have a cheerful visit. Audrey thinks you might be able to lift our spirits."

Hopper laughed. "What a coincidence. Cord was just saying he was sure hoping you two could think of something to cheer us up."

It was Audrey's turn to smile. "The main reason we want to see you is to find out if you still want to play at Miss Christmas's birthday party tomorrow. You should know if you do, you'll surely get fired."

Hopper slapped Cord on the shoulder. "You're right again, Cord. I'm cheered up already." He raised his glass. "We'd love to play some music for Miss Christmas." Audrey reached across the table and squeezed his hand.

Cord cleared his throat. "Can I be heard on this? Suppose we were to ask you two to do something for us that might cost you your jobs."

"Like what?" Abbie asked.

"Hell, I don't know. Your daddy's the chairman of the goddam board. What would you have to do to get him so pissed off he'd fire his own daughters?"

A sly smile crossed Abbie's face. "Maybe he couldn't fire us if he wanted to. Maybe in a couple of days, the ladies of the Kroneson house will have more votes on the board than he does."

Cord leaned forward, studying Abbie's face. "Is that just a maybe, or is that a fact?"

Abbie looked at Audrey, who nodded. "We can't explain everything now. We will later, if you want. But we'll be twenty-five on Saturday, which means there will be big changes in the family's financial organization. Dad has been very insistent on how things will be operated after that. He's positively furious because we're . . . well, he knows about us going to the Blue Buzzard. He knows about us inviting you to the townhouse. He says he won't have it." She tossed another meaningful glance at her sister. "I'm sure you'll respect the fact we don't want to air our family's dirty laundry in public. We . . . we . . . "

Hopper could tell he was seeing the very small tip of a very expansive emotional iceberg. Cord must have sensed it, too, as he unfolded his arms and assumed a more sympathetic attitude. They waited for Abbie to resume. Instead, Audrey took over.

"Over the last few years, our father's changed. Something about the collapse of the Penn Square Bank last year seemed to push him over the edge. He's become . . . He's, well, I guess the word is *mean*. He's terribly unkind to Mother, he's dictatorial with us, he's—"

Hopper interrupted. "Look, if this is hard for you, forget it. You don't have to explain anything." He looked at his friend. "How 'bout it, Cord? Are we going to do this gig?"

Cord allowed an uncharacteristic smile. "Yeah, I guess we are."

Abbie took another drink. "We had a bet. I thought you'd make the prudent decision. I thought you'd back out if keeping your promise would cost your jobs. Audrey said you'd keep your word no matter what. I thought she was just projecting. I was wrong."

The waitress tapped Cord on the shoulder. He ordered another shot. So did Hopper.

"So what were the stakes in this bet of yours?" Cord asked.

The two women touched their glasses together. "Sisters' secret."

When the waitress returned with their shots, Hopper raised his glass. "Now I'll make a bet. I'll bet we play for Miss Christmas, and nothing happens. Well, we might get chewed out, but that's all."

Audrey leaned forward, studying Hopper's face. "You think our father is bluffing?"

"No, I think he intends to fire us, but I think he'll get talked out of it."

"What makes you think that?"

"Redneck secret. Is it a bet?"

Abbie asked, "What are the stakes?"

"If we don't get fired, you two come to the Buzzard tomorrow night and help us celebrate."

Abbie smiled. "If you do get fired?"

"You come to the Buzzard and cheer us up. Bet?"

Audrey laughed. "Bet."

"Good." Hopper knocked back the whiskey and chased it with cold water.

Abbie and Audrey raised their glasses and sipped from straws. Cord sighed, raised his glass, and downed the whiskey.

Hopper got to his feet. "What time is the shindig tomorrow?"

"Are you leaving so soon?" Audrey asked.

"Yes, we have something we have to do tonight. It has to do with your mom's peahens." Audrey started to ask, but Hopper cut her off. "Maybe we'll explain the whole deal tomorrow night."

Audrey stood and kissed his cheek. "Come by the administration building at eleven forty-five. Miss Christmas will be there at noon."

Abbie stood and kissed him too, but her effort was more awkward. "I think tomorrow will be really interesting, no matter what happens, don't you?"

Cord stood, seeming unsure what to do. Audrey came around the table and, standing on tiptoe, kissed his cheek. He seemed paralyzed. Abbie followed her sister's lead, but she seemed uncomfortable.

Hopper slapped Cord on the shoulder. "Snap out of it, big fella. We got to go have some fun with Podd."

By the time they grabbed a bite to eat (steaks, courtesy Carla) and filled Nozetape in on latest developments, it was nearly eight o'clock. They found Podd's '66 Ford Falcon sitting in the shop's dark parking lot. Cord pulled alongside and rolled down the window. Podd rolled his down.

"Hey, Podd, what's going on?"

They couldn't see him, but his voice sounded cheerful. "Just waiting for you guys so we can get busy, looking for—you know—the cat." They heard him snicker.

Hopper spoke to Podd's darkened window. "Before we get started, let's go brew a cup of coffee."

Hopper shined his flashlight on the shop door while Cord unlocked it. As they stepped inside, Hopper turned on the lights, and Cord went to the coffeepot. Hopper sat at the card table. Podd sat across from him, smiling his lopsided smile. "Well, looks like we're going to be partners after all."

Hopper asked, "Are you a drinking man, Podd?"

"Nope. Never touch the stuff. Don't drink, don't smoke, don't chew, don't swear. I'm pure as the driven snow." Hopper and Cord exchanged a glance over the rims of their coffee cups.

"Guess you're right, Podd. Looks like we're partners after all. Problem is, we're not sure what we're partners in."

Podd frowned. "Really? You don't know what we're looking for?"

Hopper shook his head. "We were just told it was some kind of treasure."

Podd took a toothpick from his flannel shirt pocket and leaned back in his chair, clearly pleased to be in possession of superior knowledge. "Me and Feeney been around here a long time. Since I'm on the grounds crew and get a chance to go digging around, he told me to keep my eyes open for clues. He told me he knows a guy that could help us sell the stuff if we find it."

"So how did Neyland get in on the deal?" Hopper asked nonchalantly.

Podd frowned. "Feeney's real fuzzy about that. He acts like he's really got one over on me because he knows all about Neyland and I don't."

"What's Feeney tell you about how the goods will be divvied up?"

"He says Neyland has to have thirty percent, the guy that knows the fence has to have thirty percent, then the four of us split up the rest."

Hopper laughed. "The four of us?"

"Yeah, you two and me and Feeney."

"So we do all the work, find it, dig it up, haul it out, and we get ten percent each? Seems like a raw deal, don't it?"

Podd's sly grin returned. "First off, since we're the ones digging it up, how would they know if we tucked part of it away and didn't tell them?"

"For a guy that's pure as the driven show, you're a pretty shrewd cookie, Podd. If we did that, could you trust Feeney to keep his mouth shut?"

He shrugged. "If Feeney don't know nothing, he can't tell nothing."

"So is there anybody higher in the zoo organization than Neyland that knows about this?"

"Don't know. Feeney keeps all that to himself. Guess he don't trust me."

Wonder why, Hopper thought. "Hey, Podd, suppose we decide to keep it all and fence it ourselves."

Podd narrowed his eyes and looked around as if there might be someone listening. "All I can say is I wouldn't do that. Feeney says people get killed over stuff like this."

Hopper leaned back in his chair. "Well, that's all I need to know."

Podd leaned forward. "So you guys know where it's at, don't you?"

Hopper made a production of winking at Cord. "Suppose I was to say it's on the forty, and we know where?"

Podd's eyes widened like pie plates. "Well, heck, let's get over there and dig her up."

"Not so fast. What if we told you that ground really is haunted, and if someone was to go digging around in the dark . . . well, there's no telling what might creep out of there."

Podd collapsed back in his chair, frowning. Then he glared at Hopper. "You're lying."

"Okay, suppose we told you where it was and told you to go on over there and get it, by yourself, if you want to?"

"Fine, tell me, and I'll go dig it up."

"I'll do better." Hopper got a paper towel and found a pencil. "I'll draw you a map. You can just go right over and get it."

Podd got up and looked over Hopper's shoulder as he made some squiggles, lines, spirals, and finally an X.

"Walk along the south edge of the forty. About a quarter-mile in, you come to a barbed-wire fence. Follow that fence west 'til you come to a fallen corner post. It points east and west. Follow the west-pointing end about a hundred yards, and you'll come to a crocodile skull. The treasure's buried under that skull."

Cord brought a couple of trash bags to the table and handed them to Podd, who was standing with his mouth open. "You won't be able to get all of it in these. Get as much as you can. When you get back here, we'll start cutting it up."

Podd grabbed the paper towel and trash bags, obviously trying to restrain his glee. "Okay. You fellas wait right here. I'll be back soon with the boodle."

Hopper assumed an exaggerated expression of amazement. "You're not afraid to go over there—alone—at night?"

Podd extended his chin. "Course not. There ain't anything over there that'll hurt you."

Hopper shook his head. "Sure hope you're right, Podd. Anyway, we'll wait right here 'til you get back. Good luck."

Podd couldn't restrain his chuckle as he hit the door. When they heard his car start and drive off, Hopper asked, "Know what he forgot?"

Cord nodded. "Tools. But he may have some in his trunk."

"Yeah." They both bent over in fits of delicious laughter. Between laugh-spasms, Cord managed to get out, "He's laughing his ass off right now because we're so stupid. We actually thought he was going to take the map and go dig up the treasure tonight."

"Yeah, we're so dumb it never occurred to us he'd take the map, drive to the nearest phone, and call Feeney to tell him what a brilliant maneuver he just made."

They finally got control of themselves. Cord asked, "What do you think we ought to do now?"

Hopper rubbed his eyes with both hands. "I'm tired, Cord. What say we go get a few hours of sleep and come back early to be sure we keep Buntz out of trouble on that peahen deal?" Cord nodded.

Hopper fell asleep in the Rambler on the way home.

Forty-three

They got to the zoo before dawn and made a quick trip around to be sure there were no peahen carcasses to worry about. They met Buntz as they headed for the shop. He bounded off his cart and dashed up to the car window, speaking before Hopper could roll it down. "Well? Did you catch the varmint? Where is Podd? Anything happening I should know about?"

"Relax, Buntz." Hopper used his most reassuring voice. "Everything's fine. We gave Podd a map to the treasure, which was why he was assigned to keep an eye on us, and he disappeared."

Buntz sputtered. "Treasure? You gave Podd a map to a treasure? Well, that's . . . I can't believe . . . You can't just—"

"Like I said, relax. I sent him on a snipe hunt. Should keep him occupied for a few days until he figures out we ain't the ones that's the goof."

"But he might—"

"He won't say nothing. He has to consult his partners and let things settle a bit. So what's the latest on Big Ned?"

Buntz looked at his boots. "They can't do it today 'cause it's Groundhog Day, and news people show up to see what Harvey, our groundhog, has to predict. As soon as it can be done without a fuss, Ned's a goner."

When they got to the shop, the phone was ringing. Buntz hurried into his office and answered. Cord got busy making coffee. Hopper sat at the card table, trying to untangle the webs he felt wrapping around him. If he hadn't taken this job, he wouldn't be grieving for old Finn. He wouldn't be battling rage and confusion over the fate of a goddamn ox when thousands of cattle were getting slaughtered every working hour of the day. He would've been happy to live his whole life without agonizing over shit like this. On the other hand, he never would have met Audrey, and he never would have enjoyed a real-life crack at finding an honest-to-God treasure. He wondered, if he could turn the clock back, would he do it?

Again, he caught himself wondering just how the hell he got here. For an unsettling minute, he remembered what Cord said about the whole deal being a puppet show where they were dancing on strings being jerked by blind coincidence, leading nowhere but quicksand. He shrugged and chastised himself for getting spongy-brained.

Buntz came out of his office, regarding them with a suspicious eye. "Podd's in the hospital with a broken jaw. You guys didn't beat him up, did you? I'll admit he's a jerk and has an ass-whipping coming. But a broken jaw is a little harsh."

Hopper and Cord traded a glance. "It wasn't us, Buntz," Cord rumbled. "Which hospital is he in?"

"He's in the Mid-Metro, room 305. You guys sending flowers or something?"

"No, we got to talk to him. We need to know what happened."

Buntz collapsed into one of the chairs. "There's probably nothing I can say, so you guys go on. Looks like everything is going to hell around here anyway."

"Cheer up, Buntz," Hopper said, walking to the shop door. "We got to be back at eleven forty-five so we can play at Miss Christmas's birthday party."

Buntz moaned. "Please tell me you're kidding. Neyland and Mr. Kroneson will both be there. There's bound to be fireworks, and you guys will be right in the middle of it, which means the grounds crew will be right in the middle of it, which means I'll be right in the middle of it."

Hopper paused at the door as Cord stepped out. "Sorry, Buntz, but we gave our word. So we got to be there. We'll be back as quick as we can."

———

They stopped at the gift shop and bought an ivy plant. As they stepped into room 305, Podd's eyes blinked soddenly from a mask of bandages neatly wrapped around his face and head. As awareness seemed to dawn on his mind, his eyes darted around in evident panic. His legs cycled slightly as Hopper got near his bed.

"Easy there, Podd. What happened?"

Podd tried to talk through teeth apparently bound together, but the effort caused obvious pain. "Hant."

Hopper looked at Cord, who shrugged. "What are you trying to say, Podd?"

He winced. "Hat."

Hopper frowned. "Are you trying to say *Pat*?"

Podd nodded, eyes closed.

"Pat Oleg did this to you?"

Another nod.

"He was mad because you left us alone at the zoo?"

"Yee."

Hopper sat in the chair at Podd's bedside. "Okay, Podd, listen to me. First, I'm real sorry about this. I figured they'd be pissed off and give you a good tongue lashing. But I didn't think Pat would fly off the handle and put you in the hospital."

"Tanks a lah."

"Have any of them been in here to see you, Feeney or anybody?"

Negative head shake.

"Okay, if any of them show up, don't mention that we came by, okay?"

Head nod.

"Any idea how long you'll be here?"

Head shake.

Hopper stood up and followed Cord to the door. He paused in the doorway. "So long, Podd. And like I said, we're sorry this happened to you. I guess we should have tried to warn you."

"Yee."

———

Buntz showed no interest in an update on Podd's condition. So Hopper and Cord loaded their pickup and put a halfhearted effort into working on a persimmon tree on the forty. Even though a heavy negative atmosphere settled over the whole zoo, Hopper's spirits rose as Miss Christmas's birthday party drew near.

On their way to the administration building, Cord asked, "What do you think is going to happen over here, Hopper?"

"We're going to play some music, make an old lady happy, and get us a hundred dollars."

"I thought was sixty."

"That was before I turned on the Hopper charm machine."

"Well, turn on the Hopper straight-talk machine and tell me what's really going to happen."

"I'm going to try to find out if Ollie's tentacles reach all the way up to the chairman of the board."

"And this helps us how?"

"Don't know. The answer appeals to the philosopher in me."

"Well, give the philosopher a rest and unleash the escape artist. Something tells me we're about to walk into the most dangerous animal pit in the whole zoo."

———

Audrey and Abbie were walking to the front door, when Hopper and Cord arrived. Beneath their smiles, Hopper sensed there was a current of sad turmoil. "Come on, let me show you Miss Christmas's cake," Audrey said, taking Hopper's arm. Cord and Abbie followed.

A long table covered by a white cloth was set against the break room's west wall. A collection of gifts surrounded a cake, which Audrey pointed to proudly. The cake's white icing was decorated with colorful flowers and green vines. "Isn't this the most beautiful cake you've ever seen?"

Hopper nodded. "I don't see how a person with a conscience could cut up a work of art like this." Audrey's smile was angelic. "You really are a sweet man, aren't you, Dale?" This remark caught him completely off guard. He felt everyone in the place was looking at him. To his dismay, they were.

Audrey took his hand. "Miss Christmas will be coming with Dad in a few minutes. Let me introduce you around before they get here." He met the curators of grazing animals, aquatic mammals, primates, bears, and cats. Then she guided him to the punch bowl, where Feeney was skulking. "And this is Mr.—"

"Yeah, Feeney and me know each other, don't we, Feeney?"

Feeney mumbled something and scurried away. Audrey gave Hopper a quizzical look. He said before she could ask, "I'll explain everything later."

"He's not a friend of yours, is he?"

"No."

"Good."

Hopper saw Neyland glaring from the doorway. When Hopper favored him with a wide smile and wave, Neyland charged across the room as if he intended to engage him physically. Still smiling, Hopper turned slightly sideways, his weight on his right foot. If it became necessary for self-defense, he planned to execute a hard sidekick to the first of Neyland's knees to arrive on the scene. But Neyland stopped. Evidently he expected Hopper to cower. Instead, Hopper spoke cheerily.

"Well, hello, Mr. Neyland. There must be something about a party that gets you real energetic."

"What are you two doing here?" he snarled.

There was a disconnect between Audrey's sweet smile and the cool distance in her voice. "I asked Dale and Vernon to provide the entertainment for Miss Christmas's party."

Neyland's glare bordered on radioactive. It cycled between them as if he couldn't decide which of them to vaporize first. "Audrey, can I have a word in private?"

"No," she replied pleasantly. "Miss Christmas will be here in a second, and we'll need to get started."

He spoke through clenched teeth. "If you told me you wanted live entertainment, I could've arranged for a nice chamber quartet, which would be a lot more appropriate than the . . . whatever these two are offering."

Obviously exercising a level of restraint reserved for willful children, Audrey said, "Abbie and I asked Miss Christmas what kind of music she liked. She didn't mention chamber music."

Neyland turned his fury to Hopper. "You two need to take your guitars and whatever drugs you have in those cases and go back to the shop."

Audrey's pleasant façade cracked. She tensed like a bowstring drawn to its limit. There was cool authority in her voice. "That's not for you to say, Julian. Dale and Vernon are here at our request. You don't have the authority to uninvite them. Even if you did, I would have expected you to have the good manners not to."

Neyland retrained his blistering focus to Hopper. "Are you going to ignore my instructions?"

Hopper beamed his warmest smile. "Look, Neyland, you really don't want to have this conversation here. I think we both know me and Cord are staying, and you're not going to do a thing about it, not here anyway. So do yourself a favor; drink some punch."

Neyland's teeth ground audibly. Audrey regarded Hopper with a look of combined surprise and admiration. He spoke as if Neyland wasn't there. "So, Audrey, tell me about the cake." They walked away, leaving Neyland steaming.

As Cord and Abbie walked past Neyland, Cord whispered, "Like Hopper says, try the punch." Neyland stood stone-like. Hopper felt his eyes, along with all the other eyes in the place, follow as the long-haired strangers from the ground crew walked casually across the break room with the magnificent Kroneson twins.

Hopper tried to analyze his sensation. He enjoyed standing before an audience with a guitar strap over his shoulder. It was an enriching bargain. He offered the crowd the timeless, priceless gift of music, well played from the heart. In return, he received appreciation. But this was different. There may have been a bargain of some kind taking place here, but he didn't know how to value his end of it.

He felt a thickening of the atmosphere before anything else changed. Then sensed the power flux when Zack Kroneson entered the room. When he turned to look, he felt he was moving underwater. Zack and Miss Christmas stood at the door. There was a benevolent smile on Zack's face, but his eyes looked into Hopper like a sniper's scope. Zachariah Kroneson was a physically large man, larger than Neyland, maybe as large as Cord. His sandy blond hair (same color as Hopper's?) was slightly longish and curly. Even through the fabric of his superbly tailored suit, Hopper could tell the arms folded across his chest were thick. The shoulders were broad, the jaw square and hard. This was Zachariah Kroneson, eldest son of the legendary Caleb Kroneson; Zachariah Kroneson, friend and confidant of presidents, lord of one of America's great fortunes, renowned philanthropist, creator and destroyer of financial empires, master puppeteer.

Hopper's natural defiance kicked in when he realized Zack's concentrated stare was a test. Zack was reading him like an electrician would read a schematic. Hopper wasn't sure how to behave before the penetrating gaze of such a titan. Then Miss Christmas showed him the way. Her kindly eyes found him; she smiled and waved. As she was standing next to Zachariah Kroneson, Hopper's cheerful smile and wave did double duty. It conveyed messages to them both. It was a courteous response to Miss Christmas and an impertinent, informal greeting to Zachariah Kroneson.

Hopper felt himself break mentally into the clear when Zack

frowned. He couldn't explain it, but that frown rebalanced the scales. Hopper was no longer gazing up at a titan; he was looking at a pissed-off guy with an ego problem.

Audrey still hadn't seen her father come in. Hopper tapped her shoulder. "Miss Christmas is here."

Audrey took his hand. "Let's go say hello." Hopper ignored the glowering Zack Kroneson as he and Audrey stepped forward to greet Miss Christmas.

"Audrey, sweetheart, what a delightful surprise. And here's Abbie. Thank you both. But really you shouldn't have gone to all this trouble."

Audrey and Abbie took turns kissing Miss Christmas's grandmotherly cheek. She closed her eyes, obviously reveling in these kind attentions. When the Kroneson girls stepped aside, Miss Christmas took Hopper's hand in hers. She looked deep into his eyes before standing on tiptoes. He leaned to accept her embrace, and she whispered in his ear, "I heard about Finn. I understand you were very kind to him."

Hopper felt a lump forming in his throat. "I wish I could've done more. But how did you know?"

She stepped around him to Cord, who stood awkward with his hands in his pockets. "Since you're the tallest man in the room, you must be Vernon."

"Yes, ma'am."

"I've heard a good deal about you, Vernon."

"Well, I can probably explain most of it."

She chuckled and patted his chest. Hopper watched Zachariah Kroneson stride across the room in their direction. He seemed to push air toward them as he came. He stopped directly in front of Hopper, extending his big hand. "I see my willful daughters have decided not to follow my advice." His voice was deep and commanding. The grip was strong, meant to intimidate.

Hopper smiled up at the cool blue eyes. "Sorry . . . I didn't catch the name. I'm Dale Hopper."

Audrey laughed out loud. "Oh, I'm sorry. This is my father, Zack Kroneson. Dad, Dale Hopper and Vernon Cord."

Zack nodded, a look of genuine amusement on his face. "You're quick, Dale. I guess I shouldn't be surprised after all I've heard about you." Neyland appeared, as if by magic, at Zack's side. The big man glanced over his shoulder, and the two nodded to each other. Zack returned his attention to Hopper. "Let's help Miss Christmas celebrate her birthday. Then the two of us will sit down and put our cards on the table. Come to my office when we're through here." He left them and made a point of greeting everyone in the place.

Hopper noticed a disgusted expression on the twins' faces as a group of caterers began to set up a lunch buffet. He looked at the piles of brisket and ribs, the steaming pans of baked beans and corn, the trays of green salad and bowls of potato salad. "Am I missing something?"

"Miss Christmas is a vegetarian," they said in unison.

"Goofy Neyland," Audrey said, still frowning.

"Goofy, goofy Neyland," Abbie echoed. Then they put their heads together and laughed.

Hopper and Cord pretended to tune their guitars as zoo employees feasted on barbecue and its traditional western sides. Miss Christmas occupied the place of honor with Zack Kroneson and Audrey on either side. Hopper watched the interaction between Audrey and her father. There was some light cordiality, but that was it.

Zack helped himself to modest servings of everything. Miss Christmas and the twins nibbled at small helpings of corn and salad.

"What are we supposed to do?" Cord asked, working the E-string key back and forth.

"If we don't get some guidance from our hosts, I say we kick off after they sing 'Happy Birthday' and Miss Christmas blows out her candle."

Just then, Audrey signaled for someone to carry Miss Christmas's gorgeous cake to the head table. Abbie lit the single candle, and Audrey led the congregation in the traditional birthday song.

Once Miss Christmas was served, Audrey and Abbie brought generous slices of cake with a scoop of ice cream each to Hopper and Cord. They chatted for a second about the pleasures of ice cream, and Audrey called the gathering to attention.

"First of all, let's show our appreciation to Mr. Neyland for arranging this . . . plentiful birthday luncheon in Miss Christmas's honor." Courteous applause. "Then I know we all want Miss Christmas to know how much she means to us. Of all the lovely flowers in our greenhouse, I think we can agree that our very own Miss Christmas is the most beautiful of them all." The group response was heartfelt but subdued. Miss Christmas's cherubic smile drew corresponding smiles from everyone in the place, except for Feeney and Neyland. They both appeared preoccupied with distant concerns.

Audrey went on. "As a special gift to the birthday girl, we've arranged some real homegrown entertainment. We're fortunate to have Dale and Vernon on the staff of the Oklahoma County Zoo. I'm sure you've all met them by now. And we were so pleased to learn that Miss Christmas loves the very music that excites Dale and Vernon. So let's welcome our resident country and western stars, Dale Hopper and Vernon Cord!"

Evidently, everyone took their cue from Zack Kroneson, who sat, passive, his big arms crossed, a benign smile on his handsome face. Audrey, Abbie, and Miss Christmas clapped enthusiastically. Other responses were absent or anemic.

Hopper thanked everyone for their "warm welcome." They started with Hank Williams's "I Saw the Light." To Hopper's unbounded delight, Miss Christmas joined in on the first chorus with a beautiful, strong singing voice and a talent for good harmony. Hopper paused between verses and urged everyone, "Give this songbird a hand." The invitation lingered in the chilly air.

When they reached the second chorus, Audrey and Abbie added their voices. Something magical erupted over the group, and on the third chorus, almost everyone in the house embraced the joyous testimonial,

I saw the light, I saw the light,

No more sadness, no more night,
Now I'm so happy, no sorrow in sight,
Praise the Lord, I saw the light.

This time, the laughter and applause spread like contagion. Before it subsided, Miss Christmas shouted, "'Jambalaya.'" Hopper gave her a slight bow, and, again, when they reached the chorus, Miss Christmas led the group in an enthusiastic joining in. One after the other, they played requests: "Kaw-Liga," "The Battle of New Orleans," "My Bucket's Got a Hole in It," "Stay a Little Longer," "Time Changes Everything."

Hopper saw Zack look at his watch and knew it was time to wind things up. When he made the announcement, Miss Christmas pleaded with him to do "Call of the Canyon." As they finished the song, Hopper was inspired to do one more.

"Okay, okay, we could do this all afternoon, but then the zoo might learn to run itself, and the boss would see how easy it is to get along without us. So before you all stop all this nonsense and get back to work, we got one more to do." Zack looked annoyed.

They launched into Hank Williams's "Move It on Over." When they reached the line in the final chorus, Hopper improvised: "Slide over, old dog, 'cause a new dog's movin' in." He winked at Zack Kroneson, who smiled and winked back.

———

Neyland choked down as much of the bullshit music and bullshit barbecue at the bullshit birthday party as he could stand. When he thought he could exit with the lowest register on the awkward index, he skulked toward the door.

Someone spoke to his back. "Leaving already, Mr. Neyland?"

He answered without turning or slowing down. "Yes, I need to get upstairs. It's payday, and I need to sign checks." He enjoyed the wicked knowledge that no one would want to slow him down if it might mean a delay in getting their bullshit checks.

In his office, he paced back and forth across his plush gray carpet, fuming. How could this happen? How could this uneducated, uncouth, poorly groomed mule beat his time? The truth hit him like a Boeing 747. Drugs. Somehow these creeps lured the Kroneson twins into the drug scene. No doubt it happened at that seedy bar the Blue Jay—or whatever.

He stared out his window at the maned wolf padding forlornly up and down on his monotonous path. He wondered whether the wolf's endless pacing was so mindless that the creature wouldn't notice an escape if one suddenly appeared. Neyland spoke mockingly. "There's no way out for you, buddy. You're stuck. But there are solutions to my problem." He resumed pacing across his carpet.

A soft knock at the door sent him scurrying to his desk. The checks were signed already, but he pretended to be busy at the task. When he barked impatiently, "Come in," Feeney poked his battered head through the door.

"I need to talk to you, Mr. Neyland."

Neyland glanced up and then resumed his charade. "Not now, Feeney. I have to get these checks signed so everyone gets paid. You want to get paid, don't you?

"Sure, but I'd have to spend all my money on medical bills if I don't deliver Mr. Oleg's message."

Neyland nearly launched out of his seat. "Jesus Christ, Feeney, are you totally brainless? You can't mention . . . anything like that standing in the hall where anyone could hear. Come in, for Christ's sake, and close the door."

Feeney, smiling faintly, crept into the office, closing the door behind. Neyland summoned his most withering glare, which had no effect on Feeney's knowing, self-satisfied smile. "I thought I told you we were never to discuss any of this in person. If you or Ollie has anything to tell me, you're supposed to call the residence after hours."

"Ollie says he can't call, and you're not supposed to call him at the yard. Not at home neither. His phones are tapped."

First disbelief and then panic cascaded over Neyland. Once he overcame the urge to bolt through the office door, he lowered himself unsteadily into his plush office chair. "Who has his phone tapped?"

Feeney shrugged. "Don't know. He just told me to give you the message, so I did."

"That's all?"

"No."

"This is crap, Feeney," he thundered, then caught himself and lowered his voice. "This is crap. Ollie can't just send you in here and tell me something like this and then leave me hanging. I need information. I need to know what the hell is going on." Panic poured over him again. "Is mine tapped, Feeney? Are there bugs in this office and my house?"

Feeney, still smiling, shrugged again. "Can't say, Mr. Neyland. You'll need to talk to Mr. Oleg."

"Goddamn right I need to talk to Mr. Oleg," Neyland hissed. "But just how am I supposed to do that if every goddamn phone in the world is tapped?"

Feeney fumbled in his Levi's pocket, withdrawing a piece of folded paper. "Mr. Oleg says for you to call this number from a payphone at seven-thirty sharp."

Neyland bolted from his chair and glared at Feeney, who seemed to have adopted an air of annoying defiance. "Well, you tell Mr. Oleg I have plans tonight. Tell him I'll call this number at five-thirty this afternoon."

Feeney pulled a dirty handkerchief from his hip pocket and blew his nose. "I won't be talking to Mr. Oleg before five-thirty. Anyway, he'll be at the yard until seven o'clock." He stuffed the handkerchief back in his pocket. "Don't mean to be out of bounds here, Mr. Neyland. But if I was you, I'd change my plans and make that call."

Neyland stepped to the window and peered down at the wolf, still plodding along the path worn smooth by endless pacing. "Did Ollie say anything about my money?"

"Your money?"

"My money, Feeney, he owes me money. Did he say anything about that?"

"Nope, just gave me this number and told me to tell you to make the call. And I wouldn't worry about the money. Ollie always pays his debts."

Neyland whirled, glaring. "What's that supposed to mean?"

The smile disappeared from Feeney's face. He studied Neyland with a puzzled expression. "Don't mean nothing, Mr. Neyland." Feeney frowned. "It just means he pays his debts—all of 'em."

Neyland turned his gaze back to the wolf outside his window. "Okay, Feeney. Get back to work. Lunch hour is over."

Feeney started toward the door and hesitated. Neyland boomed, "What? What now?"

"Well, as long as I'm here, Mr. Neyland, how about I get my check?"

―――――――

Hopper felt a touch of vertigo when he stepped into Zack's office. A massive buffalo head affixed to the wall stared at him with dead eyes as he stood in the doorway, surveying the richness of Kroneson's sanctorum. Hopper wasn't sure if Zack detected his unsteadiness. "Have a seat, Dale. I'd offer you a drink, but you're still on duty." He poured himself a generous shot of mystery whiskey from a crystal decanter and, with an air of relaxed majesty, sat in his luxurious ox-blood office chair.

Hopper concentrated on not being overwhelmed. Almost every flat surface in Zack's office was decorated with photographs of prominent politicians and Hollywood celebrities. The walls were covered with commemorative plaques and an array of primitive artifacts: masks, weapons, painted sticks, and drums.

The north wall was dominated by the impossibly huge bull's head above the fireplace. Zack propped his exotic leather cowboy boots on his desk and sampled his drink, keeping a studious eye on Hopper.

Hopper leaned back in his chair and propped his own heavy work boots on the desktop. A frown darted across Zack's face but vanished in a blink. He cleared his throat. "Let me come to the point, Dale. I have a lot to do today, and I'm sure you'd agree when you got lots of fires to put out, you deal with those closest to home first."

He took another drink. Hopper watched. Zack smiled and nodded. "Good. No small talk. Okay, here it is. You've probably noticed my girls are headstrong. They've reached the point in their lives where they feel they have to exert some independence. I'm all for it. A strong will runs in their blood. They wouldn't be my daughter's if they didn't chafe at the bit. They're going to make mistakes. Everyone does. I just need to make sure the mistakes they make don't leave disfiguring scars. I have plans for them. I can't have them frequenting places like the Blue Buzzard Saloon." He dropped his boots from the desk and leaned forward, fixing Hopper with a steady, threatening stare. "And I can't have them seen socially in the company of men like you."

Hopper laughed. "Well, glad we cleared that up." He removed his boots from Zack's desktop and stood. "Can't say I enjoyed our chat, but it was real educational. Have a good weekend, Mr. Kroneson." He stood and started to the door, wondering if he'd made a mistake.

Just when he thought he'd miscalculated, Zack thundered, "Just a goddamn minute, Hopper. I'm not through with you."

Hopper returned to the chair and put his feet back on the desk. "You know what just happened, Mr. Kroneson? You just gave something away. You could have just fired me. But now I know that wouldn't solve your problem. What is it you want, Mr. Kroneson?"

There was deadly calm in Zack's voice. "Look over your shoulder, Hopper. That's an African Cape buffalo, the most dangerous big-game animal in the world. He's dead because I put a magnum slug in his heart.

I didn't dislike him. In fact, I admired and respected him. But I snuffed him out like a cheap candle because it suited my purpose. You follow what I'm saying?"

"Sure. You're a dangerous guy that kills animals from a distance with high-powered weapons. I repeat, what do you want?"

Zack, glaring, took another drink. "I want you to stay away from my girls."

Hopper studied Zack's rigid aristocratic features. Something wasn't adding up. Maybe Zack knew he'd be chasing his own tail if he tried to bully Audrey and Abbie. He had to know any promise Hopper made to keep his distance from the Kroneson twins was worthless if the girls wanted to come to the bar. "Just out of curiosity, Mr. Kroneson, don't you think they have something to say about all this?"

"This is between you and me." He stared into the dead eyes of the Cape buffalo. "I wanted to tell you, man to man. Personally, I don't care what kind of nefarious crap you've done and are doing now. You can overdose, go to the pen, get murdered, commit suicide—I don't care. You're entitled to a warning, and you got one."

"Well," Hopper said, getting out of the chair and stretching. "I guess that's more than this fella got," nodding to the buffalo trophy. "Guess I'll be seeing you, Mr. Kroneson."

"Don't count on it."

———

When they got back to the shop, Buntz was nowhere around. Hopper was concerned about the little guy, but, like Zack Kroneson said, he had fires closer to home to deal with. He relayed his conversation with Zack.

Cord moaned. "You think the guy was threatening your life?"

"No, I think he was threatening our lives."

"Great, so if the feds don't lock us up, and Ollie don't chop us in pieces, all we got to worry about is Zack Kroneson looking for ways to mount us on his wall. Let me ask you something, Hopper. Why couldn't you just tell the guy *okay?* Why did you have to wave a red flag in his face?"

"I'm not sure, Cord. Something tells me all this is part of a big jigsaw puzzle that won't make sense unless we get fitted in someplace."

"So you think there's a connection between Ollie and Zack."

"I don't know. Why didn't he just fire us?"

"Well, it ain't because we're valued employees, that's for damn sure."

Neyland's paranoia and troubled imagination combined to press his foot down on the gas pedal harder than prudence advised. He bypassed several pay phones in order to locate one outdoors. He needed to be sure he could talk without being overheard. An oncoming police car flashed its lights in warning as he topped the hill. He felt himself sweating until he was convinced the officer hadn't turned around to chase him. At 7:30, Neyland parked his Lincoln Mark IV beside the curbside payphone at the Conoco station on Southeast 29th and Choctaw Road.

He fed a quarter into the slot and dialed the number Feeney gave him. Ollie didn't answer on the first two rings. Neyland was certain the fat bastard delayed answering just to heighten his anxiety level.

"Hello."

"What the hell is going on, Ollie? What's all this about your phone being tapped? You haven't done anything to put me at risk, have you?"

Ollie's deep chuckle almost sounded like distant thunder. "Relax, Neyland. There's a bunch of milk-fed college boys suffering from delusions of law-enforcement competence. They got nothing, and they'll get nothing as long as you don't pee your britches and do something stupid."

"Am I under investigation, Ollie?"

"Take it easy, son. We're not going to go into all this on the phone. We need to have a sit-down where I can answer your questions. You know where the Chisholm Oaks football stadium is?"

"Have you gone crazy? If you're being followed and we meet somewhere, you'll lead them right to me."

"You want your money, don't you, genius? The only way you're going to get it is meet me at the stadium in half an hour. Don't worry, I won't be followed. Fuzzy's Heat and Air is across the street from the stadium. You get there a minute or two early and sit in the parking lot. If there's a problem, I'll pull in, do a U, and pull onto Eastern. If the coast is clear, I'll pull through and unlock the gate. You follow me in. I'll lock up behind you, and we'll be able to discuss our business without worrying about uninvited eyes and ears."

Neyland felt a loosening of the anxiety constricting his chest. Ollie was a crafty, careful man. Surely he measured every inch of his footing as he maneuvered through his complex maze of illegal enterprises. He would be mindful of every element connected to his operation, and he'd be on constant watch for any cracks that might compromise his safety. He would aggressively safeguard Neyland, not from a sense of loyalty but because Neyland exposed might snowball into other exposures. Neyland hated to salute the devil, but he had to admit, where criminal conspiracy was concerned, Ollie was a man who knew how to maneuver through the labyrinth.

All the way to Fuzzy's, Neyland imagined that headlights in his rearview mirror were cops on his tail. When he pulled into Fuzzy's, he was ten minutes early. He opened his car door and puked. Cursing, he fished around in his glove box for his TicTacs.

Ollie showed up right on time. He drove his Bronco onto the gravel road leading to the stadium. He offered Neyland a two-fingered salute as he passed. In the rearview mirror, Neyland saw Ollie silhouetted in the Bronco's headlights, closing and locking the gate. He had the distressing sensation that the devil was locking up behind him.

Neyland stepped out of his Lincoln, pulling the collar of his cashmere overcoat to cover his ears. Ollie's feet crunched on the pea gravel as he approached. "You a football fan, Julian?" Ollie trumpeted in that jovial voice of his.

"Not since I left college."

"Notre Dame, wasn't it?"

"Yes, Notre Dame."

"I made a shitload of money on Notre Dame when they busted Wilkinson's winning streak in 'fifty-seven."

Neyland wanted to take a chunk out of Ollie's butt for wasting time with smalltalk, but it's not so easy to be a tough guy when you're face to face with a man like Ollie Oleg. "Look, Ollie, I don't mean to be rude, but can we have this discussion in my car or yours? It's cold out here."

Ollie laughed. "Sure, son, let's sit in that nice warm Lincoln of yours. I'm sure you swept it for bugs and such."

Neyland felt the wind stinging his eyes. "Bugs? Shit, no. Why would there be bugs in my car, Ollie?"

"Probably not, but one might accidentally be slipped in by mistake. You want to sit in my car and talk?"

"No . . . Hell, no, Ollie. If there might be a bug in mine, how do we know there's not one in yours?"

"By God, you're right, Julian. There could be a bug in mine too. Maybe we ought to talk up in the stands. What you think?"

"Sure, you're right, Ollie."

"Follow me." Ollie pulled a small flashlight from his overalls pocket and shined a path up into the concrete stairs. He leaned on the railing and handed Neyland a paper sack. "You know how old I was before I saw twelve grand gathered up in one place?"

"Please, Ollie, it's cold, and I need information. What's with all this talk about wiretaps?"

"Relax, sonny. The FBI guys are playing with a new toy. Maybe you heard of it. It's called RICO. They're using RICO to round up racketeers and gangsters that don't know how to mind their business. The most important thing for you to know is that nobody can make a case if they got no evidence. If there ain't no documents, the only kind of evidence they can get is testimony. There ain't no criminal documents, and I know everybody's going to keep his mouth shut. See what I'm saying? No documents, no testimony, no case."

Neyland pulled his coat closer around him. "What about Feeney? How do you know he'll keep his mouth shut?"

Ollie chuckled. "Feeney ain't stupid. He might save himself some jail time if he sings, but what do you think would scare him the most: some jail time or life with no dick?"

Neyland shivered. "You wouldn't . . . wouldn't cut off his . . . his penis?"

"Don't be simple. Of course I wouldn't cut his dick off. I'd have somebody else do it."

"So I don't have anything to worry about?"

"Now I didn't say that, boy. You got plenty to worry about."

"But I thought you said—"

"That dumbass you assigned to keep an eye on my partners. He screwed the pooch, didn't he? Fell for the oldest goddamn trick in the book, a phony map. He left Hopper and Cord totally unsupervised. Hell, they coulda dug up the treasure and hid it someplace, and nobody would know a thing."

"Why don't you just cut their dicks off and make them tell you?"

Ollie grinned in the glow of the match he used to light his cigar. "Now there's a thought, Julian. It may come to that. But in the meantime, if you want to keep getting sacks of money, you better start doing a better job of making me happy."

It was Neyland's turn to laugh. "Who are you kidding? You need the zoo connection if you expect to maintain a legal façade for your enterprise. I'm in a position to acquire specimens legally. I can provide documentation of domestic origin for any specimen you want to sell. I have absolute control over the zoo's inventory records, and no one can contradict it. You need me."

Ollie's eyes twinkled. "Remember what I said about documents being evidence? What would you call them certificates of domestic origin? Suppose someone was to offer to shine a light on them certificates in return for the law's consideration?"

Neyland felt a different kind of cold coil around his heart. "You wouldn't . . . Why would you?"

Ollie slapped him on the shoulder. "That's the least of your worries, boy. Let me ask you something. You wouldn't even start to know how to threaten me, would you? Go ahead, try."

"Suppose I was to provide the testimony the FBI needs to make their case?"

Ollie's laugh was rich with genuine mirth. "Is that the best you can do? Look, son, you'd be ruined in more ways than you can count if you testify. Even if I got locked up in the federal penitentiary for years, you'd be finished in every way that's important to you. You're a smart fella, being as you're a Notre Dame grad and all. So you don't need the gory details of what might happen if you double-cross me. But you do need an antidote for your worries. Here it is. Do as you're told, mind your business, don't make no more mistakes, and you'll be fine."

Neyland didn't find this to be the antidote he hoped. He wanted to escape to the warmth of his Lincoln. He wanted to be as far away from Ollie Oleg as he could get. He never again wanted to contemplate the horrors of penile amputation. "Are we done here, Ollie?"

"Almost. You a religious man, Julian?"

"What's that got to do with anything?"

Ollie stepped close and blew cigar smoke in Neyland's face. "Just answer the goddam question."

As he choked on the rancid smell of the cheap cigar, Neyland thought it would serve Ollie right if he puked all over his faded overalls. "Yes, I'm a believer."

"So I guess you believe all the money you got in the bank is the blessings of the Lord, right? You got a clear conscience and no fear of damnation?"

Neyland's search for an answer came up empty.

Ollie sounded almost distracted. "No, you don't have no worries along them lines. Did you know people prayed to snakes for thousands of years before the Bible was wrote down?"

"The Bible says they're evil."

"The Bible ain't the whole story on how people worship, son."

Neyland stood awkwardly in the cold, waiting for Ollie to make a point. But Ollie, like a creation of the dark winter night, remained motionless and quiet.

"I have to go, Ollie."

"Yeah. Remember what I said."

The first thing that popped into Hopper's head when he walked through the door of the Blue Buzzard that night was deodorant. Not because of the way the place smelled but because Pat was uncharacteristically cordial. A pleasant, disarming mask prevented Hopper from gauging the depth of his malice. Pat's mood always ranged from sullen to downright hateful. Usually, he made no effort to camouflage the level of his malevolence. Tonight, there was no way to tell. His attitude was foul for sure. That was just Pat. But this phony joviality prevented Hopper from knowing.

"Well, evening, boys." Pat smiled as he lit his cigar. "I hear you're coming by the yard in the morning to buy some equipment."

Hopper smiled. "You're half right. We're stopping by the yard, but Ollie's giving us some equipment, free."

There was a sinister twinkle in Pat's eye. "That right? I guess Ollie's getting mushy in his old age. But if Ollie says it's free, I guess it's free." He blew a cloud of blue, foul-smelling cigar smoke over their heads. "You two play real good tonight—if you can. I'm in the mood for some laughs."

Cord paused as they walked toward the stage. "Mind if I ask what's got you so cheerful?"

Pat chuckled. "Groundhog Day. Chickenshit saw his shadow, and it scared him back into his shitty little hole."

"And this makes you happy?"

"Yeah, some critters deserve to stay underground, where they belong." His big laugh sounded more like a bellow. Cord watched him for a minute then shook his head. Pat's laughter followed them to the stage.

Little Eva, busy wiping down the bar, glanced up. Hopper waved. She returned to work without response. As they tuned their guitars, Cord glanced at the barstool where Big Pat was perched. "You know, Hopper, Pat's tilted awful funny tonight. Something's giving him a case of the friendlies. What do you think's going on?"

"Could be he's all tingly about the treasure he thinks we're going to find for them. Could be he feels he outpointed us by putting Podd in the hospital. Could be he knows something that causes a ray of sunshine to seep into that dingy heart of his."

"Could be," Cord said, his ear near the F string, "he just loves Groundhog Day."

After they were tuned, they sauntered to the bar, being careful to shield Eva from Pat's watchful eyes. She ducked behind the bar and poured shots of tequila into two beers, which she placed on the bar.

Cord asked, "What's got Pat so jolly?"

She stole furtive glimpses of Pat between the two men as she washed glasses and put them away. "Don't know. Something's up. Pat's like a yoyo. For a minute, he's cracking himself up. Then, just like that, he's a timebomb."

Cord fixed her with a stern stare. "Why don't you get out now, Eva? Just quit and make a run for it."

She wiped her eyes with a bar towel. "Can't. I owe Pat money. It will take me three or four months to pay him off."

"How much do you owe? Maybe we can help."

She shook her head. "I got myself in this mess. I'll figure a way out. Don't worry about me. You got troubles of your own—plenty. Here's another drink. You better get to singing, or Pat's mood will change again."

Cord reached across the bar and patted her cheek. "Don't worry, kiddo. We're going to get everything sorted out."

She turned her back on them as she placed glasses in the overhead drying rack. "I hope you boys can work magic, 'cause that's what it'll take."

Just as they started their second song, "Howling for My Baby,"

Hopper's heart crashed against his chest wall. Audrey and Abbie glided in. Hopper felt a hot surge when he saw Pat leering as the twins paid the cover charge.

When it was time for a break, Hopper hurried to their table. Cord chose to go to the bar instead. Audrey got to her feet. Her kiss on his cheek lingered. His fingers touched her cheek. She trembled. When he looked into her eyes, he was shocked backward by what he saw: a combination of pain and sorrow, maybe an unspoken accusation. While he groped for a way to comprehend what was happening, Abbie's lips brushed his other cheek.

He sat like a robot. Abbie spoke. "Looks like you won the bet, so we're here to celebrate."

Sandy tapped him on the shoulder. "Pat wants to buy the ladies a drink."

Hopper felt he was witnessing a defilement of some kind. Before he could say anything, Abbie spoke up. "Tell Pat, whoever he is, that we don't accept beverages from strangers. Anyway, Mr. Hopper beat him to it. Right, Dale?"

Hopper, distracted, answered, "That's right, Sandy. Rum and Coke for the ladies, tequila for me."

Sandy shrugged. "Whatever you say."

Up to that point, Audrey hadn't uttered a word. Hopper remarked, "You don't look so happy about losing the bet. Maybe we need to focus on something else to stimulate your celebration mechanism. Any suggestions?"

There was more sadness in her smile than anything else. "It's just that everything is getting turned upside down. Everyone is getting hurt. I don't want to hurt your feelings, but I need to be honest with you, okay?"

Hopper prepared himself for a kick in the gut. "Here's where a fella asks himself: 'Do I want a painful truth or a pleasing lie?' Since I figure we're friends, I'll take the truth."

Sandy brought the drinks. Audrey dipped her finger into the dark beverage. "Are we really friends, Dale? Do we know each other that well? Can a real friendship form in the few days we've known each other?"

Hopper mulled the question. "Okay, I didn't plan to get real philosophical 'til later. But if we get it out of the way, it may lighten the evening and make things easier later." He knocked back the tequila and leaned forward to be sure he was heard.

"I don't know the answer to your question. Nobody knows who their real friends are. Truth is, there really ain't many true friendships in the world. And you really don't know if you got one 'til the chips are down."

Audrey nodded. "You agree there are plenty of reasons someone might pretend to be a friend when they really want something other than friendship."

Hopper smiled. "You mean like money."

"It's happened before. So how would we know? An unscrupulous heel would have sized me up as a potentially vulnerable woman. There's a lot going on in my life that might make me an easy target for a clever bastard that knows how to make me laugh."

Hopper nodded. "True. And you ought to be real careful about socializing with clever bastards. But, believe it or not, I got no interest in your money."

Her expression was skeptical. "Really?"

"Really. And it ain't your beauty, either. I'll be honest, you're both awful pretty. But there's lots of pretty fish in the big wide sea."

The twins had the same unbelieving expression. Hopper went on. "And I can't tell you I'm interested in your mind. Oh, you got charm and personality, of course. But there's a lot about how your minds work that's a mystery to me." He leaned back in his chair. "Nope, it ain't your money, your beauty, nor your mind that makes me think we could be friends."

Both sisters frowned. Abbie spoke. "Well, don't keep us in suspense. What is it?"

"Two things: one, Miss Christmas loves you, and I'm thinking she's a good judge of character."

"And?"

"And you guys tell a hell of a good story. There's something about rich, beautiful, intelligent twins that tell a good story that . . . well, it just sweeps me off my feet."

The twins studied him for a minute. At the same instant, they burst into loud laughter. Abbie slapped her hand on the table. "I guess that settles it. Don't worry about this guy, sis. He's no clever bastard. We can take his word for it."

Hopper raised his hand. "Wait, don't get me wrong. I can be a clever bastard when I want to." The laughter was delicious.

Audrey put her hand on his knee. The warmth startled him. "If you're not afraid to be in our company, maybe we can talk when you're finished here."

"Sure. We get off at eleven-thirty."

"You remember where we live?"

"I do, but last time I showed up there, your security guard was a little too enthusiastic about keeping out the riffraff."

The twins exchanged a glance. Abbie said, "Maybe it would be better if we come to your place. Would that be alright?"

Hopper felt his heart racing and cautioned himself not to expect too much. "Yeah, sure . . . I guess that would be okay."

For the rest of the night, Hopper felt the music was bubbling up from someplace terrible and exciting. He knew the twins were drawn here by a collection of sad collapses; their uncle Lyn died under the awful shadow of Vietnam, their father was guilty of some betrayal, Big Ned was doomed, the privileged world they'd taken as a natural order of things was cracking, and they had no idea about the perils hovering over the Blue Buzzard like floating mines.

In spite of all this sadness, menace, and disappointment, Hopper was alive like never before. He played and sang with the spirit of wild abandon, like a warmup to some ancient ritual where all inhibitions disappeared and the energy of all the worshipers was focused on the savage pleasures of fertility and blood. Cord, usually the anchor of the pair, must have felt it too. Usually, he handled his guitar like an acrobat, blending his skills with Hopper's for the audience's pleasure. Tonight, Cord attacked the instrument with the fury of the pillager.

They hammered the rhythm of John Lee Hooker's "Huckle Up Baby," and their listeners became a throbbing collection of human percussion instruments. Hopper's eyes were closed, and the world, to his mind's eye, was populated by flames—infernal or celestial, he couldn't say—leaping, swaying, and clapping in obedience to the music's command. When Hopper opened his eyes, the only flames he could see were burning in Audrey's eyes.

There was only one song suitable for the night's end. The audience burst into applause when Hopper announced their closing number would be the Hopper-and-Cord, hard-driving, show-no-mercy version of Screamin' Jay Hawkins's "I Put a Spell on You."

The Blue Buzzard's appreciative patrons pleaded for an encore. But Hopper had a high fever that could only be remedied by time alone with Audrey Kroneson.

On the way home, Hopper, once again, felt he was being lifted by the hand of—what? God? Fate? Fortune? Buddha? Aimless coincidence? What? Didn't matter. He might get bumped, bruised, and bloodied along the way, but he was destined for survival and happiness.

Nozetape had the place clean and atmospheric. Black lights exposed and sharpened the colors of Led Zeppelin and Crumb posters. Colorful blobs and bubbles floated, divided, and combined in lava lamps like alien curiosities. Scented candles created dancing shadows and delicate odors suggesting someplace foreign and exotic. On the reel-to-reel, Beautiful Day sang about a white bird held captive in a golden cage.

The twins perched on the couch like a couple of rare kittens. Nozetape, seated in the rocker, kept his eye closed and moved with the music. Cord leaned back in the worn recliner. Hopper, after serving everyone chilled Strawberry Hill wine in red Soho cups, sank into the beanbag chair across from the couch. After some smalltalk about the quality of the sound system, Abbie directed a question to Nozetape.

"If I ask you a difficult question, Wendell . . . it is Wendell, isn't it?" Without opening his eyes, Nozetape nodded. "If I ask you a difficult question, would you tell me the truth?"

Nozetape stopped rocking, opened his eyes, and studied Abbie's face. "Sounds like you're leading up to something, Miss Kroneson."

"Call me Abbie."

"Tell me what's on your mind. Then ask your question again."

She smiled. "I want to ask you some questions about your two friends. If I wanted to tell them some deep, painful secrets, could I trust them to protect those secrets?"

Nozetape nodded. "If these men give you their word, they'll keep your secrets. You can believe them."

"What about you? Would you keep a promise to protect our secrets?"

The pace of Nozetape's rocking increased. "If I make promises, I keep 'em."

Hopper winked at Nozetape. "Maybe we can have a secrecy ceremony where we bind ourselves to keep everything we see and hear tonight just between us forever." He refilled his red cup as Nozetape hobbled to his room, returning with a screwdriver and an owl feather. He untwisted the handle on the screwdriver and extracted some Zig-Zag rolling papers. The twins watched as he poured marijuana from the handle onto a paper and expertly rolled a joint.

Cord mumbled, "Are you sure about this, Hopper?"

Hopper laughed. "We're all about to make ourselves vulnerable. And it's gonna be strong medicine."

As Nozetape put a match to the joint, Cord double checked the lock on the front door and made sure the curtains were tightly drawn. As they passed the joint and owl feather around, the twins, obviously expert at handling a joint, playfully confessed they'd been high before.

Hopper and Cord related tales of youthful mischief, stealing and selling hubcaps to a shady character named Ollie Oleg. "Does that name mean anything to you?" Hopper asked casually between hits.

The twins looked at each other and shook their heads. "Oh, wait," Audrey said, moving to the edge of her seat. "Remember when we were little and Dad used to tell us stories about Ollie the ogre? He was supposed to prowl the streets at night stealing peoples' money and abducting unwary children."

A chill went through Hopper as if a spider had walked across his neck. Here was a hint there might be long-standing connections between Zack Kroneson and the Oleg brothers. "Has your dad mentioned this Ollie monster lately?"

"No, he quit telling us stories a long time ago. But for years, every time we saw a semitruck, we'd shiver and say, 'There goes Ollie the ogre.'"

Hopper threw Cord a glance. He was clearly trying to connect the loose ends. Then he turned to a new subject. "What about the Alimony treasure? What do you know about that old story?"

The twins frowned in exactly the same way at exactly the same instant. Abbie spoke. "First, you tell us what you've heard."

Hopper said, "Ladies, excuse us for a minute. We have to consult on something." In the kitchen, in subdued tones, they debated the pros and cons of telling the twins everything. Cord was against it. Hopper was for it. Nozetape was the tiebreaker.

"Why do you want them to know everything?" Nozetape asked.

"I can't explain it, fellas. I just think we need to trust each other."

Cord growled. "Let's just hold on to our rule. If there's no good reason to say something, don't say something."

"But I got a feeling," Hopper said almost prayerfully.

Cord resigned. "Okay, Hopper. I don't suppose it's possible for things to get worse."

They returned to the living room and resumed their seats. Hopper cleared his throat. "Get ready, ladies, 'cause you're about to hear some wild shit, pardon my French."

He started from the beginning, that first day on the job. The twins interrupted occasionally with questions: "Can we see the boot?" "Did you really see the little man, the wet footprints?"

Cord stepped in from time to time to add detail. "I'm not sure I actually got shocked by the stick. It was probably my mind playing tricks on me."

Nozetape helped with the historical details. "Lawrence's uncle Wilhelm had a family that was just never mentioned in the stuff we saw. Old Finn was probably a grandson of Sir Lawrence's uncle."

Near the end of the narrative, Hopper paused and drew a deep breath. "Now this may hurt, but here's how it shapes up. Ollie's got hooks pretty high up in the zoo organization. They may go as high as your dad. We know Neyland and Feeney are in on it. We're betting there are lots of irregularities in the record-keeping on zoo inventory. There are probably records Neyland and Feeney can supply that would cover, if anybody caught their buyers with rare critters that aren't supposed to be sold on the open market. Everything probably looks pretty kosher on the surface, but there's got to be illegal money coming out of it somehow. And now we know Ollie and Pat are setting it up to look like me and Cord are behind everything: the drugs moving through the Buzzard, the dirty deals in exotic snakes and lizards, everything. They'll make it look like we're in it with Feeney, and I'm guessing he won't be around to contradict anybody."

There was a long silence while the enormity of the facts settled over everyone. Hopper asked, "Can you help us fill in any of the blanks?"

Audrey spoke in a quiet voice. "Now it's time for us to have a conference. Come on, Abbie." They disappeared into the kitchen, put their heads together, and spoke in muffled tones.

Nozetape scratched the back of his neck. "You know, until you laid it all, I didn't realize how much shit we're in. I sure hope someone knows what to do."

The twins returned to their seat, this time perched on the edge. Audrey cleared her throat. "Okay, starting with Mr. Alimony. We heard about him years ago. We were told he was just an old eccentric that bought land adjoining ours. He made a nuisance of himself skulking around the zoo with a shovel, trying to find some lost treasure. Dad got a restraining order against him and threatened to have him locked up if he ever came on zoo property. I think Mr. Alimony might have violated the order a time or two, and Dad had him arrested. After the party this afternoon, Miss Christmas told us she did what she could to help him over the years, but he got paranoid, and she had a hard time doing much.

"About the treasure, Dad never believed in it. He was certain Sir Alimony left it in someone's custody in England and made a phony show of hauling it out. Dad thinks these coins are in some private collection in England and will turn up someday when some rich eccentric dies.

"As for Dad's involvement with this Oleg person, we can't say. We do know he is in deeper financial trouble than he's ever been in his life. We don't know all the details, but when the Mass Square Bank collapsed last July, it sent shockwaves through America's entire banking industry. Many of Dad's lifelong oil buddies collapsed right along with that bank. Some of them are blaming him."

Abbie took over. "We'll be twenty-five tomorrow, which means on Monday, the next business day, we'll come into the inheritance left to us by Grandpa Caleb and Mom's parents. Dad's been pressuring us to put our money into the Kroneson Enterprises. But Mom is advising us against it. Dad has been a perfect shit for the last few years—pardon my French—so we've decided to manage our own money. Dad is . . . well, he's out of control."

Cord leaned forward. "So what are you going to do?"

At that moment, there was a thunderous hammering on the front door. The twins fell into the protection of each other's arms. Nozetape bolted up from his rocking chair and headed for the bathroom, carrying the screwdriver and ashtray with him. Hopper and Cord were on their feet, Cord clutching Nozetape's bois d'arc walking stick. Hopper shouted, "Who is it?"

"Audrey and Abbie, you need to come out here right now." The man's voice was loud enough to be heard but not so loud as to disturb the neighbors.

Cord stepped closer to the twins. "Do you know who that is?" Wide-eyed, they both shook their heads.

Hopper shouted again. "Maybe you didn't hear me. Who's out there?"

"None of your fuckin' business. But if you know what's good for you, you'll send Abbie and Audrey Kroneson out right now."

"If you think they're in here, dumbass, come on in and ask them to leave yourself."

Hopper took a discrete look through the curtains and saw his favorite buzzcut security guard clenching his fists and working his jaw muscles. He laughed. "I just checked the list, buddy, and you ain't on it. So get lost."

"Listen, jerkoff," the guard hissed. "Tell those girls they got about ten minutes to get out of there before the cops show up to bust up this pot party."

"I hope you're right about those cops, Sarge. That'll save me the trouble of calling them to report you being on my porch disturbing our peace."

"Wise up, you fuckin' pothead. Do you want those girls mixed up in this mess when the cops get here?"

"Do you?"

The guard hammered on the door and shouted, "Audrey and Abbie, the police are on their way. Unless you want to make headlines, you better clear out of there right now."

Abbie went to the door. "Who called them, Doug? Who called the police?"

There was a long moment of silence on the porch. "I don't know. But somebody did."

"And how did you find out the police were on their way?"

He grabbed the front doorknob and jerked. "Come out of there right now, or the shitstorm you're about to fall into will be your own fault."

Abbie's voice was cool and authoritative. "Tell your boss we're spending the night here. Tell him we don't want to be bothered by any police. Tell him we'll be at the zoo in the morning. If he wants to talk to us, tell him we'll see him then."

Hopper took the walking stick from Cord's hand and jerked the door open. Buzzcut staggered back in surprise, almost falling off the porch. Hopper stepped out with the walking stick on his shoulder.

"I'm gonna do you a favor, Sarge. I'm gonna give you the option of avoiding an ambulance ride tonight."

He could see Buzzcut's wicked smile in the light spilling through the door. His voice was calm and threatening. "Bring your stick and come on out here in the yard, tough guy. I'm gonna make you eat it."

"Sure," Hopper said as he moved toward Buzzcut, who backed down the steps into the middle of the yard, assuming a karate stance. "So you've had some training in hand-to-hand combat, and you think—"

Buzzcut executed a quick and vicious sidekick aimed at Hopper's forward knee. Hopper sprang back out of harm's way, bringing the walking stick down in a blinding arc. With a loud crack, Buzzcut collapsed in the grass, rolling back and forth, grasping his left knee.

"Like I was saying. You've had some hand-to-hand training and may even have had to try it out on some skinny, untrained Vietnamese kids. Or maybe you were MP or Shore Patrol and beat up some drunk soldiers or sailors. But what I was gonna tell you is it's a whole lot different facing a fast, tough guy with good reflexes that has a weapon and knows how to use it. I'm that guy." He stepped nearer to Buzzcut, who struggled to his feet and tried to assume his karate stance again.

Hopper smiled as he spoke. "Now I'm going to tell you two things, Sarge, and I hope you listen, because it's the last chance you're gonna have to drive yourself away from here. First, if I'd wanted to disable your dumb ass while you were rolling around on the ground, I could have done it easy, and you know it. I could still do it if I wanted to. Understand?"

Buzzcut nodded, remaining tense.

"Next, the Kroneson sisters are going to be our guests tonight—and I mean all night. Get it? And if we have any more disturbances, somebody's going to get hurt bad enough that it'll make the papers. Am I getting through, Sarge?"

Buzzcut turned and limped toward his Malibu. He snarled over his shoulder, "You'll pay for this, hotshot."

"No doubt I will, Sarge. But I got a feeling it'll be worth it."

———

She asked him to keep the lights off as she pulled off her jeans and slipped under the quilt with him. "I had an appendectomy when I was a girl. There's a scar."

Hopper caressed her shoulder in the dark. As he moved his fingers down her arm, her breath quickened, and he felt her tremble. He put his lips close to her ear and whispered, "I won't notice your scars, if you won't notice mine."

Forty-four

Saturday, February 3, 1973

Hopper felt something crushing his legs. He tried to pull his feet from under the load but couldn't. He battled a wave of nausea when he made out the enormous mass of scaly coils, piled like a pyramid of thick auto tires on the end of his bed. His automatic reaction was to get Audrey out of there. "Audrey," he shouted, but she didn't react. He shook her with all his strength, but she responded with lethargic moans, like a woman under heavy sedation.

He jerked again, desperately trying to free his legs from the crushing weight of the giant snake whose coils moved in slow motion. He tried to roll over to reach the bedside lamp, hoping to use it as a weapon. He couldn't reach it.

His jaws clenched when he heard the cool, friendly voice of Ollie Oleg. "Relax, Dale. You ain't going anyplace 'til me and you have us a little chat."

Hopper spoke through his teeth. "Ollie, get this goddam thing off me. How can I carry on any kinda conversation with my legs being crushed?" He saw Ollie's fat face above the coils.

"I guess you'll just have to concentrate through the pain, son, 'cause I'm stickin' around 'til you hear me out."

Hopper's mind spun in crazy chaos when he realized the snake holding him down and Ollie Oleg were the same creature. Ollie smiled, and an oily black tongue flicked out of his mouth. Hopper couldn't stop himself from screaming, as if the piercing vibrations of his voice might dissolve the terror slithering above his quilt, drawing nearer his face.

Ollie smiled down at him. "You and your pal Vernon think you're pretty slick, don't you? You think no matter what kind of trap I lay for you, you'll think your way out. Maybe so. But what about her?" He flicked that terrible oily tongue toward Audrey's sedated face. "Maybe you'll mind your manners if you get convinced that even if you slip away, somebody left behind will settle up with me for your double-crossing ingratitude."

Words tumbled out of Hopper's mouth in a desperate cascade. "Look, Ollie, just wait a minute. We're trying to get what you want, but—"

Ollie's snake eyes blazed as he hissed. "There ain't no *buts*, Dale. There's only 'Yes, sir, Mr. Oleg, here it is.' I got no time for *buts* or *maybes*. Understand?"

"Okay, I get it."

"Okay you get it … *Mr. Oleg.*"

Hopper exploded. "Kiss my ass, you scaly, slitherin', fuckin' freak."

Ollie smiled. 'Fine, have it your way, Dale."

Hopper's scream stuck in his throat when Ollie unhinged his grotesque lower jaw, opened his mouth impossibly wide, and lowered his head toward the sedated Audrey's beautiful face.

Hopper bolted upright in his bed, flailing at the monster's face with all his might, his heart hammering in the predawn light. He was dripping in sweat and gasping for air as the nightmare slithered away like a vapor in the dark. He threw his arms around his updrawn legs and pressed his forehead to his knees. He might have wept like a scared little boy, but Audrey put her hand on his shoulder.

"What is it, Dale? Are you alright?" She tried to entice him into a conversation, but he only responded in monosyllables. He got dressed and found Abbie and Cord having coffee. He interrupted their intimate whispering and poured himself a cup before he joined them at the table.

Without preliminaries, he asked, "That guy last night, your dad sent him, right?"

Abbie gave him a quizzical look. "Yes, I'm sure he did."

"Your dad would have made it clear that nobody else was supposed to know you stayed here last night."

"No doubt."

Cord pulled his chair up next to Hopper's. "What is it, Hopper? What's on your mind?"

Audrey appeared in the doorway with a hurt, embarrassed expression. "Do you want us to go, Dale?"

"You'd better."

She sagged in an attitude of profound sadness. "Could you at least tell me what's wrong before I go? I thought we were—"

Hopper cut her off. "Really, once we make sure the coast is clear, you two need to get out of here, pronto."

Cord frowned. "What's the rush, Hopper? There's no need to be rude, buddy."

"I think Ollie knows they were here last night. I'm afraid his warped brain is calculating how to use them in his game."

Cord leaned forward. "What makes you think Ollie knows they were here?"

"It's just a feeling, Cord. There might be lots of benefits he could squeeze if he could get his hairy hands on one or both of them."

Cord snorted. "He wouldn't dare. Old man Kroneson would have the feds on him so fast his ugly head would corkscrew. No . . . no way."

"Suppose there are reasons old man Kroneson can't call the feds."

Cord regarded him, narrow-eyed. "Like what?"

Hopper lurched out of his chair and stormed back to the coffeepot. "Hell, I don't know. That's the problem with working in the dark. We're totally blind to the possibility there are ties between these guys that might cause somebody to act desperate and crazy. I know I'd just feel better if you two disappeared until we can get all this figured out."

Abbie laughed. "Disappear? Not likely. We wouldn't let a dick like Doug scare us into hiding."

Hopper's voice was thick with impatience. "Look, I don't have time to explain everything. But that creep last night was a zero on the dangerous scale. There are people on the prowl right now that are plumb off the chart. They wouldn't have a second's heartburn at chaining you two in a cellar for the rest of your lives just for the fun of it."

Abbie protested. "Wait a minute, Dale, there's no need to—"

"Shut up and listen, Abbie," he bellowed, slamming his fist on the table and sending coffee cups crashing onto the floor. "I'm trying to—"

"Shut up yourself, Dale. In case you didn't notice, we don't just stand around and let ourselves be yelled at and bullied. Come on, Audrey. We were obviously wrong about your . . . friend."

"Wait . . ." Hopper gulped hard. "Please. I'm sorry. I'm worried about you, that's all. If there was time, I could tell you things that might convince you how much danger you're in. But there could be people at your apartment right now just waiting for you to get home. They could be on their way here—or here already—planning to grab you when you leave."

Audrey ran her fingers through her long hair. "This panic seems to have come on so quickly, Dale. Is it possible you're having a . . . an episode or something?"

Cord shook his head. "Hopper's right. We should have thought of it earlier. Is there someplace you can go and stay out of sight for a while?"

Abbie frowned. "Are you guys just paranoid, or should we really be scared?"

Hopper walked to Audrey and reached for her hand. She drew away. "I'm sorry, Audrey. I know I've been a shit this morning. If you'll give me a chance, I'll make it up to you. Tell me your plans for the day."

She stared at his face for a long moment. Then, seemingly satisfied, she outlined the day's schedule. To the zoo for a meeting this morning, shopping with Mother for birthday presents. After that, lunch with some friends and an afternoon cocktail party. Tonight, a birthday party at the Beacon Club.

"After that?"

She shrugged. "Nothing. Home to bed, get up in the morning, and get ready for church with Mom."

Hopper went to the front room window and peered out. "Is Miss Christmas going to be included in any of this?"

"Yes, she'll be at the cocktail party and the Beacon Club."

"Have you two ever spent the night with her?" They both shook their heads. "Good. If I was to ask, real polite-like, for you to stay with Miss Christmas tonight, pretty please, would you do it?"

Abbie shook her head. "I don't understand any of this."

Hopper was almost overwhelmed by the desire to berate her for her stubbornness, but knew she'd only blow up and make things more complicated. "Please just humor me. Okay? Maybe I'm a shell-shocked soldier whose brain has been fried by marijuana and LSD. Maybe I'm paranoid to the max and living a hallucination. But maybe I have a decent grasp on the situation. If I do, you girls are in more danger than you could ever get your mind around. If I'm wrong and you do what I ask, you'll be putting my unbalanced mind at ease. If I'm right, you may be saving yourselves loads of heartache, maybe saving your lives." He dropped to his knees. "Please, I'm begging you. Don't go home tonight. Be in public all day and stay with Miss Christmas tonight."

Abbie snorted. "Oh, get off your knees, Dale. This is ridiculous. Suppose we do what you ask. What happens tomorrow night and the night after?"

"We'll talk about that at lunch. You know where El Patio is?"

"We can find it."

"Come on by tomorrow after church, and we should have a better idea about what we need to do."

She looked at Audrey. "What do you think, sis?"

"I think it would be sweet to have a birthday slumber party with Miss Christmas."

Abbie shook her head. "This really is overreacting. But if it's okay with Miss Christmas, I guess it could be fun."

Hopper left by the back door and checked around the house as Cord followed his progress from the inside. He then surveyed the street and surrounding driveways. When they were sure it was clear, Hopper took Audrey in his arms and held her a long time. She returned the embrace. When they parted, Hopper noticed Cord and Abbie exchange a quick kiss. Cord whispered, "Call us when you get to the zoo."

When the twins were gone, they woke Nozetape. "Get the sleep out of your eyes and come on in the kitchen. We'll pour you a cup."

They sat around the table and reviewed the situation. Nozetape massaged his legs. "So what are you guys going to do?"

Hopper mumbled, "We're going to the salvage yard today to pick up a metal detector and try to get a feel for the timetable. Something tells me we're about out of fuse."

"What if we are?"

"We'll have a better handle after we spend a little time with the big man. In the meantime, be extra watchful. We'll fill you in when we get back."

Forty-five

As usual, when they pulled the Rambler onto the pea gravel leading up to Ollie's office, his four mongrels barked and snarled their menacing announcement. Ollie stepped onto his unpainted porch and waved his typical jolly greeting. "Come on in, boys. Got a surprise for you."

They stepped in, being sure that Hub was on one of the folding chairs where they could see him. "Have a seat, fellas," Ollie said, indicating the two chairs across from the couch, where he flopped his big body. "Go get it for 'em, Hub." As Ollie's giant minion stepped out the back door into the yard, Ollie waved toward the back of the office. "Coffee's back there if you want some. I'd get it for you, but once I get my ass on the couch, I don't like to move for at least ten minutes."

Hopper answered, "Thanks, Ollie. We're all coffeed up."

"Well, that's fine," Ollie said as Hub came in with an oily mechanical part. He put it on a newspaper page on the coffee table. "There's your solenoid. Guess as soon as we get that in your bus and put some cash in your pockets, you'll be lighting out for the promised land."

"Yep. Soon as we can tie up all our loose ends, we'll be on our way."

"Loose ends," Ollie said with a sly grin on his wide face. "I'm glad you brought that up. I want to be sure we're all in the same hymnal on exactly what loose ends I'm interested in."

"We know, Ollie. If everything works out, we ought to have the treasure by next weekend."

"Next weekend? I sorta thought you might already have it."

"No, we don't have it yet, Ollie."

"You wouldn't lie to your old partner, would you?"

"We don't have the treasure, Ollie."

All pretext of friendliness disappeared from the wide, pale face. Ollie leaned forward and barely whispered, "You must not have heard my question, Dale. You wouldn't lie to me—would you?"

Hopper shook his head and smiled. "What makes you think I would lie to you?"

"I'm gonna ask you one more time, and if I don't get a straight answer, Hub's gonna have to knock out some of your teeth. Understand? You wouldn't lie to me, would you?"

Hopper looked him in the eye. "No, Ollie. I wouldn't lie to you."

Ollie smiled and leaned back on his couch. "See, if you was to lie to me and I could prove it, I'd be justified in calling you, to your face, a lying little chickenshit, wouldn't I? I'd be justified in charging you a penalty for being a cheat, right, Hopper?"

"What are you getting at, Ollie? Let's all get our cards on the table."

"Sure, Dale. But first, Hub has the metal detector you asked for. Get it, Hub."

Hub went to the front door. Hopper kept an eye on Ollie as Cord watched Hub step behind them. He didn't go out. He locked the door and leaned against it. "Oh, yeah, before we get your metal detector, I want you to know, you lying little chickenshit, I found out about your little chat with Tiny Sunday night. So I'm calling you a goddam liar, and I'm telling you you're going to pay for that. And your dumb ass will think twice before you ever bullshit me again. Hub."

Hopper and Cord were on their feet, Cord facing Hub. Hub pulled a length of pipe from his overalls, and so did Ollie. Cord removed his belt, wrapping it around his hand, leaving the heavy buckle dangling from a foot of thick leather. Hopper kicked the coffee table, which crashed into Ollie's shins. The big man grunted and looked down long enough for Hopper to clear the coffee table and grab the pipe from Ollie's hand.

At the same time, Hub crept toward Cord, keeping a careful eye on the dangling buckle. Hopper vaulted over the couch and grabbed Ollie's overalls with both hands, pulling with all his strength. The overall bib slid up to Ollie's throat. Hopper used all his weight to choke off his air.

Just then, Pat opened the door, a key in his hand. His eyes widened as he sized up the situation, and he began to fumble in his overalls pocket. "He's got a gun," Hopper shouted as he continued to apply pressure to Ollie's throat.

Cord swung the belt buckle at Pat's hand. Pat yowled as the metal cracked his wrist. Hub swung the pipe, impacting Cord's shoulder, knocking him sprawling on the floor.

Ollie's face turned purple as he struggled to claw the bib away from his throat. Hub, pipe raised overhead, charged at Cord, still sprawled on the floor. Cord delivered a powerful kick, which smashed his boot heel directly into Hub's crotch. Hub dropped the pipe and bent over, moaning and cradling his jewels with both hands. Pat was trying, with his left hand, to wrestle a revolver from his right pocket.

Cord managed to regain his feet. He drove an expert blow into Pat's solar plexus. Pat dropped to his knees. On the way down, Cord reached into his overalls and extracted the revolver.

"Under control, Cord?" Hopper asked, loosening a bit of pressure on Ollie's throat.

Cord checked the chambers in the revolver to see there was a bullet in each one. "Under control."

"You okay?"

"Yeah, better than these three."

Hopper released Ollie's overalls as Cord joined him behind the couch, where he could cover the three fuming giants. Ollie was leaning forward, gasping for air and coughing. Hub, still cradling his jewels, puked on the floor. Pat struggled to his feet and leaned against the wall.

Hopper spoke. "Now that we've had our morning workout, when you guys are able, let's talk business."

Pat snarled, "I don't do business with dead men."

Hub wiped his mouth with the back of his hand. "You want me to shove that gun up his ass, Ollie?"

Cord cocked the revolver. "I wouldn't kill you, Hub, but for a long time after I pull this trigger, you'd wish you were dead."

Ollie, still leaning forward, started to laugh between coughs. "We're getting old, boys. Look at us. It's three to two in our favor on our home ground, and we just got our asses kicked in a fair fight." He pulled a bandana from his overalls and wiped his watering eyes. "And, to tell the truth, we had an ass whippin' coming." His laugh was rich with genuine merriment. "Yep, we got a pretty good butt stompin' to start our weekend." He tried to look over his shoulder to see Cord and Hopper, but his bulk wouldn't permit him to turn far enough.

"Okay, Hopper, I apologize for my bad manners. I got all rude and out of hand before I got your side of the story. I'm sorry. Now let's get down to business, like you said. So let's everybody make everybody else comfortable. Pat, you come over here and sit by me so Vernon can see you're not doing anything rude. Hub, you go sit at the table. Okay? You boys satisfied?"

Cord and Hopper moved to the front door. "Now I think we were all about to put our cards on the table. What do we have to do to get square with you for all this?" Hopper asked.

Ollie's eye twinkled. "*All this* being your holding out on me, then coming into my place of business, trying to choke the life out of me, roughing up my brother, and causing Hub here to puke on my floor? Is that what you mean by 'getting square for all this'?"

"Yeah, that's what I mean."

"First, I need to know, have you already dug up the treasure?"

"No."

"That the truth—for a change?"

"Yeah."

"Now don't bullshit me; when will you have it?"

"We think we're going to get it tonight."

Ollie slapped his knee. "Now that's a giant step toward getting everything square. So what's the plan?"

"If it's where we think it is, we should have it loaded by dawn tomorrow."

"Perfect." Ollie slapped his knee again. "But I'm afraid we need to renegotiate the split. I'm taking seventy percent, and you boys get fifteen percent each. Now don't raise a fuss about this. You want to get square, that's what it'll take."

"So how much of your cut are Neyland and Kroneson getting?"

Ollie's demeanor changed again. "That ain't none of your business. Who says Neyland and Kroneson are getting anything?"

"You're right, Ollie. It's none of our business."

"Now, another thing you gotta do to get square is tell me what you heard from Tiny last Sunday night."

"He told us his mom died, and he asked Cord to be a pallbearer."

Ollie growled, "Now listen . . . "

"Forget it, Ollie. We ain't talking about Tiny."

"How bad do you want to get square?"

"How bad do you want the treasure?"

Ollie threw his head back and laughed again.

"Why are you putting up with their bullshit, Ollie?" Pat thundered.

"In case you haven't noticed, baby brother, they're holding a goddam gun on us, and they're about to put one of the greatest treasures in history right in our hands. I'd say we have an incentive to put up with a certain amount of bullshit." He leaned forward and spoke with pure threatening malice. "Now this is how we play it. I'm going to give you a phone number. Once you got the treasure loaded, you call. Somebody will be waiting. We'll meet and divvy up the goods. Deal?"

"Okay."

Ollie reached into his boot and pulled out a bottle of Old Grandad whiskey. He took a long pull from the bottle and offered it to Hopper and Cord, who declined. He shrugged. "Now, we got some housekeeping

matters. Don't bother showing up at the Buzzard tonight. It's closed—
for remodeling." Pat snickered. "And I know you'd never consider a double-cross. You'd never load up the treasure and head out of town thinking
you could go to some big city and talk to somebody's cousin and make a
better deal. But just in case something like that should cross your mind,
think about this. Eva . . . that's her name, ain't it, Pat?"

"Yeah . . . Eva."

"Eva is sure hoping you boys have good luck tonight. See, she's a
sorta guarantor for you fellas. If this enterprise should fall through for
any reason, well, she might have more to lose than any of us. You get my
meaning, of course."

Cord stepped forward, pointing the revolver directly between Ollie's eyes. "Where is she, you fat prick? Tell me who has her, or I'll blow
your brains out right here."

Ollie chuckled. "You ain't gonna do nothing like that, Vernon. Anything happens to me, and you'd start a flood of bloodshed that would
spill plumb out of the banks. And that would cause Hub here to get real
irritable 'cause he hates the sight of blood. Now, I'm holding on to Eva,
and there ain't a thing you can do about it. So let's all shake hands and
part company knowing that if everybody minds his manners, we'll be
friends at the end of this, and we'll all be rich to boot. What do you say?
Shake?"

"No." Hopper and Cord spoke at the same time.

Ollie shrugged. "Suit yourselves." He picked the stub of a cigar out
of an ashtray on the floor and put a match to it. "Your metal detector's
leaning against the gate to the dog pen. Don't forget your solenoid."

Hopper asked as he picked up the oily part, "It works, doesn't it?"

"Course it does." Ollie blew foul smoke over his shoulder. "If it don't
work, you don't owe me nothing." His happy laugh followed them as
they backed down the stairs and walked toward the Rambler, stopping
to pick up the metal detector leaning against the fence. Ollie stepped out
on the porch and waved. "Oh, by the way fellas, just leave Pat's .38 on the
fender of that Buick there. Thanks. See you tomorrow."

Forty-six

There was no moon on Saturday night. It wouldn't matter anyway as a thick fog blanketed the zoo, causing the overhead lights to glow like spectral heads shrouded by halos. At least that's how it looked to Hopper.

They parked the Rambler near the zebra enclosure so they wouldn't have so far to carry their equipment: shovels, flashlight, '69 model Goldmaster 66-T metal detector, and heavy-duty trash sacks to haul off the treasure—hopefully.

Despite the ominous atmosphere, Hopper was convinced the treasure was buried in the elephant enclosure. Getting it in hand wouldn't solve all their problems, but it would accomplish two important goals. First, Ollie wouldn't get his greedy paws on any of it until Eva was free. Next, Ollie's preoccupation with the gold might keep him busy while Hopper and Cord figured solutions to the bigger collection of headaches.

They had no problem scaling the fence. After all, it was designed to keep elephants and rhinos in, not to keep treasure hunters out. Hopper climbed over the pipe fencing and dropped into the concrete moat. Cord handed the tools down and followed. Once their equipment was where they wanted it, they went to work.

They'd practiced with the metal detector and were satisfied it was sensitive enough to locate the treasure if it was buried less than four feet under the surface. Surely Pete and Sir Alimony, being in a hurry as they were, hadn't dug down too far. Cord started at the southeast corner, walking along the south edge with the metal detector. Hopper, on the northwest corner, explored the north boundary with the hazel wand. As he walked slowly, waving the wand to and fro, he mentally ticked off the list of possible outcomes. They might find the treasure, stumble onto a way to turn part of it into legitimate cash, and get away from Ollie and his schemes forever. Or they find the treasure, Ollie winds up with all of it, and his lowdown plans work out, leaving Hopper and Cord in jail for shit they didn't do. Or everything Ollie is doing boomerangs, the treasure winds up in the hands of the law, Ollie and Pat go to prison, and at the end of everything, Hopper and Cord are broke, unemployed, and stuck in Oklahoma forever. Or . . .

He felt something in the wand. His attention focused instantly and totally on the end of that stick. He walked a few steps. Nothing. He turned back and felt the wand pull to his left. He let it lead him. At a point just in front of the big door at the rear of the pachyderm building, the wand pointed straight down.

Hopper couldn't see Cord for the thick fog. He whistled and heard Cord's answering whistle. He whistled again as he might summon a dog. No response. He called in a loud whisper, "Cord, where are you?"

"Here." He saw a flashlight beam through the fog and switched on his own light. Cord whispered as he drew near, "What is it? Did you find something?"

"I don't know for sure, but the wand pointed to this spot." Hopper expected argument or protest. Instead, Cord moved the metal detector to the spot and smiled as it bleeped.

"What are we waiting for? Let's dig it up." They fell to it with enthusiasm. They laid out a five-foot circle and started shoveling. Hopper figured they had about three safe hours to work. That would give them an hour to bag up the treasure, fill in the hole, and stow the goods in the Rambler. Then they could dangle the gold in Ollie's face until he couldn't stand the pressure.

The only sound in the enclosure was shovels biting into the soil and emptying onto the growing piles. They'd been digging for a little less than an hour when Hopper's shovel struck something metallic. Cord heard it too. Hopper felt a smile spreading over his face.

"You think this is it?" Cord asked, excitement evident in his voice.

"Sure could be."

Cord shined his flashlight into the hole as Hopper dug. After a few minutes, he bent and pulled a length of heavy rusted chain from the soil. He held it up for Cord to see. Cord was ignoring the chain and shining his light off into the fog. "Cord," Hopper whispered. "Pay attention. What do you make of this deal?" Cord didn't answer, but the beam of his light was trembling. "Goddammit, Cord . . . "

Hopper followed the beam of Cord's light. What he saw looming before him in the fog caused him to stumble back in horrified shock. He felt himself shrinking into terrifying insignificance against the giant shape of an elephant looming over him. He realized how pathetically small and crushable he was at that moment.

"What should we do?" Hopper whispered.

"For starters, don't make any sudden moves."

"Okay, but after we don't make any sudden moves, what do we do next?"

"I don't know about you, but I'm thinking about leaving."

"Good idea, but I can't move."

The elephant stood motionless. No way to read its intentions.

"Just stay where you are, Hopper. I'll ease out of this hole and stroll toward the fence. If it starts to follow me, I'll make a break for it. That might clear you to run the other way. Surely I can outrun an elephant. Right? They're all real slow runners, aren't they?"

"Hell, I don't know how fast an elephant runs. But what if it doesn't follow? What if it decides to ignore you and crush my ass?"

"Well . . . well, uhh . . . that would be bad, Hopper, real bad. But most likely, it won't do that. Most likely, it'll just stand there looking at you until feeding time tomorrow."

"This is no time to be funny, Cord. If you're going to go, go. If it doesn't stomp me into a muddy pudding, bring help. I'll wait here."

As Cord was easing out of the hole, Hopper moaned. "Wait, Cord. It's moving. It's getting real close. Should I run?"

"I wouldn't."

"How come you can outrun an elephant, and I can't?"

"Because I got a head start, and you don't."

Hopper uttered another low moan as the elephant's trunk snaked over his shoulder and explored his long hair and beard. The elephant swayed from side to side and raised its trunk in the air, emitting a squeaky trumpet. Then it turned and made its ponderous way back into the building.

Cord whispered, "Let's get the hell out of here."

Hopper sat heavily on the edge of the hole. "I can't yet. I got to sit here for a few minutes."

"But what if it comes back? Next time, it might decide to make pancakes out of us."

"It's okay, really. I'll be alright in a few minutes."

"Are you okay, Hopper?" Cord shined the flashlight in his face. "You're real pale, buddy. Do you need a doctor?"

"No. I'm fine." Hopper felt he was floating in a foggy dreamworld. "When she put her trunk on me at first, I thought she was going to pick me up and squeeze the juice out of me. But she was gentle, I mean gentle like when a little baby gets hold of your finger. She stroked my hair and my beard like she was . . . like she was petting me or something. Then she breathed in my ear. Her breath was real warm and soft, Cord—just like a person. Then she touched my cheek like you'd touch your sweetheart. It's okay, she likes us. Let's go ahead and see if there's a treasure under this chain."

Neither of them spoke as they continued to dig. But the chain was all they uncovered. Controlling their profound disappointment, they finished and did their best to put the ground back like it was. As they left the pachyderm enclosure, Hopper made a solemn announcement. "I'm not ever going to eat meat again."

Cord dropped his shovel and shined his flashlight in Hopper's face. "What do you mean you're not ever going to eat meat again? What does any of this have to do with you eating meat?"

"I can't explain it, Cord. It's just that . . . well, after having Daisy touch me like this, I just can't stand the thought of eating any kind of animal ever again."

Cord snorted. "So what happens if a tomato talks to you? You going to stop eating vegetables?"

"Kiss my ass, Cord. I've had some kind of baptism here, and you're making jokes. For a second there, I thought I was about to get crushed. This was like . . . like I got pulled out of a cocoon or something. I know it don't make any sense, but if I ever tried to eat an animal after this, I'd feel like a cannibal."

Cord shook his head. "You're in shock, buddy. You had a close call. We struck out on the treasure. Your emotions are all sliced and diced. Once everything reassembles itself in your thinking, we'll laugh about this over a steak at the Sizzlin' Sirloin."

"Nope. This is final. I'm a vegetarian from now on."

"Okay, Hopper, have it your way. You can be a vegetarian if you want to. And just to be on the safe side, I'm going to keep this rusty chain as a souvenir. It might come in handy as I got no straitjacket to keep you from hurting yourself. It'll be a nice memento of your baptism."

Cord mumbled to himself as they gathered their treasure recovery gear and climbed out of the elephant enclosure. Hopper wasn't listening. He was coming to grips with the terrible reality that they'd failed to find the treasure and had no viable backup plan.

He tried to keep his disappointment from deteriorating into desperation. Without the treasure, they had no leverage. They couldn't even fabricate a decent bluff. It was taking all his discipline to keep matters from sliding into the realm of the hopeless.

Just as they got back to the Rambler with their equipment, they heard a furious commotion in the trees near the zebra enclosure. Cord asked, "What the hell do you suppose that is?"

Hopper made for the Rambler in a run. "It's the trap," he shouted over his shoulder. "Maybe we caught our varmint."

They dropped their tools at the car and used their flashlights to guide them through the tall grass to the tree where they baited the trap. Inside the wire snare, the flashlight beams played across the scarred, furious face of the aggressive peahen-killin' cat. He snarled and attacked the trap with such ferocity that Hopper thought he might hurt himself.

Hopper's disappointment at not finding the treasure diminished a bit. "How about that, Cord? We caught the bastard."

Cord grumbled as they climbed the fence to recover the trap. "Well, the night's not a total waste. At least we got a new pet out of the deal."

Hopper clapped his friend's shoulder. "Look at it this way, Cord. We struck out on the treasure, true. And by this time tomorrow, if we're not dead, we might be headed for the pen. But at least we'll know we saved Buntz's job for him."

"It's good to know our lives ain't been wasted."

They wrestled the trap down from the tree and over the fence. The old cat spun in circles, spat, snarled, and did everything he could to get at Hopper and Cord as they struggled to keep from dropping the trap. Hopper spoke to the captive. "You're not making this any easier, old-timer. You got nobody but yourself to blame if you make us drop this cage and you break your fool neck. Be cool, mind your manners, and you'll be free in a couple of days."

The message obviously didn't get through. The cat banged the sides of the cage, reaching his long, vicious claw through the wires in a desperate attempt to injure his captors.

Once they wrestled the trap into the Rambler's backseat, Cord wiped his face with a bandana. "Who says this cat's going free?"

Hopper stood with his mouth open for a second. "Why wouldn't he go free? Why wouldn't somebody just drive him out in the country where there ain't no temptation to molest any peacocks—"

"Peahens."

"And let him go?"

"You know the answer to that. Why go to the trouble? Easier to put a bullet in his head and forget it. Don't worry, though. If you are right about how karma works, you'll get kudos for your tenderheartedness, and whoever pulls the trigger will have to worry about the payback, not you."

Hopper made a tentative effort to touch the cat but recoiled when the captive laid back his ears and glared at them with an obvious desire for their blood. Cord saw the gesture. "Now don't go feeling sorry for him. Just think of him as a bloodthirsty, murdering bastard whose foul deeds caught up with him."

Hopper inhaled the cold night air. The whole situation caused an emptiness to creep over him from the inside out. "He's lived a long time and survived a bunch of hard fights. It just seems a shame that we have to be the ones to end it all." He closed the Rambler door. "So what are we going to do with him?"

"For now, we can't spend time worrying about this cat. Ollie's got Eva, and we got nothing to bargain with."

Like an enormous ill-fitting saddle, the gravity of their situation pressed down on Hopper's mind. They were out of time. The only thing that rang in his head with any clarity was the determination to get Little Eva free, no matter what might become of him. At least the Kroneson twins were in the clear.

They parked in the Holiday Inn parking lot and kicked their options around. No doubt Ollie would want them to bring him the treasure before he'd release Eva. They would be justified in demanding a straight-up exchange: the treasure for Eva. Ollie would be suspicious and careful. He'd take measures to be sure he'd get the last move in any double-cross. Bluffing him into believing they had the treasure was the only move they had. Trying to figure out where he might be hiding Eva would be a waste of time. He could have her anywhere in the Flats. If they started kicking in doors, word would get to Ollie, pronto.

The only play they had was to stall. Hopper nodded. "We'll tell him we found it but couldn't get it out. He'll have to give us another day."

"So where did we find it? Why can't we get it out?"

"We found it in the lake, and we're going to need a winch."

Cord nodded. "I like it. It's just solid-sounding enough to be the truth. It won't solve our problem, but it might buy us some time to get some helpful information and come up with a decent plan."

"Okay, let's call the number." They drove to the Quik-Mart with an outdoor phone box. Hopper made the call as he was the better bullshitter. "Hello."

"Is this you, Dale?"

"Yeah, who am I talking to?"

"Don't matter. Ollie says you got some news for me."

Hopper spun the tale about them finding the goods in the lake. "We'll need a winch. Ask Ollie how long it will take him to get us one."

"He said you was going to tell me about a treasure."

"We don't have it."

There was a long pause while the slow-witted operative decided what to do with a curve ball. "Ollie ain't gonna like it. I'll call him. Give me a number where you are, and I'll call you back." Hopper gave him the number. Click.

A few minutes later, the phone rang. Hopper answered.

"Evenin', Dale."

"Hey, Ollie."

"So you didn't find it like you promised."

"Yeah, we found it. It's just a little muddier than we thought. We'll need a winch."

"I got a wrecker in the yard. Can you get it into the zoo without causing a fuss?"

Hopper felt a wave of relief washing over him. Maybe Ollie's greed got the best of him. Maybe he was buying the story because he really wanted to. "Sure, we got a key and a license to be there at night."

"So you're sure you can get it tomorrow night?"

"No problem."

"Okay, I'll have somebody drive the winch to your place tomorrow."

"Don't bother, Ollie. We'll come by and get it tomorrow."

"We can meet you at the Skyline café for lunch and make the hand-off. Hell, we'll buy you a burger. Let's say one o'clock. What do you say?"

"Sure, Ollie. That'll work fine. See you then."

Ollie's deep, happy laugh came through the headset. "Was you able to get anything? One little coin maybe?"

"No, but we'll have the whole deal by this time tomorrow."

"You're a smart boy, Dale. We're all going to look back on tomorrow as maybe the most exciting day of our lives. See you at the Skyline at one o'clock."

"I'm bushed, Ollie. I gotta get some sleep."

"Course, Dale. You've been real busy, and you've been through a lot. Go on home and sleep tight."

Hopper related everything to Cord as they drove home.

"So we've bought one day. What are we going to do then?"

"Let's get some sleep. Maybe if we get a full night's rest, our thinking will be clear enough to come up with something."

Cord answered with a mirthless laugh. "Sure, Hopper. A good night's sleep is all we need to come up with all the answers to get us out of the cage we're locked in, just like the boxed-up killer cat we got plotting out murder in the backseat."

At their house, they put the trap on the back porch. There was still enough of the peahen carcass that they didn't have to worry about him being hungry. They'd get water to him tomorrow. Now, they needed sleep.

Hopper undressed, crawled under his quilts, and fell instantly into a glorious, dreamless slumber.

Forty-seven

Sunday, February 4, 1973

Hopper felt cold metal pressed hard, choking against his throat. When he opened his eyes, a flashlight beam blinded him. A menacing voice whispered in the darkness behind the light, "Be quiet, Dale. We got some business that won't wait 'til tomorrow. Just play it cool, and everybody comes out ahead. Now get up nice and easy. I don't want to hurt you."

He blinked, trying to get a make on the intruder's voice. "Is that you, Ollie?"

"You're a quick boy, Dale. Yeah, it's me. Don't bother with your britches just yet. Just go real quiet into the living room."

Hopper crawled out of bed and made his careful way to the living room. As he passed Nozetape's bedroom, he saw another flashlight beam and heard low talking. Same at Cord's bedroom. In the living room, Ollie shined the flashlight on the couch. "Have a seat, Dale."

He sat. He heard Nozetape bellyaching as he stubbed his toe in the dark when making his way into the living room. Someone, probably Hub, pushed him hard. He fell on the floor in front of the couch. "Get up," another voice behind another flashlight ordered. Nozetape struggled to his feet. "Sit down," the other voice commanded. Nozetape sat on the other end of the couch.

Seconds later, Cord, clutching his blanket around his waist, stepped into the living room, followed by a third intruder—Pat, no doubt. Ollie shined his light on Cord as he came in. There was raw fury on his face. Hopper knew by that expression that someone would die before this ended. He just hoped it wasn't any of the good guys.

One of the intruders pushed Cord onto the couch. Rage radiated from the big man like something nuclear. Ollie stepped forward. Pat and Hub stood behind him, shining their flashlights in the captives' faces. Ollie spoke in a quiet, calm voice. "I'm real disappointed in you, Dale. Did you think I wasn't watching everything you do? Did you think I wouldn't find a way to keep track of you guys if there was a chance you were digging up a treasure? I took you for a smart boy, but you're really kind of a dumb shit, aren't you? Now we're going for a little ride out to Piedmont. Vernon, you're going to drive your Rambler. Pat and Hub are riding with you. Dale is going to drive me and Nozetape."

Hopper spoke. "Would you tell us what's going on here, Ollie?"

"I don't want to hear nothing out of you right now, Dale. Just take my word that if everybody minds their manners and does as he's told, we're all going to be enjoying coffee and doughnuts by ten o'clock this morning after you've told me everything you know about this goddam treasure. But 'til we get someplace we can talk and work things out, I need you to shut up and behave. Okay?" Hub put a shotgun in Ollie's hands. He racked a shell into the chamber. "You first, Vernon. Go put your clothes on. No need for lights. Hub and Pat are going to be watching the whole time, so do us all a favor and take things easy. Now go on . . . go with Pat and Hub."

Cord growled. "It's too early for me to be getting dressed. I think I'll just go back to bed."

Ollie sighed. "I knew it would be you, Vernon." He stepped forward and stomped, hard, on Nozetape's instep. There was a loud crack. Nozetape shrieked and slid off the couch, grabbing at his foot. Ollie stepped away from the couch. "Sorry about that, Nozetape, but Vernon here is going to cause us all a lot of misery if he don't just get along for a little bit." Hopper heard Pat chuckling. Ollie spoke to Cord again. "Now,

Vernon, I think I broke his foot. But I swear I'll break a bunch of stuff if you don't do this the easy way. Now go get dressed. We ain't got all night."

Cord got to his feet. Ollie spoke to Pat and Hub. "Don't let him get into no drawers nor closets or nothing. And don't shoot him unless he don't leave no selection." Cord disappeared into his bedroom with Pat and Hub behind. Hopper couldn't tell which was which in the dark. They were both big, blurry blobs with flashlights walking behind his friend. Nozetape moaned pitifully, rocking back and forth on the couch.

Hopper ran through some scenarios that might open the door to escape. Any escape maneuver he cooked up came with tremendous risk that one or more good guys would get killed. For a second, he entertained the possibility that if they just went along, Ollie might offer a deal that would have them home safe and sound. No chance. No matter what he said, this was a murder detail. A necessary part of the plan had to involve three dead longhairs. He tried not to think about what was happening to Eva. He hoped, desperately, that somewhere along the way, he'd spot an opportunity to turn the tables. He considered trying to talk to Ollie but decided it was a waste.

Cord came back dressed in jeans, a flannel shirt, and boots. "Your turn, Nozetape."

"I don't think I can walk."

"Now don't be a baby. I worked a half a day chopping cotton with two toes near lopped off by a rusty hoe blade. You can walk. Go get some clothes on." Nozetape, limping a lot more than usual, disappeared down the hall, followed by Pat and Hub. Hopper shot a look at Cord, who was looking back. Ollie saw. "I know what you boys are thinking. Don't. I'd rather we part company as friends. There's no percentage in me blowing your goddam heads off. So don't make me."

Hopper knew in his bones Ollie was simply offering a pacifier to keep them manageable until everything fit into the contours of his plan.

Nozetape limped back in, fully dressed, and plopped onto the couch. "Your turn, Dale. We're almost done, so let's keep it running smooth."

Hopper, with an obedient attitude, led Pat and Hub into his bedroom. He heard Pat hiss. "You ain't so smart, and you ain't so tough, are you now, Mr. Big Mouth?"

"I can't see my clothes."

"Shine a light around, Hub, so he can find his britches."

The flashlight beam crisscrossed the room and stopped on a pair of Levi's folded on a chair by the bed. "Thanks, Hub."

"You're welcome."

"Shut up, Hub. You're not supposed to have no conversation with these guys. They got nothing to say that you need to hear." There was sullen silence behind the beam of Hub's flashlight.

Hopper took his time putting on the Levi's. As he pulled them on, he felt the knife in his hip pocket. If there was a pat-down, they'd find it for sure. His only chance was for somebody to get careless. After a few seconds, Pat gave him a rough shove. "What are you waiting on? Get dressed."

"You want to hand me my shirt and boots?"

"Get 'em your damn self."

"I would, but I can't see in the dark."

"Find his goddam boots and shirt, Hub."

Hub's flashlight played across the room and stopped next to the bed, illuminating Hopper's boots. Hopper sat on the bed and pulled them on. "Thanks again, Hub."

"Didn't I tell you to shut up?"

"What about my shirt?"

"Goddammit, find his shirt, Hub." The light searched the room for the shirt, back and forth, back and forth. "This is taking too long. Where'd you leave it?"

"In the closet."

"Why didn't you say so?"

"Didn't you tell me to shut up?"

Pat stepped forward and slugged him in the mouth. Hopper immediately tasted blood and heard loud bells ringing. Instinctively, he struck back, and Pat stumbled backward into the wall, sliding down like a limp garbage sack. Hopper heard the hammer click back on the revolver in Hub's hand. "Don't shoot, Hub. I did it without thinking." He heard Hub's heavy breathing. Ollie yelled from the living room, "What the hell is going on in there?"

Pat was struggling back to his feet. Ollie yelled again, "Somebody talk to me, goddammit."

Pat, rubbing his left eye, answered, "It's okay. The little prick cold-cocked me. But I taught him a lesson."

Hopper chuckled. "You're a lying, cowardly sack of shit, ain't ya, Pat?"

Pat slapped him on the jaw with the barrel of a pistol. "I'm gonna knock your fucking teeth out one at a time. Before I'm through with you, you'll be crying like the little baby you are."

"Sure. We'll see." There was a ray of hope. In the exchange of blows and near discharge of the pistol, nobody thought to check Hopper's pockets.

"Get him a shirt out of the closet, Hub." He grabbed Hopper by the hair and slung him through the bedroom door. Ollie shined his flashlight in Hopper's face. "Jesus, Dale, that looks like it hurts." He shined his light on Pat's face and laughed. "You're going to have a bee-ute of a shiner, little brother. That's what you get for letting old Dale here get too close. Now, I hope everybody's got all the mischief out of their system. Once we step out this door, it's gonna go real hard for anybody making trouble. Screw up, and you'll be pissed at yourself for the rest your life every time you look at the stump where your thumb used to be. Let me see your keys, Vernon."

Cord tossed the Rambler keys. Ollie inspected them. He removed a penknife from the chain and stashed it in his overalls pocket. Then he tossed them back to Cord. "Nice and easy. Here we go." He opened the door and looked down the street both ways.

Pat pushed Cord toward the Rambler. Once Hub was in the

backseat, Pat forced Cord into the driver's seat. Hub had Cord covered with a .357 Cold Python revolver as Pat climbed in.

Ollie guided Hopper and Nozetape to a Ford station wagon. "New wheels, Ollie?" Hopper asked.

"No talking, Dale. Okay?"

"How are we going to make a deal if we're not talking about something?"

"Everybody will get a chance to say his piece in Piedmont. You drive, Dale. I want both your hands on the wheel. Drive where I tell you. Do anything funny, and I'll open up this little butterfly like a can of pork 'n beans."

Hopper heard whimpering. He looked in the back floorboard and barely made out the form of Eva, bound hand and foot, a gag in her mouth. The horror of the plan hit him like a chop in the throat. They'd be forced to witness her torture until Ollie was satisfied he'd squeezed everythin' out of them he could.

It took about forty minutes of slow driving in a zigzag pattern before the Rambler and the station wagon pulled behind an abandoned farmhouse.

Pat and Hub covered the prisoners as Ollie pulled Eva up from the floorboard. The prisoners stood by the cellar door as Ollie disarmed the shotgun boobytrap. He unlocked the heavy metal door and started down speaking over his shoulder. "Come on down, boys and girls. I got something to show you. Watch your step now. I don't want nobody falling down the stairs and breaking something."

Cord refused to move. "I ain't going down there." Pat clubbed him savagely on the head with his pistol butt. Cord sank to his knees. On pure instinct, Hopper leapt into the air and kicked at Pat's head with all his might. He saw Pat stumble backward, blood pouring from his face. Hopper cushioned his fall with his right arm. As he struggled to regain his footing, the heavy blow fell on his head, and his lights blinked out.

When Hopper came to, he, Cord, Nozetape, and Eva were seated at a card table, their arms tied to the folding chairs they sat in. His vision was blurry, but there was nothing wrong with his sense of smell. The odor was overpowering and familiar. His focus returned at the same instant his mind made the connection. The snake house. This place smelled just like the bowels of the snake house. He looked around to see the walls lined with cages full of snakes, frogs, and lizards. Blood streamed down Cord's face. Eva, trembling, looked at Hopper, her eyes pleading. Hub had them covered with a shotgun.

Hopper looked around for Ollie and Pat. Not here. Hub spoke. "Got anything you want to say, tough guy?"

"You the one that put me to sleep?"

"Yeah, and that's just for starters."

"You guys are planning on leaving us down here, I suppose."

Hub nodded his big head. "Don't take you long to get the picture, does it?"

Eva wailed, "Please, mister, I'm not part of any of this. Please let me out of here. I can't stand it."

Cord mumbled, "Quiet, Eva. Just be calm. Everything's going to be okay."

"No, it isn't." She sobbed. "Nothing's ever going to be okay again."

Cord spoke soothingly. "Trust me, Eva. You won't help anything by getting hysterical. We need you to keep your head. Can you do that?"

"I'll try," she whimpered.

Hopper spoke up, drawing the big man's attention. "Hey, Hub, they left you down here all by yourself to do the dirty work, huh?"

Hub grunted. "Pat's still out where you put him. He hit his head on the bumper of the station wagon. Ollie's trying to bring him to. Pat might be hurt real bad."

"I'm real sorry to hear that." Hopper did his best to survey the cellar for a way out. He saw two shotguns suspended from the cellar ceiling pointing at the door. But being tied up like he was and with Hub covering them, prospects were slim. Hopper felt nauseous at the idea of Little

Eva being killed and left to rot in a room full of reptiles. It just couldn't happen like this.

Hub moved around where he could see Hopper's face. "Too bad you didn't find that treasure. Maybe you wouldn't be in the mess you're in now."

Hopper broke into uncontrollable laughter. Hub frowned. "What the hell's so funny? I don't see that you got a goddam thing to laugh about."

"So the Oleg brothers told you we didn't find the treasure, and you believed them, you dumbass."

Hub stomped over and rammed the shotgun barrel into Hopper's chest. "I'll show you whose the dumbass, you . . . you dumbass."

"Sure, they're real sorry there ain't no treasure, but they'll make it up to you, right? And you believe that?"

Hub frowned, "Course I believe it." He thought a minute, then leaned into Hopper's face and growled. "What are you saying, that you guys found it, and Ollie's lying to me?"

Hopper laughed despite the pain in his chest where Hub rammed him with the shotgun. "Oh, no, Hub, they'd never lie to you. Just because they bullshit everyone else if it puts a dollar in their pockets, you're different. You're too smart. They'd never cheat you, would they?"

Hub stood quiet while the possibilities rolled around in his big head. Hopper, not knowing how much time they had before Ollie came down, pressed his advantage. "Why do you think they were so hyper about you not talking to us, Hub? It's because they're afraid the truth will come out, and you'll catch on to their scheme."

"No, that ain't it. It's just that . . . " Hub shook his head, as if that might make the puzzle pieces fall into place.

"Listen, Hub. Here's what's going to happen. Ollie's going to tell you to blow our heads off."

Eva wailed.

"Shut up, you," Hub snapped.

"But before you get out of here, they'll either blow your brains out or just lock you down here with what's left of us . . . and these snakes, of course."

Hub shot a nervous glance at the array of reptiles all around the cellar. Hopper went on. "If you don't believe me, take a look in my back pocket. There's a key to a trunk that's in our attic. That's where the treasure is."

Hub snorted. "How dumb do you think I am? I ain't gonna untie you so I can look in your back pocket." A malicious grin crossed his wide features. "Why don't I just blast your ass and get it after you're dead?"

Hopper assumed his best look of deep disappointment. "You got me there, Hub. You could blast me, get the key, and deal with Pat and Ollie however you want. I didn't think of that."

Hub chuckled, triumphant.

"Except for one thing. You're afraid of blood, ain't you, Hub? A hemophobic, Ollie said?"

"Yeah, so what? I can do what I gotta do."

"But if you blast me, you'll have to go digging around in my pockets, sopping wet with blood. Won't that make you sick?"

Hub frowned as he thought it over. Then the light came on, and he grinned. "There don't have to be no bloody pockets." He laid the shotgun aside. "I'll just choke you down, and it'll be all nice and clean, and the way you're hogtied here, there ain't a goddam thing you can do about it."

He stood over Hopper and wrapped his giant hands around his throat, thumbs on Hopper's Adam's apple. His smile broadened as Hopper's legs began to cycle wildly and his face turned purple. Hub's smile broadened as he was clearly enjoying the sport.

Cord shouted, "Well, hello, Ollie, where you been so long?" Hub loosened his grip and raided up to look at the cellar stairs. Hopper, gasping and coughing, kicked the heel of his boot, with all his might, into Hub's knee. The joint was forced backward beyond its limit. Hub stumbled backward, clutching his knee. Cord leapt to his feet, chair and all, and charged forward. Hub started for the shotgun, but his leg wouldn't support him. He looked up just as the crown of Cord's head rammed into his face. Hub collapsed on the floor, blood dripping through the fingers covering his nose and mouth. Cord fell back on the floor, stunned.

Hopper, still gasping, stumbled toward Hub, who was trying to recover. He unleashed a savage barrage of bone-crushing kicks to Hub's face. Hub rolled over on his back, blindly raising his arms in a vain effort to shield his face. Hopper stomped on his throat. The big hands fell reflexively. A sickening gurgle issued from Hub's mouth as Hopper continued to stomp his face until there was no question that Hub was no longer a threat.

Nozetape spoke for the first time since they'd come into the cellar. "Hopper, that's enough. You're going to kill—"

Cord interrupted. "We got to get out of these ropes before Ollie comes down here."

Hopper brought his boot down one more time on the pulp that used to be Hub's face. He tried to tell Cord there was a pocketknife in his hip pocket, but his damaged throat would only allow a whisper.

Cord wasn't paying attention anyway. He was in a vain, all-out struggle to get free of the ropes. Hopper tried to get close enough to speak into Cord's ear, but he pushed him away. "You got to get out of the way, Hopper. If I don't get loose, we're done for."

Hopper wanted to kick Cord's shins but doubted it would do any good. He turned his attention to Eva, head down, weeping. He stumbled to her side and whispered in her ear, "There's a knife in my back pocket. I'm going to put my butt against your hands. I ain't being fresh. I just need you to get that knife out of there." He moved behind her chair and positioned his rear end so she could reach the pocket. She found the knife and managed to inch it up and out.

Nozetape saw it. "Cord, there's a knife."

Hopper stepped aside as Cord dropped to his knees, retrieving the knife with his teeth. Hopper offered his tied hands. Cord pushed the knife against his palms. Hopper opened the blade and did considerable damage to his hands and arms cutting the ropes. Just as he got his right hand free, the cellar door opened, and Ollie's big body came hurrying down the stairs.

"We got to finish this up, Hub. Pat may be hurt bad, and we need to . . . Hub?"

Hopper, still tied to the chair, made an awkward dive for Hub's shotgun. The cellar exploded as Ollie opened a barrage of random shotgun blasts, destroying several cages, which toppled over, spilling an assortment of shot-riddled dead and dying snakes onto the cellar floor. Hopper fired. Ollie tumbled down the stairs, moaning and grasping his mangled right arm. As he fell, a Colt .45 model 1911 spilled out of his overalls pocket and spun across the floor. When it came to rest, it was in the middle of a mass of mangled snakes writhing on the bloody concrete.

Ollie sat up and reached for the pistol on the floor in the middle of the bloody snakes squirming in death agony. The longest was approximately six feet with its head almost severed by the shotgun blast. When Ollie reached over it, the snake raised its bleeding head off the cellar floor and hooded out. Cobra.

Ollie tried to roll away, but the snake struck, sinking its fangs into his cheek. He swatted at the dying snake with his left arm, but the snake held. Ollie grasped the body and pulled as hard as he could. The head detached and remained fastened to Ollie's face.

Ollie shrieked and battled in blind terror, trying to dislodge the cobra's head. He finally managed to pull it free. Hopper dodged as Ollie flung the severed snake head in his direction. Blood trickled down Ollie's cheek from the fang punctures. He placed his fingers to the bite marks on his face. "Hopper . . . Hopper, listen to me. You got to get me to a hospital."

Hopper kept Ollie covered as he cut Cord, Nozetape, and Eva free. Just then, the cellar door slammed shut. They all heard someone trying to attach the lock. Hopper croaked, "Pat's trying to lock us in here." Cord deftly snatched the .45 from the writhing serpent mass and bounded up the stairs, crashing his shoulder against the door. It gave a bit, but Pat was using all his enormous weight to keep it closed as he tried to fasten the lock.

Eva screamed, "Don't let him bury us in here, Vernon."

Ollie yelled, "Pat, is that you? Help me, Pat. I'm snake-bit. I got to get to a hospital, fast."

Cord focused all his strength against the door. It opened a crack and then burst wide open. There were shots fired. Cord fell down the stairs, and the door slammed shut. Hopper thought he heard the locks snap into place. They were entombed.

Ollie's whisper was weak. "Pat, little brother—help me."

Blood dripped from Cord's left arm. Even so, he bounded back up the stairs. "Come on, Hopper. Help me with this door. I can't move this by myself."

Hopper guided Eva through the chaos of dead and dying snakes. He joined Cord on the stairs. Cord said, "On three, push with all your strength. One, two . . . three." They groaned and strained. Nothing happened.

Hopper shook his head and croaked, "I'm afraid the sombitch locked us in."

Cord put his hand on his friend's shoulder. "No, he didn't. He's dead. The only thing keeping us in here is that the tub of guts is laying on the door. So you gotta push, buddy. Push with everything you got, and let's get the hell out of here."

Hopper took a deep breath. He and Cord, together, summoned all their strength and focused it on that door. Hopper's heart was about to burst, when there was a slight movement. With this encouragement, they heaved again, and Pat's body rolled off, the lock still clutched in his right hand.

The door opened, allowing fresh air to rush into their lungs and across their upturned faces. Hopper spoke as loud as his voice would allow. "Come on up out of there, Eva. Let's get you someplace safe."

Whimpering, she hurried up the steps and disappeared, Nozetape close behind.

Ollie crawled toward the stairs, calling Hopper's name. Hopper clutched at Cord's sleeve and croaked, "Come on, Cord. Help me get this barrel of blubber up the stairs."

"Leave him." There was cold fury in Cord's voice.

"Can't do it, Cord. We gotta get him to a doctor."

"You're wasting your time. He'll never make it."

"We gotta try. He may be the only guy that can clear us."

Cord shook his head. "He'll never tell the truth, even if we could get him out of here alive. We're more likely to wind up behind bars if Ollie's around to spout his bullshit."

Ollie whined, "Listen, Vernon, see that door?" He pointed to the heavy door at the rear of the cellar. "I got a key around my neck that'll open that door. Get me to a doctor, and you can have it all. There's a fortune in there. It's enough for you all to live like kings for the rest of your lives. You've got to help me."

Cord watched as Hopper descended the stairs and tried to raise Ollie's huge body. But his feet slipped in the mixture of Oleg and snake blood. Hopper looked past Cord. "Nozetape, give me a hand here." Nozetape, lingering at the top of the cellar door, pushed past Cord and limped down the stairs.

They tried again to get him up, but Ollie sagged and then went rigid. Flecks of foam bubbled from his lips, and he died. They left him there and came out into the fresh air again.

Hopper surveyed the damage to Cord's left arm. He might be crippled up a little bit, but he'd be alright. Cord looked over Hopper's head to the golden rays of the rising sun. "You know what almost happened down there, don't you?"

"Let's not think about it. Let's get Nozetape and Eva out of here."

Nozetape looked at the yawning cellar that almost turned out to be his grave. He blinked in the dawning light. "What do we do now?"

Hopper said, "I need to go back down there."

Nozetape shook his head. "Not me. I've been down there enough. And you shouldn't go neither."

"I'll be fine. Wait here. I'll be up in a minute. Give me the Rambler keys, Cord."

"They're in Pat's pocket." Hopper fished the keys out of Pat's overalls. He opened the Rambler's trunk, emptied some tools from an oily canvas bag, and went back into the cellar.

———

They stopped at the first service station they found. Hopper called the local FBI office and left a message for Smalley and Tillis. When he got back in the Rambler, he spoke to Eva. "Listen, sweetheart, you probably don't need to have any part of what happens next. If we leave you here, can you call someone to come and pick you up?"

She broke down sobbing, "Hopper, Cord, I don't . . . thank you. I'll never be able to—"

Cord said, "Come on now, Eva. We'll have a chance to talk it all over later. But there's going to be lots of law enforcement headaches, and you need to go home and get some rest. Don't mention any of this to anyone. Okay?"

She nodded and got out of the car. "I'll call Sandy. She'll come."

Cord patted her cheek. "Tell Sandy to forget anything that happens this morning. It'll be best for everyone."

Hopper removed his boots. "On the way home, find an out-of-the-way dumpster and get rid of these." Eva blinked, waiting for an explanation. "Just do it and forget it, please, Eva." She paused once as she walked to the station and then disappeared inside.

Hopper smiled at Nozetape in the backseat. "We're taking you to the hospital, buddy. We need to see about your foot and Cord's arm. And you may be having a heart attack."

"I don't get it."

"We just left the scene of a triple homicide. If you're having chest pains and trouble breathing because of all the stress, the natural thing for us to do is get you out of there and rush you to a hospital."

Nozetape nodded. "I get your point. Now that I think of it, I am having some indications of a heart attack: chest pain radiating into my arm, shortness of breath. Get me to the hospital, *stat*." After a few minutes, Nozetape asked, "If they ask me what brought this on, how much do I tell them?"

"Tell them the truth as best you can in every detail. The only thing you need to leave out are the parts about Eva, and don't say nothing about me going back down there."

"Why did you go back?"

"We'll go over all that later. Right now, you just concentrate on having a heart attack."

———

Smalley and Tillis showed up at the hospital at 9:15. Hopper and Cord were drinking coffee in the coronary care waiting room. Both of them had bandages on their heads, and Cord had stitches in his left arm. The agents scribbled furiously in their notebooks as Hopper related what happened. "So we loaded Nozetape in the Rambler, and here we are."

Smalley gave him a sly grin. "You know we're going to take you guys back out there."

"Yep."

"And when we do, your story better match up with what we find on every tiny point right down to the cobra head."

"We'll be glad to help in any way we can."

Smalley told Tillis to notify the Oklahoma City Police Department and the Oklahoma and Canadian County Sheriff's Offices. He turned his attention back to Hopper. "Okay, where is the slaughterhouse?"

"It's a farmhouse out in the country near Piedmont."

"Can you narrow that down a bit?"

"Look, it was dark when they took us out there. They didn't take us in a straight line. We took three or four wrong turns trying to get out of there. Maybe Cord can retrace his steps."

"How about it, Mr. Cord, can you guide us back there?"

"I think so."

"Let's go."

Hopper nodded. "We'll have to go without Nozetape. He might be having a heart attack." Smalley looked at Hopper's bare feet and frowned. Hopper shrugged. "They didn't give me time to put my shoes on before they dragged us out. My feet are freezing." Smalley gave him a sideways glance and started to say something but shrugged instead.

Tillis spoke to a doctor at the nurse's station. When the doctor verified that Nozetape's condition was unknown but potentially dangerous, Smalley pointed to the elevator.

The motorcade was comprised of two FBI sedans, two cruisers from the Oklahoma City Police Department, two from the Oklahoma County Sheriff's Department, two from the Canadian County Sheriff's Department (in case the farmhouse was on the Canadian County side of the line), and two ambulances. Cord led the whole convoy to a dead end twice.

When they finally arrived at the widow's farmhouse, Hopper and Cord refused to go back into the cellar.

Smalley snapped, "Don't tell me you two guys are that squeamish."

Hopper spoke through gritted teeth. "Squeamish has nothing to do with it. There's dead guys and snakes down there, and it stinks. If it wasn't for me having so much good karma piled up, our bodies would be locked up down there, and no one would find us for a generation or two. I'll be having nightmares about that place for the rest of my life. So we'll just stay up here in the fresh air while you guys do your investigating, if you don't mind."

They didn't get back to the hospital until three o'clock. Hopper and Cord had to relate their story separately to every law enforcement agency on the scene. The doctor gave Smalley and Tillis ten minutes to question Nozetape and promised he'd discharge him the next day if the labs were clean and no symptoms recurred.

Hopper asked, "Can we go now?"

Smalley put his notebook back in his pocket. "Can you guys tell us what this was all about?"

Hopper said, "I can give you my theory."

"Go ahead."

Forty-eight

When they showed up for work on Monday, Buntz was sitting in the parking lot on the hood of his pickup, looking at the toes of his boots. Hopper could tell something was seriously wrong. "Hey, Buntz, what's up?"

He wiped his nose with his sleeve and didn't look up. "I'm afraid I've got some bad news, boys. We're all out of a job."

Cord stepped closer. "I think my ears are playing tricks on me. I thought you said we're all out of a job."

"We are. The dozers will be on the forty tomorrow. They're going to flatten everything we didn't get out."

Hopper rubbed the back of his neck. "I thought we had until April."

Buntz regarded them with sad resignation. "Where were you guys? We tried to get hold of you all day yesterday. The FBI was all over this place with dark suits and search warrants. The whole damn organization was here from the Kronesons on down. They even called Junior out of church and made him show up. They interviewed everybody on the staff—even poor Sid, who ain't got the emotional preparation for that kind of excitement." He frowned. "Where were you guys, anyway?"

Hopper answered, "Well, Buntz, I suppose you could say we was at a honest-to-God come-to-Jesus meeting."

Buntz cocked his head to one side. "I didn't know you guys was religious."

"Never mind, Buntz. Just tell us what happened."

"From what I hear, they had Feeney in one of their sedans. I guess
he was squealing like the rat he is. I guess he started off claiming you two
was the masterminds behind his schemes. He admitted making off with
the zoo supplies to feed the animals he stole. I guess there never was any
bona fide way to inventory everything they had in that place, and nobody in the head office knew or cared how to monitor how many mice
and crickets they actually needed. I guess they broke him down quick.
Evidently there was some murders involved, and to keep from getting
tied to homicide charges, he spilled everything, which wound up getting
you boys off the hook."

Cord asked, "Did anybody mention Ollie Oleg?"

Buntz rubbed his chin as he thought. "I know I heard that name
sometime, but I don't know if it had anything to do with this."

"Sorry, Buntz. Go ahead."

"Turns out the feds done a bunch of homework before they showed
up here, and they knew the whole story. They was really interested in you
two, but the timing didn't work out. Turns out the money tap turned on
for Feeney and this other guy when Neyland took over. Feeney figured
out how to use Neyland's contacts with suppliers and zookeepers all
over the world to move snakes and other crawlies along back channels
where no one could keep track of what was going on.

"Zack Kroneson bellowed like he was going to kick the place down.
There was lawyers lined up at the gate, and every phone line at the zoo
had a senator on the other end of it." He stopped to take breath. "Anyway, I guess Feeney got a lawyer, and by the time his story got straight,
Neyland didn't have nothing to do with nothing. The whole deal was
masterminded by a couple of guys that's dead now and can't contradict
anything Feeney says."

Cord scratched his jaw. "How does all this add up to the dozers
showing up tomorrow?"

Buntz cleared his throat. "When Zack Kroneson found out Neyland went outside usual hiring procedures to get you guys on, he made up his mind you two was somehow up to your eyeballs in the mischief. So he told me to . . . " He looked at the toes of his boots. "He told me to tell you that you got a week's severance pay coming, and you're . . . you're both fired. And then he fired me too."

Hopper wasn't surprised that the ax fell on him and Cord. And he was sorry the west forty's appointment with the dozers was moved up. But when he heard Buntz was fired, it boosted his anger index off the charts. "Why fire you, Buntz? You aren't guilty of nothing but doing the best you could to attend to their plants for them."

Buntz took a deep breath. "Well, I talked back to Mr. Kroneson. I talked back pretty rough."

"Exactly how did you talk back?" Hopper tried to imagine Buntz, with his unruly red mop and freckles, trying to stand toe to toe with Zack Kroneson. He couldn't make the picture materialize in his brain.

"I told him he had no call to fire you guys. When I tried to explain, he looked at me like I sprouted feathers between my eyes, and turned his back. I hurried around and stopped in front of him. I tried explaining again. He stepped back and asked me if I was crazy. I told him no, I just thought he had you guys all wrong. I told him you might have made mistakes in your past, but where the zoo was concerned, you're both straight as a plumb line. I know he was hacked about you and his daughters. But, hell, they're grown women, and the stuff they do after hours is their own business. He got all narrow-eyed and asked why I was so all-fired determined to keep you guys on the payroll. He said maybe I have fingers in the misdoings, and that's why I was trying so hard to protect you. I don't know what got into me. I told him the only thing I was trying to do was persuade him to take a minute and try to think like a decent guy." Buntz wiped his nose with his sleeve. "Then he fired me." He looked past them, his eyes lingering on the zoo premises in the background. "I'm sure going to miss being here."

Hopper felt like an acid bubble was building up in his heart. "What will you do, Buntz?"

"I don't know. Maybe I'll start a lawn care business. That would keep the bills paid and food on the table." He looked back down at the toes of his boots. "I guess I owe you boys an apology."

"For what?"

"Well, I sorta promised I'd get you on permanent. Hell, I couldn't even keep you on temporary."

Hopper put a hand on Buntz's shoulder. "You don't owe us nothing. You've been a straight-up guy ever since we set foot in this place. I'd be proud to shake your hand."

Buntz's eyes reddened, and he choked up a little bit. He shook Hopper's hand twice, then Cord's.

"Well, I guess that's it. Be seeing you, Buntz."

"Yeah, be seeing you." He jumped off the hood of his truck, got in, started the engine, and drove away from the zoo.

Hopper and Cord stood in the parking lot, looking at each other. "Well," Cord said, watching Buntz's pickup disappear down the access road. "There goes the treasure."

Hopper listened to the sound of the winter birds in the trees north of the shop. "How long have we been working here, Cord?"

"Less than three weeks."

"Seems longer, doesn't it?"

"Yep."

"Well, let's pack and head to California."

Forty-nine

The bus was almost packed and ready to go. A black sedan pulled up in front of their house. Smalley and Tillis got out. "Going somewhere?" Smalley asked.

"California," Hopper answered.

"In a hurry?"

"Not really."

"Mind if we have word?"

"No, come on in."

They came in the house and surveyed the rooms bereft of any furniture. "There's no place to sit."

"Like I said, we're going to California. We got rid of everything we can't fit in the bus. Is there something we can do for you?"

"We got a couple complications."

"We're listening."

"See, we found that vault full of gold and cash down in that cellar. There might be some missing. No way to tell for sure, of course. You know anything about that?"

"Why do you ask?"

"Just wondering."

"No, don't know a thing about any missing riches."

"I have to tell you that technically you're the finders, so part of it may turn out to be yours. There's no way to tie any quantifiable amount to any particular criminal acts. And we can't say whether some of it is part of a tax evasion scheme. So who gets a share of all this is real uncertain at the moment. I'm supposed to leave you these forms. It's too complicated to say right now, but you'll need to fill those out just in case. Of course, if some of it does turn out to be yours, you'll owe taxes on it."

Cord shook his head. "Taxes, huh? I knew it. There's a catch to every goddam thing."

Tillis mumbled, "Yeah, tough luck." He put on his sunglasses. "Okay, I guess that's it. You can thank Benjamin Lucan you're in the clear."

"Who?"

"Tiny. When he was sure the Oleg brothers were going to give him up, he told us about the whole operation, at least as much of it as he knew." He gave them a hard stare. "We have some evidence that might incriminate you two in some of this. But it's weak, and with Tiny's statements, we'd never get a conviction."

"Ask them about the Rambler," Smalley muttered.

"Oh, yeah." Tillis cleared his throat. "Technically, we should have given your car a good going-over before we let you drive it off. After all, it was part of a crime scene. Mind if we take a look now?"

Cord smiled. "Knock yourself out, if you can find it. We sold it to a guy named Droop. Can't say where he's at now."

Smalley rubbed his eyes. "Never mind."

Cord asked, "I don't suppose you guys know what became of Tiny?"

Tillis shook his head. "Not yet. We're looking. I don't guess you guys can help us there."

They shook their heads. Tillis studied their faces and sighed. "I'd say everything worked out pretty good for you two." He cleared his throat. "Well, I guess that's it. Fill out the forms. They might make you rich. Enjoy California."

Hopper and Cord watched the agents as they stepped into the yard. Halfway to the car, Smalley turned. "One more thing." He walked back to the porch, where Hopper and Cord were standing. He spoke in low tones that no one but Hopper and Cord could hear. "We've identified the remains we found in the freezer in that cellar. He was an undercover federal agent. If I thought for one minute you two had anything to do with that or knew anything about it and were holding back, I'd dedicate the rest of my life to putting you on death row."

"You'd be right to do that, Agent Smalley."

"Good day, gentlemen."

As the federal agents left, an Oklahoma County squad car drove up. A grim-faced officer approached. "Vernon Cord and Dale Hopper?"

"What can we do for you, Officer?"

He presented them both with papers. "I'm serving you with restraining orders directing you to stay away from any part of the Oklahoma County Zoo premises. Good day, gentlemen."

Hopper watched him go. "Why do you reckon that every law enforcement guy that talks to us today wants us to have a good day?"

Cord sighed. "What gives them the idea we're gentlemen?"

Hopper made several attempts to call Audrey at the zoo, but his calls were never put through. Even when he claimed to be a reporter with the *Daily Oklahoman*, he was asked to leave a number and told she would return the call. She didn't.

He read a small item in the newspaper reporting that the wild ox that caused the death of Gary Bennett at the Oklahoma County Zoo had been "put down." Hopper felt a stab of regret. He mumbled to himself, "His name was Big Ned, and he wasn't wild; he just wasn't domesticated."

On the morning they were leaving, the postman knocked on their door and asked them to sign for identical letters from Mr. Thorson:

Dear Mr. Hopper (Cord):

This will serve to advise that this firm has been employed to handle the probate of the estate of Felix Alimony. As you know, shortly before his death, Mr. Alimony changed his will. The amended document leaves Mr. Alimony's estate to you and Mr. Cord (Hopper). At this time, we are unable to prove any definite information concerning the extent of his estate or whether there are any assets at all. We anticipate there will be considerable delay in processing these matters as it will be necessary to make inquiries into possible holdings in Great Britain.

As for Mr. Alimony's debts, we are unaware of any existing obligations, but we are seeing to the publication of all legally required notices.

We understand that you may be traveling out of Oklahoma soon. Please keep us informed as to your whereabouts as we will need to provide you with formal notices as this case proceeds through the probate court. If you have any questions, please feel free to contact me here at the firm.

On a personal note, I'd like to express my appreciation for the kindness and considerations you offered Mr. Alimony in the closing days of his life. Per his request, there will be no funeral services. His body has been transferred to the US Army for internment in Arlington Cemetery. Please accept my sincere regards.

Yours truly, Jude Thorson

Hopper and Cord drove the peahen-killing cat all the way to the western edge of Canadian County. On the way, Cord asked, "Have you figured out exactly how we're going to handle this?"

"Sure. We're going to open the trap and let him out."

"Suppose he decides some payback is in order. Suppose he decides to stick around long enough to whip our ass."

"Why would he?"

"'Cause he's a maniac, that's why. This may be the sickest psycho cat on the planet. He may be having fantasies right now about biting chunks out of our butts and making us sorry we ever lured him into this trap."

"He ought to be grateful he didn't get a bullet in the brain."

"You see anything in that varmint's face that makes you think he has a thankful fang in his head?" Cord asked.

"What do you think we should do?"

"Hell, I don't know, man. This is your deal."

"Can you think of any way we can open the door by remote control?"

"Nope."

"Okay."

They drove a county road to a point near the Canadian River. When they removed the trap from the school bus, the cat flew into another furious frenzy, trying to get at them. They carried the trap to a barbed-wire fence and rested it on a sturdy fence post.

Hopper and Cord stood on either side of the trap, looking at each other. Finally, Hopper said, "Okay, here's what we do. We'll stand on this side of the fence and open the door facing the other side. As soon as he jumps out, we make a break for it."

"What if he comes after us?"

"He can't catch us both."

"Oh, I get it. He catches whichever of us is the slowest runner."

"I'm opening the gate, so you have a head start."

"Thanks, and bet your ass I'll take it."

"Now hold the cage steady so it doesn't fall on him. Ready?"

"Ready."

The cat made a grab for Hopper's hand as he reached for the trap-door. Hopper jumped back and laughed nervously. "Ready?"

"Ready."

He made a rapid grab for the latch, and the door opened. The cat hit the door like a brown blur. Cord was in full stride when Hopper released the cage and followed at a dead run. Cord shouted over his shoulder, "Is he coming?"

Hopper, gaining, yelled, "I don't know."

They reached the bus at the same time and scrambled inside, slamming doors behind them. They scanned the brown grass behind them for signs the cat was in pursuit.

"There he is." Cord pointed to a dirt pile on the other side of the barbed-wire fence. The cat threw a belligerent look their way and disappeared.

Hopper slid open one of the windows and shouted, "You're welcome, asshole."

Made in the USA
Columbia, SC
14 February 2022

55733216R00236